白蛇传·雷公传·少林寺

雷峰塔下的传奇·唐代传奇·天下武学的殿堂

MADAM WHITE SNAKE · THUNDER GOD
SHAOLIN TEMPLE

The Legend underneath Leifeng Pagoda
The Legend in TANG Dynasty
The Palace of Gongfu

蔡志忠／编绘

李乔思　吴靖宇／译

中国出版集团
现代出版社

图字：01-2006-1449

图书在版编目（CIP）数据

白蛇传·雷公传·少林寺：汉英对照 / 蔡志忠编绘；李乔思，吴靖宇译．-- 北京：现代出版社，2013.12
（蔡志忠漫画中国传统文化经典：中英文对照版）
ISBN 978-7-5143-2051-0

Ⅰ．①白… Ⅱ．①蔡… ②李… ③吴… Ⅲ．①漫画－连环画－作品集－中国－现代 Ⅳ．①J228.2

中国版本图书馆CIP数据核字（2013）第291917号

蔡志忠漫画中国传统文化经典：中英文对照版

白蛇传·雷公传·少林寺

作　者	蔡志忠　编绘 李乔思　吴靖宇　译
责任编辑	袁　涛
出版发行	现代出版社
地　址	北京市安定门外安华里504号
邮政编码	100011
电　话	010-64267325　010-64245264（兼传真）
网　址	www.1980xd.com
电子信箱	xiandai@cnpitc.com.cn
印　刷	北京诚信伟业印刷有限公司
开　本	710×1000　1/16
印　张	22.5
版　次	2014年1月第1版　2014年1月第1次印刷
书　号	ISBN 978-7-5143-2051-0
定　价	38.00元

目录
contents

白蛇传
Madam White Snake

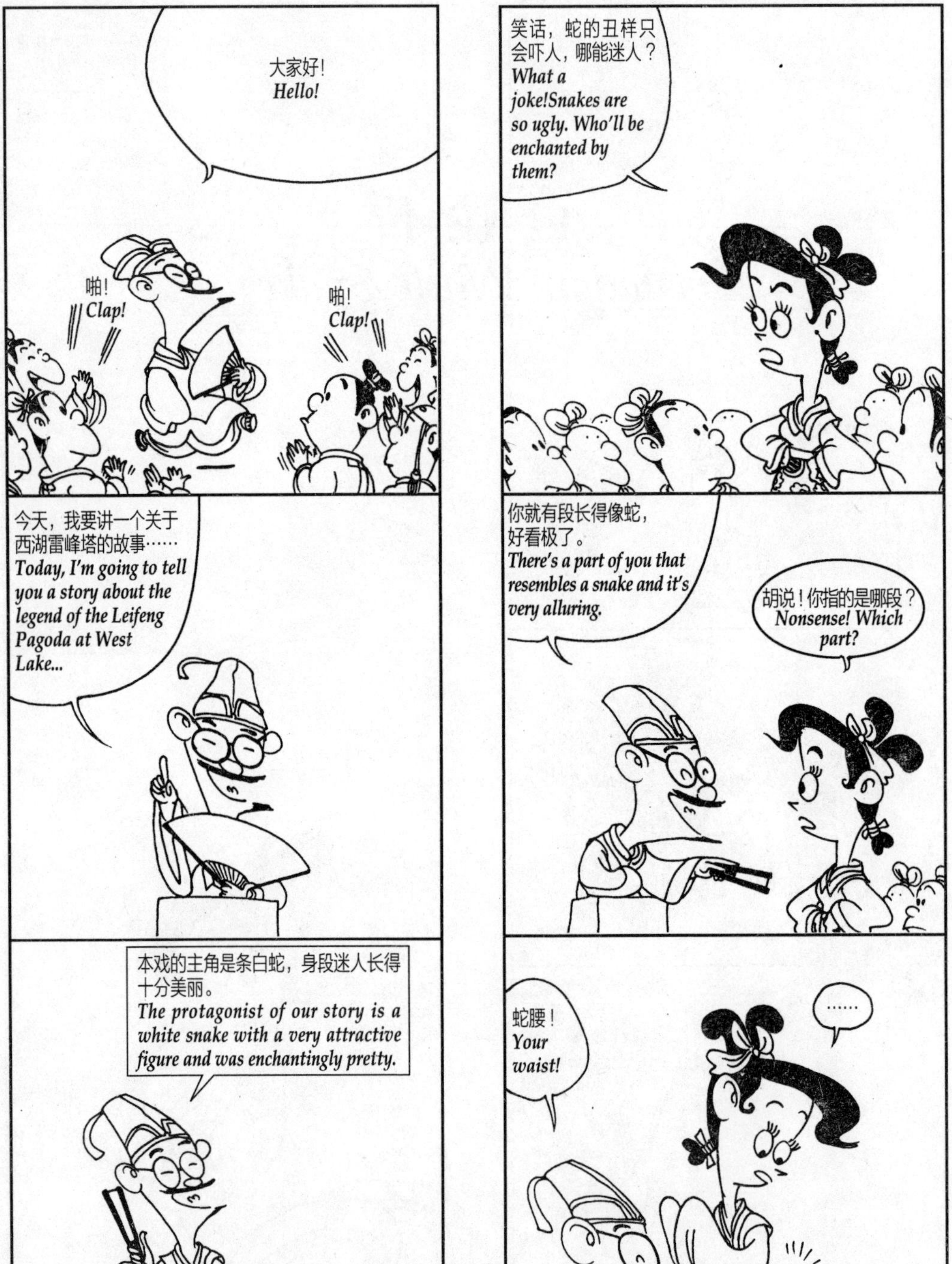

大家好！
Hello!

啪！
Clap!

啪！
Clap!

今天，我要讲一个关于西湖雷峰塔的故事……
Today, I'm going to tell you a story about the legend of the Leifeng Pagoda at West Lake...

本戏的主角是条白蛇，身段迷人长得十分美丽。
The protagonist of our story is a white snake with a very attractive figure and was enchantingly pretty.

其实蛇不但不可怕，蛇还是人类的祖先。
Far from being frightening creatures,snakes are in fact, the ancestors of mankind.
排湾山胞就是以百步蛇为他们的始祖。
The natives of Paiwan worship snakes.
中国的龙正是由蛇演变而成。
The Chinese dragon is said to have evolved from the snake.
创造人类的女娲娘娘也是人头蛇身。
Nu Wa, the mythical creator of mankind, had a human head and the body of a snake.

开天辟地以来，第一个懂得广告推销术的也是我们。
Since time immemorial, we have been the first to make use of sales gimmicks.
朋友！来一个好吃的苹果吧。
Hey pal! Have a delicious apple.
不不！我不吃苹果。
No, no, I don't eat apples.
吃它一个，你就能像上帝一样万能！
Just eat one and you'll be like God!
真的？我买一个。
Really? I'll buy one then.
嘻嘻嘻！推销成功。
Hee! Hee! I've made a sale.
好吃！
It's delicious!
伊甸果园
自产自销
Orchard of Eden

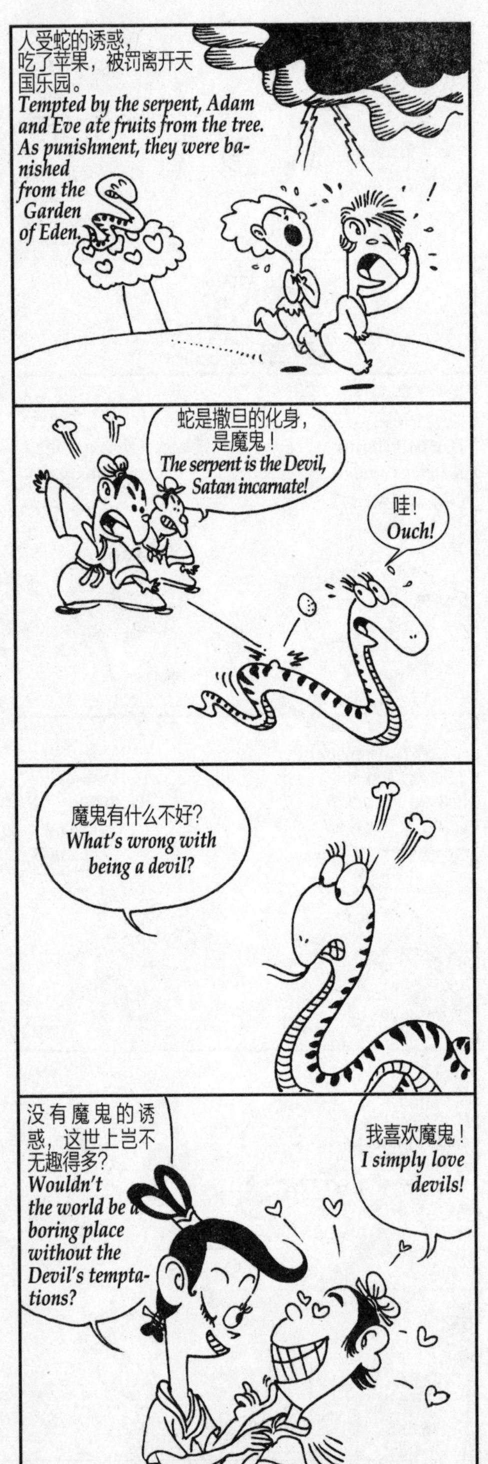
人受蛇的诱惑，
吃了苹果，被罚离开天
国乐园。
Tempted by the serpent, Adam and Eve ate fruits from the tree. As punishment, they were banished from the Garden of Eden.
蛇是撒旦的化身，
是魔鬼！
The serpent is the Devil, Satan incarnate!
哇！
Ouch!
魔鬼有什么不好?
What's wrong with being a devil?
没有魔鬼的诱惑，这世上岂不无趣得多?
Wouldn't the world be a boring place without the Devil's temptations?
我喜欢魔鬼！
I simply love devils!

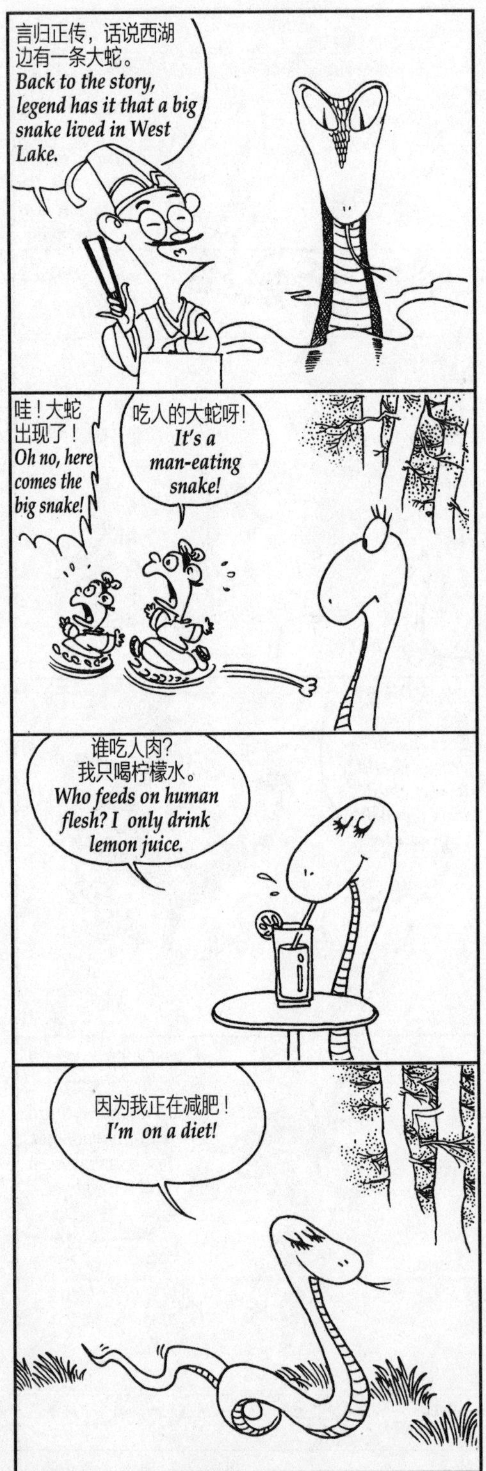
言归正传，话说西湖
边有一条大蛇。
Back to the story, legend has it that a big snake lived in West Lake.
哇！大蛇
出现了！
Oh no, here comes the big snake!
吃人的大蛇呀！
It's a man-eating snake!
谁吃人肉?
我只喝柠檬水。
Who feeds on human flesh? I only drink lemon juice.
因为我正在减肥！
I'm on a diet!

这条白蛇身材标致，长得十分美丽。
This white snake is blessed with a lovely figure and great looks.
可惜全身光溜溜。
It's a pity her body is so bare.
我洞内有八十多套蛇皮大衣呢！
I have more than 80 pieces of snake skins in my cave!
蛇一年蜕一次皮，由此可知她的年纪。
Snakes moult once a year, so we can tell her age.
露出蛇脚了！
Oh no, I've given myself away!

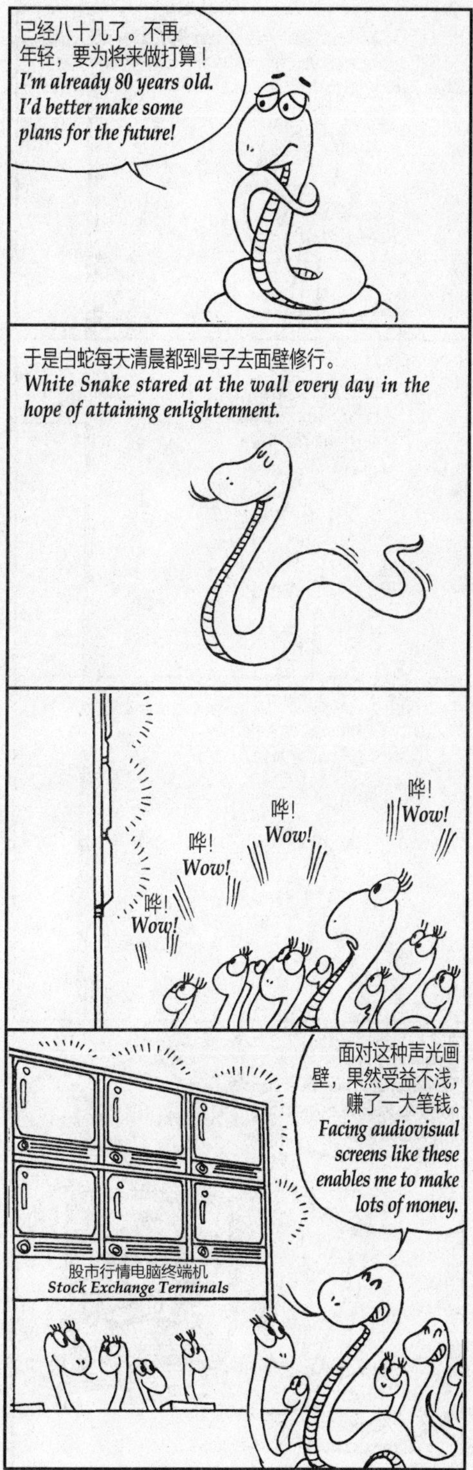
已经八十几了。不再年轻，要为将来做打算！
I'm already 80 years old. I'd better make some plans for the future!
于是白蛇每天清晨都到号子去面壁修行。
White Snake stared at the wall every day in the hope of attaining enlightenment.
哗！Wow!
哗！Wow!
哗！Wow!
哗！Wow!
面对这种声光画壁，果然受益不浅，赚了一大笔钱。
Facing audiovisual screens like these enables me to make lots of money.
股市行情电脑终端机
Stock Exchange Terminals

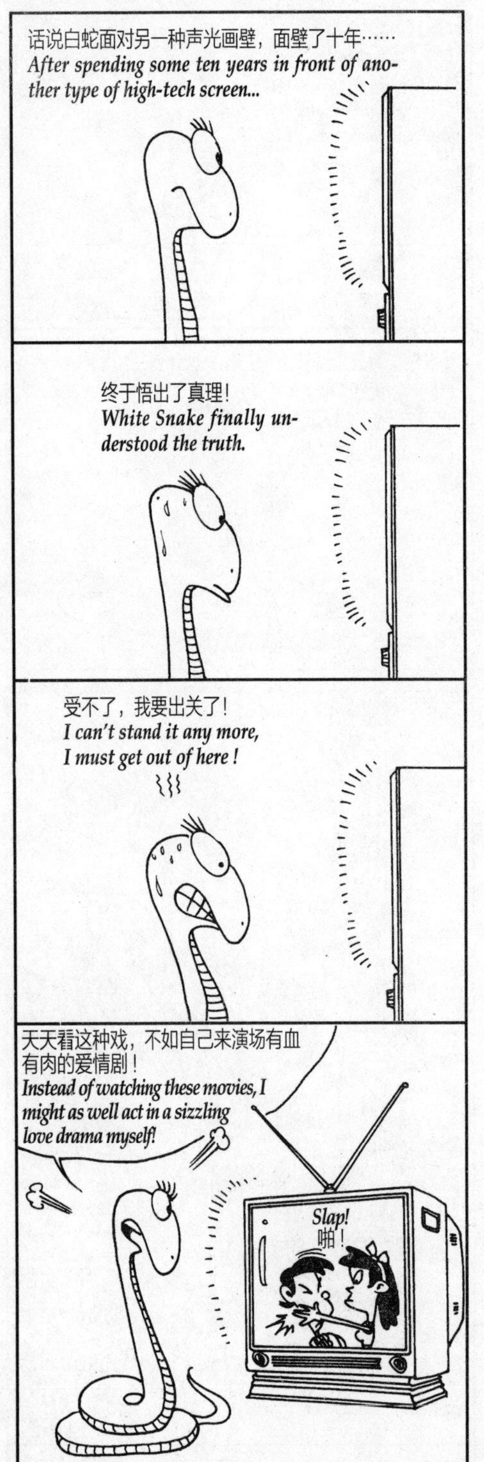

要演戏当女主角，首先得变成个女人才行。
To be the lead actress, I must first turn myself into a woman.

只要肯花钱，要变成女人绝对没问题。
As long as you're willing to spend some money, it can be done.

我炒股票赚了不少，钱不是问题。
I've made a pile from the stock market. Money is not a problem.

那就好。
That's good.

Cosmetic Surgery Hospital
美容整形医院

先得做丰乳、隆鼻、隆臀，共二百万元，保证让你成为真正的女人。
The implants for the breasts, nose and buttocks will cost 2m units of cash. I guarantee you'll become a real woman.

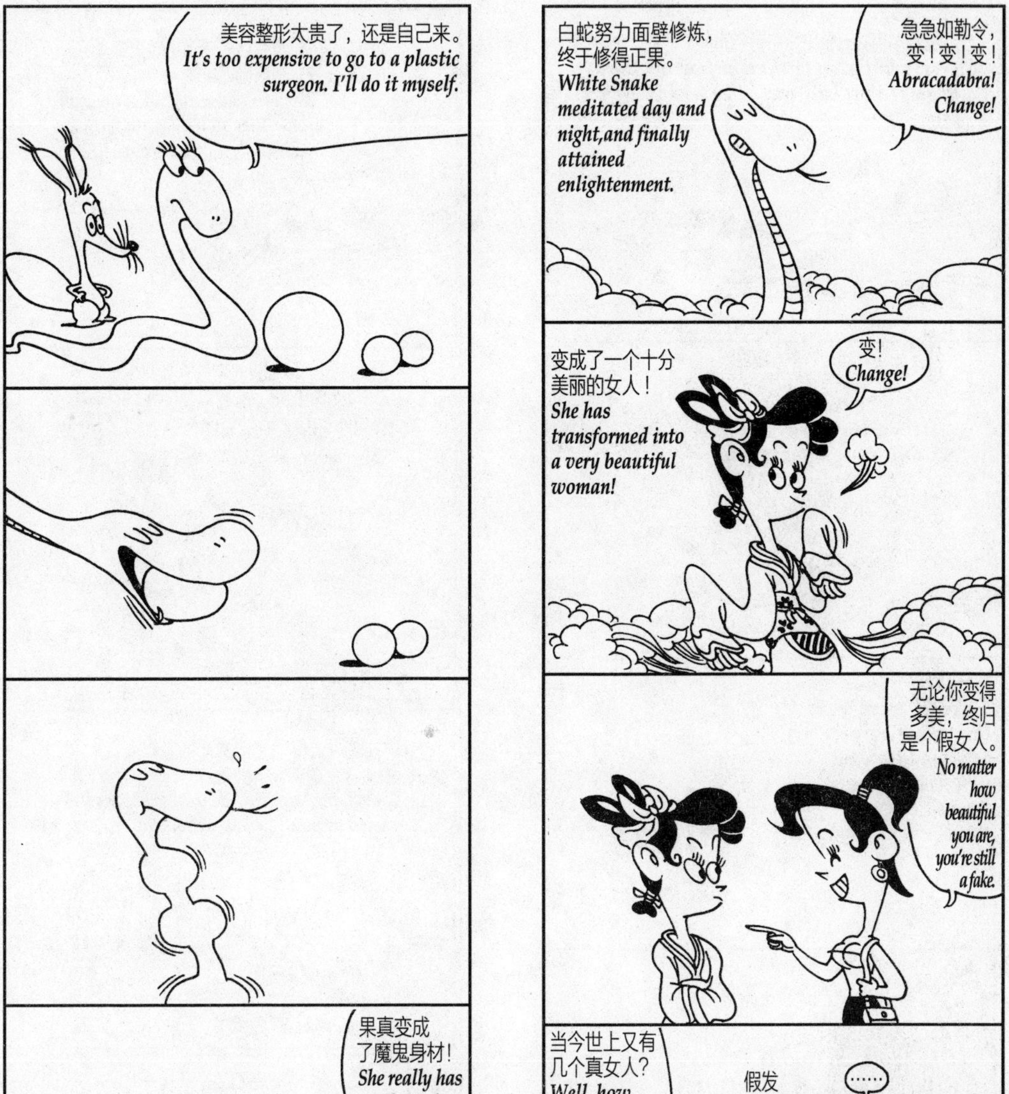

美容整形太贵了，还是自己来。
It's too expensive to go to a plastic surgeon. I'll do it myself.

果真变成了魔鬼身材！
She really has an hourglass figure now!

话说西湖内第三桥下潭内有条千年的青鲤。
Living in the waters just below the third bridge in West Lake was a thousand-year-old carp.
住在西湖好处多多，游客多，食物不会匮乏。
I like it here. Many tourists visit the lake, so there's no shortage of food.
假日加菜打牙祭，兼玩死亡游戏。
On Sundays and public holidays, I get to eat more food,and to play the game of death.

千年青鲤终日在湖中游来游去，快乐逍遥无比。
The thousand-year-old carp spent all her time swimming in the lake and leading a very carefree life.
姑娘十八一朵花，尚未找到好婆家……
I'm a beautiful girl of eighteen who has yet to find a good husband...
青鲤姑娘长得十分美丽，可惜却有恼人问题。
Though the thousand-year-old carp was a great beauty, she had a problem.
遗憾的是漂亮脸蛋上竟长了胡须。
Oh, why must there be whiskers on my beautiful face?

浪里的鱼悠游自得，
这就是鱼的快乐。
Look at all those fish swimming in the water. They look so happy.
你不是鱼，怎么知道鱼是快乐的呢？
You are not a fish. How do you know that they are happy?
...
你不是我，怎么知道我不知鱼是快乐的？
You're not me. How do you know that I don't know if they are happy?
为这种问题也要争吵，所以我知道人是不快乐的。
Fancy arguing over something like that! I know for sure that human beings are not happy.

小池之鱼，当然是不快乐的喽。
You're just a fish in a small pond. You must be unhappy.
你又不是我，怎么知道我不快乐？
You're not me. How do you know that I'm not happy?
我证明给你看。
I'll prove it to you.
哇！
Wow!
不能决定自己的生死，怎么能快乐？
You can't even control your own destiny. How can you be happy?
承认，我承认不快乐！
Okay, I admit that I'm not happy!

面壁修行了三周，大概可变成人形了吧？
I've been meditating for three weeks. Can I transform myself into a human being now?
你修行只达一半，大概不成。
Probably not, since you're only halfway through.
我有千年修行的底子，应该可以。
But I've been practising for a thousand years.
好吧。
All right.
急急如勒令，变身！
Abracadabra! Change!
隆！
轰！
...
半分努力只能有半分成果。
Put in half the effort, and you'll only get half the results.

娘娘为我再作法一次，一定变身成功！
Please use your magic powers again!
再试一次看看。
Let's try again.
急急如勒令，
叶呢嘛哪呀哇变身！
Abracadabra! Abracadabra! Change!
果然变身成功，
变成细眉大眼的美娇娘！
It really worked! You've transformed into a beautiful girl with fine eyebrows and big eyes!
美中不足，
是个鲤须姑娘！
Except for the whiskers!

*A popular Taiwanese singing group.

脸蛋是变得可爱了，不知身材变得如何？
You've got a beautiful face now, but what about your figure?
扑！
Poof!
快把门窗关上，否则三点穿帮！
Quick, close the windows!
现在大家关心的是万点，谁看你的三点？
Everybody is interested in the stock index nowadays. Who cares to peep at you?
哗！
Wow!
哗！
Wow!
庆祝股票指数冲破一万点
A celebration to mark the 10,000-point index!
证
券
哗！
Wow!
哗！
Wow!
哗！
Wow!

今后我就是白娘娘，你则是我的婢女小青。
Henceforth, I shall be Madam White Snake and you, my maid, Xiaoqing.
不公平！为何你是主人，我是婢女？
It's unfair! Why should you be the mistress, and I, the maid?
因为我年龄比你大。
Because I'm your senior, that's why.
这也只能以姐妹相称，何用分主婢？
That only makes you my big sister, not my mistress.
因为你是我变身的。
Well, I was the one who turned you into a human being.
我宁可变回原形也不要当你的丫头。
I'd rather be a carp than be your maid.
变回原形，我还是主人，你还是丫头。
Even if it's so, I'll still be the mistress, and you, my maid!
还是她的嘴上肉……
I'm still at her mercy...

当鱼当蛇可吃喝不愁，当人可要工作，否则哪能生活？
As a carp or a snake, we needn't worry about our livelihood. But as human beings now, we have to work for a living.
我们是在工作赚钱的呀！谁说没有？
That's exactly what we're doing now.
坐着聊天也算是工作？
What? You call sitting around and chatting work?
我们是在万象版演漫画白蛇传！
Well, now we're appearing in the comic strip, Madam White Snake.
登场一次可得报酬两千文钱！
Every time we make an appearance, we get 2,000 units of cash!
联合报会计处
Lianhe Bao Accounts Section
稿费

洗手做羹汤，做道名菜给娘娘尝尝。
I'll prepare some food for my mistress.
清蒸田鸡。
Steamed Frogs.
是我最爱的食物！
That's my favourite dish!
明天换我下厨做菜给你吃。
For a change, I'll do the cooking tomorrow.
你知道我爱吃什么食物？
Do you know what I like?
我当然清楚。
Of course I do.
哇！活蚯蚓！
Wow! Live earthworms!

小青的烹饪技术没话说，料理一等一！
Xiaoqing was a super cook whose culinary skills were unsurpassed!
真好吃！
This is delicious!
但有时闹情绪，也会恶作剧。
But occasionally, when she was in a bad mood, she would play a joke on her mistress.
……
这算哪门子料理？
What is this?
清蒸蛇汤
Snake Soup
今后参照这本食谱做菜，保证令我满意。
Just refer to this cookbook from now on it contains recipes of my favourite food.
食谱
Cook-book
是。
Yes.
……
红烧鲤鱼
Braised Carp
清蒸石斑
Steamed Garoupala

整天窝在家里，真无聊！
It's so boring to stay at home all the time!
说得也是。
You're right.
找个好男人来谈谈爱情也不赖。
We should look for some decent men to fall in love with.
娘娘思想太老旧了，不合潮流。谁说爱情一定要一男一女？
Madam, you're too old-fashioned! Who says only man and woman can fall in love?
两个女人当然也可以。
Two women will do too.

找男伴应该门当户对，个性相投，条件相当。
When choosing a partner, it's important that we find someone from a similar background, with a well-matched temperament.
刚好有个人选，我马上带来。
I know of someone who fits the bill! I'll get him here right away!
果然眉清目秀、一表人才。
He's indeed a fine-looking man.
龙配龙，凤配凤……
As the saying goes, a couple has to be well- matched...
蛇娘娘配蛇郎君当然是门户相当。
Since you're Madam Snake and I'm Mister Snake, we're definitely well-matched.

话说杭州临安府有个许姓人家在开药店卖药材。
It's said that in Lin'an county in Hangzhou, there lived a Xu family who owned a medical hall.
许家三代单传，只生个宝贝蛋。
The Xu family had only one male heir in three generations.
许仙，传宗接代要靠你了。
Xu Xian, we're counting on you to carry on the family name.
爹。
Father.
两个恰恰好，一个不算少，应该颁奖给你当模范。
"Two is ideal, one is good enough!" You deserve this award.
这……万万不敢当！
Oh no, I don't deserve this honour!
家庭计划模范
Model of Family Planning
其实早在先前连生十女，才生下许仙这个宝贝蛋。
Actually, my wife had already given birth to ten girls before we had Xu Xian.
...

爹!
Father!
许仙年少时，父亲便因病去世了……
When Xu Xian was still a young boy, his father died of an illness...
爹！为何你去得这么急?
Father, why did you die so soon?
忌
哇！
Wah!
我也觉得没道理。
I feel it's unfair too.
才演两集就要我死去，这是谁的主意?
Why did I have to die after two episodes? Whose idea was it ?
抱歉，因为你非主戏，红包送你冲喜。
Sorry, it's because you're not the lead actor. Here's a red packet for you to ward off the bad luck.
红包
Money

姐弟一行将父亲出殡，草草办完丧事……
Xu Xian and his sisters gave their father a simple burial...
父母早死，我们姐弟顿时失去了依靠。
Now that both our parents have passed away, we have no one to rely on.
我是男人还好，姐姐们的后半辈子要依靠谁?
I'm a man, so it's still all right for me. But my sisters, who are you going to depend on?
我们女人找个人嫁了，吃饭没问题。
All we have to do is find ourselves a husband.
该担心的倒是弟弟你一人!
Brother, you should worry about yourself!

话说杭州府管钱粮的军需官，名叫李仁，他看上了许仙的姐姐，想与她结婚……
Li Ren, the quartermaster attached to Hangzhou County Office, fell for Xu Xian's sister, and wished to marry her...
我家贫，父母又双亡，办不起嫁妆，对不起！
My family is poor and my parents are dead. Sorry, I can't afford any dowry!
我爱的是你的人，没嫁妆没关系。
It's you that I love. It doesn't matter if you don't have any dowry.
还有样东西陪我进夫门。
However, I am bringing something along.
有总比没有好。
Well, it's better than nothing.
孤苦伶仃的弟弟一名。
My orphaned and helpless brother.
是只拖油瓶！
One additional mouth to feed!

拖油瓶当然被看不起，受的是不平等待遇……
Needless to say, the unwelcome addition to the family was not treated fairly...
许仙，端酒过来！
Xu Xian, bring me the wine!
是！姐夫……
Yes! brother-in-law...
砰！
Bang!
姐夫李仁经常借故欺负他……
Li Ren seized every opportunity to bully him...
这个碍眼的拖油瓶，愈看愈生气……
The more I look at him, the angrier I get...
"摔小瓶"骂人！
Li Ren often vented his anger by smashing bottles!
啪！

靠人不如靠自己，还是去跟叔叔做生意。
Instead of depending on others, I'll make my own living... I'll help Uncle in his business.
李家草药铺
Li Medical Hall
叔叔，我想跟你学做草药生意。
Uncle, I'd like to learn about the medicinal trade from you.
当然欢迎。
You're wel-come.
大汉药材的将来得靠你们年轻人加入才能抵挡蛮人的入侵。
The Chinese medicine industry badly needs young people like you to help us withstand the onslaught of foreign medicine.
武田
Takeda
田边制药
Takeda Tanabe Pharma-ceutical Company-tique
安非他命
Anvitamins
李斯德林制药
Listerine Phar-macy maceutique
强生大药
Qiang Sheng Medical Hall
草药铺
安田大药厂
Anda Pharmaceuti-cal Company
××商行
不然只有灭亡一途了！
Otherwise, we'll be wiped out!

李家草药铺
Li Medical Hall
叔叔的草药铺果然生意不好。
Business is bad.
叔叔，咱们度小月时也来兼做别的生意如何？
Why don't we do so-mething else during the slack season?
好啊。
Good idea.
咱们是草药铺，兼差也不要离开本行。
But it must be rela-ted to our medicinal trade.
当然。
Of course.
是兼这个差？
Is this our sideline?
蔬菜也算是草药啊。
Well, vegetables can be considered medicinal herbs too.

*The Tomb-sweeping Festival

清明天气惯会作弄人，有诗为证。
Poems have been written about the unpredictable weather during Qing Ming.
清明时节雨纷纷，
A light drizzle begins to fall during Qing Ming,
路上行人欲断魂。
It dampens the spirit of passers-by.
借问酒家何处有？
Where can I find a wineshop?
牧童遥指杏花村。
The cowherd points to the Apricot Village.
五月花酒家
May Flower Wine-shop
新加坡
Singapore
黑美人酒家
Black Beauty Wine-shop

群芳过后西湖好，狼藉残红，飞絮蒙蒙……
The flowers wither and the leaves fall but West Lake is as lovely as before...
垂柳栏杆尽日风。
The weeping willows sway in the breeze.
笙歌散尽游人去，始觉春空，垂下窗栊，
The visitors leave as the music fades. As the shutters are closed, silence falls,
双燕归来细雨中。
A pair of swallows appears in the drizzle.

好黑的皮肤！
What tanned skin!
好白的肤色！
And what fair skin!
黑是健康美！
Such tanned skin is a sign of good health!
白是因为贫血。
Such pale skin is a sign of anaemia.

在下姓许名仙，排行第一，家住过军桥黑珠儿巷。
My name is Xu Xian. I'm the eldest in my family. I live in Black Pearl Alley near Guojun Bridge.
奴家姓白名素贞，家住箭桥附近。
My name is Bai Suzhen and I live near Arrow Bridge.
她是我的丫鬟，名叫小青。
This is my maid,Xiaoqing.
小青贵姓？
What's her surname?
阶级歧视不公平！
Class discrimination —it's unfair!
婢女只是个下人，有名已是不错了，岂能有姓？
She's only a servant girl. It's good enough that she has a name.

我生肖属蛇。
I was born in the year of the snake.
我生肖也属蛇。
So was I.
想不到咱们还真是同年呢！
We are of the same age fancy that!
是啊。
Exactly.
小生今年刚满二十二。
I'm twenty-two years old.
我多了两轮，今年四六一枝花。
I was born 24 years before you, so I'm forty-six years old.
是个老娘……
She's an old hag...

真是艳福不浅，交上了两个美娇娘。
I'm lucky to have made the acquaintance of two beautiful ladies.
求求老天爷帮忙牵红线，拉近我们的距离！
Oh heaven, please be my matchmaker, so that I may get to know them better!
有求必应，果然灵验。
Heaven has answered my prayer.
沥沥沥
Pitter-Patter
沥沥沥
Pitter-Patter
沥沥沥
Pitter-Patter
小雨来得正是时候！
What a timely shower!
沥沥沥
Pitter-Patter

你俩娇滴滴淋不得雨，这把雨伞借你们遮雨。
You two delicate ladies mustn't get caught in rain. Here, take my umbrella.
你把伞借了我们，你怎么办？
Oh,what about yourself?
没问题。
Don't worry.
我可以找个自然的小伞代替。
I'll find myself a small "natural" umbrella.
如此岂不更加诗情画意？
Now, isn't this more roman-tic?

寒舍就在箭桥双茶坊巷口，明日请到寒舍取伞。
My humble abode is at Arrow Bridge. Do come and collect your umbrella.
一定去！
I'll be there!
想不到出来扫墓，竟交得桃花运。
Who would have expected a visit to the tomb to lead to such a romantic encounter?
希望美梦成真，早日尝到爱的果实。
I hope my dream comes true and I'll be able to taste the sweetness of love soon.
当！
Dang!

第二天，许仙果真如约到箭桥双茶坊巷口找白娘子。
The next day, Xu Xian made a trip to Arrow Bridge to look for Madam White Snake.
请问这附近可有座白王府？
Could you tell me if there's a White Mansion in the vicinity?
这是贫民区，哪来王府？只是昨日突然增多一座豪华的大屋。
This is a slum area of course there's no mansion here. But strangely enough, a very grand house sprang up here overnight.
一日造成，真有这等怪事？
A house built in just a day?
造样品屋当然快速，要不要进来参观订一户？
Such model houses can be put up in no time?
西湖建筑工地
West Lake Buliders Construction Site
样品屋
Model House

白娘娘的家可真是豪华惊人！
Madam White's residence is indeed grandiose!
相公果然如约而至，真是有信之人。
You've kept your promise to come.
你们这巨宅可真漂亮得吓人！
What a grand house this is!
只是门面好看，里面可惨不忍睹。
This is only a facade.
拍片搭景，只须搭半边屋。
It's just a prop, so you don't need a complete structure.
...

许公子真劳驾你了。
Master Xu, sorry to have made you come all the way here.
白娘娘你别客气。
Not at all, Madam White.
你请坐，我吩咐小青泡茶。
Please have a seat. I'll get Xiaoqing to make you some tea.
想办法尽量把他留住。
Do your best to make him stay here.
这个我会。
No problem.
请喝茶，有乌龙、普洱、铁观音、龙井，请慢慢品尝。
Have some tea. We have many types Oolong, Pu'erh, Tiekuangyin and Longjing. Happy sampling.
...

...
我家白娘娘喜欢你，欲把终身相托，不知官人可愿意？
My mistress has fallen in love with you, and is willing to spend the rest of her life with you. Are you willing to marry her?
你们两人年貌相当，天生一对，结成百年夫妻好不好？
You're both very compatible in terms of age and appearance. You make a perfect couple.
可是……可是……
But... but...
再说白娘娘家财万贯，陪嫁的现金不说，外加洋屋一栋送给你。
Besides, Madam White comes from a very rich family. Other than cash, you will also have a big house.
可是……可是……可是……
But... but...
别再可是了，最后"一个条件"买一送一！外加青春婢女一个你还不满意？
No more buts! I'll make you one last offer. Buy one and get one free. Marry her and you'll have me as well. What more can you ask for?

可是我家中贫困，哪来的钱讨老婆成亲？
I come from a very poor family, and cannot afford to take a wife.
原来是为了这个……
Don't worry about money...
没钱简单！这两锭银子你先拿回去。
You may have these two silver ingots.
谢谢小青姐姐看得起，来日有钱再还你。
Xiaoqing, thank you for thinking so highly of me. I'll return you the money some other day.
算你抵押贷款十分利，抵押品当然就是你。
I'll charge you 10% interest for the loan and of course, you're the mortgage.
十分利
10%
Int

青姐，我这就回去，马上请媒人来提亲。
Xiaoqing, I'll go home and get a matchmaker to ask for Madam White's hand.
慢着！口说无凭无据……
Just a minute! We should put this down in black and white.
先把订婚证书签了。
Both parties will need to sign an engagement certificate.
现在可以走了吧？
Can I leave now?
等着！还差一道手续。
Hold on!
还得再签一纸银子的借据。
You'll have to sign an IOU.
……

来一只
烤鹅！
One roast goose, please!
许仙为求姐姐替他说媒，于是在街上买了鲜鱼精肉提回去……
Xu Xian decided to ask his sister to be the matchmaker, so he bought some fish and meat from the street market...
老板！最上等好酒来两瓶。
Two bottles of the best liquor, please.
是！
Okay!
最好的酒要数这种XO级，每瓶八千六百七十一。
XO, our best brand of liqour. Each bottle costs 8,671 units of cash.
XO
好酒果然真够劲，
光听价钱就醉了！
This is indeed a strong brew. The mere mention of its price is enough to knock him out!
XO

姐姐、姐夫请坐下来喝酒吃肉。
My dear sister and brother-in-law, join me in the feast.
日常不见酒盏面，今天有何喜事，为何花大钱？
You hardly ever touch liquor. Why the sudden splurge?
好事容后再说，来！先喝酒。
I have some good news to announce, but let's have a drink first.
干！
Cheers!
干！
Cheers!
XO
弟弟请我喝酒，到底是为哪桩？
Brother, you still haven't told us the good news.
对啊！
到底是为了什么事？
Gosh, I can't remember what it is!

于是许仙把清明扫墓，雨中遇佳人，借伞定奇缘从头细说一遍……
Xu Xian recounted how he had met the two women after a visit to the cemetery.
希望姐姐姐夫同意，我将她们两人娶进这家门。
I hope to marry the young lady and her maid. May I have your consent?
我举双手赞成，并还答应替你分摊一半责任。
You have my full support. I'll share the responsibility with you.
将她们两人娶进门，你照顾一人，我照顾一人！
I'll take care of one lady and you, the other!

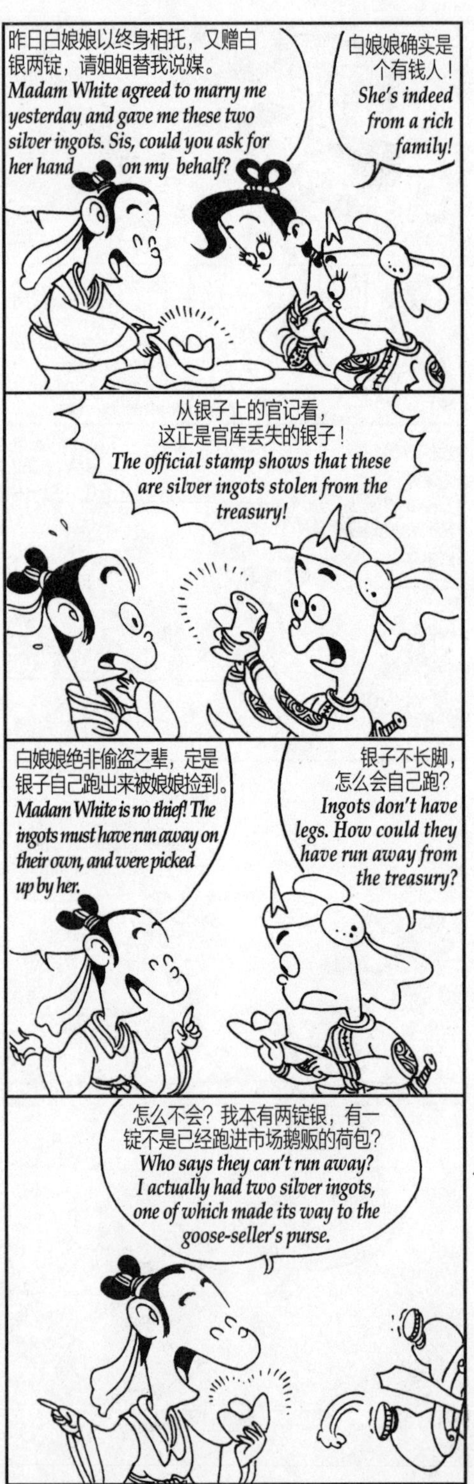
昨日白娘娘以终身相托，又赠白银两锭，请姐姐替我说媒。
Madam White agreed to marry me yesterday and gave me these two silver ingots. Sis, could you ask for her hand on my behalf?
白娘娘确实是个有钱人！
She's indeed from a rich family!
从银子上的官记看，这正是官库丢失的银子！
The official stamp shows that these are silver ingots stolen from the treasury!
白娘娘绝非偷盗之辈，定是银子自己跑出来被娘娘捡到。
Madam White is no thief! The ingots must have run away on their own, and were picked up by her.
银子不长脚，怎么会自己跑？
Ingots don't have legs. How could they have run away from the treasury?
怎么不会？我本有两锭银，有一锭不是已经跑进市场鹅贩的荷包？
Who says they can't run away? I actually had two silver ingots, one of which made its way to the goose-seller's purse.

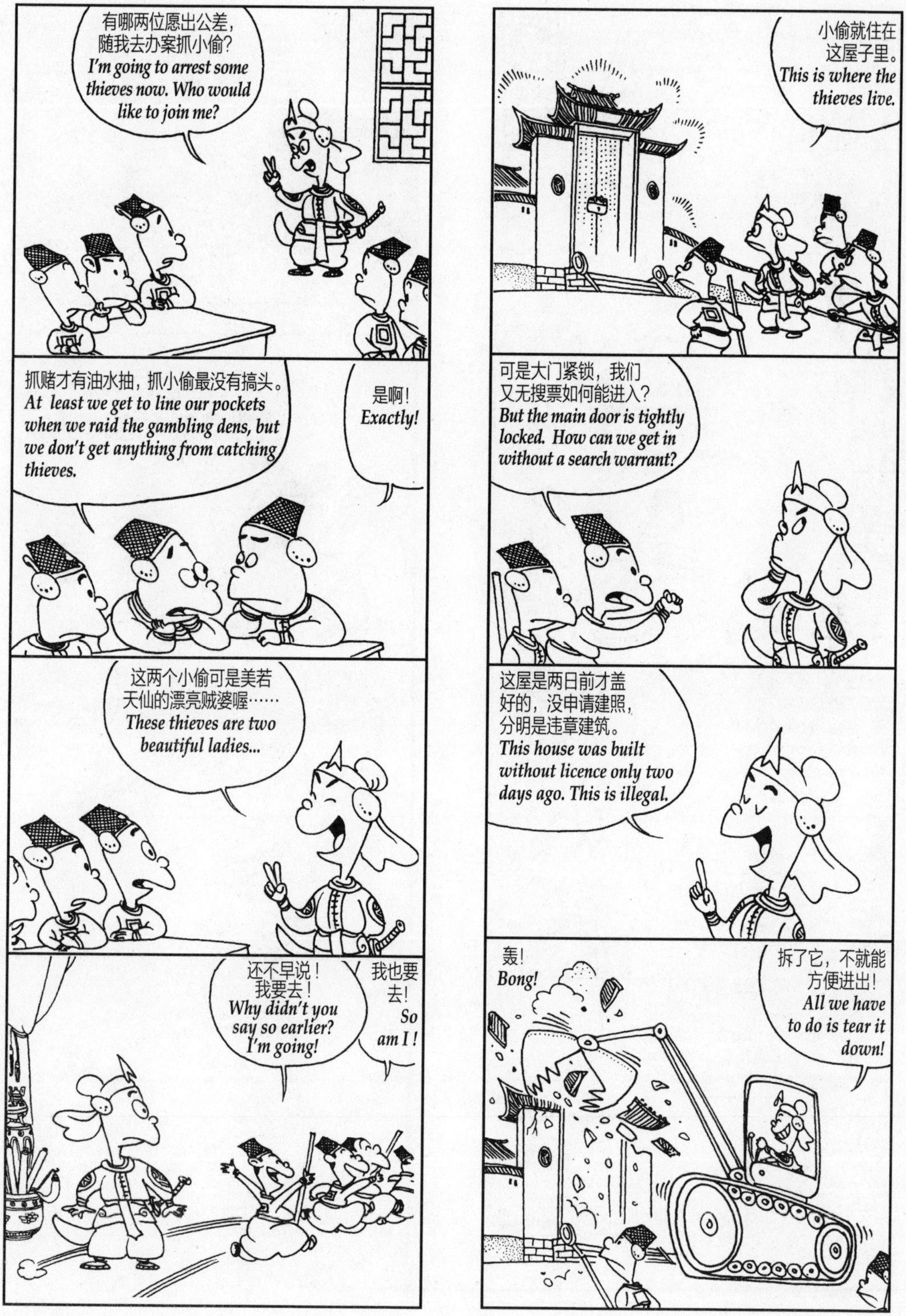

有哪两位愿出公差，随我去办案抓小偷？
I'm going to arrest some thieves now. Who would like to join me?

抓赌才有油水抽，抓小偷最没有搞头。
At least we get to line our pockets when we raid the gambling dens, but we don't get anything from catching thieves.

是啊！
Exactly!

这两个小偷可是美若天仙的漂亮贼婆喔……
These thieves are two beautiful ladies...

还不早说！我要去！
Why didn't you say so earlier? I'm going!

我也要去！
So am I!

给我仔细地搜查！
Make a thorough search!
库银完好地放在这里。
The silver ingots from the treasury are still intact here.
报告长官！找不到贼婆，库银却在床上找到。
Sir, we can't find the two women except for the silver ingots on the bed.
逮不到主谋，这个案子如何销案了结？
How am I going to close the case?
把库银押回去起诉，罪名是"不假外出"。
Bring the silver ingots back to be prosecuted. They shall be charged with absence without leave.
冤枉！
We're innocent!
哇！
Wah!

县官对许仙从轻发落，发配镇江为民……
Xu Xian received a light sentence and was banished to Zhenjiang...
可怜的弟弟，小小年纪就得远离家门到镇江去。
My poor brother-fancy being banished to such a faraway place at such a young age!
相公这么做，为的是什么？
Why did you do such a thing?
把他发配到镇江为民，正是我出的主意。
It was my idea.
麻烦的亲戚离得越远越可喜！
Troublesome relatives should be kept at arm's length!

许仙来到镇江，蒙姐夫的
推荐，暂居在何员外家中。
Xu Xian's
brother-in-law had
arranged for him to
stay with Squire
He for the time being.
光阴似箭，
匆匆又过了半年……
Half a year went by...
平白让许仙住了半年，
对我们有什么好处？
What do we gain by letting
Xu Xian stay here?
当然好处多多！
We have
plenty to gain
from it!
他是本剧的主角，他不住在我们家，
哪轮到我们上台演出？
He's the protagonist in the story. If he
hadn't come to stay with us, would we
have the chance to appear on stage?
说得也是！
You've got a
point there!

请问是否有位
许公子住在这里？
Excuse me, is there a
Master Xu staying here?
有啊！
请进。
Oh yes. Please
come in.
你这个贼婆为何不放
过我，还要苦苦缠我？
You thief! Why won't
you leave me alone?
Stop pestering me!
许仙！你真是不知好歹，
人在福中不知福！给她们缠
有什么不好？
Xu Xian, you fool! You don't
know how lucky you are!
Isn't it good to be pestered
by them?
...
要是她们肯缠我，
那有多好！
I'd love to be in
your place!

你清白无辜？
为何给我官府失窃的银子？
If you were innocent, why would you give me silver ingots stolen from the treasury?
公子，这是误会啊。
Master Xu, this is a misunderstanding.
这些银子是先夫留下来的，为何是赃银，我也不知……
My late husband left me the silver ingots. I have no idea they were stolen property.
这件事害我惹上官司，差点坐牢。
Did you know I almost had to go to jail because of those ingots?
可惜你没坐牢……
It's a pity you didn't go to jail.
不然可借题诉求，年底也参加竞选民意代表。
Otherwise, you'd have a good excuse to stand for election as a people's representative.

酒
第二天，小青受命到街上找房子。
The next day, Xiaoqing set off to look for a place to stay.
我把三百个房间的旅馆租下来了！
I've booked all the 300 rooms in this hotel!
我们只有三个人，为何租这么大饭店？
There are only three of us. Why did you do so?
多下来的房十倍价钱转租别人好赚钱！
We can sub-let the other rooms and make a profit from it!
当然得先把旅馆改成医院，客房当病房好收钱。
But we'll have to convert the hotel into a hospital first. Then we'll make money.

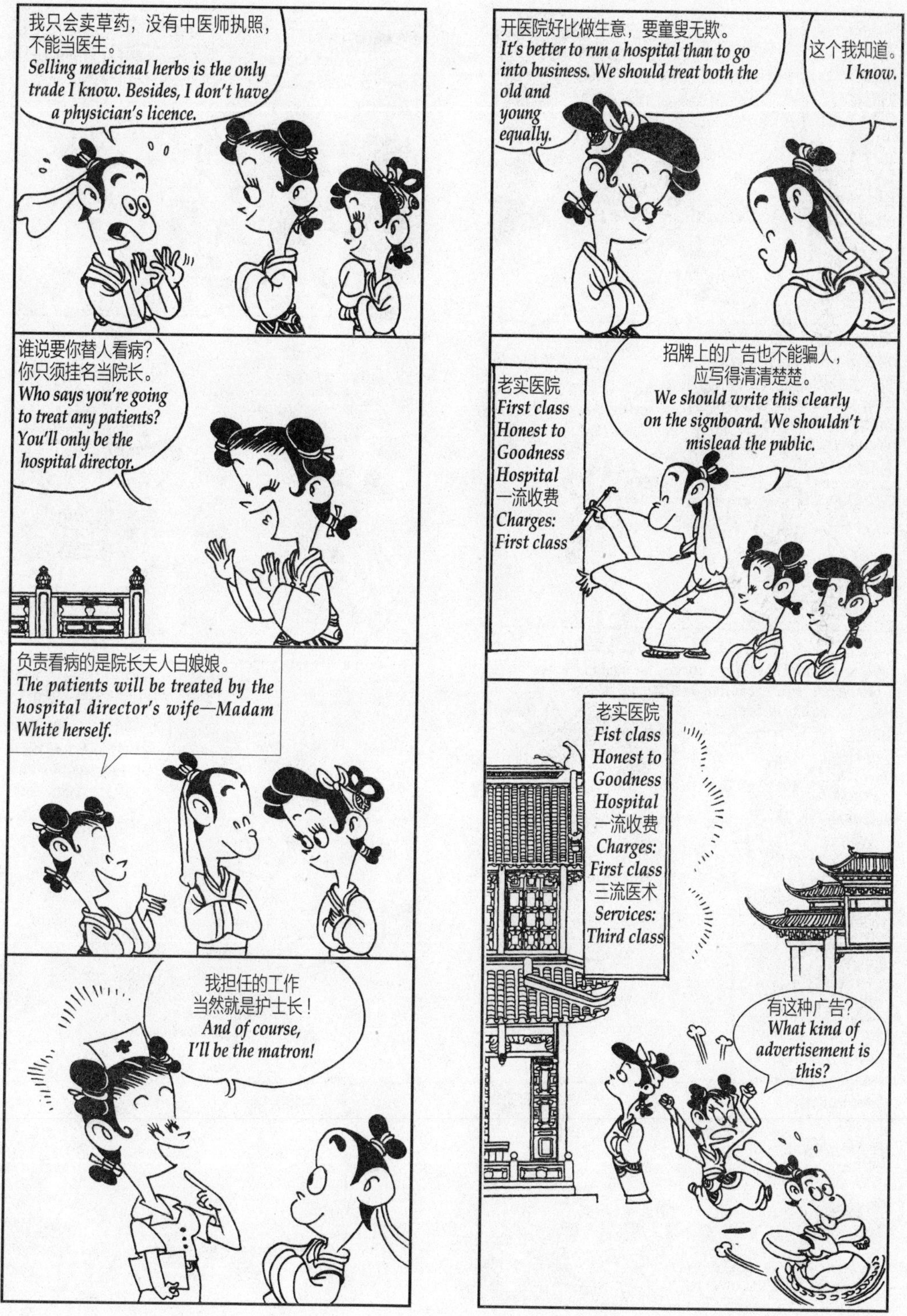

我只会卖草药，没有中医师执照，不能当医生。
Selling medicinal herbs is the only trade I know. Besides, I don't have a physician's licence.

谁说要你替人看病？你只须挂名当院长。
Who says you're going to treat any patients? You'll only be the hospital director.

负责看病的是院长夫人白娘娘。
The patients will be treated by the hospital director's wife—Madam White herself.

我担任的工作当然就是护士长！
And of course, I'll be the matron!

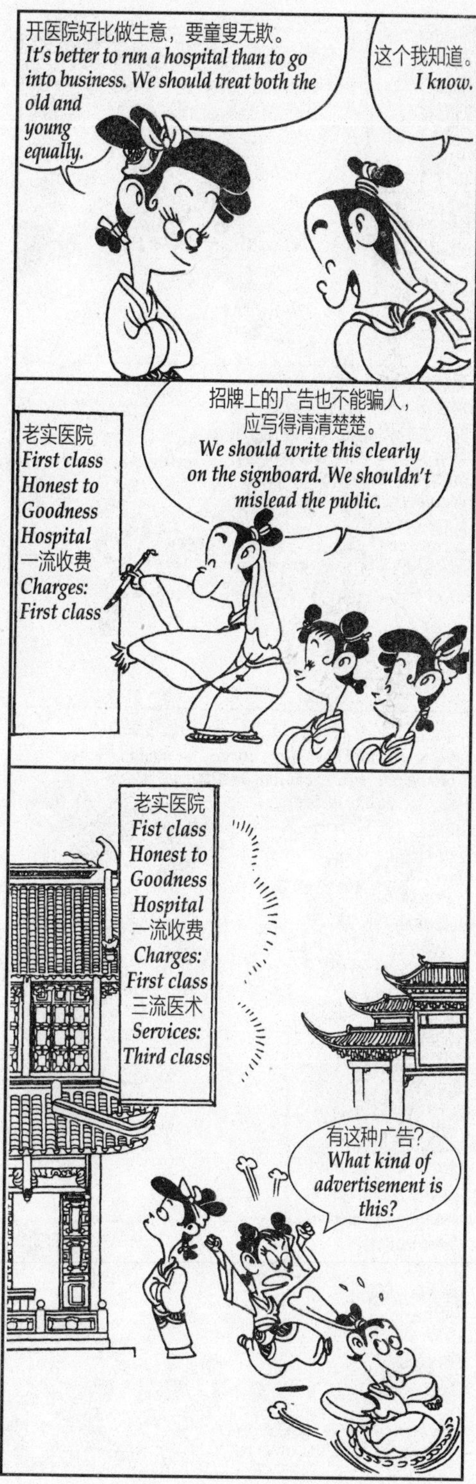

老实医院
生意不好，没病人来。
Business is so poor. We hardly have any patients.
自从开了医院，希望人人都生病，真怀疑自己是否变坏了心肠？
Ever since we set up the hospital, I've been hoping that everybody will fall ill. Have I really become that wicked?
开棺木店希望人死，这是人之常情……
Well, if you were a coffin-maker, you'd naturally hope that more people would die too...
既然别人不生病，我们改变经营，专看没病的病人。
Since we don't have any patients, we should change our management style, and treat those who are healthy instead.
没病也要上医院？
Perfectly healthy people go to hospitals too?
老实美容整形医院
Honest to Goodness Cosmetic Surgery Hospital
果然真有这种病人！
There really are such people!

你要做隆鼻、薄唇、去斑的手术。
You need to have the bridge of your nose raised, your lips made thin, and the freckles on your face removed.
是！
Yes!
小青，我的午餐呢？
Xiaoqing, where's my lunch?
哈哈，太忙了竟忘了做饭。
Ha! Ha! I've been so busy that I forgot to fix lunch.
没时间到市场买菜了，只好就地取材。
I have no time to go to the market, so we'll have to make do with whatever is available.
克补、维他命丸、葡萄糖等，吃了保证够营养！
Capsules, vitamin pills and glucose sweets-they provide you with all the nutrition you need!
!

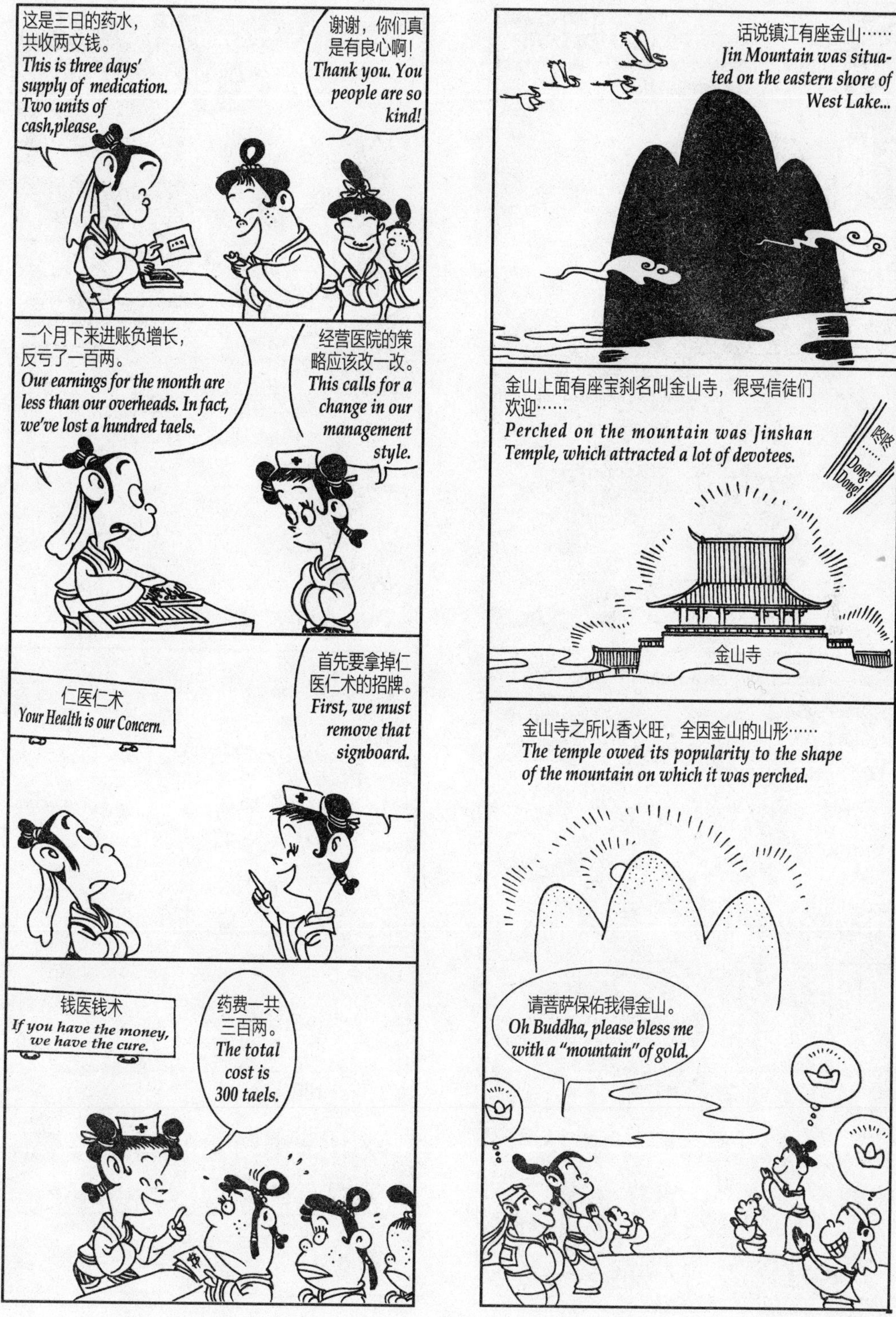

这是三日的药水，共收两文钱。
This is three days' supply of medication. Two units of cash,please.

谢谢，你们真是有良心啊！
Thank you. You people are so kind!

一个月下来进账负增长，反亏了一百两。
Our earnings for the month are less than our overheads. In fact, we've lost a hundred taels.

经营医院的策略应该改一改。
This calls for a change in our management style.

仁医仁术
Your Health is our Concern.

首先要拿掉仁医仁术的招牌。
First, we must remove that signboard.

钱医钱术
If you have the money, we have the cure.

药费一共三百两。
The total cost is 300 taels.

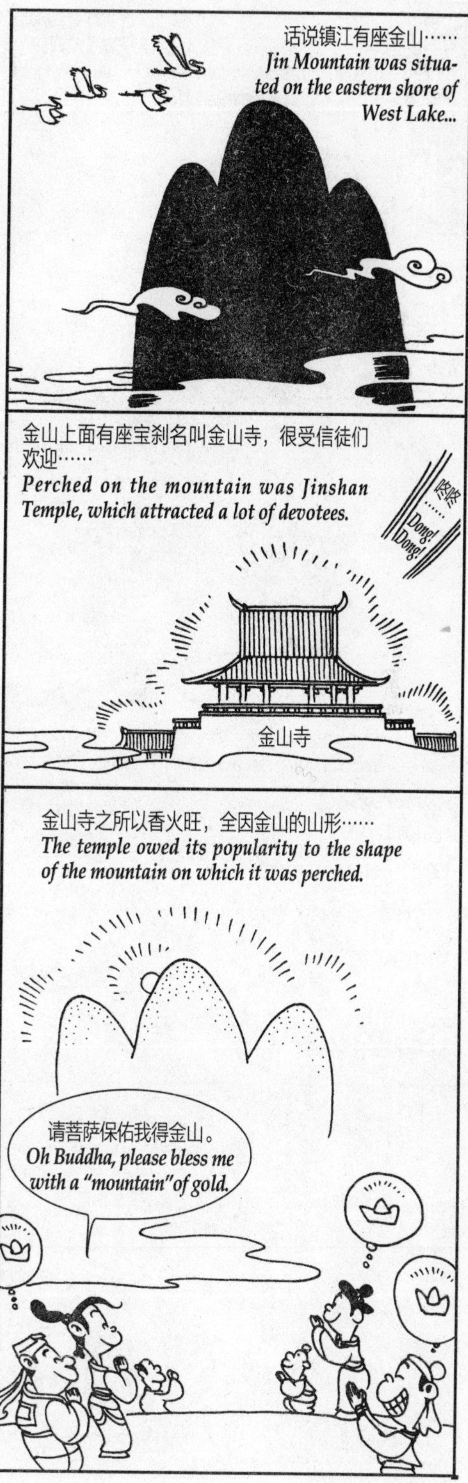

* One zhang=3.33 metres.

这么多善男信女来求神保佑。当然是希望能有求必应。
Our temple attracts so many devotees.
不知信徒所求的，神明有没有达成他们的心愿。
Of course, we hope to meet all their needs.
不过我却从信徒中，求来了纯金神明。
But I wonder if the gods will really answer their prayers. Anyway, through them, I've managed to get a Buddha made of pure gold.

啊！镇上一股妖气冲天……
Ah! There's a foul smell from the town...
妖气原来是从白蛇精开的医院冲出来的。
It's from the hospital run by the white snake spirit.
待我下山为民除去此害！
I must leave the temple and rid the town of the scourge!
现在民智已开，用不着师父出头下山除害。
People are more aware of their rights now. You can save yourself the trip to town.
抗议！
Protest!
抗议！
Protest!
老实医院焚化炉
Honest to Goodness Hospital Incinerator
抗议
Protest!
抗议空气污染
Against Pollution!
环境保护
Save our environment!
生活品质破坏！
Don't destroy the quality of our life!
抗议黑烟公害！
Against Pollution!

白娘娘乃是峨眉山蛇妖所化，小青是西湖鱼精所变的妖怪！
Madam White is actually a snake spirit from Mt Emei, and Xiaoqing, a carp spirit from West Lake!
白蛇、青鱼这两个妖孽胆敢私下红尘，为师誓将她们除去，从地球上消失！
They had the audacity to sneak their way into the mortal world! I vow to destroy them and make them disappear from the face of the earth!
其实蛇与鱼并不丑恶狠毒，他们也有权生存在世。
Actually, snakes and carps are neither ugly nor venomous creatures. They have the right to be in this world too.
你怎会替它们求情？平日念的是什么经书？
Whose side are you on? What Buddhist books did you refer to?
徒弟念的是这本《可爱的动物》。
"The Wonderful World of Animals!"
…
可爱的动物

法明，命你即刻设法启度许仙，拆散他们的姻缘。
Fa Ming, I want you to rush to Suzhou and warn Xu Xian of the danger he is in! Break up his marriage too!
是。
Yes.
俗话说："促成一段姻缘胜造七级浮屠。"
As the saying goes, "Bringing a couple together in marriage is better than giving offerings to the gods."
师父何苦要做坏人，硬生生地拆散他们的幸福？
Teacher, why do you insist on being a villain and breaking them up?
我不入地狱谁入地狱！
Well, somebody has to do the dirty work!

这日，法明禅师奉命来找许仙……
Under the orders of his teacher Fa Ming made his way to Suzhou in search of Xu Xian...
挂号处
Registration Counter
阿弥陀佛，我有急事找许先生。
Amitabha, I wish to see Mr Xu regarding a very urgent matter.
你姓甚名谁？今年几岁，家住哪里？
What's your name? How old are you? Where do you live?
我叫法明，今年廿一，家住金山寺。
My name is Fa Ming. I'm twenty-one and I live at Jinshan Temple.
挂号处
Registration Counter
这是你的挂号证，请缴急诊挂号费三两银。
This is your number, and the fee for the Emergency Department is three taels of silver.

贫僧法明，奉师命特来为许施主消灾解厄。
My name is Fa Ming. My teacher sent me here to get you out of trouble.
这位师父，有急事找我吗？
Sir, what can I do for you?
施主被妖孽所缠，夫人白娘娘是千年蛇精，婢女小青是个鲤鱼精。
Sir, you've been bewitched by an evil spirit. Your wife, Madam White is actually a thousand-year-old snake spirit, and your maid Xiaoqing, a fish spirit.
真的？
Really?
可恶的妖和尚，敢来此搬弄是非，指我是个妖精！
You wicked monk! How dare you tell tales, and accuse me of being a fish spirit!
妖孽！在本法师面前还不现出原形！
Witch,you'd better reveal your true self!
让你瞧瞧我的本相，敢说我是鱼精？
Very well, I'll let you have a look at my true self! How dare you call me a fish spirit?
确实是条美人鱼精！
My God! What a superb figure she's got! She's really a beautiful fish spirit!

我们主仆三人，在此安分守己地过着幸福的日子。
The three of us have always minded our own business and led a peaceful life.
你何苦来到这里，破坏我们的幸福？
Why did you travel all the way here to disrupt our happiness?
我奉命来此，就为了能让故事延续，能多演几集。
I was sent here so that the story can continue for a few more episodes.
否则你们三人从此过着幸福的日子，岂不没戏了？
If the three of you lived happily ever after, then there wouldn't be anymore drama, right?

原来白娘娘是蛇妖，小青则是鲤鱼精……
Madam White is actually a snake spirit, and Xiaoqing, a fish spirit...
我今天才知道家里的老婆竟是蛇……
I only found out today that my wife is actually a snake...
老婆是蛇算什么？小意思。
So what if your wife is a snake?
一点都不可怕。
That's nothing frightening.
还不可怕吗？
It isn't?
惧内协会
我家的母老虎才吓人……
The tigress in my home is more frightening...
我家有只河东狮！
And I have a virago at home!

端阳节那天你让白娘娘喝雄黄酒，待她醉了便可知道她是不是蛇精！
On the day of the Dragon Boat Festival, give your wife some liquor with realgar added to it. When she's drunk, you'll be able to tell if she's indeed a snake spirit!
好办法，我回去试试便知。
Good idea, I'll give it a try.
与你相谈，心宽了不少。
I feel so much better after talking to you.
请付谈话费三千文。
That will be 3, 000 units of cash, please.
你算哪门子江湖术士，跟你谈两句话还要收钱？
Are you some kind of charlatan or what? Why should I pay you for this conversation?
我不是江湖术士，而是正牌律师。
Well, I'm not acharlatan, but a licenced lawyer.
谈话费，一个时辰收三千文。
My counselling fees are 3, 000 units of cash per hour.
法律博士律师
Doctorate of Law

端阳节那天，许仙果然买回雄黄酒想灌醉白娘娘，试她一试……
On the day of the Dragon Boat Festival, Xu Xian bought some realgar from the market. He hoped to make Madam White drunk to find out if she was really a snake...
娘子，端阳佳节陪我一同喝杯雄黄酒好避邪。
Dearie, it's the Dragon Boat Festival. Why don't you join me for a drink? It will help ward off evil spirits.
抱歉！我不能陪你喝酒。
Sorry I can't join you.
依法规定，未成年不能喝酒。
The law forbids all minors from drinking alcohol.
都快七老八十喽，还未成年少女呢？
You're almost eighty. Are you still a minor?
可是肚子里的小孩才满六个月呀！
But the baby in my womb is barely six months old!

过节破例喝点有什么关系？再不喝酒我要生气了！
This is such a happy occasion. Can't you make an exception and drink a little? If you don't, I'm going to be very angry!
好吧，我就陪你喝一口。
Very well, I'll just take a sip.
酒
这样才听话嘛，嘻嘻嘻嘻嘻……
That's more like it! Hee Hee...
两杯下肚，果真有变化……
She really looks different now...
咕！
Hic!
既然开了酒戒，就喝它个痛快！
I might as well drink to my fill!
干！
Cheers!
果然现出原形！
She's revealed her true colours!
酒

我扶你到床上躺一下。
I'll help you to the bed and you can get some rest.
酒喝得太多了，怕要出丑态现出原形来……
I've had too much of a drink. I'd better stop before I make a fool of myself.
咕！
Hic!
娘子你安心休息。
Dearie, have a good rest.
奇怪，并没有如我所料变成蛇精。
Strange, she hasn't turned into a snake as I've thought she would.
但还是现出原形……
Still, I've seen her for what she really is...

偷偷瞧一瞧，看看是否真变成原形……
Let me take a peek and see if she has really turned into a snake...
哇！果真是蛇精！
Wow! She really is!
砰！
Bang!
哎呀！
Ouch!
演得太逼真了……
He's really good...
No! 暂停录像！
No good! Stop rolling!

相公已吓得失魂，除非得南极仙翁的仙草才能回春。
He's been frightened out of his wits! Only the magic herbs of the South Pole can save him now.
我要到海外仙岛盗仙草，速替我准备行李！
I'm going to the South Pole to steal the magic herbs! Get my luggage ready quickly!
是。
Yes.
这是机票和外钞，还有你的护照。
This is your air ticket, your passport and some foreign currency.
最重要的是你的蒙面罩。
But the most important thing is your mask.
...

急急如勒令，有请筋斗云载我到仙境盗仙草！
Abracadabra! Please take me to the South Pole so that I can steal some magic herbs!
云来！
Come here, Cloud!
你坐前座，还是后座？
Do you want the front or back seat?
有什么差别吗？
What difference does it make?
...
头等舱多十两银子。
A first-class seat costs ten taels of silver more.
南极仙翁就住这里。
The Deity of the South Pole lives here.
谢谢你了。
Thank you so much.
不客气。
Not at all.
不见半个人影，会不会是弄错地方了？
There isn't a single soul here. Have I come to the wrong place?
这里确是南极。
Yes, this is the South Pole.

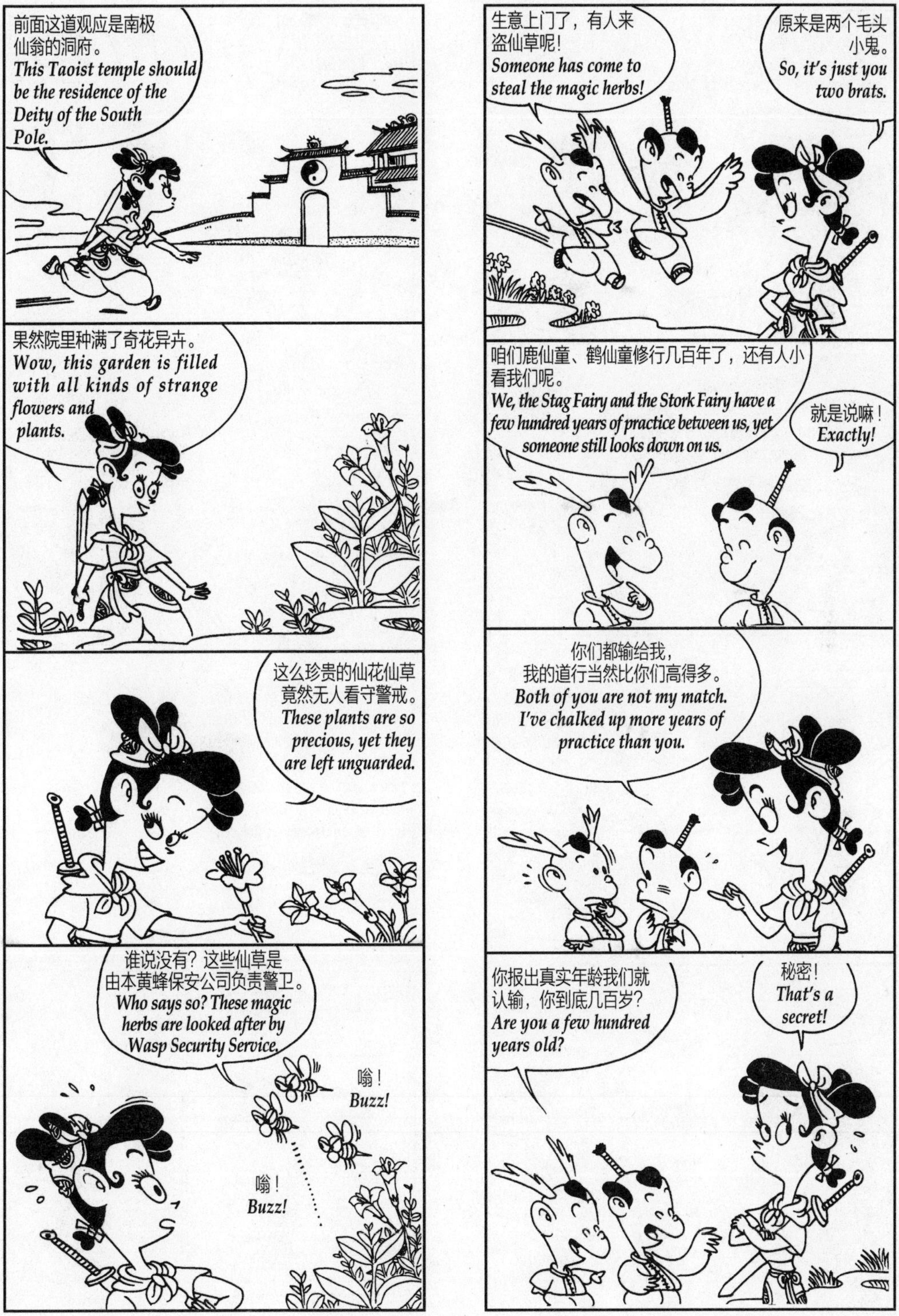

前面这道观应是南极仙翁的洞府。
This Taoist temple should be the residence of the Deity of the South Pole.

果然院里种满了奇花异卉。
Wow, this garden is filled with all kinds of strange flowers and plants.

这么珍贵的仙花仙草竟然无人看守警戒。
These plants are so precious, yet they are left unguarded.

谁说没有？这些仙草是由本黄蜂保安公司负责警卫。
Who says so? These magic herbs are looked after by Wasp Security Service.

嗡！
Buzz!

嗡！
Buzz!

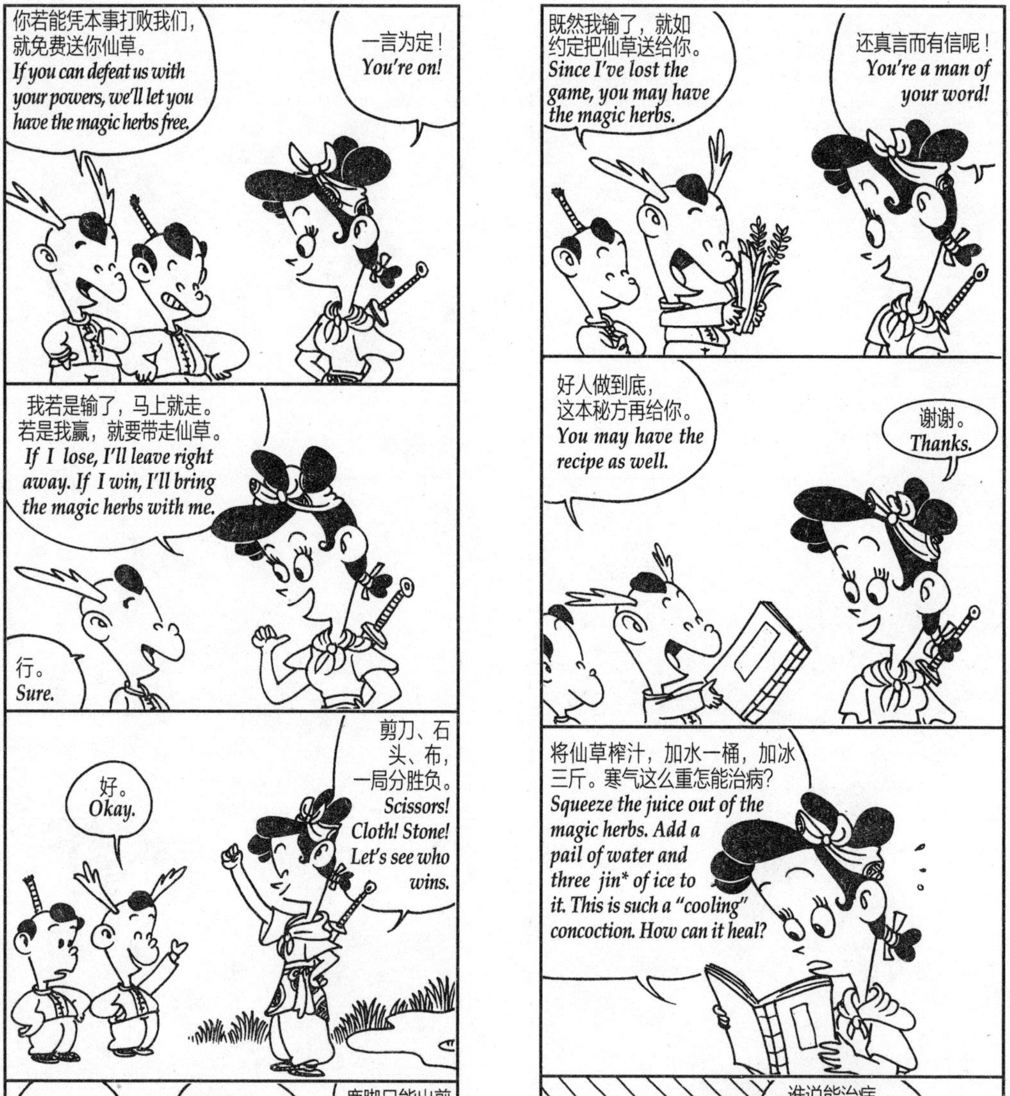

你若能凭本事打败我们，就免费送你仙草。
If you can defeat us with your powers, we'll let you have the magic herbs free.

一言为定！
You're on!

我若是输了，马上就走。若是我赢，就要带走仙草。
If I lose, I'll leave right away. If I win, I'll bring the magic herbs with me.

行。
Sure.

剪刀、石头、布，一局分胜负。
Scissors! Cloth! Stone! Let's see who wins.

好。
Okay.

石头！
Stone!

啊！输了……
Ah! I've lost...

鹿脚只能出剪刀，当然要输！
Just look at his hoof! There's no way he can win the game!

1 *jin*=0.5*kg*

白娘娘，你不在深山修炼，为何跑到我洞府放肆？
Madam White, what are you doing in my cave instead of meditating in the mountains?
仙翁救命，家夫因受惊吓而昏迷不醒，求南极仙翁大德救救命！
Immortal, my husband is unconscious after being frightened out of his wits! Please save him!
我是修道者，如何能替人治病？
I'm just a practitioner of the Tao. I know nothing about the art of healing.
仙翁请慈悲为怀，你不援手救家夫，叫我送他到哪里去？
Immortal, please have pity on me. If you don't save my husband, where can I send him to?
速去台大医院急诊处，不就可以了？
Just send him to the Emergency Department of Taiwan University Hospital.

求仙翁赐我仙丹，好让我带回给家夫吃了治病。
Immortal, please give me an elixir. My husband is really very ill. Only the elixir can save him now.
我修行只做超级静坐，并不炼药制仙丹。
I only know the skill of meditating. I know nothing about making elixirs.
只要能救命就行。
It does not matter as long as it can cure my husband.
中国仙丹难找，外国仙丹倒是到处都可以买到。
Chinese elixirs may be hard to find, but foreign ones can be found everywhere.
买三粒美国仙丹阿斯匹灵。
Three tablets of American elixirs—aspirins please.
西药房
Pharmacy
伤风
Flu
一粒五块钱。
Each tablet costs $5!

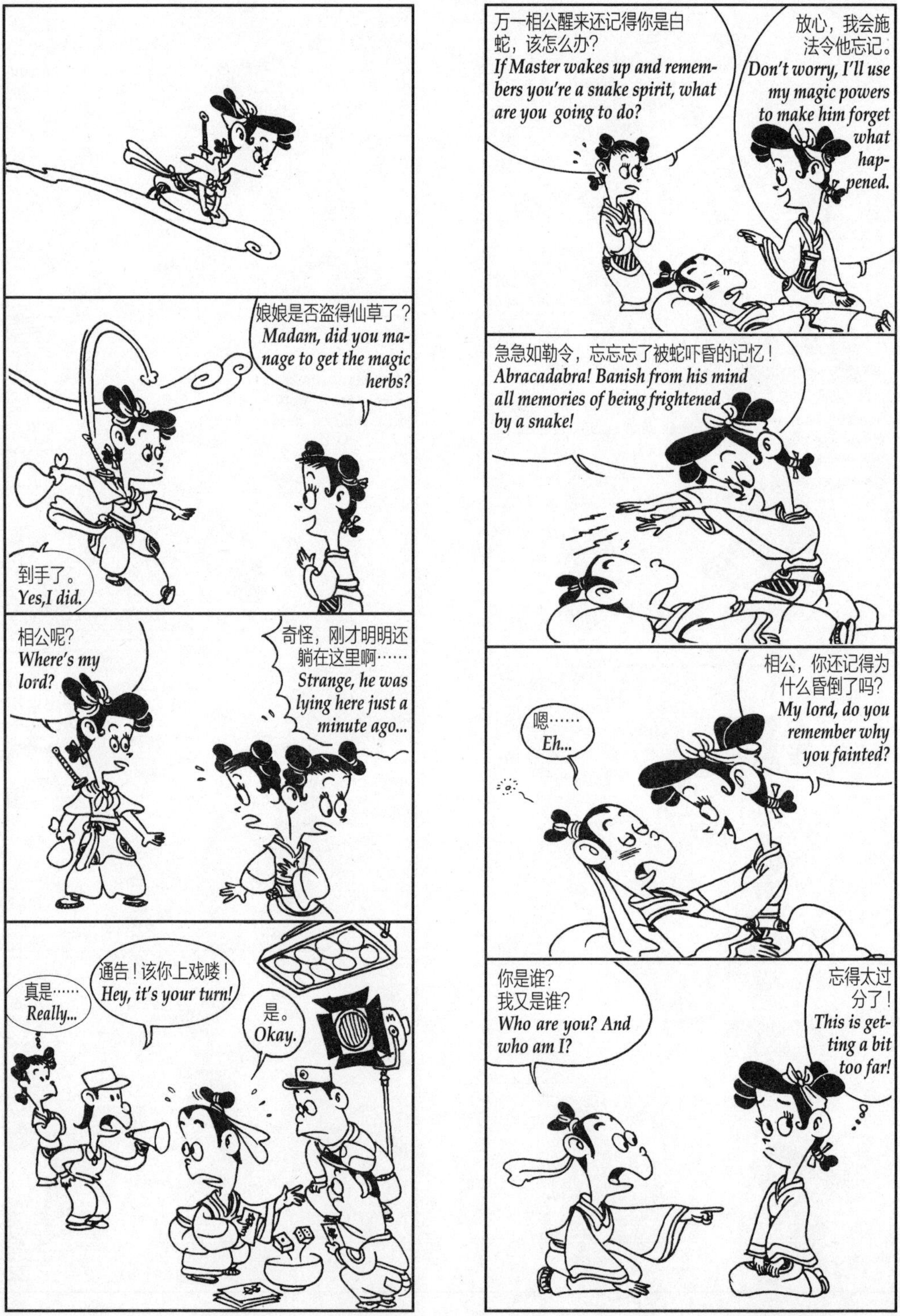

娘娘是否盗得仙草了？
Madam, did you manage to get the magic herbs?
到手了。
Yes,I did.
相公呢？
Where's my lord?
奇怪，刚才明明还躺在这里啊……
Strange, he was lying here just a minute ago...
真是……
Really...
通告！该你上戏喽！
Hey, it's your turn!
是。
Okay.

日复一日年复一年，日子过得不新鲜。
Day after day, year after year, life goes on in the same old way.

光阴似箭，匆匆又过了半年……
Before we knew it, another six months had passed...

整天待在屋子里，闷得人要发慌了……
I'm cooped up in the house all day. This is driving me crazy...

原来你也得了这种婚姻病，看来病情还不轻。
So you've caught the 'marital disease'. Looks like it's rather serious.

我生病了？得的是什么病？
I'm ill ?What am I suffering from?

七年之痒症！
The seven-year-itch!

许仙不知不觉间，来到金山寺上香。
Somehow, Xu Xian made his way to Jinshan Temple where he burnt some incense.
这位施主，本寺住持有请。
Sir, our abbot wishes to speak to you.
哦！
Oh!
原来是法海师父找我。
Reverend Fa Hai, I'm pleased to meet you.
施主请坐。
Sir, please take a seat.
不敢，我站着就行。
No, thanks. I'd rather stand.

上回你用酒将那蛇妖灌出原形，难道你忘了？
Have you forgotten how that woman revealed her real self after she got drunk?
奇怪，这件事我一直想不起来，不记得……
It's strange, but I don't seem to recall...
定是她施法让你忘了这段剧情。
She must have used her magic powers to make you forget it.
不过我已将证据保留下来。
But I've kept the proof.
请看八月二十九日的《联合报》万象版就能证明。
Take a look at this report in Lianhe Bao on Aug 29.
果然！
Really!

可怕啊，娘子果然是白蛇，师父你要救救我……
Oh, this is so terrible. Madam White is actually a snake spirit. Teacher, please help me...
那当然。
Sure.
你暂时在此住三天，蛇妖上门来要人时，我会施法将她制服。
Stay here for three days. When she's here to look for you, I'll use my magic powers to deal with her.
三日太久了，一日还差不多。
Three days is a bit too long, Will one day do?
咱们家里妻管严，一日未归保证明天就会赶到这里。
My wife is very strict with me. She'll rush here if I don't go home for just a day.

你随小沙弥到禅房小住两天。
Follow him. He will show you to the meditation room.
是。
Yes.
住在这里真不错，景观好，空气好！
It's not a bad idea to stay here. The scenery is beautiful and the air is fresh!
禅房好，竹床好。
The room is nice and the bed is comfortable too.
价钱也好！
The price is right too!
啊……
Aahh...
上等禅房
日租十两
Superior Meditation Room Rate: Ten taels per night.

相公出去一日未归，想必是被法海老贼留住……
Xu Xian made a trip to West Lake and didn't come home last night. Fa Hai must have kept him at the temple...
娘娘该想个办法对付，别让他们以为我们好欺负！
Madam, you'd better do something about this, or Fa Hai may think we're a pushover!
冤有头，债有主！
Every injustice has its perpetrator, every debt, its debtor!
首先登报警告逃夫，不履行夫妻同居义务。
First of all, I've issued a warning to Xu Xian for running away and not fulfilling his duty as a husband.
Waming to Runaway Husband

法海老贼！我白娘娘与小青特来向你要人！
Fa Hai, my maid Xiao-qing and I have come to demand the release of my husband!
你胆敢把我的夫君留下来当和尚，快快放他出来！
How dare you keep my husband to turn him into a monk! You'd better hand him over!
我没有留许仙当和尚，你错怪了好人。
I've not accepted Xu Xian into my order. You've got it all wrong.
我宁可让他当个捐钱的居士，不要他做个吃粮的入室弟子。
I'd rather he remained a lay Buddhist so that he could donate money to us, than have him as a disciple.

娘娘别与他耍嘴皮，来硬的，水淹金山寺，教他尝尝厉害！
Madam, just flood Jinshan Temple and teach him a lesson!

好。
Right.

我白蛇修行八百年，好不容易才变成人形与许仙成亲……
It was only after eight hundred years of practice that I managed to transform my self into a human being and marry Xu Xian...

无端遭你破坏人家夫妻和睦，哇！
Why did you have to break up our marriage?

我真命苦哇！
Oh, woe is me!

真的水淹金山寺……
Jinshan Temple is really flooded...

有请李天王及三十六天罡星、七十二地煞星降临来助我！
Deity Li, and you warriors up there, please come to my aid!

白蛇精休猖狂！
Don't you try anything funny!

咚！
Dong!

咚！
Dong!

咚！
Dong!

咚！
Dong!

普天之下难道无人能助我孤立无援的弱女子？
Is there no one in the world who's willing to help a damsel in distress?

本会的宗旨就是帮助弱女子，打败这些沙猪。
Our organization's mission is to champion women's rights and to fight against male chauvinist pigs.

主妇联盟
House Wife League

女性救援联盟
Women's Coalition

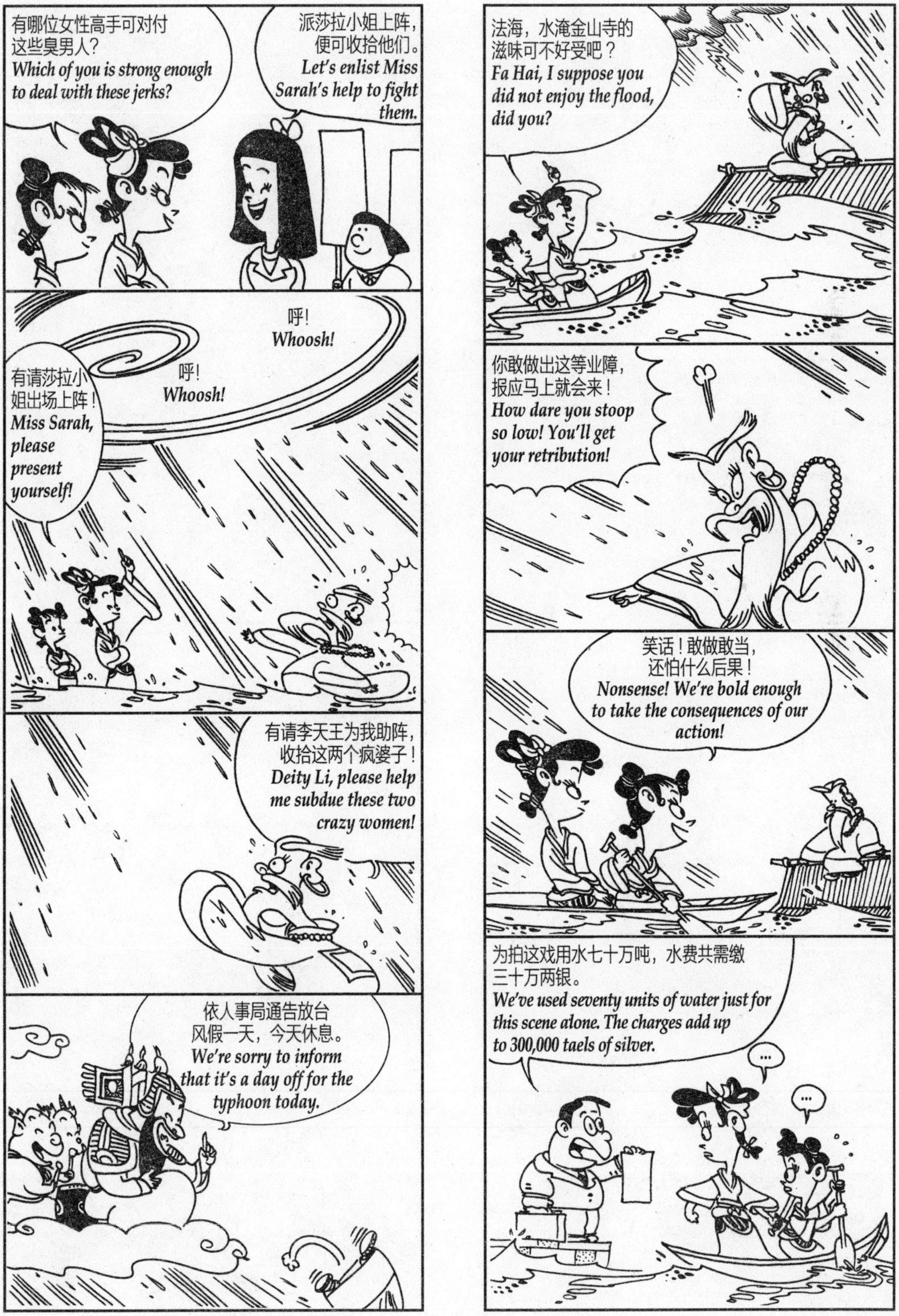

有哪位女性高手可对付这些臭男人？
Which of you is strong enough to deal with these jerks?

派莎拉小姐上阵，便可收拾他们。
Let's enlist Miss Sarah's help to fight them.

呼！
Whoosh!

有请莎拉小姐出场上阵！
Miss Sarah, please present yourself!

呼！
Whoosh!

有请李天王为我助阵，收拾这两个疯婆子！
Deity Li, please help me subdue these two crazy women!

依人事局通告放台风假一天，今天休息。
We're sorry to inform that it's a day off for the typhoon today.

李天王你要替我收拾这个白蛇精!
Deity Li, please help me deal with Madam White Snake!
杀鸡不须用牛刀，要治这蛇精自有专家上阵。
That's easy! All you need is an expert.
有请华西街大佬!
The butcher of Hua Xi Street!
杀蛇抓蛇请我来，可真找对了人!
I'm an expert at catching and killing snakes!
哇!完了……
Wah! Help!

法海老贼，今日且饶过你，改日再找你算账。
Fa Hai, you old rogue, I'll let you off today! But I shall return to settle the old score.
师父您管闲事。惹得水淹金山寺，真得不偿失啊!
Because of your interference, our temple has been flooded. Don't you think you've lost more than what you've gained?
经历这事也有一收获，使我悟得一真理。
I did gain something from this experience – I've realized a truth.
什么真理?
What's that?
女人的确是祸水!
Women spell nothing but trouble!

白娘娘水淹金山寺，把这里搞得一塌糊涂……
The flood has turned this place into a mess...
师父，这一切全因我而起，佛门圣地蒙尘实在是我的罪过。
Teacher, I'm the cause of all this trouble. The temple's holy ground has been sullied because of me.
解铃还需系铃人，你要赎罪也可以。
Well, you can make amends.
师父，我应该怎么做？
What should I do?
清洗全寺的污泥。
Clean up the mess in the temple.

光阴似箭，匆匆过了三个月……
Another three months passed...
师父，我决心离开白娘子，请让我留在寺里当和尚吧。
Teacher, I've made up my mind to leave Madam White Snake. Please let me stay here to be a monk.
许施主你大错特错了，你把佛门净土看做什么？
Master Xu Xian, what did you think we are?
你以为佛门是情场失意的避难所？
Did you think our temple is a refuge for the heart-broken?
...

白娘子即将分娩，不便收取，
待她生产后我再下山收拾她。
Madam White is about to give birth—it's not right for me to capture her yet. I'll deal with her after the baby is born.
你先回去，待小孩生下后，
速上山通知我。
You may go home. Let me know when the baby is born.
我一定尽快地向您报告，因为我也很好奇……
I will. Actually, I'm very curious to find out...
人蛇相交，到底会生下什么样的小孩……
I wonder what a child of mixed parentage will be like.
蛇头人身
Snake head/human body
人头蛇身
Human head/snake body

你带回此钵，待白蛇梳妆之际将钵合在她头上即可收妖。
Take this alms bowl back with you. When White Snake is putting on her make-up, find an opportunity to put this over her head.
啊！
Ah!
师父！这个任务太重，
我无力胜任啊……
Teacher! I'm afraid I can't shoulder this heavy responsibility...
这么轻而易举的事都办不到，算什么男人？
You can't even handle such a simple task. Are you a man?
谁说轻？
我真抱不动它呀！
Who says this bowl is light? I can hardly lift it!
...

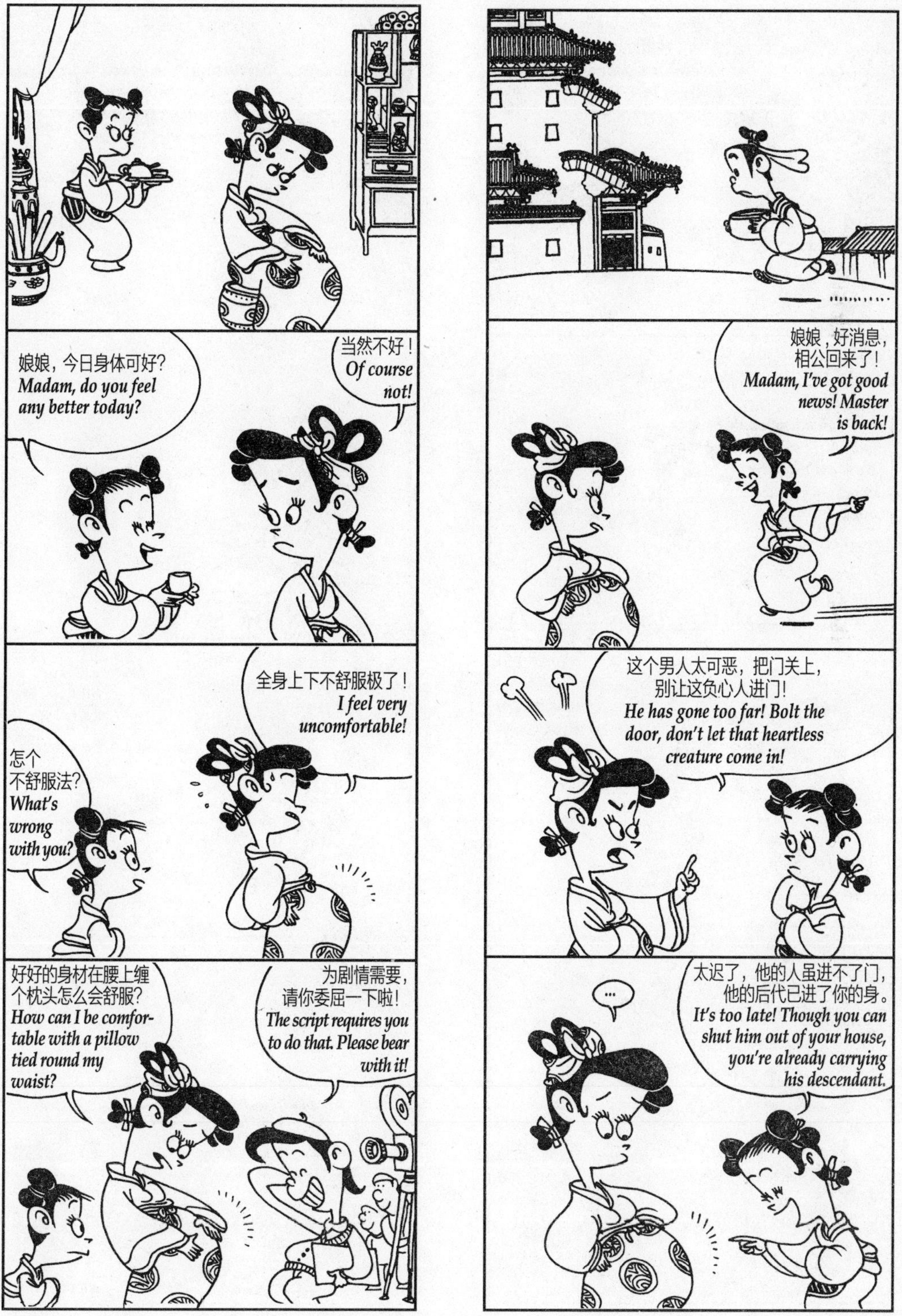

娘娘，今日身体可好？
Madam, do you feel any better today?

当然不好！
Of course not!

全身上下不舒服极了！
I feel very uncomfortable!

怎个不舒服法？
What's wrong with you?

好好的身材在腰上缠个枕头怎么会舒服？
How can I be comfortable with a pillow tied round my waist?

为剧情需要，请你委屈一下啦！
The script requires you to do that. Please bear with it!

你听信谗言，把夫妻恩情抛于脑后，还敢回来见我？
You believed in slanders and cast aside our love. How dare you come back!
我听说娘子怀有身孕，即将临盆，我抱子心切才赶快回来的。
I heard that you would be giving birth soon! I can't wait to carry my son, so I rushed home.
孩子都还没生下，怎么能抱子？
The child is not even born yet. How are you going to carry him?
连妈妈一起抱，不就可以了？
All I have to do is carry the mother as well!
...

娘子的预产期是今日，初为人父真是紧张死了……
My wife is going to give birth today. I'll be a father soon—I'm really excited...
啊！孩子生下来了！
The baby is born!
哇！哇！
Wah! Wah!
宝宝竟是一个布娃娃，真是怪事！
Strange, how did the baby turn out to be a rag doll? How did this come about?
怎么会这样？……
How did this come about?...
依《广电法》规定，婴儿不能上台演戏，只好以布娃娃代替。
The law does not permit infants to act in movies, so we have to make do with a rag doll.
...

白娘娘自生下娇儿，心满意足，
而许仙也身前身后殷勤伺候……
After giving birth to a son, Madam White became a contented mother. As for Xu Xian, he became a loving husband and doting father.
从此一家三口，圆满幸福地过日子……
And the family lived happily ever after...
故事演到这种结局，
我岂不成了多余的？
If the story were to end here, wouldn't I be redundant?
请别走，尾场法海收妖还需要你演，才能散戏。
Please don't go! We'll need you in the last act when Fa Hai subdues the demon.

白娘娘正对镜梳头，
这是个好机会。
She's looking into the mirror now. Here's the chance I've been waiting for.
娘娘原谅我！
Dearie, please forgive me!
哇！
Wah!
啊！
Ah!
相公，
你干什么？
My dear, what are you doing?
在为你做产后新发型呀！
It's a new hairdo for you after your confinement!
果然不错，还真时髦年轻了许多。
Not bad at all! It's fashionable and makes me look younger.

白蛇拿命来！
Meet your doom!

是法海老贼……
It's that rogue, Fa Hai...

你口口声声说爱我，却私下串通外人来害我，真是没心肝的男人！
You claimed that you loved me, yet you secretly plotted with an outsider against me! You heartless creature!

这不是我本意……
This wasn't my intention...

忠于剧本演出，我才做出卑鄙的事陷害你。
I had to stoop to such despicable means in order to keep to the script.

其实戏外……我是真心地爱着你！
In real life, I'm actually secretly in love with you!

NG!
No good!

白娘娘，现出你丑恶的原形来！
White Snake, reveal your true self!

不要！不要！
No! No!

哇！
Wow!

你也现出原形来才公平！
To be fair, you should reveal your true self too!

不要！不要！
No! No!

蛤蟆虽丑，却也是为民除害的益虫！
The toad may be ugly, but it helps get rid of pests, hence it's a very useful creature!

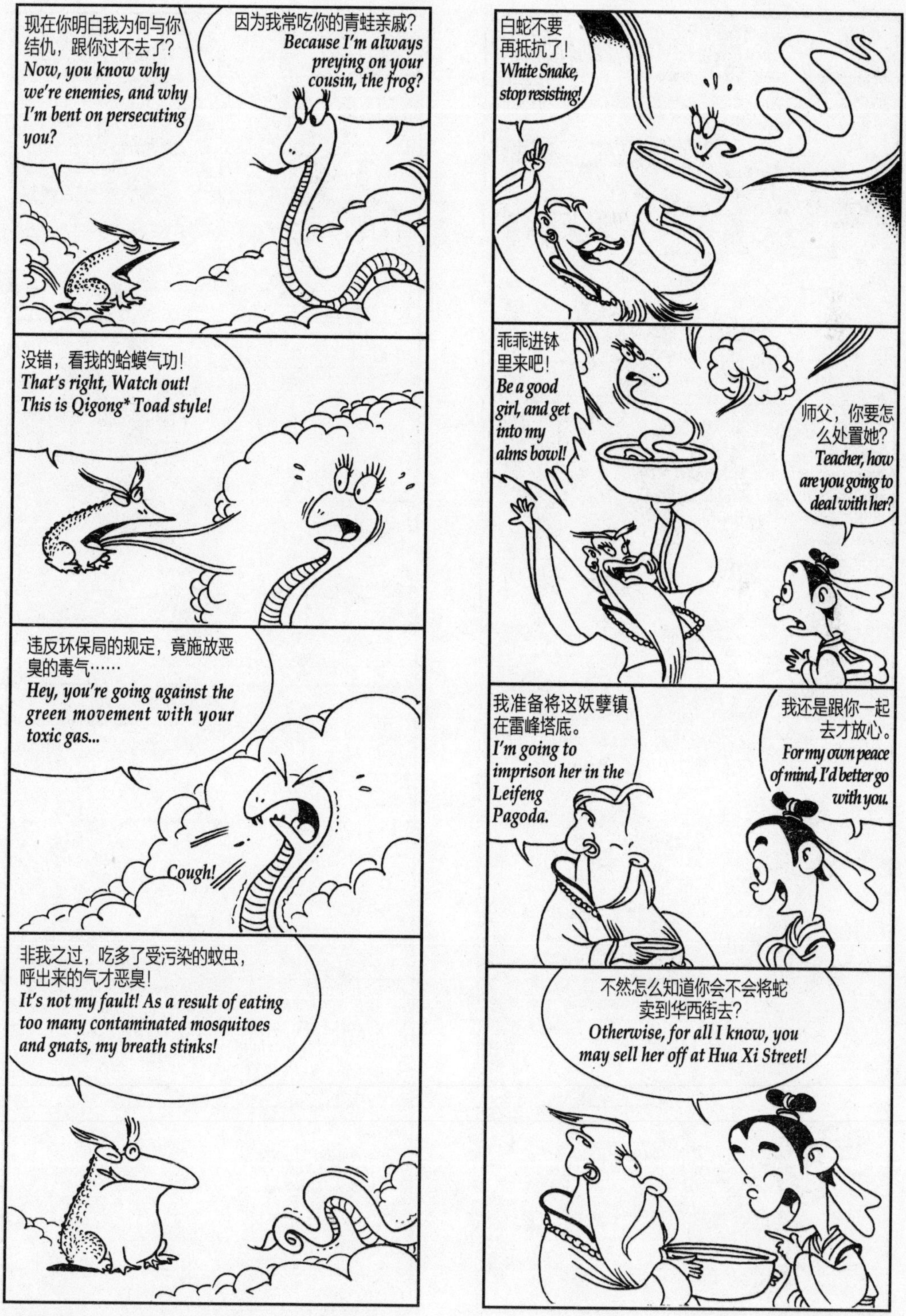

现在你明白我为何与你结仇，跟你过不去了？
Now, you know why we're enemies, and why I'm bent on persecuting you?

因为我常吃你的青蛙亲戚？
Because I'm always preying on your cousin, the frog?

没错，看我的蛤蟆气功！
That's right, Watch out! This is Qigong Toad style!*

违反环保局的规定，竟施放恶臭的毒气……
Hey, you're going against the green movement with your toxic gas...

Cough!

非我之过，吃多了受污染的蚊虫，呼出来的气才恶臭！
It's not my fault! As a result of eating too many contaminated mosquitoes and gnats, my breath stinks!

** Qigong is an exercise that makes use of the vital energy or qi in the body to help one keep fit.*

* A Taiwanese movie of the 1960s.

白蛇你就收心在此
服刑赎罪吧。
Madam White Snake, you'd better resign yourself to your fate.
看来我只好孤独寂寞
地在此度过此生……
Looks like I'll be spending the rest of my life here all alone...
不会的，保证每天会有
人排队来探监。
Don't worry, you will have many visitors every day.

师父，如今可为弟子剃度，
让弟子正式皈依佛门了吧？
Teacher, can I have the tonsure now, to be a member of your order?
好吧。
All right.
我终于明白师父确实是位
有道的高僧……
I know that Teacher is an eminent monk...
……但却不是个好理发师！
...but you're certainly not a barber!
...

当和尚无凡间俗事纷扰，轻松多了。
A monk leads a more carefree life since he doesn't have to worry about things in the mortal world.
做一天和尚撞一天钟，这是每天的功课……
One must be pious as a monk. This is what you need to do every day...
是！
Yes.
行深般若波罗蜜多时，照见五蕴皆空。度一切苦厄。舍利子色不异空，空不异色，色即是空，空即是色。受想行识，亦复如是。舍利子是诸法空相，不生不灭不垢不净不增不减。
The virtue of wisdom is the principal means of attaining Nirvana. There is an emptiness in all things. The immaterial is the material. Nothing is added and nothing is taken away. When there is no desire, there is no pain, no gain or loss.
当和尚反而不轻松……
It's not easy to be a monk after all...
师父您插手凡尘俗事，收妖做好事，但却多了仇人小青一人。
Teacher, though you did a good deed by subduing Madam White Snake, you've got Xiaoqing as your enemy.
诸法空相，不生不灭，不垢不净，不增不减。
There's no gain, no loss, no life, no death.
收了白蛇虽增加仇人小青一人……
Though I've got myself one more enemy in the form of Xiaoqing...
仇人数目
Number of disciples
弟子数目
Number of disciples
但也增加门人许仙一人，所以不得不失。
I've got myself another disciple, Xu Xian, so I've neither gained nor lost.

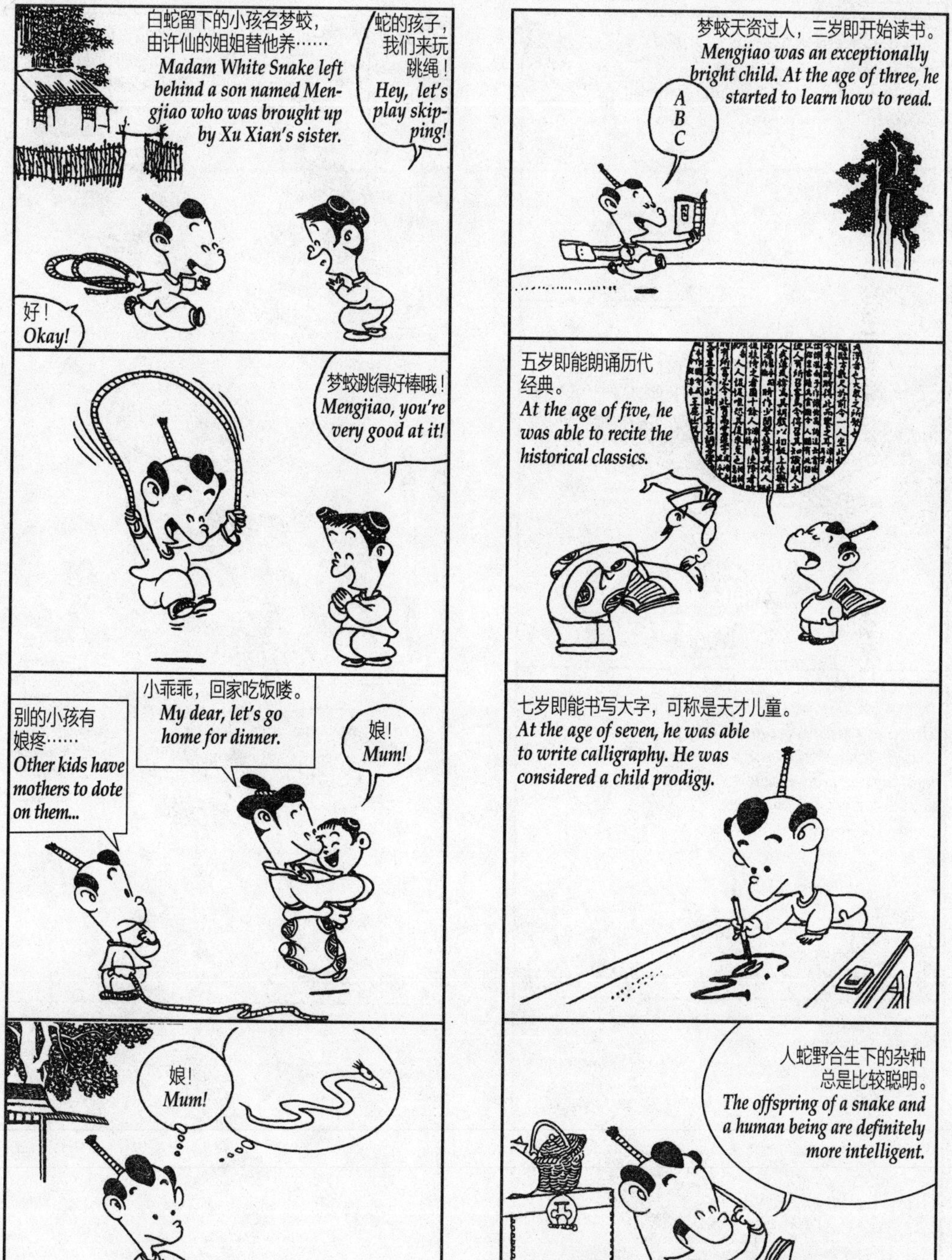

白蛇留下的小孩名梦蛟，由许仙的姐姐替他养……
Madam White Snake left behind a son named Mengjiao who was brought up by Xu Xian's sister.

蛇的孩子，我们来玩跳绳！
Hey, let's play skipping!

好！
Okay!

梦蛟跳得好棒哦！
Mengjiao, you're very good at it!

别的小孩有娘疼……
Other kids have mothers to dote on them...

小乖乖，回家吃饭喽。
My dear, let's go home for dinner.

娘！
Mum!

娘！
Mum!

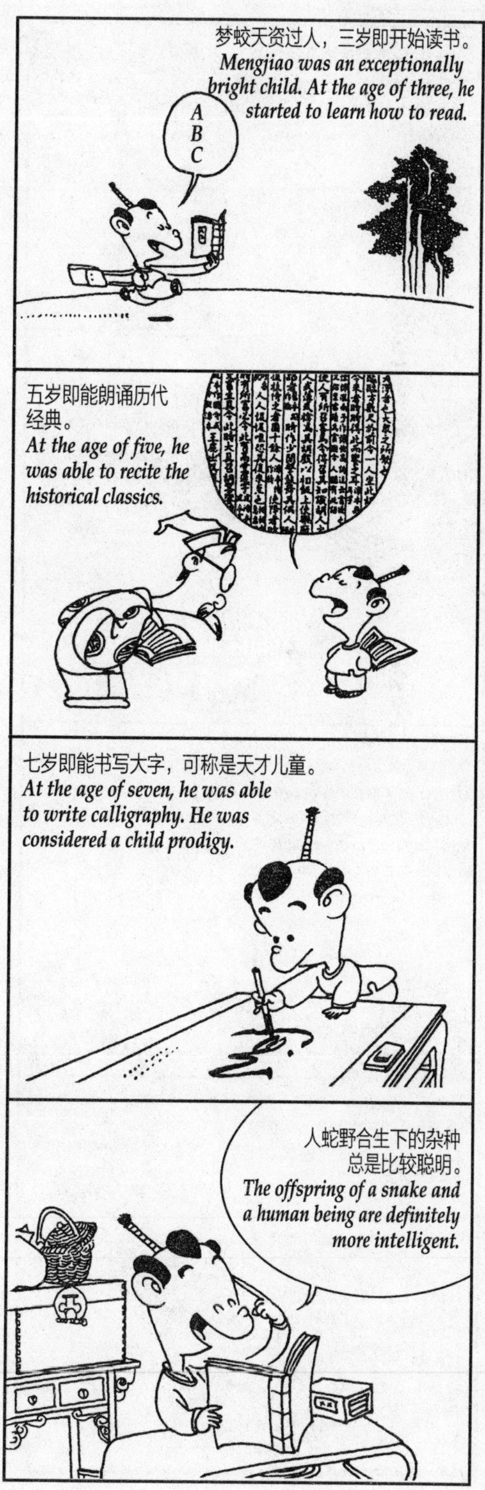

许梦蛟十九岁那年，赴京应举。
When Mengjiao was nineteen, he sat for the imperial examinations.
他不负众望，一举考中了状元。
As expected, he passed with flying colours and became a scholar.
梦蛟文章的确好，写的故事动人，文词并茂！
Mengjiao's essay is very well-written. It narrates a very touching story. It's excellent in both content and language.
只因为考题正合我意罢了。
That's because the topic happens to be my pet subject.
作文题目：我的母亲
Essay topic: My Mother

娘！ Mum!
状元爷又在想亲娘了，好可怜呀！
The top scholar is thinking about his mother again! Poor thing!
娘！
Mum!
睹物思情，真令人感动……
Every small thing reminds him of his mother. How touching...
娘！
Mum!
娘！
Mum!
这就太过分了……
But this has gone a bit far!

明天我想回家省亲，至雷峰塔探望母亲。
I'm returning to Zhenjiang tomorrow to visit my relatives. I plan to visit my mother at Leifeng Pagoda.
大人新科中举，衣锦返乡，要不要办个大游行?
Sir, you're the top scholar in the imperial exams. Are you going to hold a procession when you return home?
正是。
Sure.
为官知法守法，集会游行得事先申请。
As an official, I understand the legal requirements. I will apply for a permit to hold the procession.
法海大师！限你24小时内放出我母，否则包围你金山寺!
Fa Hai, you'd better release my mother within 24 hours or I'll have Jinshan Temple surrounded!
反恶势力
Against totalitarianism!
反极权
Against evil forces!
抗争!
Protest!

你娘的刑期可真遥遥无期啊……
Looks like your mother may really have to stay here indefinitely...
除非西湖水干，雷峰塔倒，白蛇永不脱身。
法海上
Unless the waters of West Lake dry up and Leifeng Pagoda collapses, Madam White Snake will not regain her freedom.
娘，你真命苦，这一关要关到几时才能出来啊?
Oh poor Mother! How much longer will you have to stay in captivity?
大人别哭了，再哭就坏事了!
Sir, you mustn't cry anymore, or you'll make things worse!
为什么?
Why?
西湖水干你娘才能出塔，你的泪水又使西湖增高了几分。
Your mother can leave the pagoda only when the lake is dry. Your tears have raised the water level of the lake.

许梦蛟你来得正好，今日雷峰塔要拆，可放你母亲出来。
Xu Mengjiao, you've come at the right time. We're going to demolish Lefeng Pagoda today, so we can release your mother.
大人当了官毕竟不同，经过关说就有效果。
Sir, things are different once you're an official. All it took was a little persuasion on your part.
是啊！
That's true!
这事不涉及关说案……
This has nothing to do with your persuasive powers.
拆塔为的是要建高尔夫球场。
We need to make way for a new golf course.

只要从 10 至 0 念一遍，即能解咒放你母亲升天。
To break the curse, all you need to do is count backwards from ten to zero.
咒语这么简单？
It's that simple?
10, 9, 8, 7, 6, 5, 4, 3, 2, 1……
轰！
0！
Zero!

哈哈，被
关十九年，
终于还我
自由身！
Ha! Ha! After 19
years in captivity,
I'm finally free!
娘，我是你儿
梦蛟呀！
Mum, I'm your
son, Mengjiao!
想不到你竟能考取
功名当起大官来。
I've never thought
you would
become a scholar
and now an
official.
儿如今已是朝廷重臣，娘有
何冤屈？……
Mum, now that I'm a court
official, would you like me to
redress any injustice you've
suffered?...
当然有！
Of
course!
首先替我翻案，
重审当年白蛇案。
First, I want you to
reverse the verdict and
reopen my case.
要求平反！
Redress
my
grievance!

恭喜白娘娘服刑完毕出了狱！
Congratulations on your
release from the prison!
你就是薄幸
男子许仙？
You're that
heartless creature,
Xu Xian?
许仙已随红尘去，
贫僧法号道宗上人。
Xu Xian has passed
on. The monk Dao-
zong has taken his
place.
这位可就是我儿梦蛟？
Is this my son,
Mengjiao?
梦蛟已随岁月去，
他是新科状元许大人。
Mengjiao has passed on.
The top scholar has taken
his place.

许仙，我为了爱你，
这一生被你害得好惨呀！
Xu Xian, my love for you has ruined my life!
受陷害被关在雷峰塔十九年，
这期间你从未来探监。
Because of you I have been imprisoned in Leifeng Pagoda for 19 years, but you have never visited me.
如今见了面，你竟连抱歉
也不说一声？
Now that we meet again, you didn't even apologise.
竟有这样的男人……
I've never met a man like him...
"爱"就是不需要
说抱歉。
Love means never having to say you're sorry.

我千年修行完毕，
如今可乘祥云升天去。
I've completed a thousand years of meditation, it's time I ascended to the heavens.
娘！
Mum!
梦蛟再见了！
Goodbye, Mengjiao!
娘，再见！
Goodbye, Mum!
阿弥陀佛！
Amitabha!
娘又变蛇，你不再害怕了？
Mother has turned into a snake again. Aren't you scared anymore?
当然不。
Of course not.
同样的情节看多了，不稀奇。
I've seen the same old story enacted time and again. It's not surprising any more.
...

娘，上天保佑你！
Mother, may heaven watch over you!
阿弥陀佛！
Amitabha!
《白蛇传》到此告一段落，谢谢各位读者收看。
We've come to the end of the story of Madam White Snake.
观众一向爱看悲喜剧，看了人人都满意。
Thanks for tuning in. Viewers love tragicomedies. Everybody is satisfied.
至少我没白娘娘那么不幸。
At least, I'm not as ill-fated as Madam White Snake.
至少我比许仙有情！
At least, I'm better than Xu Xian!
白蛇传 END
Madam White Snake The End.
至少我比梦蛟幸福。
At least, I'm happier than Mengjiao.

附录·延伸阅读

APPENDIX Further reading

此部分为本书图画页的延伸阅读，
各段首所示的页码与图画页对应。

P1 本书故事选自《警世通言》第二十八卷。白娘子的故事是流传很广的一个民间故事，几乎家喻户晓。关于白蛇化身为人，蛊惑男人的故事虽然可以上溯到唐代的传奇小说，但是，真正将白蛇写成一个很有人性的女妖，却是从这一篇《白娘子永镇雷峰塔》才开始。在六十家小说所收的话本《西湖三塔记》里，白蛇也仍然只是个专门吃人的可怕妖怪。从《白娘子永镇雷峰塔》这篇以后，所有的白蛇故事，才都将白蛇写成一个善解人意的可爱女性。

P2 下面让我们先来看看“蛇”究竟是什么样的动物：

蛇类是在二亿三千万年前由类似蜥蜴类的动物演化而来的。

蛇属于爬虫类。

P3 蛇身上的鳞片是它的外层“皮肤”，十分坚韧，却不会长大，因此需要蜕皮。

蛇嘴的骨头与骨头之间连系着可缩可放的韧带，因此能吞食大东西。

P4 大部分的蛇是卵生，少数则卵胎生。

蛇没有耳膜，因此听不到空气中传来的音波，但它们却可以感觉到从地面传出的轻微脚步声。

P5 蛇没有胸骨，若将蛇倒提着抖一抖，它的脊椎骨便会脱臼，脊髓受到严重损害，蛇就会一命呜呼了。

蛇身上的鳞片，是保护它身体的“盔甲”，也是爬行时唯一依靠的工具。

P6 蛇类的祖先曾过穴居生活，猎食小毛虫、白蚁、地鼠……后来地面上的哺乳类动物已经进化繁殖得体形大、数量又多……蛇类才放弃穴居生活，为了生存下去，形体也就愈变愈大了。

P7 蛇身上的外皮很松弛，爬行时，身体内部先向前滑动，外皮再随着往前移；若将蛇放在光滑的地板或松软的沙滩上，它就无法爬行了，分布在寒冷地区和在水中生活的蛇，为卵胎生。

P8 山外青山楼外楼，西湖歌舞几时休?

暖风薰得游人醉，直把杭州作汴州。

杭州西湖的胜景，自古天下闻名，不只山光秀丽，水色宜人，更多的是名胜古迹，引人幽思。

这些名胜古迹之所以引人幽思，使人流连，是因为在它们的背后，往往有一个悠远的传说，或美丽的故事。

P9 金山寺、涌金门的由来，据说就是因为在晋朝咸和年间，有一次山洪爆发，水势汹涌，惊涛骇浪冲入西门。眼见全城即将遭殃，忽然水中涌现一头全身金色的牛，不久洪水即退。而那只金牛随水流到北山之后，便不见了。杭州城的人认为这是神灵显化，便在山腰立了一个寺庙，这就是金山寺。而西门从此便叫“涌金门”。

P10 飞来峰的神话也很神奇。听说以前有一位西域来的僧人，名叫浑寿罗，云游到杭州西湖，观赏山景之余，看到这一座突出的山峰，便说："印度灵鹫山前的一座小峰，忽然不见，原来就是飞到这里。"当时的人都不相信，僧人说："我记得灵鹫山前的这座峰岭，叫做灵鹫岭，上面有一个山洞，洞里有只白猿。不信的话，让我呼叫它出来。"一呼叫，果然跑出了一只白猿。从此，大家便称这座山峰为飞来峰。

P11　西湖中有一座山，叫做孤山，旁边有一条路，东接断桥，西接霞岭，叫做孤山路，便是宋朝的隐士林和靖先生筑的。另外又有白公堤、苏公堤。

P12　白公堤就是唐代大诗人白乐天来做刺史的时候筑的，南接翠屏山，北至栖霞岭。苏公堤则是北宋大文学家苏东坡在那儿当太守的时候修的。两座堤上都栽满了桃柳，每当春景融和的时节，桃花飘香，杨柳依依，真是美丽非常，堪描入画。

P13　各位读者，或许你们会说，正经儿的故事不说，却讲这些古迹传说干什么！这有个缘故，本书要说的这一篇故事，正和西湖一个古迹的传说有关，所以在正题儿未讲之先，便先引这几个有关名人古迹的传说，来做个开场。

P14　我们今天要说的故事，就是西湖雷峰塔的传奇。雷峰塔是杭州的名胜，这是各位都知道的。但是，为什么有这雷峰塔？各位恐怕就不一定清楚了。原来雷峰塔的建立，关联着一个稀奇古怪、美丽风流，却又有些悲怨凄怆的故事。

故事就发生在南宋绍兴年间的杭州府。

P15　话说杭州城中官巷口李家草药铺中，有一位年轻的伙计，名叫许仙，今年二十二岁，尚未成亲。这许仙上无兄、下无弟，父母就单单生下他和一个姐姐，按排行来说，也算是老大，因此家人便又叫他小乙。

P16　小乙的爹原也是开草药铺的，不幸在他十五岁那年，父母相继病亡，当时姐姐又已出嫁，家中便落得孤孤凄凄的小乙一个人，好不可怜。亏得姐姐、姐夫怜他一个少年人家，无人照管，便将他接过来同住。

P17　小乙的姐夫姓李名仁，家住城中过军桥黑珠巷内，是邵太尉手下一名小小的军需官，平常也替邵太尉管钱粮。这种军需官在当时又称募事官，所以人家便叫他李募事。

P18　官巷口李家草药铺的主人李员外，就是小乙的表叔，因为小乙从小跟随父亲，耳濡目染，对草药生意这一行倒也懂了一些，所以在他住到姐姐家不久之后，李员外便叫他来到铺里当助手。小乙白天到药铺里照管生意，晚上便回姐姐家睡，日子平平淡淡的，倒还过得安稳。如此过了六七年，小乙渐渐长大成人了。

P19　就在这一年的清明节前夕，小乙回家之后，吃过了晚饭，对姐姐说："今天保叔塔的和尚到店里去，叫我明天到寺里烧香，追薦祖宗。我想明天向表叔告个假，去走一趟。"

姐姐说："爹娘过世多年了，这也是应当的。"

第二天早起，便先去买了蜡烛、冥钱、纸马、香枝等东西。准备妥当，换了新鞋袜、新衣服，然后才到药铺里来，对李员外说："我今天要到保叔塔去烧香，追薦祖宗，来给叔叔告个假。"

P20　谁知这清明天气，惯会捉弄人。忽然云生西北，雾锁东南，下起微微的细雨来了。不一会儿，雨渐下渐大，正是清明时节，少不得天公应时，催花雨下，那阵雨下得绵绵不绝。

眼见得地下湿了，小乙可惜新鞋袜，便脱了下来，赤脚走出四圣观来寻船，却没见到半只。正不知如何是好，只见一个老儿，摇着一只船过来，小乙认得是张阿公，大喜，叫道："张阿公，载我过湖去，拜托。"

P21　船刚摇离了岸七八丈远，忽然岸上有人叫道："公公，拜托一下，我们要搭船过湖。"原来是一个妇人和一个丫环。

张阿公将船又摇过岸边，接那妇人同丫环上船。小乙见那妇人头上梳着孝髻，身上穿一件白绢衫儿，上穿一条细麻布裙。丫环头上一双角髻，身上穿着青色衣服，手中捧着一个包儿。

P22　那妇人说："不敢动问官人，尊姓大名？"

小乙答道："在下姓许名仙。"

妇人说："府上何处？"

小乙说："寒舍住在过军桥黑珠儿巷，白天在一家草药铺帮人做点生意。"

那妇人问过了，小乙想到自己也该问她一下，便说："不敢拜问娘子，尊姓？府上哪里？"

P23　那妇人说："奴家白氏，亡夫姓张。亡夫年前不幸过世，就葬在雷岭这边。今天清明，带了丫环来坟上祭扫，刚要回去，不巧就遇上了这场雨。如果不是搭了官人的便船，不知该如何是好！"

小乙付过船钱，搀那妇人上了岸，雨还是淅淅沥沥地下着。

那妇人说："寒舍就在箭桥双茶坊巷口，若不嫌弃，请到寒舍奉茶，一并送还船钱。"

小乙说："这点小事何须挂怀。天色晚了，容改天再来拜望吧！"

P24　小乙至草药铺借了伞，刚走到后市街巷口，忽听得有人叫道："小乙官人！"小乙回头一看，只见沈公巷口，小茶坊屋檐下站着一个人——正是搭船的白娘子。

小乙说："娘子怎么一个人在这里？"

白娘子说："雨下个不停，鞋儿都踏湿了，不好走，叫青青回家拿伞和鞋子去了，到现在还没来。天色已经不早，官人如果方便，送奴家一程，不知可好？"

P25　隔天，小乙离了店，一路便到箭桥双茶坊巷口来，找白娘子。问了半天，并没一个人认得。

正在那儿不知所措，青青正好从东边走来。小乙说："你家在哪里啊？我来拿伞，找了好久都找不到啊。"

青青说："官人跟我来。"带着小乙走了一段路，来到一家楼房门前，说："这里便是。"

青青说："官人，请到里面坐。"又向里面悄悄地叫声："娘子，许官人来了。"

白娘子在里头应道："请官人进里面奉茶。"

P26　小乙坐下。白娘子给他倒了一杯酒，劝他喝了，又倒一杯，带着满面春风，娇滴滴地说："官人，奴家看你是个老实人，真人面前说不得假话。奴家的丈夫过世经年，想必你我宿世有缘，才有这番巧遇。而且一见便蒙错爱，正是你有心我有意。如不嫌弃，就请央一个媒人，共成百年姻眷。不知意下如何？"

小乙说："实不相瞒，只因在下身边窘迫，不敢从命。"

白娘子说："这倒不须官人烦恼，奴家身边还有些余财，可以用得。"便叫青青："你去取一锭白银下来。"

P27　隔天，小乙把伞送还了李员外，仍照常到铺里照管生意。到得下午，又给李员外告个假，到市场买了烧鹅、鲜鱼、精肉、嫩鸡、果品等提回家来了。又买了一樽酒，安排了一桌酒席，来请姐夫和姐姐吃酒。

那天刚好姐夫也早些回来，听说小乙摆了酒席请他，好生奇怪，想道："小乙平常俭省得不得了，今天不知为了什么事？"

喝了几杯，姐夫憋不住闷葫芦，便说："小乙，无缘无故地花钱，有什么事吗？"

P28　小乙说："姐夫、姐姐照顾小乙多年，小乙感谢良多。小乙年纪已经不小，长此下去，终不是了局。现在有一头好亲事，小乙不敢自作主张，望姐夫、姐姐给小乙做主。"

说完，便到自己的房中，拿出白娘子给他的银子，递给姐姐，说："我只要姐夫替我做主，钱已经准备了。"

姐姐就将银子递给丈夫。李募事拿在手中，翻来覆去地看着，忽然大叫一声：“不好了，这下子全家遭殃！这是官银啊！”

P29 他的妻子听得目瞪口呆，出声不得。

李募事当时拿了银子到府里出首，府尹听说有了贼赃，整个晚上再也睡不着。第二天上堂差捕头何立前去抓人。

何立带了一班衙役，火速赶到官巷口李家药铺，见了小乙，不由分说，绑了就走。即刻解到府里来。

府尹见了，也不问话，只喝声：“打！”

P30 小乙将遇见白娘子的事情，前前后后说了一遍。

府尹说：“白娘子现在何处？”

小乙说：“住在箭桥边，双茶坊巷口，秀王王府对面的楼房。”

府尹随即叫何立带领从人，押着小乙去捉白娘子。

一行人扰扰嚷嚷地赶到秀王府对面楼房一看，门前一堆垃圾，也不知堆了多久了：大门一条竹竿横架着，哪里像是有人住的样子？众人都呆住了，小乙更是惊得合不了口。

P31 小乙被发配到苏州，后来住在王主人家，时当九月下旬，有一天，王主人正在门口闲站，看街上人来人往，忽然一乘轿子，旁边一个丫环跟着，来到门前停了下来。那丫环向前问道：“借问一下，这里是王主人家吗？”

王主人说：“这里就是，不知你找谁？”

丫环说：“我找杭州府来的许仙官人。”

主人说：“你等一等，我去叫他出来。”便走到里面叫着：“小乙哥，有人找你。”

P32 小乙听了，忽走出来，到门前看时，那丫环正是青青，轿里坐的正是白娘子，不禁气往上冲，连声叫道：“死冤家！你盗了官库银子，劳累我吃了多少苦！有冤无处申！如今落得如此下场，你还来干什么？不羞死人么！”

白娘子道：“官人，不要怪我，这次来，是特地来给你分辩这件事的。让我们到主人家里面说。”说着，便叫青青取了包裹下轿。

白娘子解释过后，王主人说：“既然当初曾许嫁小乙哥，那就更不用回去了，你就留下来吧！”

P33 光阴一瞬，早到吉日良时。白娘子取出银两，央王主人备办喜筵，二人拜堂成亲。异地完婚，别是一番情味，新婚之乐，自不必说。以后生活，都是白娘子拿钱出来用度。日往月来，自从两人成亲，又是几个月过去。时当春景融合，花开似锦，街坊上车马往来，热闹非常。小乙问主人家道：“今天是什么日子？怎地如此热闹？”

主人说：“今天是二月半，大家都去承天寺看卧佛。你也好去逛逛。”

P34 小乙说：“我和妻子说一声。”便上楼来对白娘子说：“今天二月半，大家都去看卧佛，我也去逛逛，一会儿就回来。”

白娘子说：“有什么好看的？在家里不是很好吗？去看做什么！”

小乙说：“我去走走，马上就回来。反正在家也是闲着没事。”出了店，便往承天寺去。到了寺里，各处闲走了一回，刚要回家，寺外一个道士在那儿卖药，散施符水，小乙便也挤到人丛中去看。

P35 只听那道士说道：“贫道是终南山道士，到处云游，散施符水，救人病患灾厄。有事的，请向前来。”

忽然在人丛中看见了小乙，便叫他近前，对他说：“近来有一个妖怪缠你，为害不轻！我给你两道灵符，救你性命。一道符三更烧，一道符放在你的头发内。”

小乙自已也想道：“我也有几分怀疑她是妖怪，听他说来，毕竟是了。”接了符，纳头便拜。回到家中，只装作平常一样，不动声色。

P36　等到晚上三更，小乙料想白娘子和青青都睡熟了，便起身将一道符放在头发内，正要将另一道符烧化，忽听得白娘子叹了一口气："小乙哥，做夫妻那么久，一向我待你也不薄，为什么你老是疑神疑鬼，随便就相信别人的话？半夜三更，你烧符干什么？是不是要来镇压我？你就烧吧！"

说罢，也不等小乙回答，一把夺过符来，就在灯前烧化了，却全无动静。白娘子说："看看，我是妖怪吗？"

小乙说："这不干我事，是承天寺前一个云游道士教我的，他说你是妖怪。"

白娘子说："我以前未嫁时，也学了些道术，明天便同你去看，是怎么样的一个道士。"

P37　第二天清早，夫妻两人梳洗罢，白娘子穿了素净衣服，吩咐青青在家，便一同往承天寺前来。那个道士仍在那儿散施符水，旁边围了一群人。

白娘子对小乙说："我先试他道行看看。"走到道士面前，大喝一声："你好无礼！出家人怎么随便说人家是妖怪！你画符来我看看！"

那道士说："我行的是五雷天心正法，凡有妖怪，吃了我的符，即刻便现出原形。"

P38　白娘子说："众人在此，你且画符来让我吃吃看！"

那道士画一道符，递给白娘子。白娘子接过来，一口吞了下去。众人看看并没些影响，便起哄说："一个好好的妇人家，怎么说是妖怪呢？"大家你一言我一语地骂那道士。道士被骂得目瞪口呆，说不出话来，惶恐满面。

白娘子说："他欺骗无知便罢，还血口喷人，实在可恶！我从小也学了些戏法，就和你玩玩试试。"

P39　只见白娘子口中喃喃的，不知念些什么，那道士忽然好像被人擒住一般，缩作一团，悬空而起。众人看了，都吃一惊，小乙却呆住了。

白娘子说："如果不是看众位面上，我便吊他一年半载！"喷口气，那道士立刻恢复原状，只恨爹娘少生了两条腿，飞也似的走了。众人看完好戏，也就散了，他夫妻两人回家，仍如以往度日，不在话下。

P40　不久之后，小乙拿了银子，约了隔壁的蒋和做伴，到镇江渡口码头上去租了一间房子。这蒋和也没什么正经职业，平常就帮人打杂，算得上是个帮闲。小乙叫他帮忙，很快地置办了药橱、药柜，到十月前后，种种药材都陆续采办齐全，便择吉开张，做起自家的生意了。

小乙开店以后，生意倒是不错，一天比一天兴旺。不觉冬尽春来，眼见夏节又至，有一天，一个和尚拿了化缘簿子进来说："小僧是金山寺和尚，七月初七是英烈龙王生日，希望官人到寺烧香，布施些香钱。"

P41　小乙说："不必记名字了，我有一块上等的好降香，就舍给你去烧吧。"

和尚谢了，说："到时还希望官人来寺里烧香。"念声佛号走了。

白娘子看见，说："你倒真大方，把这么一块好香送给那贼秃去换酒肉吃！"

小乙说："我一片诚心施舍给他，他要不正经地用了，是他的罪过。"

P42　一转眼，不觉已是七月初七，小乙刚开店门，只见街上人来人往，好不热闹。那帮闲的蒋和走过来说："小乙哥，你前天不是布施了香吗？今天何不到寺里走走？"

小乙说："你等一下，我收拾好了和你一道去。"

忙忙地收拾了，进去对白娘子说："我和蒋和去金山寺烧香，家里你照顾一下。"

白娘子说："人家说，无事不登三宝殿，你没来由放着生意不做，去干什么？"

小乙说："我来镇江这么久了，金山寺是什么样的，连看都没看过，趁着这个机会，去看一看。"

P43　白娘子说："你既然要去，我也阻挡不了，只是要答应我三件事。"

小乙说："哪三件？"

白娘子说：“第一，不要到住持的房里去。第二，不要与和尚说话。第三，早去早回。如果你稍晚一点回来，我就去找你。”

小乙说：“三件都没问题，我去一下就回。”

立刻换了干净衣服鞋袜，带了香盒，和蒋和到江边搭船，往金山寺去。

P44 到了龙王堂烧了香，寺里各处走了一遍，随着众人信步走到住持所住的方丈门前，猛然猛省道：“娘子叫我不要到里面去。”立住了脚，只在外面张望。

蒋和说：“进去瞧瞧，不碍事的，她在家里，怎么会知道你进去了没有？回家不说就是了。”说着，拉着小乙进去看了一会儿，便又出来，却也没什么事。

却说方丈里面当中座上坐着一个和尚，方面大耳，一派庄严，看那样子，倒像是个有道行的高僧。一见小乙走过，便叫侍者：“快叫那年轻人进来！”

P45 原来小乙早就走出寺外，在那儿等船。这时候风浪颇大，大家都不敢上船，要等风停了才走。忽然江心里一只船，飞也似的来得好快，小乙对蒋和说：“风浪这么大，这里的船家没人敢开船，那只船却怎么来得那么快？”正说之间，那只船已将近岸，看时，是一个穿白的妇人，和一个穿青衣的女子。来到岸边，仔细一认，原来就是白娘子和青青。小乙这一惊非同小可。白娘子来到岸边，对小乙说：“你怎么还不回去？快来上船！”

P46 小乙正要上船，忽听得背后有人大喝一声：“孽畜！想要干什么！”小乙回头一看，是一个大和尚，旁边的人说：“法海禅师来了。”

禅师说：“孽畜，敢再来残害生灵，老僧手下便不留情！还不快走！”

白娘子见了禅师，不敢逞强，摇开船，和青青把船一翻，两个都翻到水底下去了。

小乙回身看着禅师便拜：“求师尊救弟子一命！”

P47 禅师说：“你怎么遇上这妇人？”

小乙将事情前后说了一遍。禅师说：“这妇人正是妖怪，现在你就回杭州去。如果再来缠你，你便到西湖南岸净慈寺来找我。”有诗四句：

本是妖精变妇人，西湖岸上卖娇声。汝因不识遭他计，有难湖南见老僧。

小乙拜谢了禅师，和蒋和下了渡船回家。回到家时，白娘子和青青都不见了，小乙更相信她们就是妖精。到了晚上，独自一个人不敢睡，便叫蒋和相伴过夜。可是心里烦闷，哪里睡得着，整夜地辗转反侧。

P48 第二天早起，叫蒋和看家，他一个人走到李克用家来，把昨天的事说了一遍。李克用说：“我生日那天，她去净手，我无意中撞了进去，就撞见这妖怪，当时把我吓昏了，我又不敢告诉你。既然如此，你那里也住不得了，还是搬到我这里住，大家有个照应。禅师叫你现在就回杭州，可是刑期未了，还是不能走的。”

小乙依了李克用的话，把那边的店收拾了，便搬到他家来住，白天仍到铺里相帮。

P49 两个月后，正值高宗策立孝宗为太子，大赦天下，除了人命大事，其余小事，尽行赦放回家。小乙过赦，欢喜不胜，拜谢了李克用、李妈妈一家，以及东邻西舍，央蒋和买了些土产，便兴冲冲地作别回乡。

一路饥餐渴饮，夜住晓行，不到几天便已到家。见了姐姐、姐夫，拜了几拜。却见姐姐、姐夫脸上并无色，好生奇怪，只见姐夫绷着脸说：“你这个人也太欺负人了，我们一向怎么待你，谅你心里明白！怎么你在镇江娶了老婆，连写封信来通知一下都没有，难道我们是外人吗？真是无情无义！”

P50 小乙听了这没来由的话，如坠五里雾中。忽然想到白娘子，心中一阵忐忑，硬着嘴皮说：“我没有娶老婆呀！”

李募事说："亏你说得出口！你的妻子和丫头现在就在家里，难道会假！你的妻子说你七月初七那天到金山寺烧香，却一去不回，害她找了好久，找不到人。后来听说你遇赦回乡，她才赶了来，已经等你两天了。"说着，便叫人请出小乙的妻子和丫头。

P51　小乙顿时目瞪口呆，两脚发软——果然是白娘子和青青。心中无限惶恐，又无限委屈，欲待要说，舌头却似乎结住了，一句话也说不出来。李募事看此情形，更认为他是心虚，说不得话，着着实实地埋怨了他一场。

当晚，李募事便叫小乙和白娘子同住一房。小乙心中只是害怕，站在房门口，不敢进去，僵持了一会儿，看着白娘子笑吟吟的，不由得向前一步，跪在地下，说："不知娘子是何方神圣？乞饶小人一命啊！"

P52　白娘子面带笑容，无限温柔地上前扶了他起来，说："小乙哥，你莫不是疯了吗？我们多年的恩爱夫妻，难道我有什么地方做错了？你讲这些是什么话？"

小乙说："以前的种种，也不必说了。那禅师说你是妖怪，你见了禅师，便跳下江去，我只道你死了，想不到你又好端端的。我到什么地方，你便到什么地方，如果我有什么地方冲犯了你，也是无心，求你慈悲，饶我一命！"

P53　白娘子听了，登时变脸，说："小乙，这样说来，你是信了那妖僧的话了？你也不想想，我和你做了夫妻，有什么亏待你之处？一切的一切，还不都是为了你好！谁知你一再相信别人的闲言闲语，一再地怀疑我！我如果真的另有他图，又何必如此苦苦地跟着你？"

说得小乙半晌无言可答，怔在当地。白娘子的话句句是实，自己孑然一身，她即使是妖是怪，跟定了自己，又有什么好处？可是，大江中风浪涛涛的那一幕，法海禅师一再交代的那些话……难道是我小乙前生罪孽，今生冤孽……

P54　青青看着两人僵持不下，走上前来说："官人，娘子对你是一片痴情，一番真心，你们夫妻也一向恩深情重，听我说，不必再有什么疑虑，和睦如初，一切便都没事了。"

小乙还是发怔，对青青的话好像全无知觉。

白娘子忍不住气，圆睁怪眼说："是妖也好，不是妖也好，反正大家扯开了。我老实对你说，如果你愿意听我的话，欢欢喜喜，大家没事。如果你要动歪念头，我叫你满城波涛，人人手攀洪浪，皆死于非命，让你后悔不及。我不知道我对你好，是犯了什么罪过，要人家屡次地来破坏！"

P55　这些话，小乙听得句句扎实，大吃一惊，不禁叫了起来："我真是苦啊！"

这时小乙的姐姐正在天井里乘凉，听得小乙叫苦，以为他们小两口吵架，连忙走到房前，将小乙拉了出来。白娘子也不来辩解，关了房门自睡。

小乙把前因后果，一一向姐姐说了一遍，只说自己心中的疑惑，并不说她是妖是怪，刚好李募事在外面乘凉回来，姐姐说："他两口儿吵架了，不知她睡了没？你去看一看。"

P56　李募事走到房前看时，门窗关得紧紧的，只好将舌头舔破窗纸，朝缝里看，不看万事皆休，这一看，连李募事这种胆大的人，都吓得半死。原来房里不见了白娘子，只见一条吊桶大的蟒蛇，睡在床上，伸头在天窗上纳凉，鳞甲内放出白光来，照得房内一闪一闪的。

李募事大吃一惊，回身便走，当着小乙姐姐的面，暂不说破，只说："睡了，丫头也睡了。"当晚小乙就躲在姐姐房中，不敢过去，姐夫也不问他。

P57　第二天一早，李募事将小乙叫到一个僻静的所在，问他："你妻子从什么地方娶来的？实实在在地对我说，不要瞒我。昨天晚上我过去看，亲眼看见她是一条大白蛇，我怕你姐姐害怕，所以不提。你要实实在在地告诉我！"

小乙说："姐夫，现在该怎么办？"

P58　李募事说："唯一的办法，就是你住到别处去，不让她知道。她不见了你，自然就离开了。西湖南岸赤山埠前张成家欠我一千贯钱，你就先到他那儿去，租间房子住下，慢慢地再想法子。"

小乙无计可施，只得答应。和李募事回到家里，静悄悄地没啥动静。李募事写了信，和借据封在一起，叫小乙拿了去见张成。

这时白娘子却出来了，将小乙叫到房中，气愤地说："你好大胆！你把我当成什么了？你叫捉蛇的来干什么？我昨天告诉你的话，你得好好想一想，别到时后悔！"

P59　小乙听了，不敢作声。袖里藏了书信借据，踱出房来。走到门外，三步作两步地便往赤山埠来找张成。见了张成，正要去袖中拿借据，却不见了！这一惊非同小可，心中叫苦，慌忙转身来找。一路上来回走遍了赤山埠路，却哪里找得到！正气闷不已，来到一个地方，想坐下休息，抬头一看，是一座寺庙，上写"净慈寺"三字。小乙登时心中一亮，想起了法海禅师吩咐的话："如果那妖怪再来缠你，你就来净慈寺找我。"

P60　小乙急忙跑进寺中，问寺里的和尚："请问，法海禅师到宝刹来了没？"

那和尚说："没有。"

小乙听说禅师没来，心里郁闷，折身出来，有气无力地，一步一步走到长桥，自言自语说："时衰鬼弄人，像这样活下去有什么意思！"望着一湖清水，便要往下跳，正是：

阎王判你三更到，定不留人到五更。

P61　小乙正要往湖里跳，忽听得背后有人叫道："男子汉何故轻生？有什么看不开的事？"

回头一看，正是法海禅师——背驮衣钵，手提禅杖，原来真个才到——也是小乙命不该绝，若再迟一步，早作湖底游魂了。

小乙见了禅师，如获救星，纳头便拜，道："师尊救命！"

禅师说："孽畜今在何处？"

P62　小乙将最近的事向禅师说了。禅师听了，从袖中拿出一个钵盂，递给小乙说："你现在回去，这个东西不要让那孽畜看见，等她不注意，悄悄地往她头上一罩，紧紧地按住，不要害怕，我随后就来。"小乙将钵盂藏在袖中，拜谢了禅师，先自回家。

P63　回到家中，白娘子正坐在房里，口中喃喃地不知说些什么。小乙走到她背后，趁她不注意，拿出钵盂，往她头上一罩，用尽平生力气按了下去，随着钵盂慢慢地按下，不见了女子身形。小乙不敢松手，紧紧地按着。只听得钵盂内道："和你多年夫妻，你怎么如此无情！求你放松一些！"

P64　小乙正不知如何是好，忽听得外面有人说："一个和尚说要来收妖。"小乙连忙叫李募事去请那和尚进来。小乙见了法海禅师，说："救救弟子！"不知禅师口里念的什么，念毕，轻轻地揭开钵盂，只见白娘子缩做七八寸长，如傀儡一般大小，双眸紧闭，蜷做一团地伏在地下。

P65　禅师喝道："是何方孽畜妖怪？怎敢出来缠人？详细说来！"

白娘子答道："祖师，我是一条大蟒蛇，因为风雨大作，便来到西湖安身，同青青一处，不想见了许仙，就动了凡心，化作人形。一时冒犯天条，也是出自一片痴情，却从不曾杀生害命，望祖师慈悲！"

P66　禅师又问青青来历。白娘子说："青青是西湖内第三桥下潭内千年成精的青鱼，是我拉她做伴，诸事与她无干，并望祖师怜悯。"

禅师说："念你千年修炼，免你一死，可现本相！"

P67　白娘子不肯，抬头呆呆地望着小乙。禅师勃然大怒，口中念念有词，大喝道："护法尊神何在！快与我把青鱼怪擒来，并令白蛇现形，听吾发落！"

禅师话刚说完，庭前忽起一阵狂风，风过处，豁剌剌一声响，半空中坠下一条青鱼，有一丈多长，在地上拨剌剌地跳了几跳，缩作尺多长的一条小青鱼。看那白娘子时，也现了原形——变了一条三尺长白蛇——依然昂着头瞧着小乙。

P68 禅师将白蛇、青鱼收了，放在钵盂内，扯下长袖一幅，封了钵盂口，拿到雷峰寺前，将钵盂放在地下，令人搬砖运石，砌成一塔。

后来小乙也看破红尘，随了禅师出家，到处化缘，将原来的小塔改砌成七层宝塔，这便是雷峰塔。

P69 禅师见宝塔峰砌成，留偈四句：

西湖水干，江湖不起，

雷峰塔倒，白蛇出世。

从此千年万载，白蛇和青鱼永不能出世，除非雷峰塔倒！

P70 法海禅师留偈四句之后，又题诗八句，以劝后人：

“奉劝世人休爱色，爱色之人被色迷。

心正自然邪不扰，身端怎有恶来欺。

但看许仙因爱色，带累官司惹是非，

不是老僧来救护，白蛇吞了不留些。”

P71 法海禅师吟罢，大家都各自散去。只有许仙情愿出家，礼拜禅师为师，在雷峰塔剃度为僧，修行数年，直至坐化而去。

众僧将许仙遗体烧化，造了一座骨塔，千年不朽。

P72 许仙坐化之前，也有诗四句留以警世：

“祖师度我出红尘，铁树开花始见春。

化化轮回看化化，生生转变再生生。

欲知有色还无色，须识无形却有形；

色即是空空即色，空空色色要分明。”

P73 《警世通言》所收的《白娘子永镇雷峰塔》，其来源为《出唐人白蛇记》，这篇白蛇故事，有着其特殊的意义和价值，是一篇拟话本。

后来《西湖佳话》的《雷峰怪迹》一篇，和清人的《雷峰塔传奇》以及种种白蛇小说，和义妖传弹词，都是由这一篇衍化而来。

如果以宋人话本的分类来说，应属灵怪类的小说。

雷 公 传
Thunder God

我是千里眼。
My eyes can see objects miles away.
我是顺风耳。
My ears can hear voices a long way off.
我的眼睛很特别，可以看十里以外的报纸。
I have unusual eyes.They can read a newspaper placed several miles from me.
是超级远视啊！
You are superfarsighted!
不是远视而是近视。
No,not farsighted, but nearsighted.
但附有伸缩功能的眼珠。
But my eyeballs function like zoom lenses.

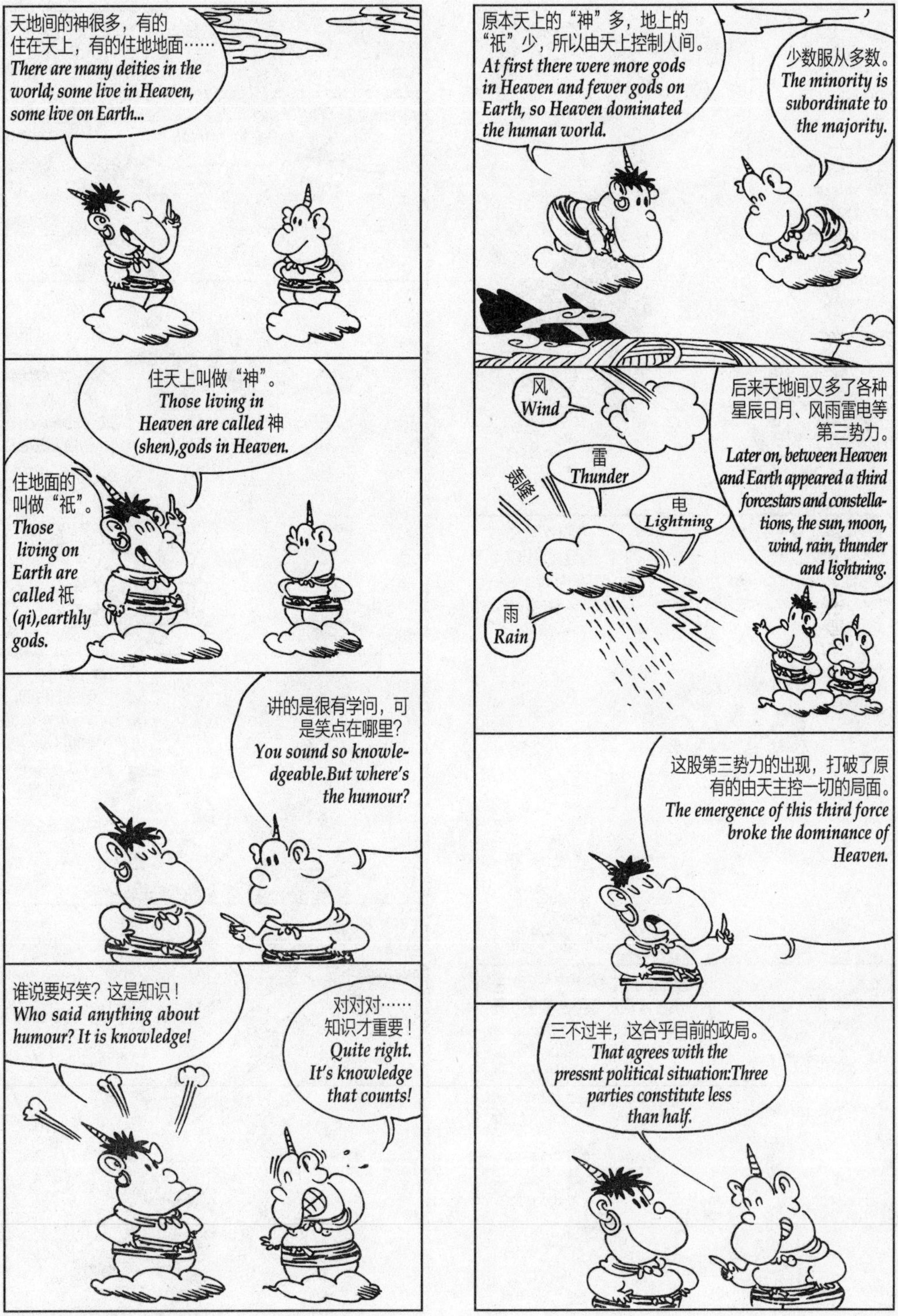

天地间的神很多，有的住在天上，有的住地地面……
There are many deities in the world; some live in Heaven, some live on Earth...

住天上叫做"神"。
Those living in Heaven are called 神 (shen),gods in Heaven.

住地面的叫做"祇"。
Those living on Earth are called 祇 (qi),earthly gods.

讲的是很有学问，可是笑点在哪里？
You sound so knowledgeable.But where's the humour?

谁说要好笑？这是知识！
Who said anything about humour? It is knowledge!

对对对……知识才重要！
Quite right. It's knowledge that counts!

这第三势力日月星辰、风雨雷电诸神，关系到人的生活。
The third force of the sun,moon, stars and constellations,and the gods of wind,rain,thunder and lightning have influence on the life of Mankind.
风
Wind
雨
Rain
雷
Thunder
隆隆隆
电
Lightning
所以自古以来人类常用三牲酒礼祭祀风雨雷电。
Therefore,since ancient times men have offered sacrifices of catle,sheep and pigs as well as wine to these gods.
为什么要祭拜风雨雷电？
Why do they offer them sacrifices?
为了答谢供水供电，一年缴一次水电费也是应该的。
To thank them for providing water and electricity.Paying for water and electricity once a year is the right thing to do.

民间祭拜风雨雷电其实有不同的目的，祭雨师为的是求它降雨。
Actually people offer sacrifices to the gods of wind,rain,thunder and lightning for different purposes.They offer sacrifices to the Rain God to beg for rainfall.
求您滋润干旱的大地。
Please come and water the parched earth.
祭拜风伯则是为了相反的目的。
They offer sacrifices to the Wind God to beg for the opposite.
我不受人欢迎呢！
So I am unwelcome!
呼！
Hoo!
求求您别再来啦，让风止息。
I beseech you not to come any more.Please let the wind stop.
呼！
Hoo!
呼！
Hoo!
呼！
Hoo!

原本风伯、雨师、雷公、电父四位神祇都是男神。
It turns out that the four gods were all male.

太不尊重女性了……
So disrespectful to the fairer sex...

后来才将电父改为电母，使得风雨雷电中也有个女神。
Later,the Lightning God became the Lightning Goddess,so that there was one female among the four gods.

这创造了中国第一个妇女保障名额的案例?
Was that how the reserved candidacy for women originated in China?

不!
No!

这创造了先进科技变性的第一例。
This was the first instance of sexchange surgery.

雨 *Rain*

雷 *Thunder*

电 *Lightning*

风 *Wind*

本栏漫画要说的故事主角，正是他们四位中的一位。
One of them will be the main character in this comic story.

为了公平起见，咱们就用投标决定。
For the sake of fairness, we will select him or her by throwing a dart.

Wind 风 *Rain* 雨 *Thunder* 雷 *Lightning* 电

很公平。
That's fair.

少演戏了，看上面《雷公传》的刊头也知道主角早就内定。
Stop acting!We know from the title that the protagonist has been chosen already.

被看穿了……嘻嘻嘻……
Hee,hee.The game is up...

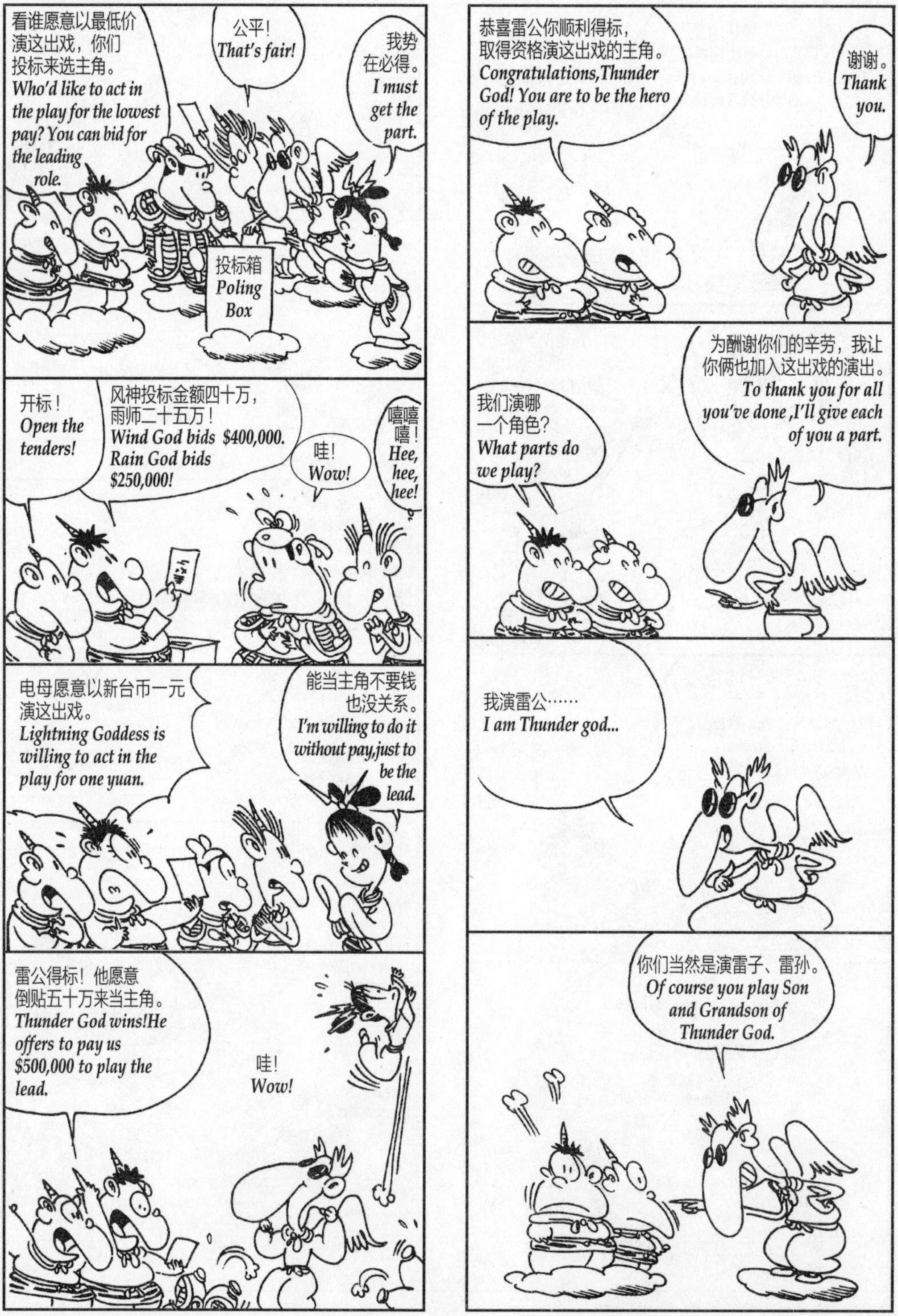

看谁愿意以最低价演这出戏，你们投标来选主角。
Who'd like to act in the play for the lowest pay? You can bid for the leading role.
公平！
That's fair!
我势在必得。
I must get the part.
投标箱
Poling Box

开标！
Open the tenders!
风神投标金额四十万，雨师二十五万！
Wind God bids $400,000. Rain God bids $250,000!
哇！
Wow!
嘻嘻嘻！
Hee, hee, hee!

电母愿意以新台币一元演这出戏。
Lightning Goddess is willing to act in the play for one yuan.
能当主角不要钱也没关系。
I'm willing to do it without pay,just to be the lead.

雷公得标！他愿意倒贴五十万来当主角。
Thunder God wins!He offers to pay us $500,000 to play the lead.
哇！
Wow!

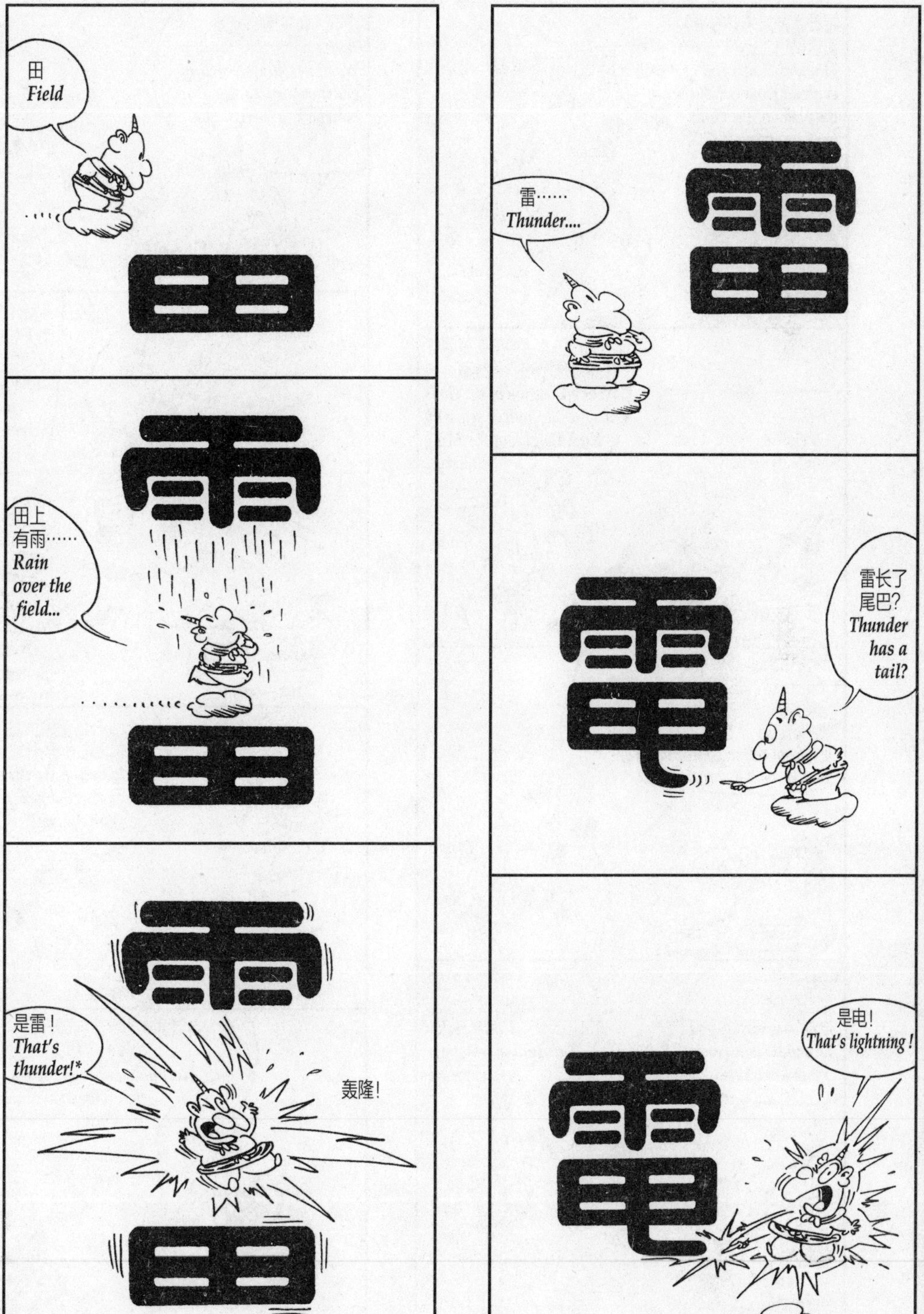

田
Field

田上
有雨……
Rain over the field...

是雷！
*That's thunder!**

轰隆！

**The Chinese word for "thunder" is made up of two parts:the upper part means "rain", and the lower part means "field".*

雷公本是从《封神榜》里雷震子衍生出的气候神。
Thunder God,a god of weather, evolved from Lei Zhenzi in Creation of the Gods.

哦……
Oh...

!

错了！《封神榜》是明代许仲琳编出的神话故事……
Wrong!Creation of the Gods is a mythological story by Xu Zhonglin of the Ming Dynasty...

正确的说法，雷公应是从佛经《天龙八部》里的大鹏金翅鸟演变而来的。
The origins of Thunder God may be traced to the gold-winged roc in a Buddhist scripture.

是由印度来中国打工的外国神祇？
So he's an earthly god from India who came to work in China?

没错，不信有天竺国的护照为证。
That's right. This Indian passport here is proof.

中国人有中国的神祇，怎会信仰外国神？
We have Chinese earthly gods;why would we believe in a foreign god?

这不奇怪！
What's wrong with that?

就像中国人拜的诸天如来菩萨原本就是外国神。
Tathagata whom we Chinese worship was originally a foreign god.

至少孙悟空是我们本地的神祇吧！
At least the Monkey King is an indigenous god of ours!

不！我原本也是来自印度教神话故事的人物。
No!I am also originally a character in a Hindu myth.

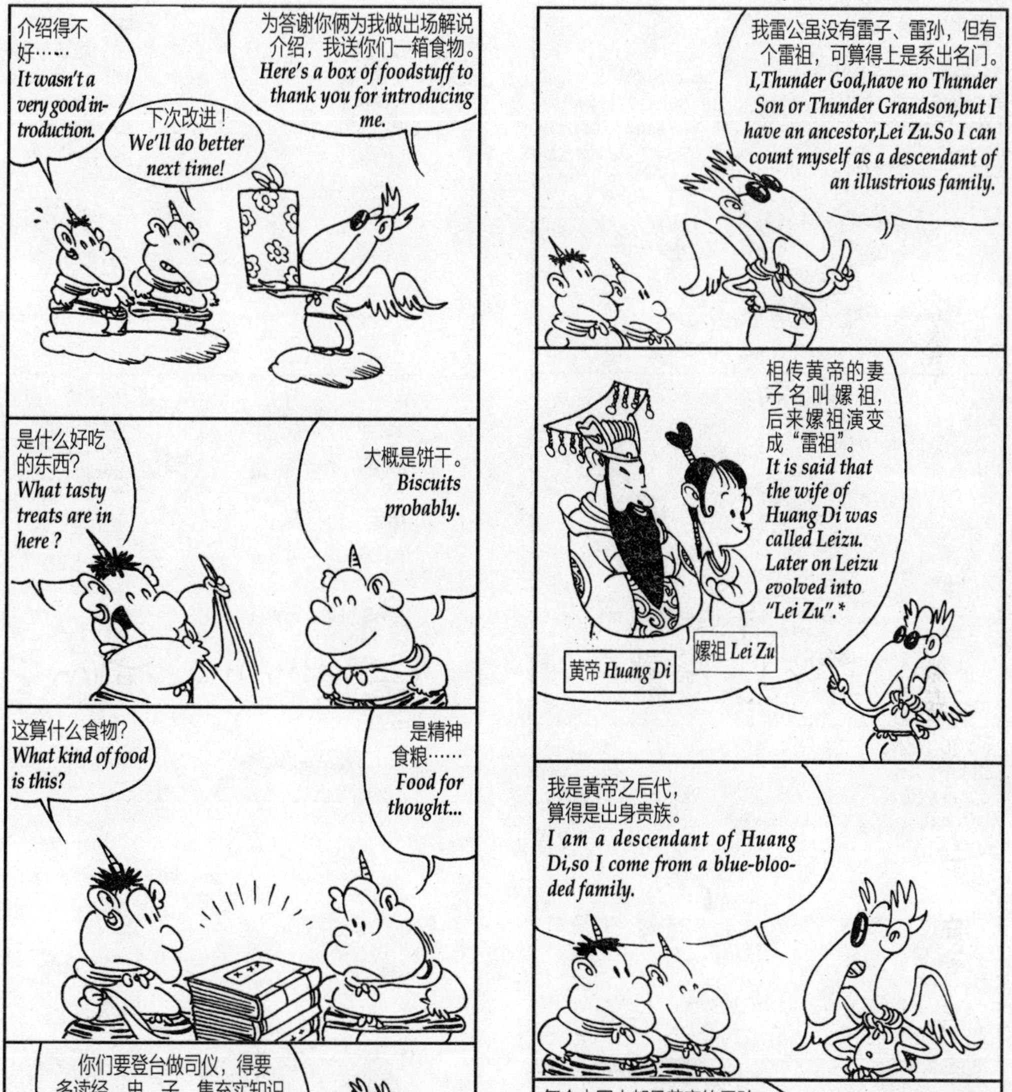

介绍得不好……
It wasn't a very good introduction.
下次改进！
We'll do better next time!
为答谢你俩为我做出场解说介绍，我送你们一箱食物。
Here's a box of foodstuff to thank you for introducing me.
是什么好吃的东西？
What tasty treats are in here ?
大概是饼干。
Biscuits probably.
这算什么食物？
What kind of food is this?
是精神食粮……
Food for thought...
你们要登台做司仪，得要多读经、史、子、集充实知识。
To go on stage as emcees,you should read more historical classics to enrich your minds.

*The name of the wife of Huang Di 黄帝 ,one of the Three August Ones,was Lei Zu 嫘祖 ,the patron saint of silkworm breeders.The Chinese for Thunder God is 雷祖。

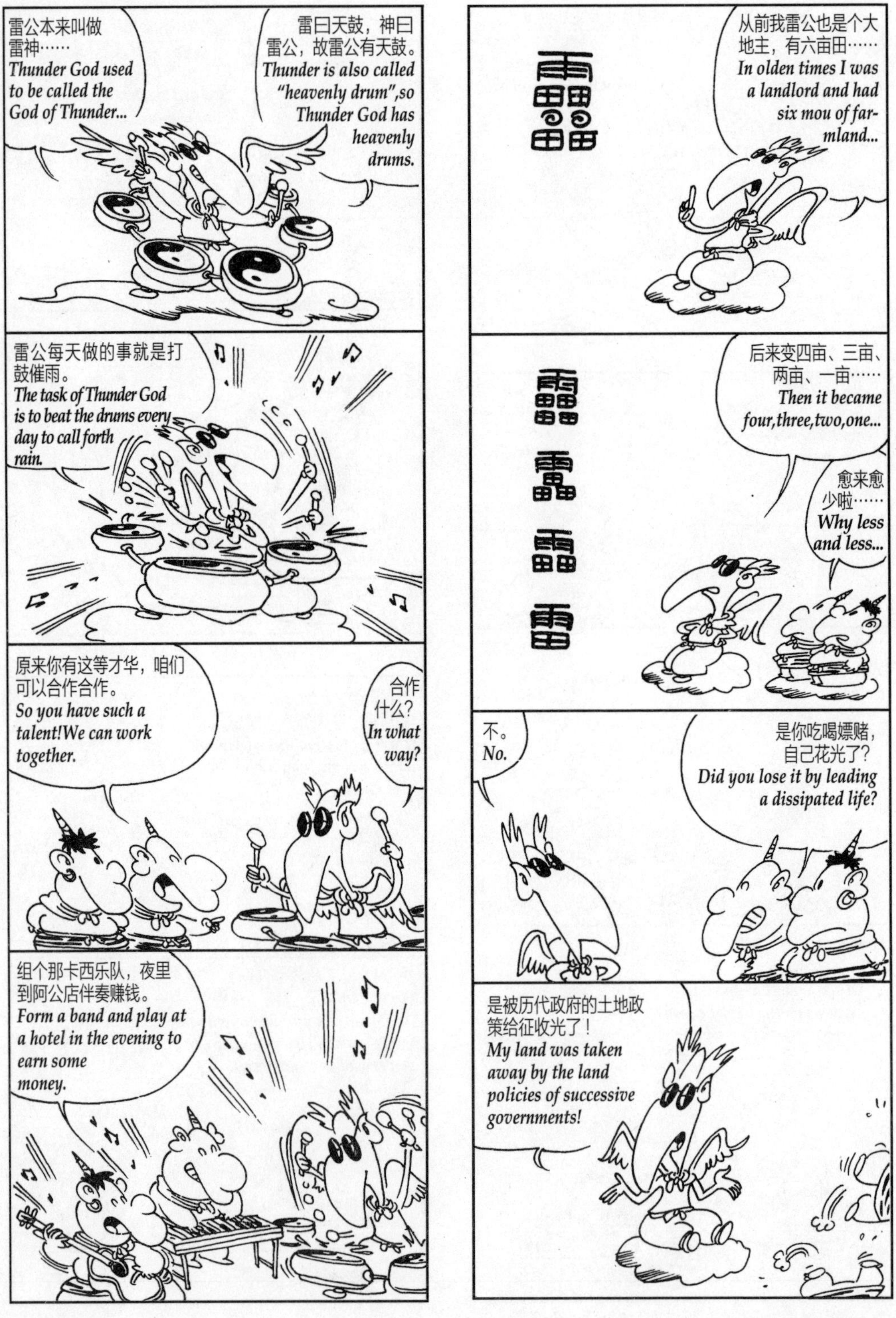

雷公本来叫做雷神……
Thunder God used to be called the God of Thunder...

雷曰天鼓，神曰雷公，故雷公有天鼓。
Thunder is also called "heavenly drum",so Thunder God has heavenly drums.

雷公每天做的事就是打鼓催雨。
The task of Thunder God is to beat the drums every day to call forth rain.

原来你有这等才华，咱们可以合作合作。
So you have such a talent!We can work together.

合作什么？
In what way?

组个那卡西乐队，夜里到阿公店伴奏赚钱。
Form a band and play at a hotel in the evening to earn some money.

道教之书曰："雷公名江赫冲，电母名秀文英。"
A Taoist book states thus:The Thunder God's name was Jiang Hechong,and the Lightning Goddess was called Xiu Wenying.
可惜我的老婆电母受不了我的雷性，早就与我离婚啦！
It's a pity that my wife the Lightning Goddess divorced me long ago because she couldn't stand my thundering!
是受不了你的脾气"暴跳如雷"？
She could not bear your hot temper?
不。
No.
是不能忍受我的鼾声如雷！
She could not stand my thunderous snores!

我雷公不但背生有翅能飞，最厉害的法宝要数手中的一钉一锤！
I not only have wings and can fly, but my most powerful weapons are the hammer and chisel in my hands!
隆！
隆！
隆！
哈！钉锤又迫不及待地准备上工……
Ha! my hammer and chisel can't wait to start work...
有好戏可看了，他要去杀坏人啦！
Something interesting is starting!He's going to kill a scoundrel!
不！是到石窟雕石打工。
No!I'm going to make statues in the ghetto.

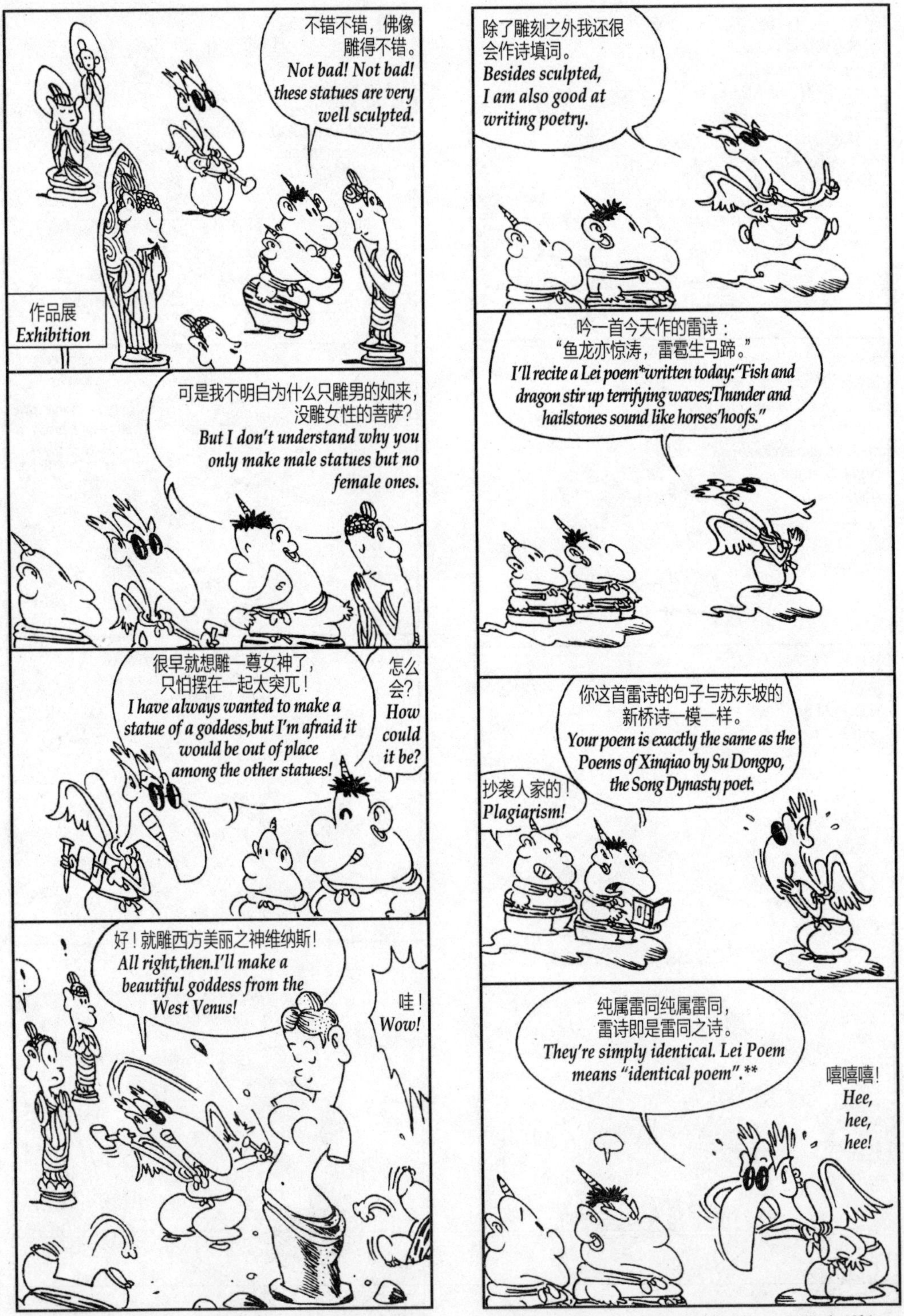

不错不错，佛像雕得不错。
Not bad! Not bad! these statues are very well sculpted.

作品展
Exhibition

可是我不明白为什么只雕男的如来，没雕女性的菩萨?
But I don't understand why you only make male statues but no female ones.

很早就想雕一尊女神了，只怕摆在一起太突兀！
I have always wanted to make a statue of a goddess,but I'm afraid it would be out of place among the other statues!

怎么会?
How could it be?

好！就雕西方美丽之神维纳斯！
All right,then.I'll make a beautiful goddess from the West Venus!

哇！
Wow!

**The Chinese word for "thunder"is pronounced"Lei".Lei poem means"poem written by Lei",just as poems by famous poets Du Fu and Li Po are called"Li poems"and"Du poems".*

***This is a play on words.The first character in the Chinese word meaning"identical" 雷同 is the same as the Chinese word for"thunder".*

我雷公还有一宝，就是声音洪亮，如雷贯耳。
I have another asset.It is my sonorous voice.It reverberates like thunder.
破嗓子没什么用处……
What's the use of a lousy voice...
啊！
Ah!
谁说没用？声音大就是有用！
Who says it's useless? A loud voice can be of great use!
果然有妙用。
It does have magical effect.
失火啦！
Fire!
KTV

其实打鼓、雕刻、作诗只是我个人的兴趣……
As a matter of fact,beating the drums,sculpting and writing poetry are just my hobbies...
我的正业是替民间打雷司雨！
My job is to supply thunder and rain to the world!
隆！
隆！
隆！
隆！
风雨雷电各司其职，雷公也能司雨？
The wind,rain,thunder and lightning each has its own job. Do you supply rain too,Thunder God?
不能。
No.
我只能替民间求雨信士关说而已……
I can only lobby on behalf of human believers for rain...

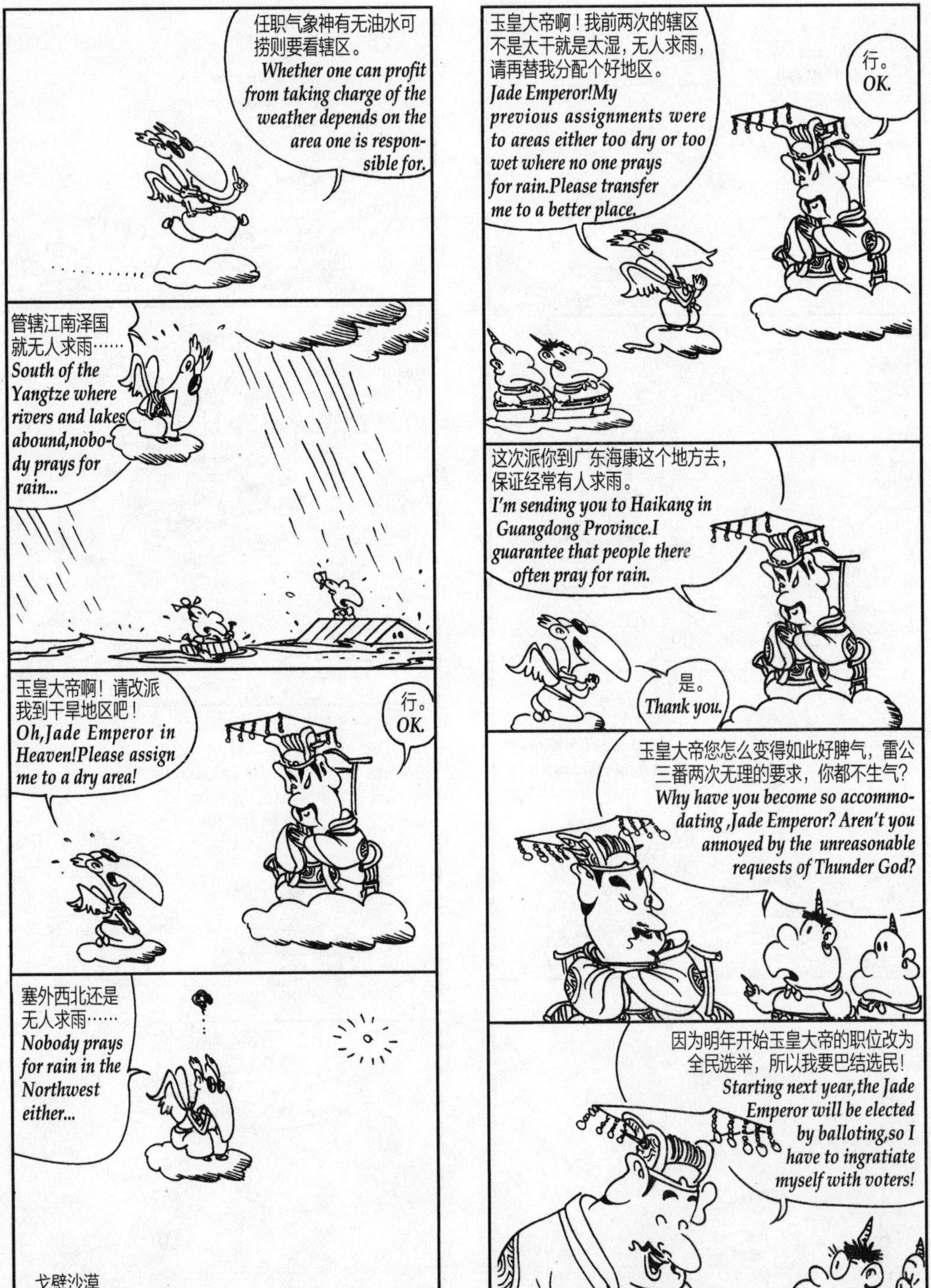

任职气象神有无油水可捞则要看辖区。
Whether one can profit from taking charge of the weather depends on the area one is responsible for.

管辖江南泽国就无人求雨……
South of the Yangtze where rivers and lakes abound,nobody prays for rain...

玉皇大帝啊！请改派我到干旱地区吧！
Oh,Jade Emperor in Heaven!Please assign me to a dry area!

行。
OK.

塞外西北还是无人求雨……
Nobody prays for rain in the Northwest either...

戈壁沙漠
Gobi Desert

*The Chinese terms for sea mines and land mines are 水雷 and 地雷 respectively.

**Torpedo is known as 鱼雷 in Chinese.

雷神啊，求求你降雨吧……
Oh,Thunder God! Please give us rain...

好吃好吃！
Mun... Delicious!

吃人供品，与人消灾。
Having eaten his sacrifice,I've got to solve his problem.

雨师啊！求求你降雨吧！
Rain God! I beg you to dispense some rain!

雨师
Rain → God

天上包青天
Justice Bao of Heaven

雷公除了负责打雷催雨，还兼任执行司法正义……
Besides providing thunder and rain,he also administers law and justice...

你没良心，敢为私怨在溪水里下毒，这么做不怕雷公打死你？
You put poison in the stream to redress your personal grievance.Aren't you afraid of being struck by the Thunder God?

嘻嘻嘻。
Hee,hee, hee.

雷公啊！请以五雷轰顶打死那个恶徒！
Thunder God, please strike that rascal dead!

行！执行一个案子请付白银二百五。
All right.I charge 250 ounces of silver for each case I handle.

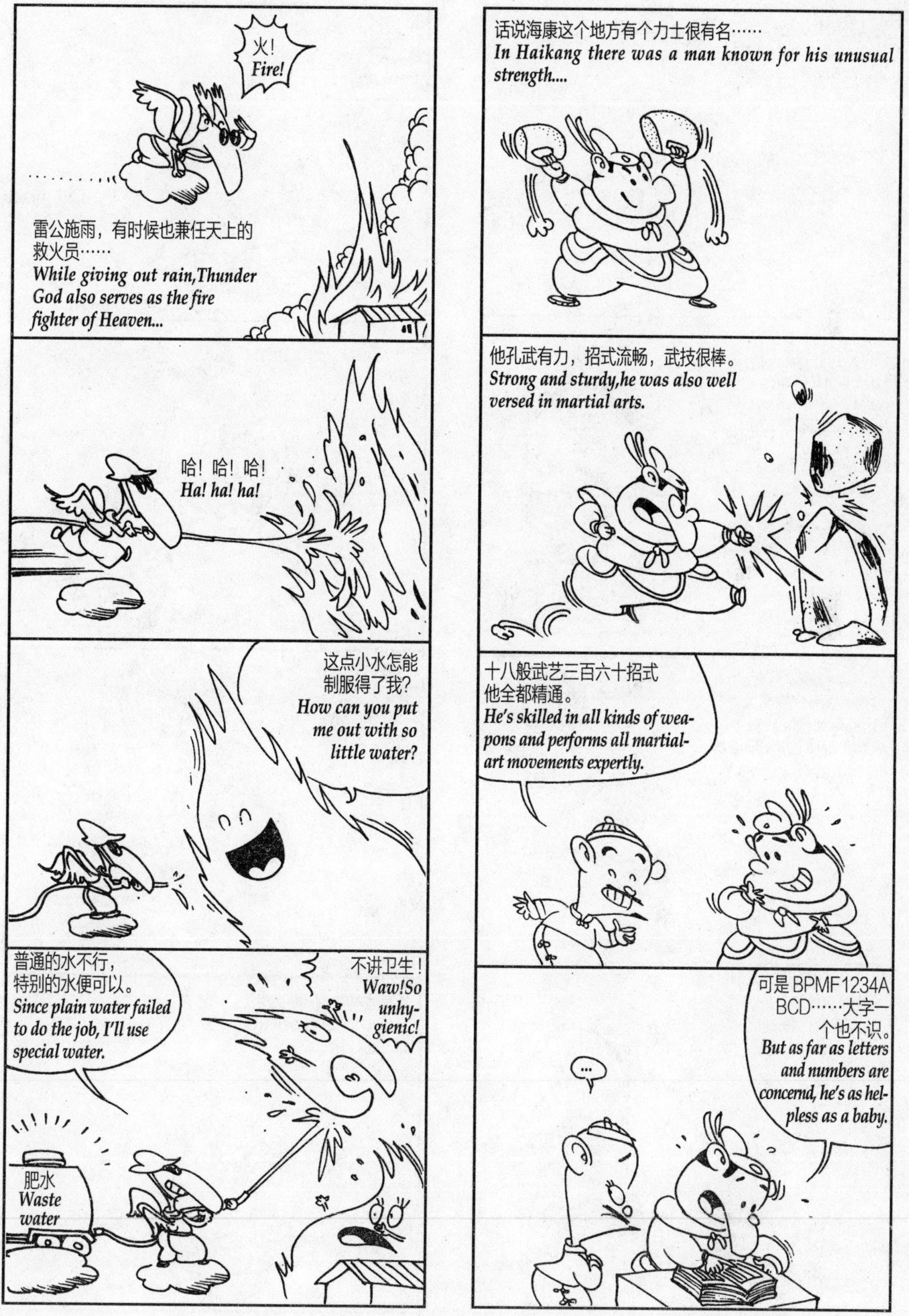

火！
Fire!

雷公施雨，有时候也兼任天上的救火员……
While giving out rain,Thunder God also serves as the fire fighter of Heaven...

哈！哈！哈！
Ha! ha! ha!

这点小水怎能制服得了我？
How can you put me out with so little water?

普通的水不行，特别的水便可以。
Since plain water failed to do the job, I'll use special water.

不讲卫生！
Waw!So unhygienic!

肥水
Waste water

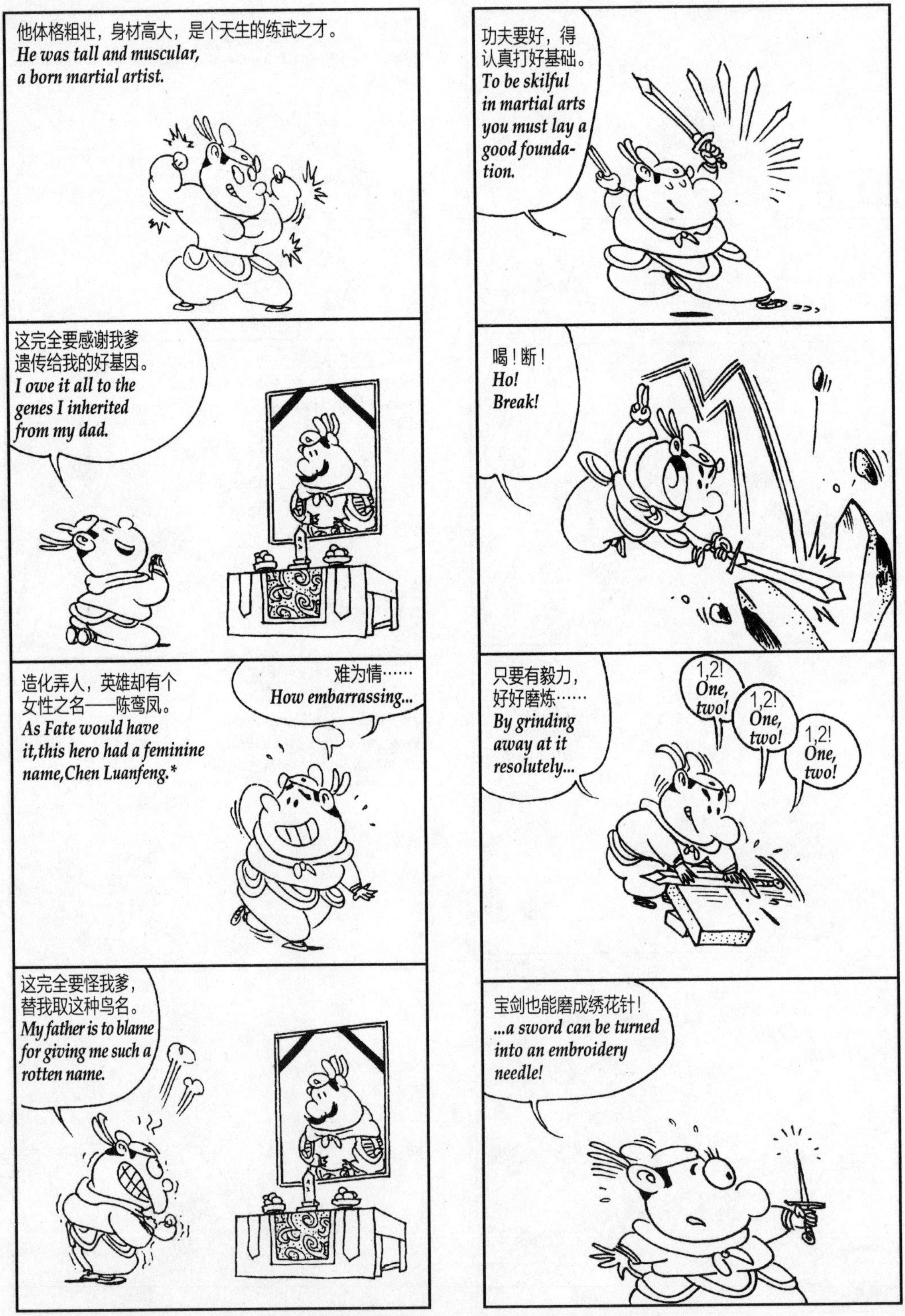

他体格粗壮，身材高大，是个天生的练武之才。
He was tall and muscular, a born martial artist.

这完全要感谢我爹遗传给我的好基因。
I owe it all to the genes I inherited from my dad.

造化弄人，英雄却有个女性之名——陈鸾凤。
*As Fate would have it,this hero had a feminine name,Chen Luanfeng.**

难为情……
How embarrassing...

这完全要怪我爹，替我取这种鸟名。
My father is to blame for giving me such a rotten name.

**The literal meaning of Luanfeng，鸾凤，is"phoenix".So it is often used to name girls.*

十年磨一剑，霜刃未曾试，今日把示君，谁有不平事？
I spent 10 years honing this sword;its keen edge is yet untested.I am showing it to you today;Could you tell me where there is injustice?

路见不平，拔刀相助。
Seeing injustice, I draw my sword to assist.

是有不平的事……
There is injustice...

路的这里不平，能否摆平它做做善事？
The road is bumpy here.Will you be good enough to level it?*

This is a pun."不平"in the idiom"路见不平"means "injustice",but when used by itself,it means "not level".

酒
wine
三杯不过冈
No crossing the ridge after three cups

这里有吃人的老虎?
Are there tigers that eat people?
酒
wine
乱石冈
Stony Ridge

老虎多得是，它们现在全都在这屋子里。
There are lots of tigers. They're all inside.
什么!
What!

只是它们现在不吃人，而是专门给人吃。
Only they do not eat people now.They are to be consumed by people.
虎骨酒
Tiger Bone Wine
Wine

你这三杯不过冈的招牌是什么意思?
What does that sign mean?
三杯不过冈
No crossing the ridge after three cups

就是说如果喝了本店三杯酒，就过不了乱石冈。
It means after three cups of our wine,you won't be able to cross the ridge.
哦!
Oh!

喝了这区区小小的三杯酒还不简单?
Drinking these three tiny cups in no problem at all?

喝是容易，只是买单付钱可不简单。
Drinking is no problem, but paying for your drinks is a problem.
价目表 Price list
三杯酒三十两银
30 ounces of silver for three cups of wine.

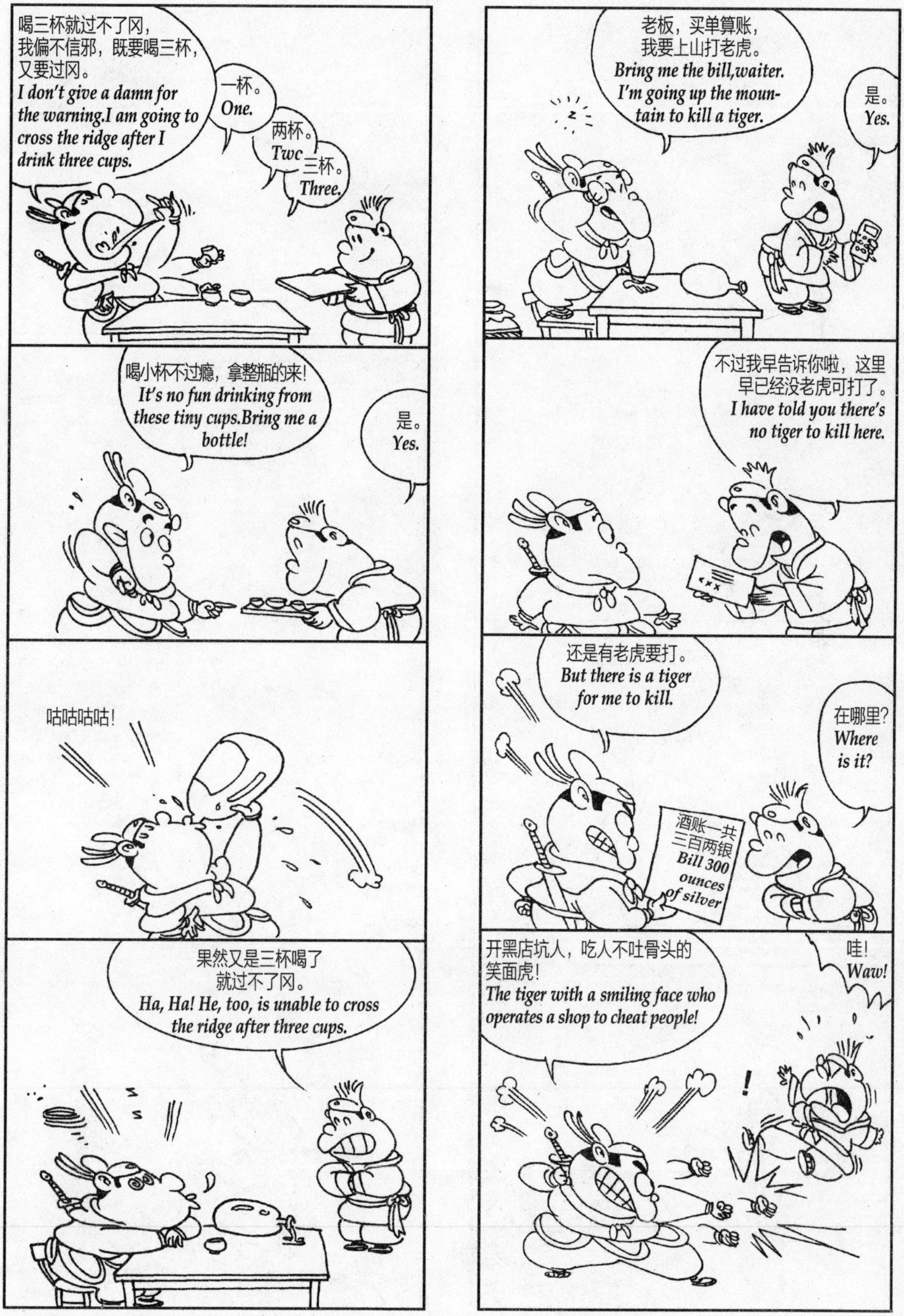

喝三杯就过不了冈，我偏不信邪，既要喝三杯，又要过冈。
I don't give a damn for the warning.I am going to cross the ridge after I drink three cups.
一杯。One.
两杯。Two.
三杯。Three.
喝小杯不过瘾，拿整瓶的来！
It's no fun drinking from these tiny cups.Bring me a bottle!
是。Yes.
咕咕咕咕！
果然又是三杯喝了就过不了冈。
Ha, Ha! He, too, is unable to cross the ridge after three cups.

乱石冈
Stony Ridge

呵！
Hoo!
呵！
Hoo!
呵！
Hoo!
呵！
Hoo!

呵！
Hoo!
呵！
Hoo!
呵！
Hoo!
呵！
Hoo!
呵！
Hoo!

!

大胆狂徒，敢在我鬼弟兄的地盘睡觉，竟不怕我鬼类。
This daredevil dares to sleep in my territory.He's not afraid of ghosts.

你是什么鬼？
What kind of ghost are you?

因为我自己也是个鬼，鬼当然是不怕鬼喽！
Being a ghost myself,of course I'm not afraid of my kith and kin.

酒鬼！
A drinking ghost!*

...

*"Drinking ghost"is the literal translation of the Chinese term 酒鬼 ,which means "drunkard".

*A jocular colloquial Chinese term for untidy handwriting is 鬼画符, literally translated as "a magic figure drawn by a ghost".

**Zhong Kui is a deity who catches demons.Therefore, his pictures are pasted on doors to ward off evil spirits.

***The Chinese word for gall bladder 胆 is the same as in 胆大, meaning "courageous" or "bold".

你癌症末期只剩两年生命，胆肿大只能活一年，高血压严重只能活三年，肺痨第三期只能活四年，右心房萎缩只剩一年可活……
You have terminal cancer and have only two more years to live.You have only one year to live because of swollen gall bladder.Because of high blood pressure,you have only three years.For third-stage Tuberculosis,four more years.For atrophy of right atrium, only one more year...

两年加一年加三年加四年加一年加六年加八年加十年，一共还可活三十五年。
Two plus one plus three plus four plus one plus six plus eight plus 10;altogether you have 35 more years to live.

陈鸾凤打鬼成名，于是改行专门为人驱鬼捉妖。
Having established his reputation as a demon-battering hero,Chen Luanfeng decided to make exorcising evil spirits his occupation.

打鬼英雄
Demon-battering Hero

脚踏北泽魍魉，拳打南山鬼魅！
With my feet I tackle the demons of North Lake.With my fists I bash the ghosts of South Mountain!

打鬼英雄
Demon-battering Hero

你专门治鬼，瘟神也能治吗？
You specialise in dealing with ghosts. Can you deal with the God of Plague too?

行！你的症状是贫血、体重过轻，治疗秘方是多运动、多喝猪肝汤。
Yes!You are anaemic and underweight.My secret prescription for your ailment is lots of exercise and plenty of liver soup.

*The Chinese term for "god of plague"is 瘟神.When the radical meaning "disease"is removed from the word,the inside part is left and the word becomes 温,which means "gentle".

打鬼英雄
Demon-battering Hero

陈英雄，你什么鬼都能打吗？
Hero Chen,can you deal with every kind of ghost?

体重轻的鬼叫魖，身高的鬼叫魁，独脚的鬼叫魈，梦中的鬼叫魇，山林中的鬼叫魅，你要打的是哪一种？
Ghost that are underweight are called 魖 Tall ghosts are called 魁 .One-legged ghosts are 魈 .Demons in dreams are 魇 and demons in mountains and forests are called 魅 .Which kind of ghost do you want me to bash?

可是我要请你打的不是这种活生生的厉鬼。
I don't want you to bash any of these evil spirits that are alive.

鬼当然是死的啊！
Ghosts are of course dead!

正是，我要请你治的是家中那个只顾吃喝不养家的“死鬼”！
That's right.I want you to deal with the devil in my home that eats and drinks but does not provide for the family!*

啊！又是练武的时辰到了。
Oh!It's time for martial-art exercise agiain.

咕

武要练得专精，得选对了练武的环境。
To get good results I must practise under the right conditions.

我的办法叫做“寓教于食”。
My method is to combine instruction with practice.

第一式，力斩猛牛。
The first move is to attack a tough bull.

三分熟牛排
A rare steak

* 死 鬼 *is a term often used jocularly and sometimes as a term of endearment.*

*熊心豹子胆 is a Chinese phrase often used to mean "unusual courage",as the word 熊 meaning "bear"is a homonym of 雄 and 雄心 means "great ambition".

再大的厉鬼、神祇我都不怕，还会怕雷公？
I'm not even afraid of ferocious devils and earthly gods,what is the Thunder God to me?

普天之下的鬼神你都不怕吗？
Aren't you afraid of any ghosts and gods?

不！
No!

只有一种神我不敢得罪！
There's only one god I dare not offend.

什么神？
Which one?

招财进宝
Let riches and treasures come into the house.

财神！
God of Wealth!

你真的什么神鬼都不怕，连雷公你也敢治？
Is it true that you are not afraid of any gods or demons and have the nerve to punish the Thunder God?

当然。
Of course.

好极了，请你替我治治一个雷公瘟神。
Very good! I'd like you to punish this thunder god of plague.

行。
All right.

天杀的死鬼，不好好上班赚钱奉养老娘，还敢带朋友到家里来！
You devil! You don't support your old mother.And now you even dare to bring home a friend!

砰！
Pang!

当！
Dang!

看我不杀了你，千刀杀的！
Just wait and see how I'm going to kill you!

这种母雷公连我都怕！
Even I am scared of this kind of thunder goddess!

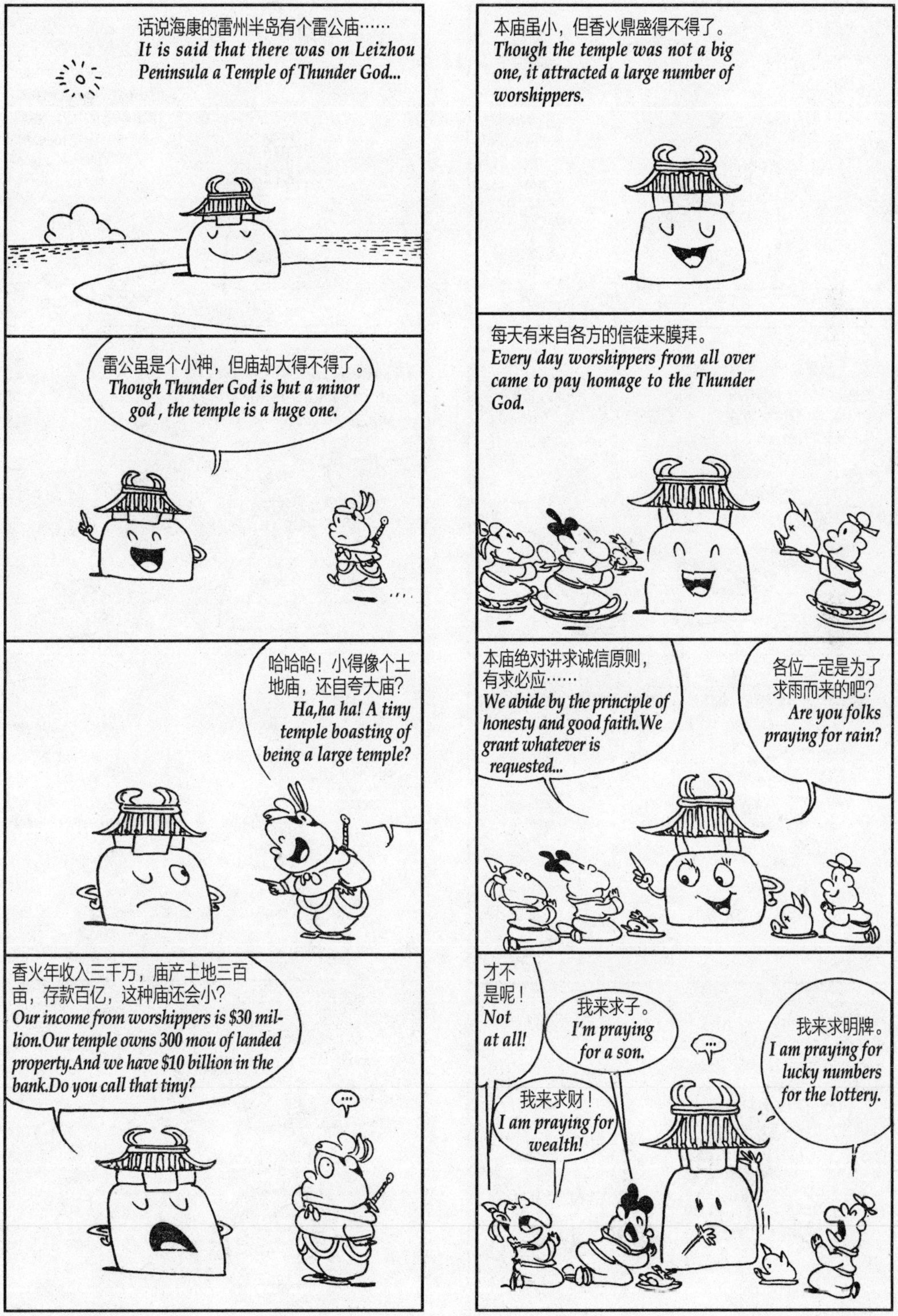

话说海康的雷州半岛有个雷公庙……
It is said that there was on Leizhou Peninsula a Temple of Thunder God...

雷公虽是个小神，但庙却大得不得了。
Though Thunder God is but a minor god , the temple is a huge one.

哈哈哈！小得像个土地庙，还自夸大庙？
Ha,ha ha! A tiny temple boasting of being a large temple?

香火年收入三千万，庙产土地三百亩，存款百亿，这种庙还会小？
Our income from worshippers is $30 million.Our temple owns 300 mou of landed property.And we have $10 billion in the bank.Do you call that tiny?

听说雷公庙灵得很是吗?
I hear that this temple is efficacious. Is it true?

本庙上达天意无疑，当然是很灵喽。
Of course.We have no communication problem with Heaven.

何以证明?
How do you prove it?

喂！天庭吗？雷公在吗?
Hello! Is that Heaven?May I speak to the Thunder God?

!

雷公本人来跟你证明，请你来听……
Let the Thunder God himself prove it to you .You answer the phone...

哇!
Waw!

信士陈某供奉一只烧鸡，请雷公保佑让我发财。
Devotee Chen offers you a chicken,Thunder God. Please bless me with wealth.

求财得财，有求必应。
All requests are granted.You beg for wealth,you'll get it.

轰!
Boom!

咦？才一锭银而已……
What? Only one silver ingot...

一只鸡多少市价你明白，得银一锭还有什么不满意?
You know very well the price of a chicken. Why are you not satisfied with one silver ingot?

…

信士王氏求雷神赐子，佑我怀胎。
Thunder God,please bless me with a son.

抱歉！现在天庭实施正风专案力扫弊病，求子之为不得行。
Sorry! A campaign is on in Heaven at the moment to wipe out malpractice. I can't help you get a son.

这与我求子有何关系?
What does the campaign have to do with my getting a son?

天庭严禁神人之间的不伦关系。
Heaven strictly forbids immoral deity-human relationships.

天罗神、地罗神、人离难、难离身，一切灾殃化为尘。
Heavenly gods,earthly gods,Let Man and trouble be separate. Let all sufferings be turned into dust.

你是求平安?
Are you praying for peace and safety?

是。
Yes.

请在合约上签字。
Please sign on the contract.

月缴保费三千，雷公接你这笔平安人寿保险。
Thunder God will underwrite your life insurance.The monthly premium is $3,000.

海康雷公庙香火鼎盛，信徒常来求子、求财、求明牌……
The Thunder God Temple at Haikang was visited by many worshippers.They came to beg for sons,for wealth,for success in gambling...

雷公庙正事不做，忘了施雨的本分。
This temple does not attend to its proper business. It neglects its duty to adminster rain.

你可知道我远道而来，为的是什么事？
Do you know what I have come all the way for?

为了老农津贴预算案？
For the third reading of the Veteran Farmers' Subsidy Act at the Legislative Council?

我是来求明牌，求雷公赐我下一期的六合彩数字。
Thunder God,please give me the winning numbers of the next lottery draw.

有求必应，显现一组数字图形。
All requests are granted. Now show a set of figures.

从0到9统统有，怎么组合你自己猜！
They're all here,from 0 to 9.You can guess their combinations!

我老农是为
求雨而来的。
I have come to beg for rain.

你可知道老天已经整
整六年没下过雨了?
Heaven has not given us any rain for six long years. Do you know that?

这个简单,
马上办!
That's easy. I'll see to it at once!

省政府吗?请为海康地区发放天灾补助,
并申请六年地价税免征。
Is that the provincial government? Please grant disaster subsidy to the Haikang district and apply for exemption of land tax for six years.

求求你施法降雨吧,不然
这茬稻子又要枯死……
Please use your power to give us rain. Otherwise, our crops will fail again...

天灵灵,地灵灵,
勒令下雨不停!
Please,gods in Heaven and on Earth,give order for incessant rain!

哈哈哈,
有雨了!
Ha, ha, ha! It's raining!

慢着!这小雨是给我自
己用的,祈雨前要净身。
Wait! This drizzle is for me to clean myself before I pray for rain.

我来跳一段印第安祈雨舞，保证有雨。
I'll do an Indian "rain dance"and rain will come.

嘿呦！嘿嘿呦！呼啦啦呼啦啦呦！
Hey-you!Hei-hei-you! Hoo-la-la-hoo-la-la-you!

呼呼呼啦啦啦！呜呜呜！哈哈哈！
Hoo-hoo-hoo-la-la!Woo-woo-woo! Ha, ha, ha!

没有雨呀？
Where's the rain?

有的，汗淋如雨！
It's here.My sweat is dripping like rain!

雷公庙不能为民祈雨，留它何用？
You cannot get rain for the people. What's the use of this temple?

劈了它！
I'm going to pull it down!

急急如勒令！
Hocus pocus!

轰！
Boom!

求雨祈福不灵，降灾可很灵。
Though I can't bring you rain, I can bring you disaster.

你这恶庙光知收礼，不为百姓祈雨。不如劈了你！
Evil temple ,you only accept offerings,but do not pray for rain on behalf of the people. Might as well chop you into pieces!
根据大唐文化部法令，谁都不得动本庙一瓦一砖。
According to decree of the Ministry of Culture nobody is allowed to lay hands on any bricks or tiles of this temple.
!
因为本庙建自初唐，是国家重要古迹。
This temple was built in the Tang Dynasty,so it is an important national relic.
一级国家古迹
First-grade national historic site
老农不如老建筑物。
An old farmer is not as precious as an old structure.
一级古迹
First-grade national historic site
寺庙够老有文化部保护，老农够老有谁保护？
When a temple is old enough it is protected by the Ministry of Culture. Who protects an old farmer?

可恶的邪庙欺善怕恶，不为人民祈福消灾……
This vicious temple bullies the virtuous and fears the wicked.It does not send up prayers for the welfare of the people...
这种无用的庙不如一把火烧了它。
Might as well burn it down.
!
请先等我打通电话……
Please wait till my call gets through...
打电话给雷公讨救兵?
You're calling Thunder God for help?
打给 119 消防中心。
I'm calling the Fire Department.

雷公啊！你再不现身施雨，
我就一把火烧了你的庙！
Oh, Thunder God! If you still will not make your appearance and give us rain,I'm going to set fire to your temple!
你烧吧！我不但不会阻止反对，还要感谢你呢！
Go ahead!Not only will I not stop you ,I will be very grateful to you!
因为我已替我的这座庙投保火险五十亿。
Because I have taken out a five billion yuan fire insurance.
既然雷公也同意，
我就一把火烧了你。
Since Thunder God has given his consent, I'm going to set fire to you.
咦？不怕火烧？
Huh? Aren't you afraid of being burnt?
哈！
Ha!
哈！
Ha!
哈！
Ha!
这是守法的好处。
Being law-abiding has its advantages.
本庙依政府规定，全部使用防火建材建造。
In accordance with government regulations,this temple was built entirely with fireproof materials.

虽然你不怕烧，又是一级文物古迹，我还是有办法对付你。
Though you are fire-resistant and you are a first-grade historic structure,I still have a way to deal with you.
文物资讯快报！这里有座早唐的建筑，位置偏僻又无人看管。
Cultural Relic Information Bulletin! This is an early Tang Dynasty structure.
瓦当刻的是四灵祥兽！
Wow! Han Dynasty glazed tiles!
哇! 是汉代的琉璃瓦！
Auspicious animals are carved on the edge!
每一块砖瓦都是国家级的珍宝啊！
Each of the bricks and tiles can be rated a national treasure !
三两下就被古董商盗个精光。
In a matter of minutes it is stripped to the ground by antique dealers.
雷公啊！我已将你的庙拆了。看你能拿我怎么办?
I have demolished your temple,Thunder God!What are you going to do with me?
感恩不尽，真是谢谢你！
Thank you very much.I'm very grateful.
我正想卖这块地，多谢你免费为我做地上物的清理。
I was contemplating selling this piece of land. Thank you for clearing it for me free of charge.
土地出售　雷公上
Property for Sale Thunder God

雷公你吃了人家鱼肉供品，
应该为人施雨！
Thunder God,you've eaten so many fish offered by the people,you ought to give them some rain!

雨来！
Come, rain!

来了！
Coming!

是鱼……
It's a fish!

雷公你身为雷神，
应为天下庶民施雨！
As the Thunder God,you should bring rain to the common people!

请你降雨，大雨小雨不管什么
雨都成，否则我绝不放过你！
Please let us have ain,heavy rain,light drizzle whatever. Otherwise,I won't let you have a moment's peace!

雨来了！
Rain is coming!

是箭雨……
A rain of arrows...

大胆狂徒敢与我雷公作对，看我来收拾你！
Impudent rogue,you have the audacity to set yourself against me !See how I'm going to deal with you!
呵！Ah!
呵！Ah!
呵！Ah!
呵！Ah!

啊！原来雷公是只人形大鸟……
Oh! Thunder God is actually a big bird in human shape...

现在知道已经太迟啦！
Now you know that,but it's too late!
绝不太迟！
Not at all late!

我随身带好装备，随时不放弃赏鸟机会。
Being well equipped, I never lose a chance for birdwatching.

停电期间我改用自己制造的土制炸弹对付你。
Meanwhile I'll deal with you with a homemade bomb.

接着！
Take this!

哇！
Wah!

锵！
Chi –ang!

果然是纯土制成的炸弹……
*It is indeed a bomb made entirely of earth.**

哈！
Ha!

哈！
Ha!

哈！
Ha!

哈！
Ha!

好吧！咱们就停战三十分钟。
OK.Let's have a 30-minute truce.

停战 30 分
30-minute truce

趁机会补充一点水分。
I'm taking the chance to have a drink of water.

我也借这停火时间去充充电。
*I'm taking advantage of recharge my batteries.***

打败人类的方法……
Ways to defeat Mankind...

《完全制胜手册》
Handbook of Complete Victory

* *The basic meaning of the first character in 土制 ,which means "locally made"or "home -made"is "earth"or "soil".*

** *In modern colloquial Chinese, 充电 ,which originally means "to recharge a battery",is often used to mean "to take a crash course".*

*Duke Zhou was the son of King Wen of Zhou Dynasty.It was mentioned in The Analects of Confucius that Confucius once dreamt of meeting Duke Zhou,so the Chinese often use "meeting Duke Zhou" to mean having a dream.

睡香吃饱精神好，
拳脚快速有劲无人敌。
After a good sleep and a good meal,my boxing movements are so swift and forceful that no one is my match.
况且居高临下空对地，这场决斗你输定了！
Moreover,I am fighting from a high position while you are on the ground;you are doomed to lose.
难说。
It's hard to say.
哇！
依我看胜负是五五开，没打不知晓结果！
As I see it,our chances are 50-50.You can't predict the outcome now!

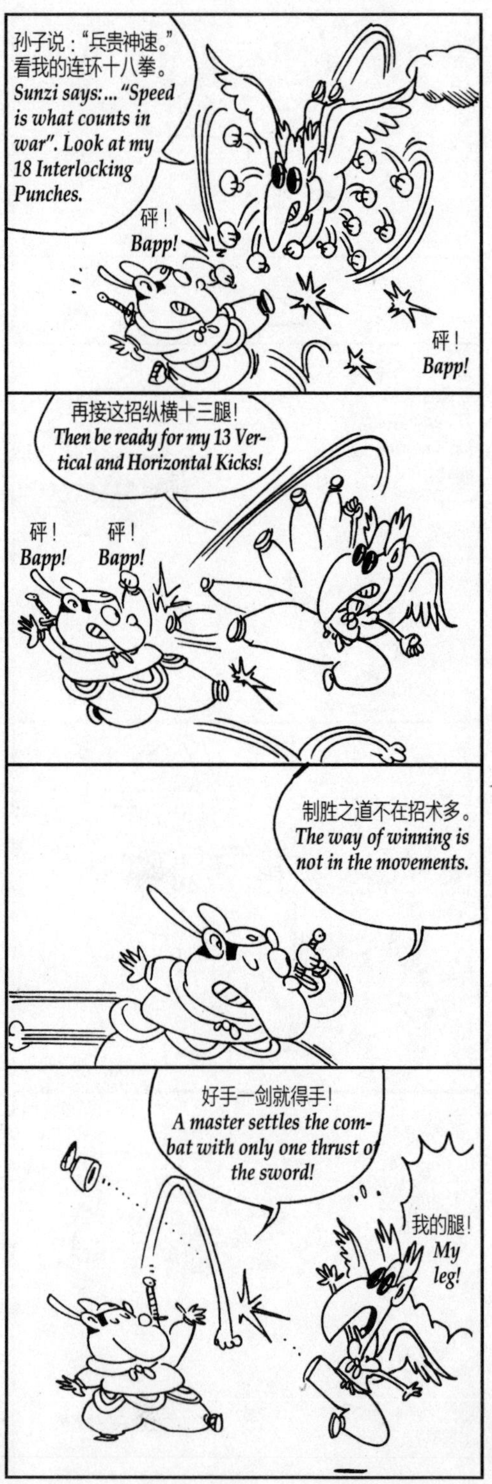
孙子说："兵贵神速。"看我的连环十八拳。
Sunzi says:... "Speed is what counts in war". Look at my 18 Interlocking Punches.
砰！
Bapp!
砰！
Bapp!
再接这招纵横十三腿！
Then be ready for my 13 Vertical and Horizontal Kicks!
砰！
Bapp!
砰！
Bapp!
制胜之道不在招术多。
The way of winning is not in the movements.
好手一剑就得手！
A master settles the combat with only one thrust of the sword!
我的腿！
My leg!

我是输了，输得很彻底……
I have lost, totally lost...

你是输了，这不用怀疑。
There's no doubt about that.

想不通啊！神怎么会输给人呢？
I really cannot understand how a god could lose to a man?

因为编故事的作者是人！
Because the story was made up by a man!

人袒护人是天经地义的事。
It's only natural that a man sides with a man.

各位父老乡亲们快来看哦！我已经抓到雷公啦！
Elders and fellow townsmen,come take a look! I have seized the Thunder God!
雷公空享香火不管乡民死活，你们说该怎么处治它？
He's been enjoying our offerings and paying no heed to our welfare. How should we deal with him?
我有个好主意。
I have a good idea.
你说！
Tell me!
把它油炸料理，做成汉堡快餐香酥鸡！
Let's fry him and turn him into crispy chicken!
哇！
Waw!
它是鸟类，不能杀！ 
He's a bird.You shouldn't kill him!
陆上的兽可以吃，水里的鱼可杀，但天上的鸟被立法保护。
It is legal to kill animals on land and to eat fish in the water ,but there is a law protecting the birds in the sky.
法律是公平的，为何兽可杀、鱼可吃，而独厚鸟族？
The law should be fair.Why does it allow killing animals and eating fishes yet treat birds so kindly?
因为咱们全世界的鸟族花钱游说保护团体，申请立法保护。
Because we birds paid money to lobby for bird protection legislation.

它虽有翅，但有手有脚，算不上是鸟类，当然可以杀来吃。
Though he has wings,he also has hands and feet.So he's not a bird. Of course we can eat him.

有翅又有手有脚，更是不能杀！
Having wings and also hands and feet makes me even more unkillable!

因为我是稀有动物！
Because I am a rare species!

瞧！你们人类自己订的《动物保护法》规定稀有动物更要保护！
Look ! The law you made yourself stipulates that rare species should be protected!

手不会写字可以改用脚写悔过书。
You can't write with your hand,but you can write with your foot.

脚怎么写？
How?

照着写在地上的字，来回跑十遍！
Just run 10 times tracing the two characters written on the ground!

我不用手不用脚，而用翅膀写吧……
I won't write with my hand or with my foot. I'll write with my wings...

SORRY

雷鸟特技飞行出SORRY的字样……
The word "sorry"is produced by Thunderbird stunt flying...

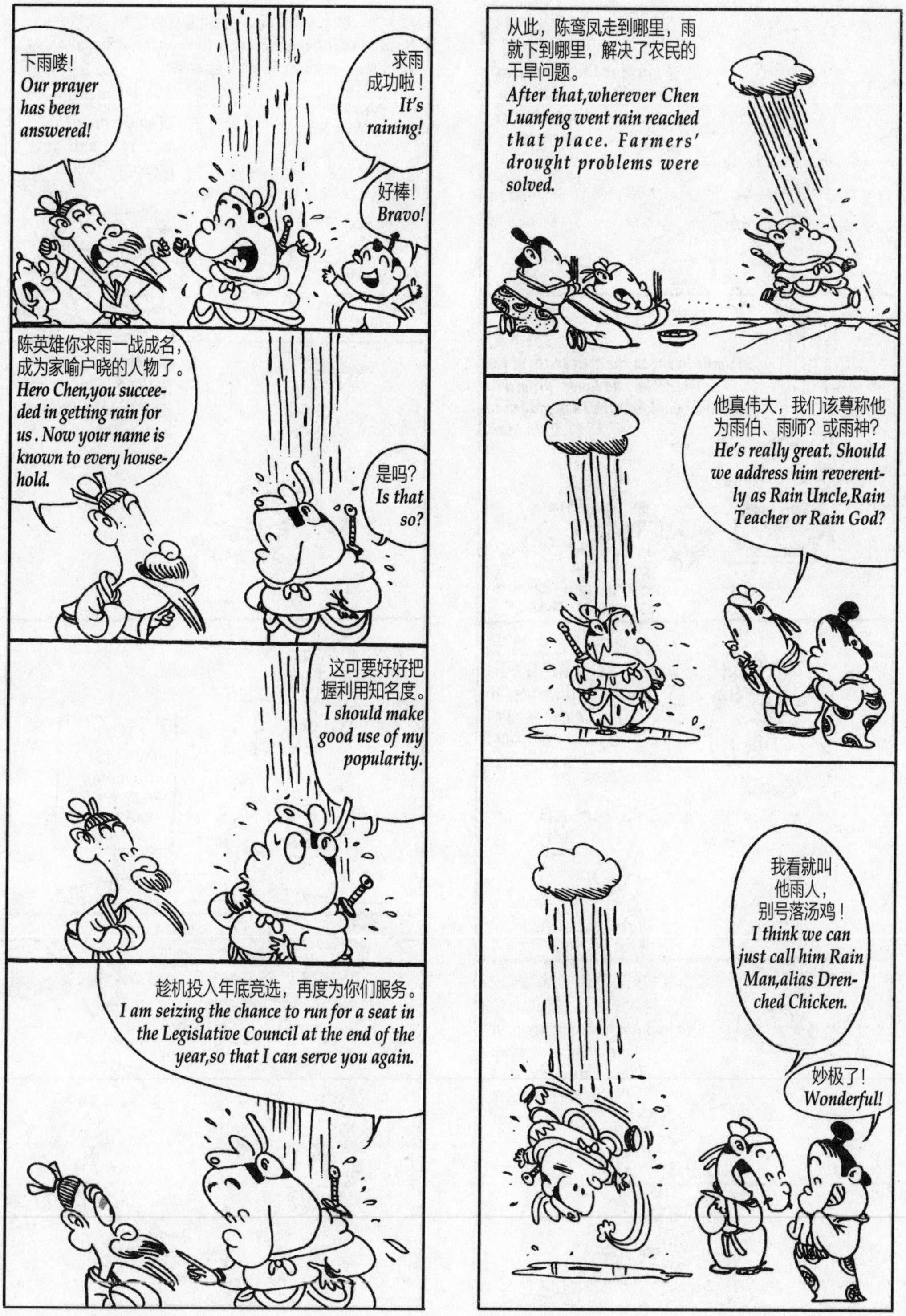

下雨喽！
Our prayer has been answered!

求雨成功啦！
It's raining!

好棒！
Bravo!

陈英雄你求雨一战成名，成为家喻户晓的人物了。
Hero Chen,you succeeded in getting rain for us . Now your name is known to every household.

是吗？
Is that so?

这可要好好把握利用知名度。
I should make good use of my popularity.

趁机投入年底竞选，再度为你们服务。
I am seizing the chance to run for a seat in the Legislative Council at the end of the year,so that I can serve you again.

雨人陈鸾凤为人带来甘霖，
专司民间水利问题。
Rain Man Chen Luanfeng brought rain to Mankind and specialised in water conservancy.

江南地区的人们求雨不再拜雷公，
而改拜雨人。
People living in the area south of the Yangtze River no longer prayed to Thunder God for rain.They prayed to Rain Man.

你太过分了，连我的职位也被你霸占顶替了！
You are really going too far! You've usurped my position!

不不！我只是当你凡间的经纪人，抽两成求雨的贡品而已。
No,no.I am just your agent in the mundane world. I take only 20 per cent of the sacrifices offered to you.

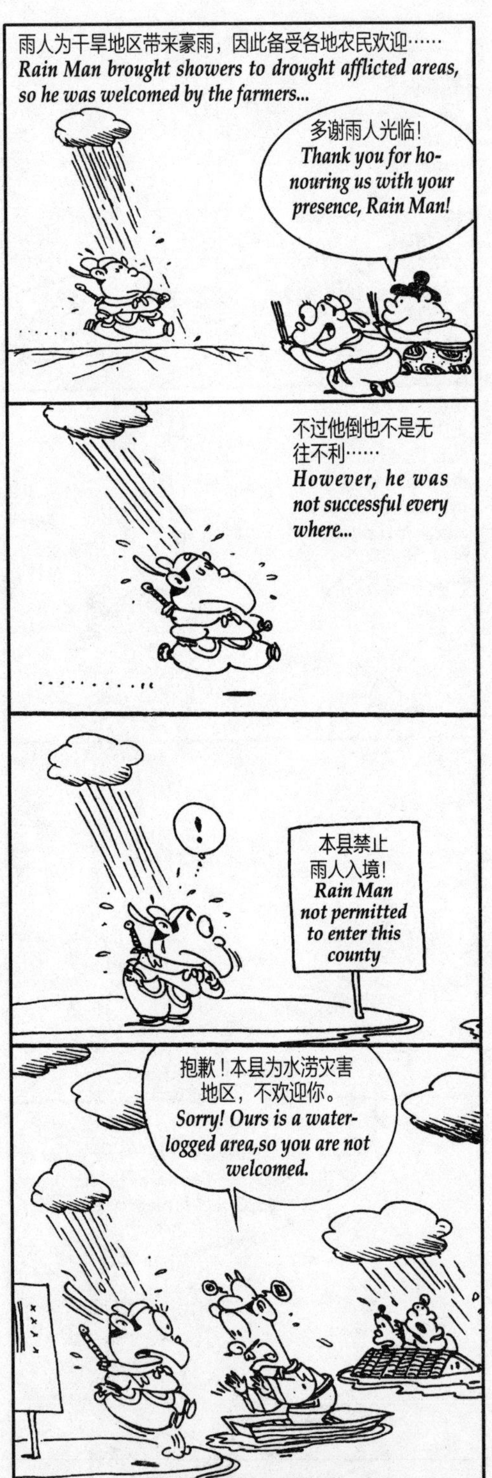

蛇天师
Snake Master

*The Chinese word for "valley"is 谷 .By adding the radical 亻 that means "man"to 谷,the word becomes 俗 . 俗人 can be translated as "layman".

**By adding the radical 亻 meaning "man"to the Chinese word for "Mountain",the word becomes 仙 . 仙人 is a celestial being.

*The terms 麻婆，麻子 (pockmark), 大麻 (marijuana), 麻辣 (the taste of brown peopper and Chinese prickly ash) all have the word 麻.

我麻婆算来也是职业妇女上班族。
I also count as a professional woman.

男人的职业有三百六十行，女人能做的无非是三姑六婆。
Men have 360 trades to choose from,but women can only be "three aunts and six grandmas".That is to say a woman can only make a living through dishonest means.

哪三姑六婆？
*Which three aunts and six grandmas?**

三姑是尼姑、道姑、卦姑；六婆是牙婆、媒婆、师婆、虔婆、药婆、稳婆。
The three aunts are:nuns,Taoist nuns and priestesses.The six grandmas are yapo, woman trafficking in young girls; meipo, matchmaker; shipo, sorceress; qianpo, procuress; yaopo, female druggist; and wenpo, midwife.

那么你做的是哪一个工作？
What's your occupation then?

我干的是稳婆……
I am a midwife...

稳婆虽不错，但我最想做的倒是"富婆"！
Though it's a pretty good occupation,what I really want to be is a fupo,a wealthy lady.

**The first three Chinese terms all have the word 姑 and the latter six all have the word 婆 ,so they are often lumped together and referred to as 三姑六婆.*

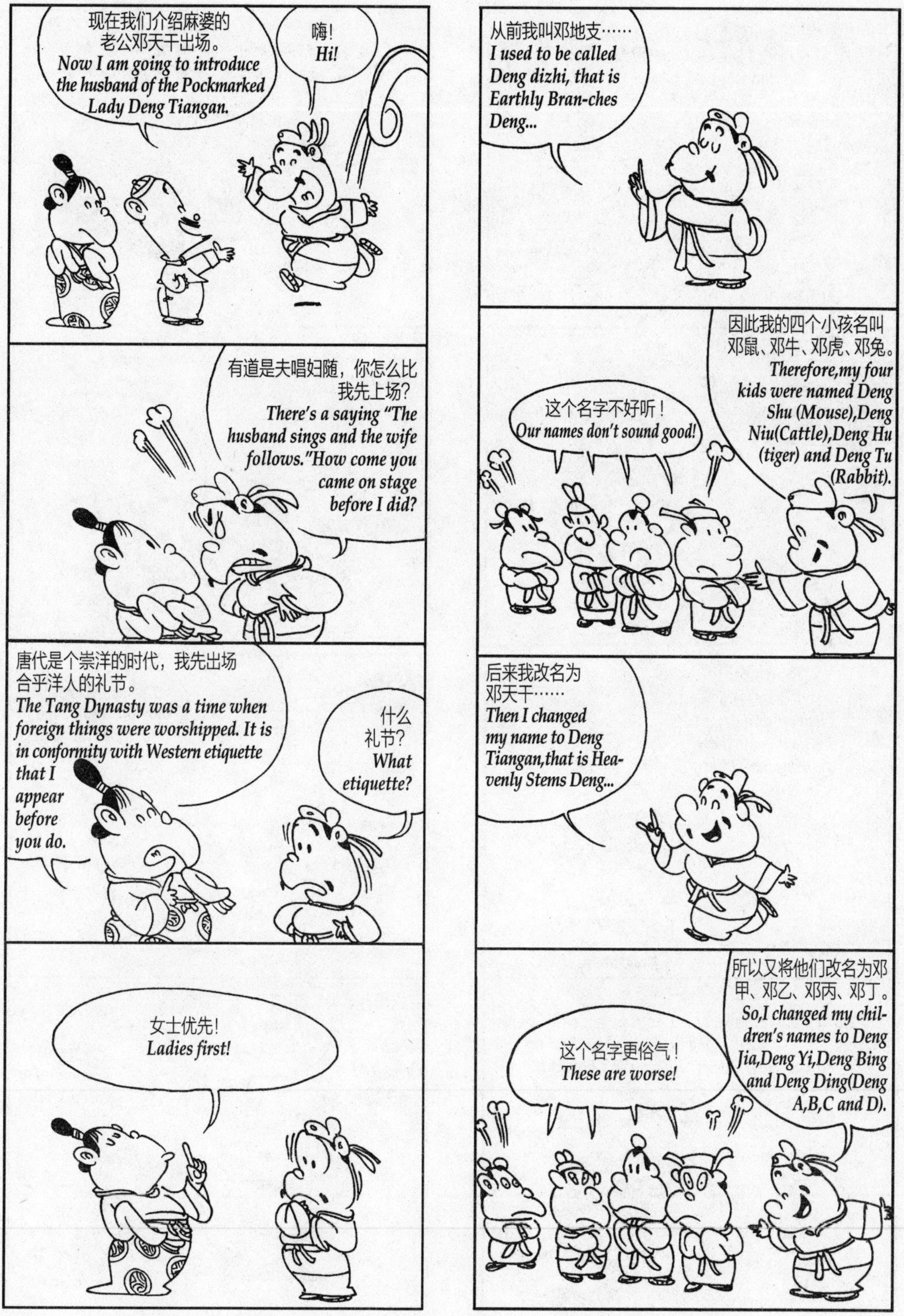

现在我们介绍麻婆的老公邓天干出场。
Now I am going to introduce the husband of the Pockmarked Lady Deng Tiangan.

嗨！
Hi!

有道是夫唱妇随，你怎么比我先上场？
There's a saying "The husband sings and the wife follows." How come you came on stage before I did?

唐代是个崇洋的时代，我先出场合乎洋人的礼节。
The Tang Dynasty was a time when foreign things were worshipped. It is in conformity with Western etiquette that I appear before you do.

什么礼节？
What etiquette?

女士优先！
Ladies first!

邓天干非常宠爱小孩儿……
Deng Tiangan doted on his children...

来来来！
Come here! Come here!

哈，哈，哈！
Ha, Ha, Ha!

哎呀！都爬到头上去了，真不像话！
My! They are sitting on his head!Really shocking!

哈！
Ha!

哈！
Ha!

哈！
Ha!

这才对得起自己的姓，不愧为邓家子弟。
They are doing right by their name,these worthy Deng boys.

你说的是什么意思？
What do you mean?

"邓"就是登上耳朵，不是吗？
The left part of the word "Deng" is 登, which means "climb", and the radical on the right side means "ear". Doesn't it mean to climb to the ear?

邓家小孩虽名为甲乙丙丁，但个个有才情……
Though the boys are named by the prosaic 甲乙丙丁, all of them are talented.

我是智慧第一。
I am the knowledgeable champion.

我是多问第一。
I am the champion in asking questions.

我是多言第一。
I am the talkative champion.

我是多闻第一。
I am first in resourcefulness.

四子登科。
Father Deng is a champion father.

邓爸爸是"多子第一"。
Four sons bring honour to the family.

邓妈妈当然是……
Mother Deng is of course a...

多产第一！
I'm in the family way again!

哇！又有啦！
Champion in productivity!

大儿子邓甲的专长是“多闻第一”。
The special talent of the eldest son,Deng Jia,was his vast knowledge.

多闻就是知道得多。证明看看？
Being knowledgeable means having plenty of information. Can you prove it?

好的。
OK.

左闻右闻前闻后闻……
*I sniff around...**

妈妈今晚准备的好菜是红烧豆腐、清炒竹笋与酸菜肉丝汤！
Mother is preparing good dishes like braised tofu,stir fried bamboo shoots and pickled vegetable soup!

…

秀才不出门，能知天下事，是多闻的好处。
A scholar does not leave his home,yet he knows everything happening in the world.That's the advantage of being knowledgeable.

可是多闻的成本很贵……
But it costs a lot to be knowledgeable...

收报费！
Receiver fee!

各大报刊一共三十六份，合计三千六百文。
The Union Daily,The Minsheng Daily,Economic Daily, ..36 newspapers cost 360 wen.

**The Chinese word 闻 can mean 见闻 ,which means “knowledge”or“information”. Usually when someone is 多闻 it means the person is knowledgeable.But 闻 itself as a verb means “to smell”or “to sniff”.*

二儿子邓乙的专长是“多问第一”。
Second son Deng Yi was Number One in inquisitiveness.

其实我只能算第二，“多问第一”
非屈原莫属。
Actually,I am only Number Two. The first place has to go to the ancient poet Qu Yuan.

遂古之初，
谁传道之？
Who made it known to later generations what the Universe was like at the very beginning?

上下未形，何由考之？
How can it be proved what the Universe was like before Heaven and Earth were separated?

瞢暗冥昭，谁能极之？
Who can explain the chaotic situation without the distinction of night and day?

承让了。
That's true.

他在《天问》篇中一共问了
一百七十二个问题，才真是
天下第一多问。
He asked 172 questions in his poem Questions for Heaven.He was Number One in the world.

*The Chinese term for "knowledge"or "learning"is made up of the charaters" 学 "and " 问 " .Taken separately they mean"learn"and "ask".

**The Chinese words 智 and 痣 are homonyms.The former means "wit","wisdom"and "intelligence",while the latter means "a mole".

*In the old days,the Chinese 甲，乙，丙 and 丁 were used for grades in the same way A,B,Cand D are used in most schools today.

"多智第一 IQ 一百七。
Champion of resourcefulness has an IQ of 170.

创意书生多才多艺！
Versatile scholar with creative ideas!
天生的点子王。
Aborn idea man.
主意人！
Idea man!

你真是会自我吹嘘呀！
You are really good at selfglorification!
抱歉！是我的职业病又犯了……
Sorry,it's caused by my job...

因力我正开始去广告公司上班当创意人。
Because I am starting a new job with an advertising agency as a creative director.

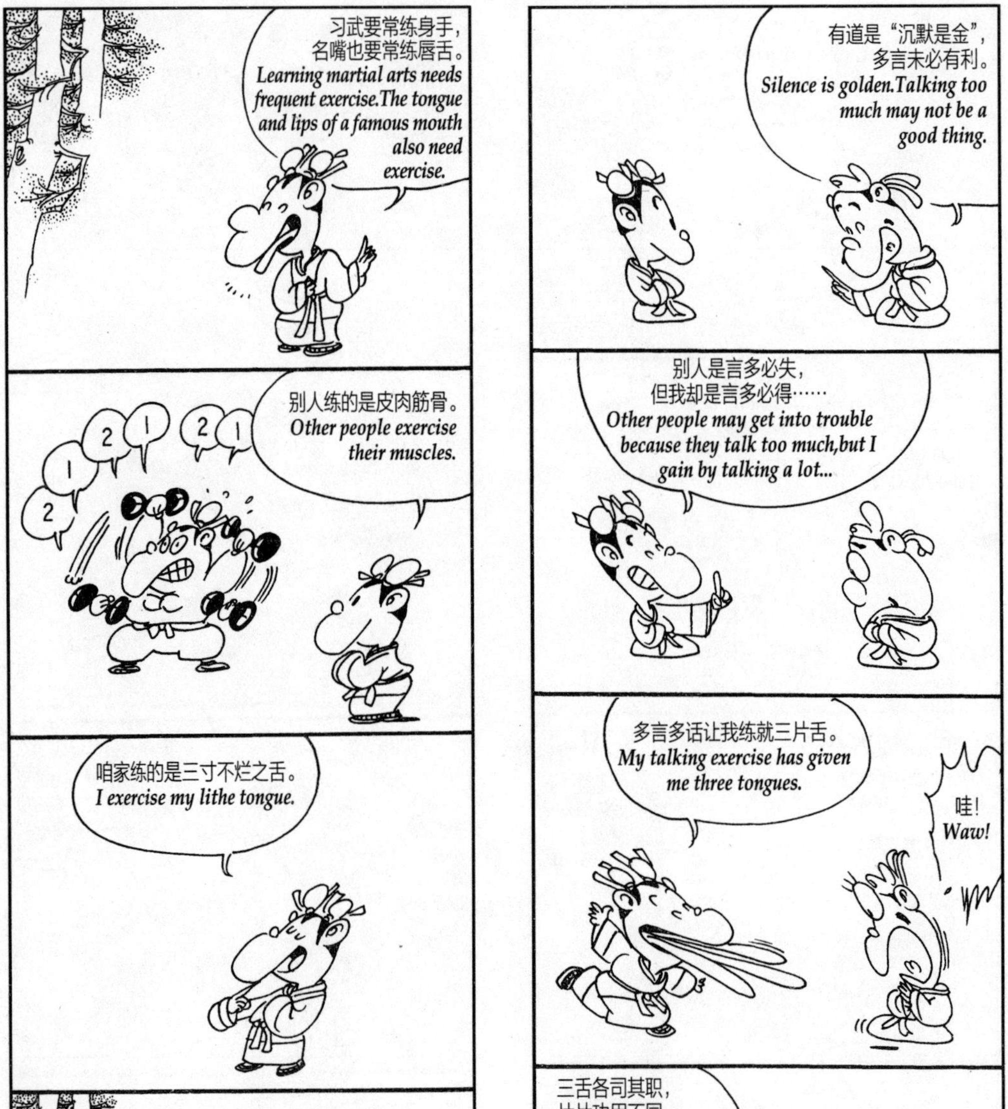

有道是“沉默是金”，多言未必有利。
Silence is golden.Talking too much may not be a good thing.

别人是言多必失，但我却是言多必得……
Other people may get into trouble because they talk too much,but I gain by talking a lot...

多言多话让我练就三片舌。
My talking exercise has given me three tongues.

哇！
Waw!

三舌各司其职，片片功用不同。
Each of the three tongues has a different use.

吃饭用。
One tongue for eating.

接吻用。
One tongue for kissing.

说话用。
One tongue for speaking.

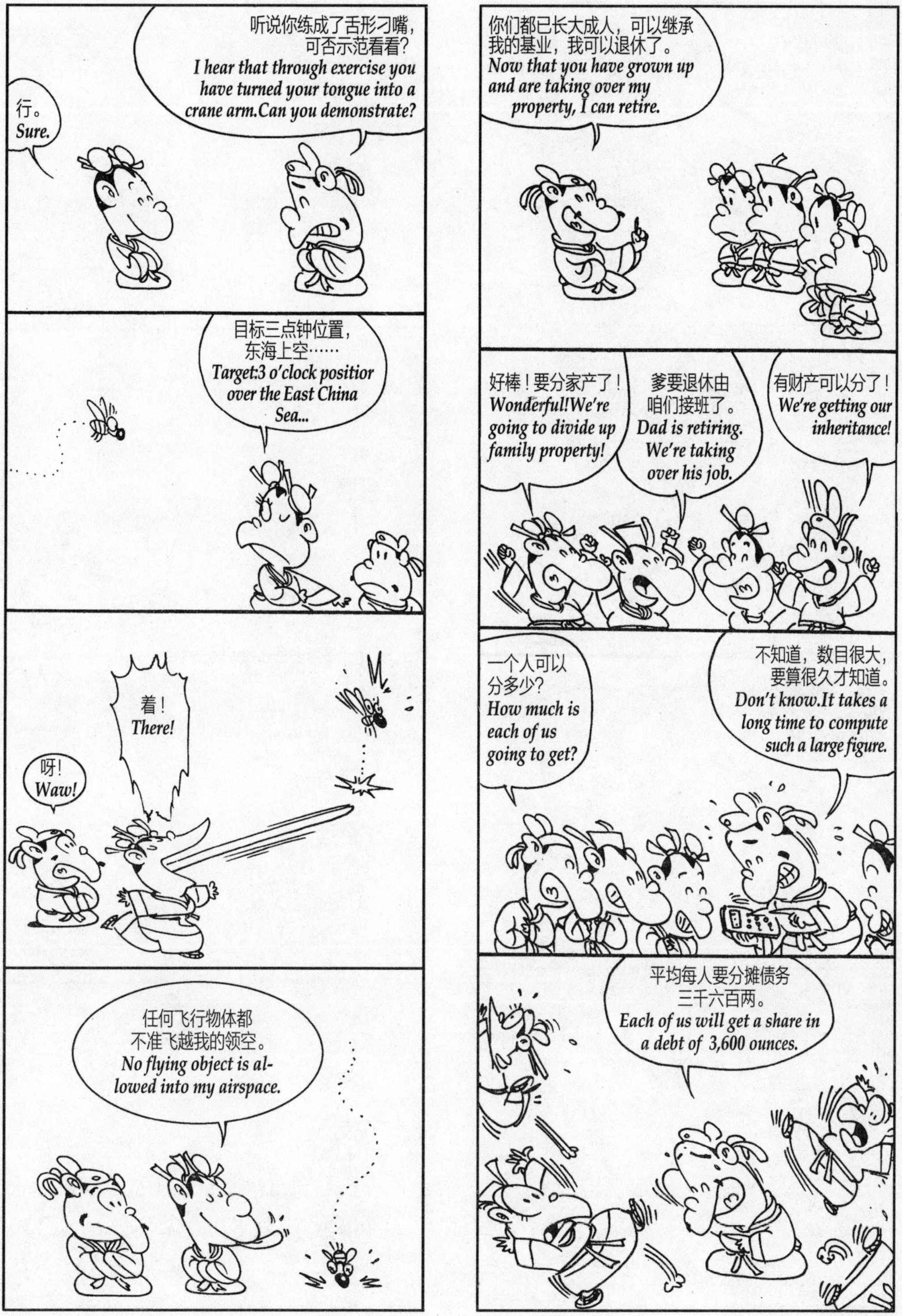

听说你练成了舌形刁嘴，可否示范看看？
I hear that through exercise you have turned your tongue into a crane arm.Can you demonstrate?

行。
Sure.

目标三点钟位置，东海上空……
Target:3 o'clock positior over the East China Sea...

呀！
Waw!

着！
There!

任何飞行物体都不准飞越我的领空。
No flying object is allowed into my airspace.

你们瞧，这是一杯水，一口就被喝掉了。
Look,this is a glass of water.I'll drink it in a single gulp.
……
……
……
……
如果四杯水合在一起，就没有人能一口气喝掉。
If we pour four glasses of water together,no one can drink it in one gulp.
由此，你们分家产后知道应怎么做?
Therefore,you know what to do after you have divided our family property?
知道!
Yes,we do.
喝水一次只喝一杯，不要四杯一起喝。
We should drink one glass of water,not four.

爹今天跟你们四位谈合作团结的好处。
Dad is telling you the advantage of unity and cooperation.
瞧！这是一根筷子，一折就断。
Look! One chopstick breaks when it is bent.
这是四根筷子，你们说会怎么样?
Now we have four chopsticks here.What do you think will happen to them?
也是一折就断。
They will also break when they are bent.
…

*The Chinese terms for"orator", "politician"and "strategist"all end with the character家，which when used by itself means"home".

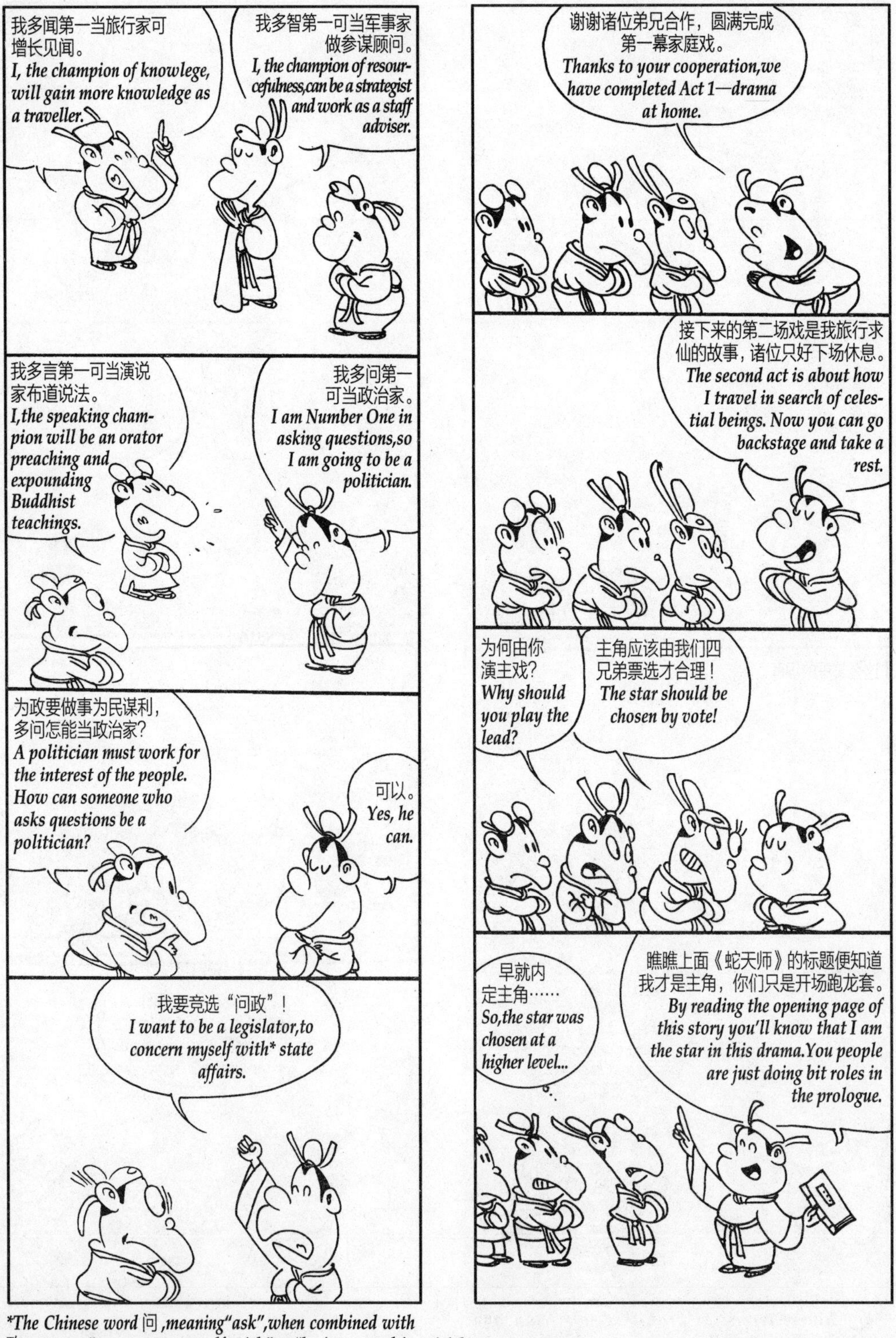

我多闻第一当旅行家可增长见闻。
I, the champion of knowlege, will gain more knowledge as a traveller.

我多智第一可当军事家做参谋顾问。
I, the champion of resourcefulness,can be a strategist and work as a staff adviser.

我多言第一可当演说家布道说法。
I,the speaking champion will be an orator preaching and expounding Buddhist teachings.

我多问第一可当政治家。
I am Number One in asking questions,so I am going to be a politician.

为政要做事为民谋利，多问怎能当政治家？
A politician must work for the interest of the people. How can someone who asks questions be a politician?

可以。
Yes, he can.

我要竞选"问政"！
I want to be a legislator,to concern myself with state affairs.*

**The Chinese word 问 ,meaning"ask",when combined with 政 ,means "to concern oneself with"or "be interested in "politics or state affairs.*

爹！娘！我要上山求仙去了，告辞了。
Goodbye,Dad! Mom! I am setting out in search of celestial beings.

别急，爹为你准备三百两银子送给你。
Wait, I have here 300 ounces of silver for you.

...

这么笨重的银两怎能提上山去？
How can I carry such a heavy load on my trip?

这趟旅行要花钱的，我有妈给的塑胶货币。
Mom has given me this plastic money to cover my travel expenses.

!

邓甲要远行，父母弟兄分别送他礼物为他送行。
Beng Jia's parents and brothers gave him farewell presents before he left.
弟弟们合送他一套《蜡笔小新》"随身看"。
His brothers gave him a set of new crayon pictures.
爸爸送他一台"随身听"！
His father gave him a Walkman.
妈妈则送他一份重礼"随身洗"。
His mother gave him an expensive mini washing machine.

爹娘！我上山求仙学道去了！
Mom and Dad, I am off to study Taoism!
再见！
Godbye,Son!
儿子呀！你此行往西往南往北皆吉，千万可别往东海去！
My son,it is auspicious for you to travel towards the west,south or north,but do not go east!
东边方位不利?
What's wrong with the east?
因为东海有飞弹演习不安全。
Because it is unsafe in the East China Sea.

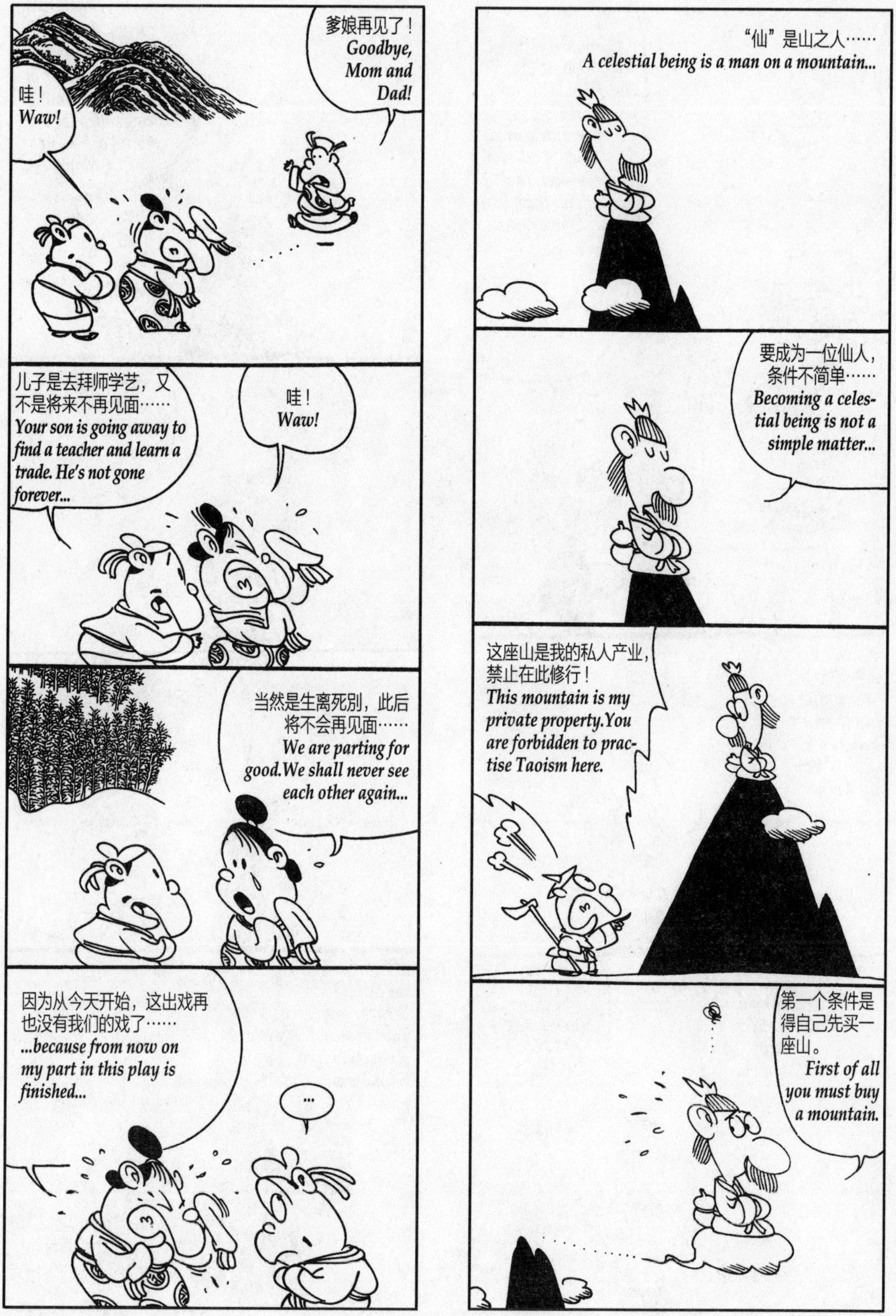

爹娘再见了！
Goodbye, Mom and Dad!
哇！
Waw!

儿子是去拜师学艺，又不是将来不再见面……
Your son is going away to find a teacher and learn a trade. He's not gone forever...
哇！
Waw!

当然是生离死别，此后将不会再见面……
We are parting for good.We shall never see each other again...

因为从今天开始，这出戏再也没有我们的戏了……
...because from now on my part in this play is finished...
...

仙人有很多种：有上仙、高仙、大仙、玄仙、天仙、真仙、神仙、灵仙、至仙……

There are various kinds of celestial beings. Taoists divide them into nine ranks...

其实天下的仙人只有两种……

As a matter of fact,there are only two kinds of celestial beings in the world...

一种是“真人”！

One kind is the “true Man”!*

另一种是“假仙”！

The other is “Fake Celestial”!

**True Man as an official Taoist title is a man who has attained immortality.At the same time ,in ordinary usage, a true man is just a true man.*

***This is a form of self-address used by Taoist priests.*

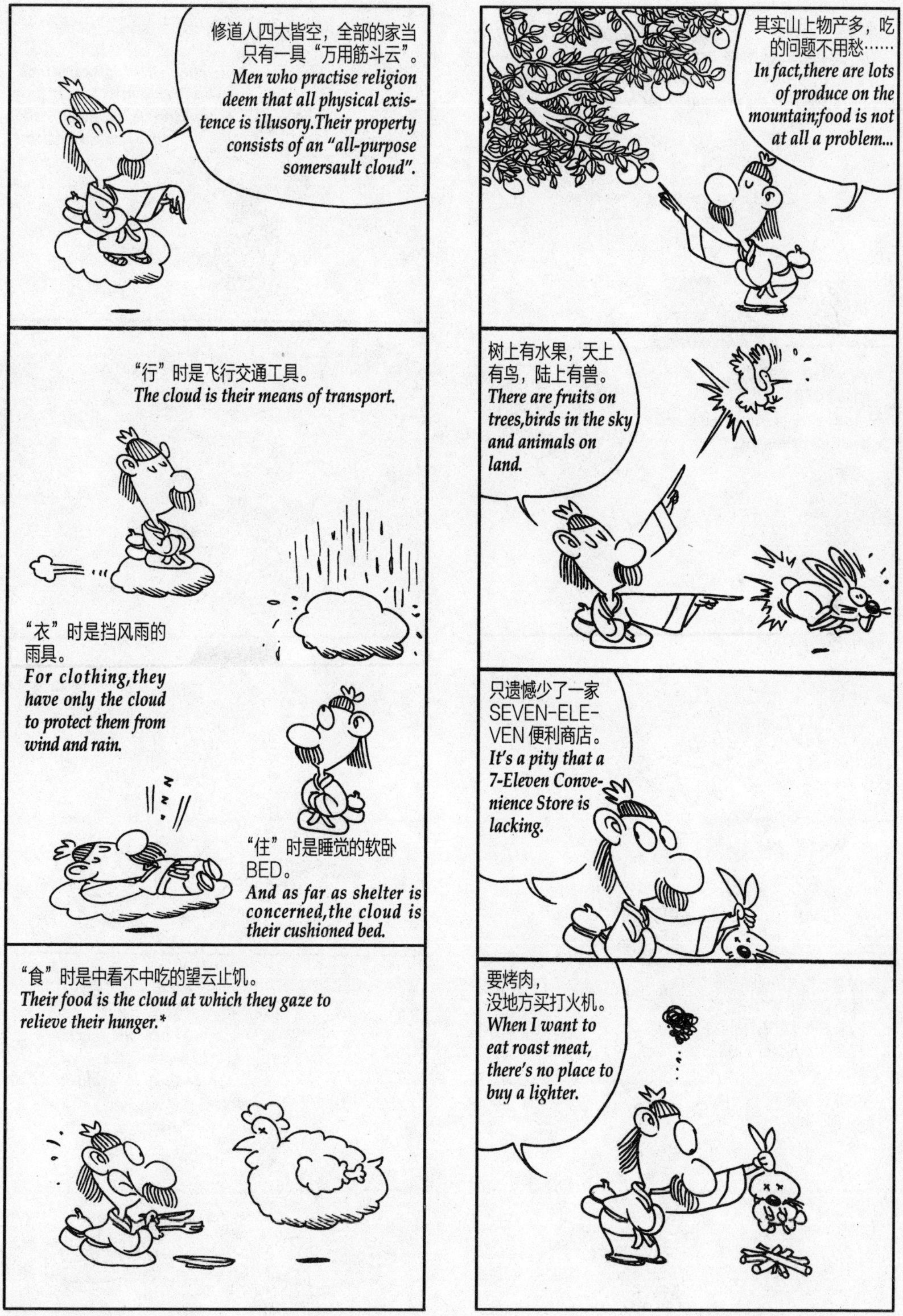

修道人四大皆空，全部的家当只有一具“万用筋斗云”。
Men who practise religion deem that all physical existence is illusory.Their property consists of an “all-purpose somersault cloud”.

“行”时是飞行交通工具。
The cloud is their means of transport.

“衣”时是挡风雨的雨具。
For clothing,they have only the cloud to protect them from wind and rain.

“住”时是睡觉的软卧BED。
And as far as shelter is concerned,the cloud is their cushioned bed.

“食”时是中看不中吃的望云止饥。
*Their food is the cloud at which they gaze to relieve their hunger.**

**This is a parody of the Chinese saying:“To quench one's thirst by gazing at a plum”.*

茅山仙人修道有成，无论是外功、内功都练得很成功。
The Immortal of Maoshan Mountain had achieved self-cultivation.He was successful in practising gongfu,whether the external or the internal way.
他的外丹功、内丹功、气功、轻功样样都精通……
He was very skiful in each and every type of gongfu...
轻功！
Light skill!
气功！
Qigong.
最厉害、为人所敬佩的是京剧玩票的……
He was highly esteemed for his terrific skill as an amateur Peking opera singer.
唱功！
Singing skill!
闲来无事，不如乘云采药补充药材。
Since I have some free time, I will ride on a cloud to pick herbs on the mountain to replenish my medicine chest.
云来！
Come cloud!
云来！
Come cloud!
闲来无事，不如睡觉补充元气。
Since I have nothing else to do, I might as well take a nap to regain my vigour.

东胜神州傲来国
Aolai of the Dongsheng Divine Land

找到仙山了，找到仙人拜师了！
I have found a celestial mountain.I'm going to find a celestial being to be my teacher!

东胜神州傲来国
Aolai of the Dongsheng Divine Land

抱歉！我只收猴子，不收人做徒弟。
Sorry!I only accept monkeys as my students, not men.

...

如果你是真仙人，必定能渡我登山去。
If you are really an immortal, you must be able to ferry me across to you.

行。
Sure.

就坐这个上来吧。
Sit on that and come up here.

哇！要乘云上山？
Wah! Am I to ride on the cloud?

原来是云形登山吊具……
It's actually a cloud-shaped lift...

小伙子你上山来做什么？
What are you here for,young man?

想拜您为师学法术。
I want to learn magic skills from you.

年轻人主动积极，勇气可嘉……
You are a spirited and energetic young man, and have admirable courage...

可是要是我不答应你，怎么办？
But what if I refuse you?

您若不收我为徒，我就实施三不政策！
I will adopt the "Three No's" policy if I am rejected!

什么三不政策？
What "Three No's" policy?

一、不吃；二、不睡；三、长跪不起不离开此地。
One,no eating.Two, no sleeping. Three, kneeling here and no standing up to leave.

厉害……
He's good...

学仙得每天餐风饮露，你可消受得了？
While practising selfcultivation you'll have to eat the wind and drink the dew. Can you bear the hardship?

吃喝简单我不怕。
I don't mind simple food.

我早已自己准备出方便面一年份，这些孝敬你老人家。
I have prepared instant noodles to last me a whole year.These are an offering to you.

谁要吃你这种食物！
Who wants to eat this stuff!

餐风饮露是吃欧“风”大餐，喝的是韩国真“露”。
I meant eating European-style food and drinking genuine "Dew"from Korea.

一年下来账单可受不了……
The bill is going to be hefty...

要跟我学法术得先通过入学考试。
You must first pass an entrance examination.

三七六〇〇加七八〇〇〇加六三二八〇合计是多少？
How much is 37,600 plus 78,000 plus 63,280?

这难不倒我，二五得十……一共是一七八八八〇！
That's easy!Two times five is ten... The total is 178,880.

37600
78000
+ 63280
178880

答对了！入学考试通过。
Correct! You've passed the exams.

报名费
Registration fee 37600
学杂费
Tuition&miscellaneous 78000
食宿费
fees Board & lodging 63280
合 计 *Total* 178 880

这个正是一年的学杂费金额，请付钱来！
The figure is your tuition and miscellaneous fees for one year. Now pay up!

一年学杂费才十七万多，比美国学校还便宜……
The annual fees are about $170,000, much cheaper than American colleges...
那就快缴钱注册吧？
Then why not pay your fees and register now?
刷 VISA 卡行吗？
Can I pay with a VISA card?
别生气……不收信用卡没问题……
If you don't accept cash or credit card,...
改付您三个月期支票行吗？
...can I pay with this cheque?
哇！
Waw!
你今年几岁？
How old are you?
今年二十三！
Twenty-three.
教育部规定四岁上幼儿园，七岁进小学，十三岁上初中，十六岁上高中，十九岁上大学……
The Ministry of Education stipulates that children enter kindergarten at four, primary school at seven,junior high school at 13, senior high school at 16, and go to college at 19...
你已经二十三岁，来得太迟了太迟了……
You are already 23. It's too late, too late...
那怎么办？
What shall I do than?
倒过来读，由研究生读回去！
Reverse the order and start with graduate studies!

我二十三岁，敢问师父您今年贵庚？
May I ask how old you are, Master?
三十年前是“耆”，二十年前是“耋”，十年前是“耄”，今年是“毫”。“毫”？
Thirty years ago I was 耆.Twenty years ago I was 耋. The years ago I was 耄, and now I am 毫.
毫是几岁？毫（mao）？
How old is that?
耆是六十，耋是七十，耄是八十，毫是九十岁。
Storyteller 耆 is 60.耋 is 70. 耄 is 80,and 毫 is 90.
哇！有学问。
Waw! Really a man of great learning.

我授课实施“三多教学”政策……
In my teaching I adopt the "Three Lots" policy...
哪三多？
Which three lots?
学费多，
Lots of fees,
功课多，
... lots of homework,
校规多。
... and lots of rules.
我爹教我求学的方法也是三多方针。
My dad also taught me a "Three Lots" policy in learning.
多听，
Lots of knowledge,
多闻，
... lots of listening,
多问。
... and asking lots of questions.

*The basic meaning of the word 功 is "skill" or "achievement". When used in the context of martial arts, it refers to specific skills being practised. The phrase 好大喜功 has a derogatory connotation, meaning "have a fondness for the grandiose".

人、鬼、仙的分别只是阴阳而已……
The difference between man,ghost and celestial being is that of yin and yang...
纯阴无阳者，鬼也。纯阳无阴者，仙也。阴阳相染者，人也。
The ghost is purely yin without yang. A celestial being is yang without yin,while man touches on both yin and yang.
所以要成仙，首先得戒女色?
Therefore,to be a celestial being one must first of all give up relations with women?
对。
Right.
我还是喜欢当阴阳调和的人类。
I prefer to be a man who has harmonious relations with both yin and yang.
贫道，峭岩仙人是也……
I am a poor cleric named Immortal of the Steep Cliff...
贫道，邓甲是也……
I am a poor cleric named Deng Jia...
...
咱们自称“贫道”是什么意思?
Why do we refer to ourselves as “poor clerics”?
贫道，当然是贫穷的道人!
A poor cleric is of course an impoverished Taoist!
没错!
Quite right!

贫道，峭岩仙人是也！
I am a poor cleric named Immortal of the Steep Cliff!

…

师父，这是我这学期的学费三十两银子。
Master,here is 30 ounces of silver, my tuition for one semester.

如此一来贫道人就不穷了……
Now the poor cleric is not poor any more...

正是。
Quite right.

"富"道，峭岩仙人是也！
I am a rich cleric named Immortal of the Steep Cliff!

嘻嘻！
Hee,hee!

哎呀！蚊子……
Aiya! A mosquito...

着！
Shoo!

没打到。
You missed it.

啪！
Crack!

嘻嘻！
Hee,hee!

将它的凶器缴械了。
I've stripped it of its lethal weapon.

*The Chinese term for "Taoist skill"is 法术.The word 法 is made up of 去 plus the radical 氵,which means "water", 去 when used as a verb means"rid of".

**The word 悟 is made up of 吾,that means "my"and the radical 忄 meaning "heart".

眼观鼻，鼻观心，进入悟境……
Eyes focus on nose.Nose focusses on heart.Then I reach the state of awakening.
悟即是觉醒，
悟的反面即是睡……
悟 means awakening.
The oppsite is asleep...
睡者，目垂也！
Asleep means "eyes are shut"!
进入梦境……
I am in dreamland...
悟。
Awakening.
悟。
Awake.
悟。
Awake.
悟。
Awake.
悟。
Awake.
悟。
Awakening.
迷。
Dazed.

* 手印 are signs formed by the hand when Buddhists chant incantations.It also means "fingerprints"in the ordinary sense.

**These terms with special Taoist meanings form an incantation.

天罡天元，坎水八玄，
四目神仙，金童传言。
Blah,blah,blah,blah,four-eyed god,the golden boy brings a message.*

边做手印边诵咒，
心想事成十分灵验。
Making signs with your hand while chanting incantations is quite effective in granting wishes.

真的会灵吗？
Does it really work?

钱来钱来，手印第一式！
Come,money. come,money.The first sigh!

这是什么印？
What sign is that?

金钱印，请缴手印课程学费五百元。
Money sign.Please pay 500 yuan for the lesson on finger signs.

真的灵……
It does work!

药火。
Yaohuo.

右剪。
Right Scissors.

降魔杵。
Demon-subduing Club.

神虎。
Divine Tiger.

小泰山！
Little Tarzan!

!

西方人也懂得手印？
Do Westerners understand these finger signs?

哈！这个手印西方很流行！
Ha!They are quite popular in the West!

F印……
F-sign...

骂人的 ×× 印。
An abusive ×× sign.

**The terms with special Taoist meanings form an incantation.*

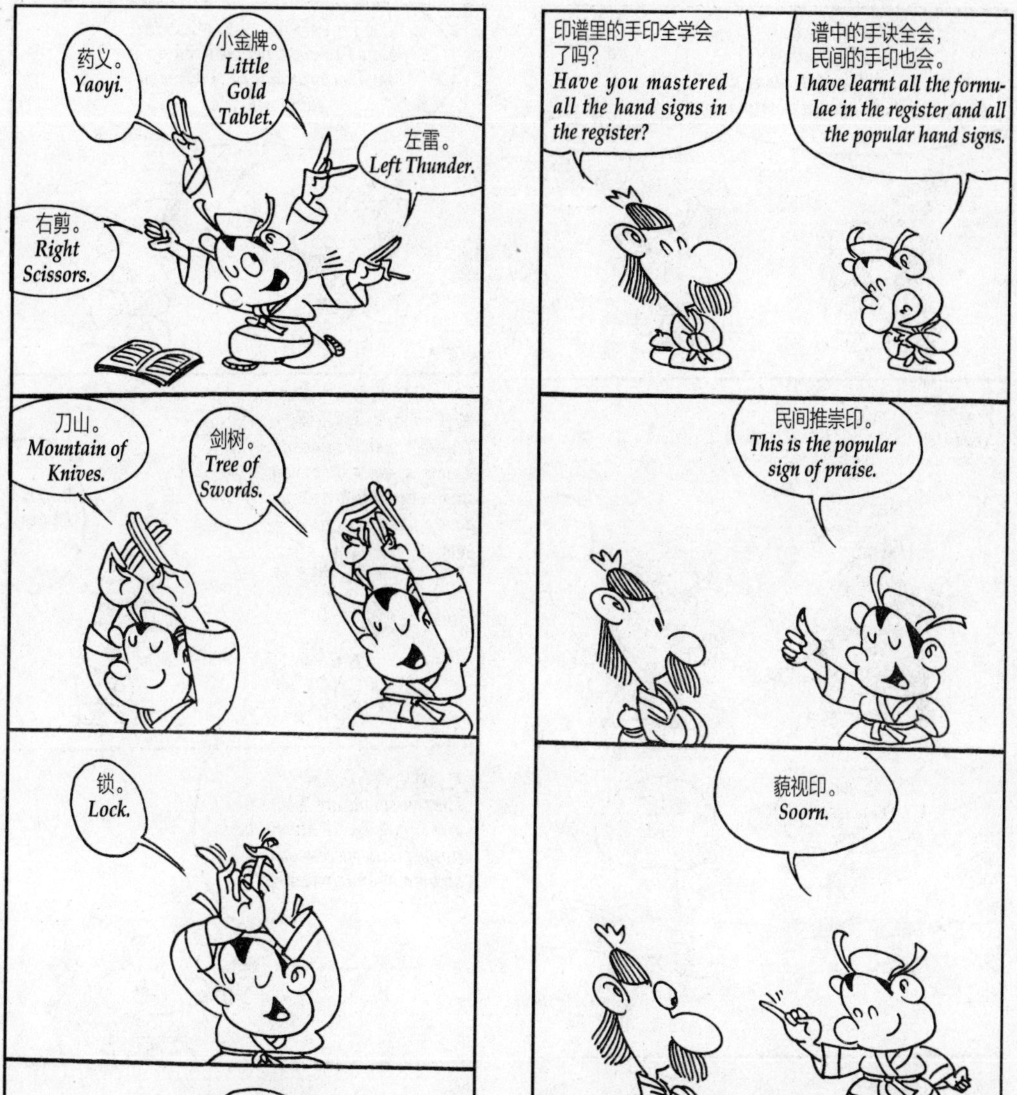

药义。
Yaoyi.
小金牌。
Little Gold Tablet.
左雷。
Left Thunder.
右剪。
Right Scissors.

刀山。
Mountain of Knives.
剑树。
Tree of Swords.

锁。
Lock.

锁住了！
My fingers are locked together!

*All three Chinese idioms have in them the word 风 that means"wind".

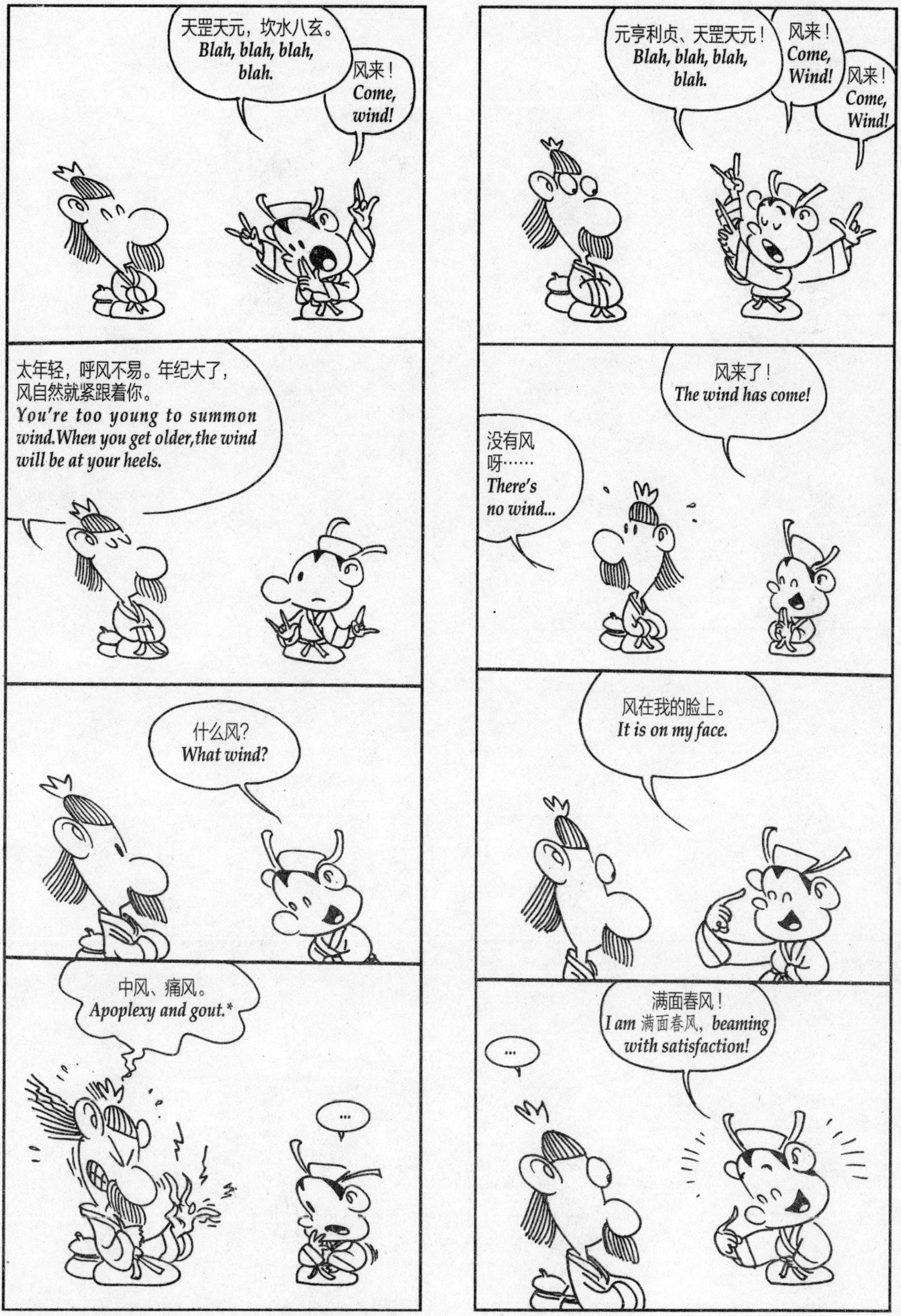

天罡天元，坎水八玄。
Blah, blah, blah, blah.

风来！
Come, wind!

太年轻，呼风不易。年纪大了，风自然就紧跟着你。
You're too young to summon wind.When you get older,the wind will be at your heels.

什么风?
What wind?

中风、痛风。
*Apoplexy and gout.**

...

**The Chinese words for "apoplexy"and"gout" 中风 and 痛风 both include the character 风 which when used alone means"wind".*

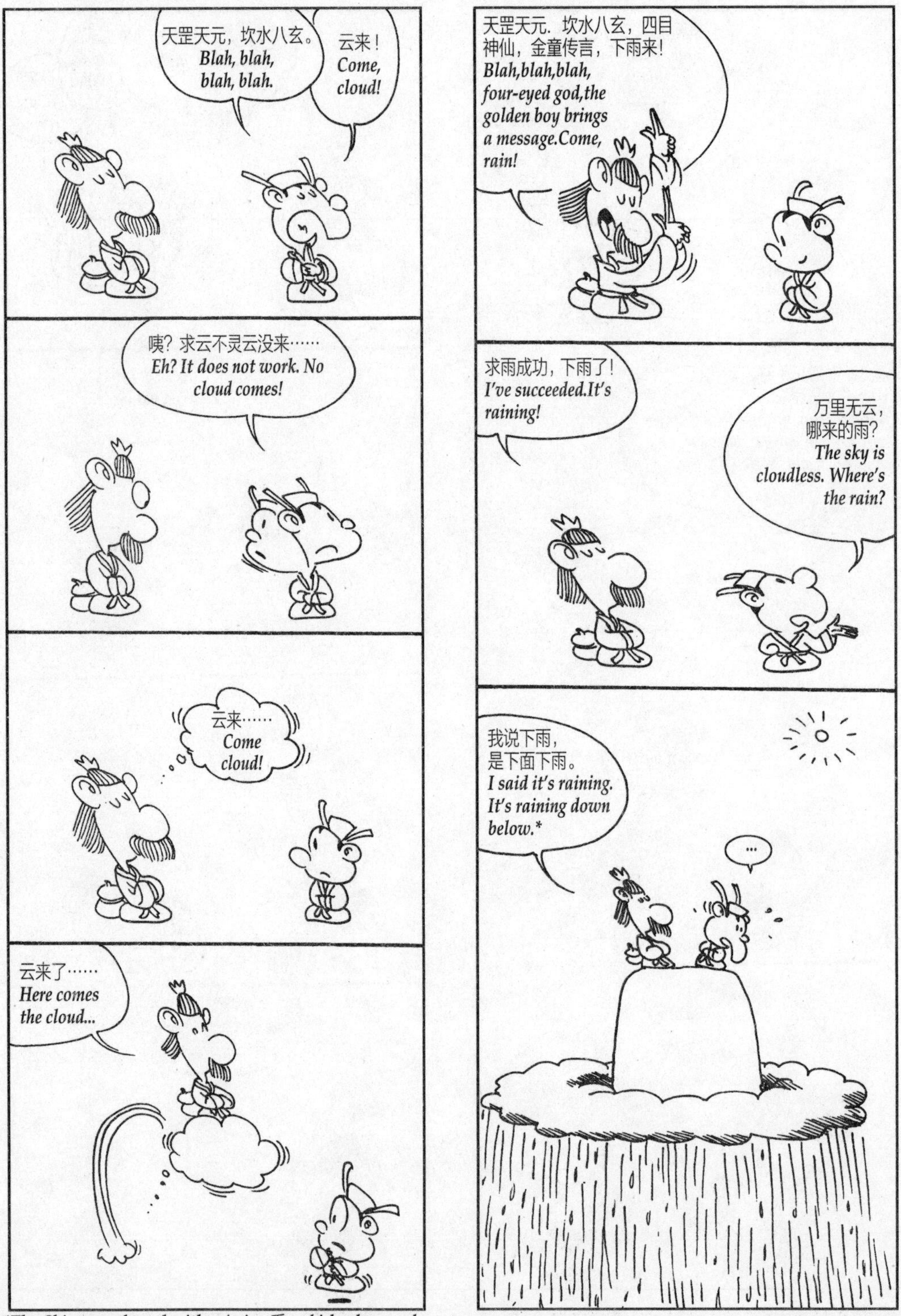

天罡天元，坎水八玄。
Blah, blah, blah, blah.

云来！
Come, cloud!

咦？求云不灵云没来……
Eh? It does not work. No cloud comes!

云来……
Come cloud!

云来了……
Here comes the cloud...

The Chinese verb used with rain is 下 ,which,when used independently,means "below"or"under".

天罡天元，坎水八玄，四目神仙，
金童传言，下雨来！
Blah, blah, blah, blah, four-eyed god, the golden boy brings a message. Come, rain!

下雨下雨，下雨来！
Come,rain!come! Come rain!

雨是下啦！
It is raining!

哇！为什么我持咒就不会
下雨呢？
Waw!Why doesn't rain come when I recite the incantation?

泪下如雨！
His tears fall like rain!

...

今天为师要教你一种新功夫。
Today I'm going to teach you a new skill.

是。
Yes Master.

把身上的银子全部拿出来。
Take out all the silver on you.

又要付学费啦?
Am I to pay for tuition again?

身上无银一身轻。
*You feel lighthearted and happy when you have no silver on you.**

今天要学的是轻功。
Today we are going to learn the light skill.

老年人学轻功比较难。
It is difficult for an old man to learn the light skill.

因为老年人稳重、庄重、德高望重，样样重。
Because old men are 稳重 *(steady),.* 庄重 *(serious),* 德高望重 *(of noble character and command universal respect).Everything about him is* 重 *(heavy).*

有道理。
True.

少年人学轻功易。
It's easy for a young man to learn the light skill.

怎么说?
How so?

因为少年人年轻、轻率、轻浮，样样轻。
Because he is 年轻 *(young),* 轻率 *(indiscreet)and* 轻浮 *(frivolous).Everything about him is* 轻 *(light).*

**This is a parody of the popular Chinese saying* 无官一身轻 *,that means "happy is the man who is relieved of his official duties".*

要学好轻功你得行孔子的师生之礼。
To master the light skill,you must abide by the Confucian rules of etiquette.
怎么做?
How?
有事，弟子服其劳。有酒食，先生馔。
When there's work to do, the pupil does it.When there is wine and food,the teacher has them.
这个跟学轻功有什么关系?
What does that have to do with light skill?
不吃东西光做事，身体自然就轻了，学轻功自然易。
When one works without eating his body becomes light .It'll be easy for him to master the light skill.

学轻功要先把脚练得轻盈。
To learn light skill,you must first exercise your feet and make your footsteps light.
是。
OK.
脚要轻，得加重头的重量训练。
To make your footsteps light, you need to have weight exercise on your head.
轻功是脚的事，跟头的重量有什么关系?
Light skill is a skill of the feet. What does it have to do with the weight on the head?
因为头重……脚就轻。
Because when your head is heavy,your feet become light.You're top-heavy.

轻功能身轻如燕，
履浮云如踩在地面。
The light skill makes you as light as a swallow.You can tread on a cloud as if standing on the ground.

我不能履浮云如踩地面，
但能踩地面如虚空。
I cannot tread on a floating cloud as if standing on the ground,but I can stand on the ground as if it's a void.

你如何办得到？
How can you do that?

嘻！
Hee!

学迈克尔·杰克逊，
跳太空漫步舞。
I do the Moonwalk like Michael Jackson.

...

今天要开新课程，
要教的是"气功"！
Today we are starting a new lesson,qigong!

学气功学费比较贵。
Fees for learning qigong are higher.

还没教就要收学费？
You ask for payment before you start to teach?

先缴学费可舒解我
荷包的经济不景"气"。
Prepaid tuition will help relieve the slump* of my purse.

而我得到的
是一肚子
怨"气"。
But what I get is empty air.

*The Chinese for "slump" 不景气 includes the character 气 as in 气功 "qigong".

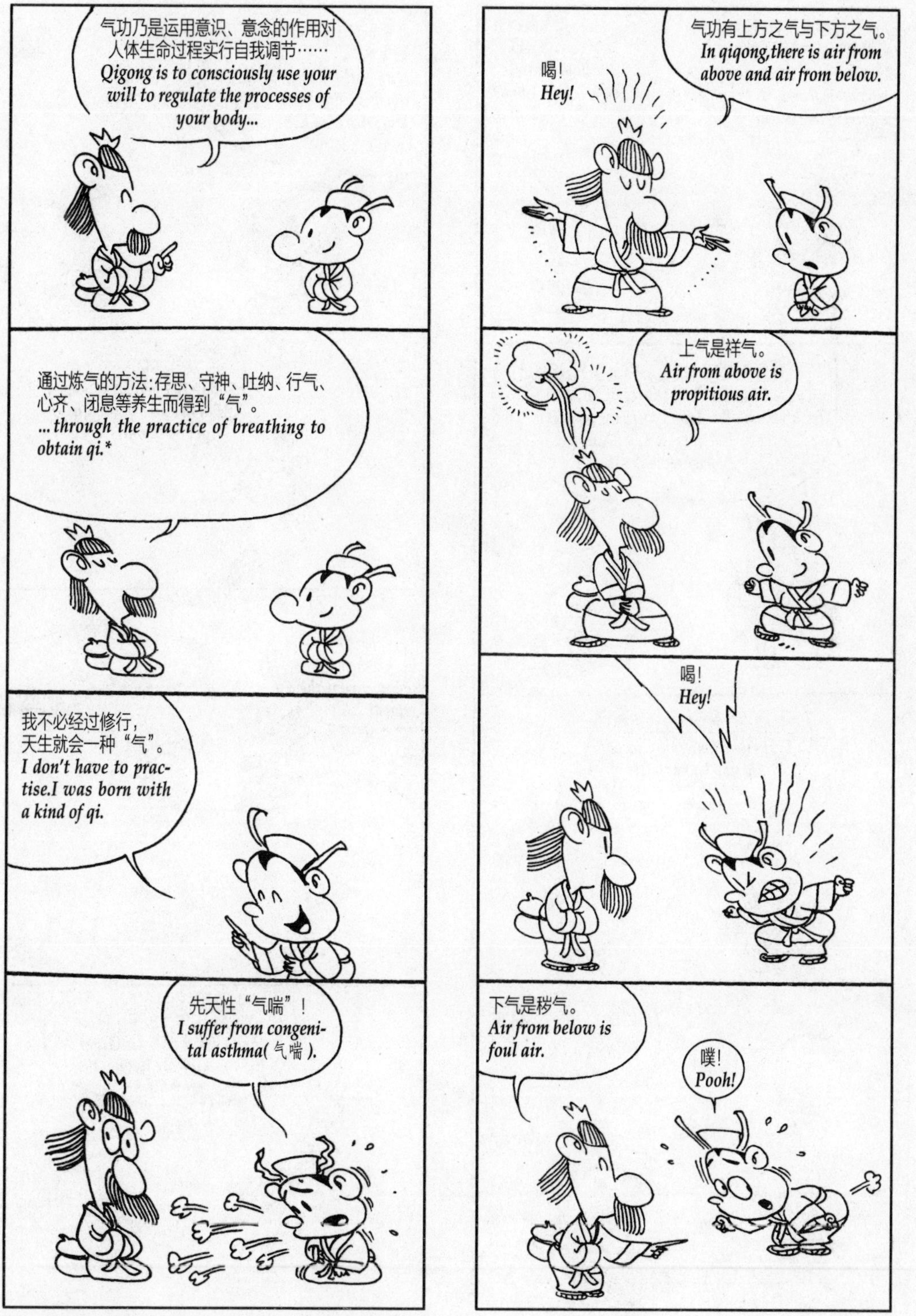

气功乃是运用意识、意念的作用对人体生命过程实行自我调节……
Qigong is to consciously use your will to regulate the processes of your body...

通过炼气的方法：存思、守神、吐纳、行气、心齐、闭息等养生而得到"气"。
*...through the practice of breathing to obtain qi.**

我不必经过修行，天生就会一种"气"。
I don't have to practise.I was born with a kind of qi.

先天性"气喘"！
I suffer from congenital asthma(气喘).

**The Chinese word 气 means "air","gas","odour"as well as "breath": hence it is used in different senses in the following dialogue.*

人一出生就天生有气，但气有好的气与坏的气。
Man has qi as soon as he enters this world,but there is good qi and bad qi.
坏的气是闷气、赌气、喘气、叹气。
Bad qi are 闷气（sulk）, 赌气 (pique), 喘气 (gasp)and 叹气 (sigh).
好的气是骨气、客气、福气、才气、豪气、正气。
The good qi are 骨气（integrity）, 客气 (politeness), 福气 (good fortune), 才气 (talent), 豪气 (heroic spirit)and 正气 (righteousness).
这是哪一部气功经典里写的?
From which qigong classic did you learn that?
…
是汉语字典里有关气的词句。
I learnt all these terms from the Chinese dictionary.
不但只是人有气，天地万物皆有气。
Not only humans have qi,everything in the Universe also has qi.
今天天、地、人三者，气皆不顺……
Today,Heaven,Earth and Man are all 气不顺（in a bad mood）...
天生雾气，地有湿气……
There is 雾气（mist）in the sky and 湿气 (dampness)on the ground...
而我正生闷气，所以今天停课放假休息。
And I am 生闷气 (sulking) today,so we are having the day off.

儒家观人观其眸，道家观人观其气。
Confucians observe a person by looking at his eyes.Taoists observe a person by focussing on his qi.

气也能看一个人的特征?
Qi also shows a person's character.

当然。
Of course.

例如我呢，是老“气”横秋、英雄豪“气”。
For instance I am 老气横秋（*lacking in youthful vigour*）*but have* 英雄豪气 *(heroic spirit).*

而你则是怪里怪“气”、孩子“气”。
And you are 怪里怪气（*eccentric*）*and* 孩子气 *(childish).*

…

气功除了能养生外，还有无限的妙用。
Besides keeping you in good health,qigong has numerous other uses.

天纯阳热气！
Blah,blah,blah,heat!

喝！
Ya!

感受到气功的作用了吧?
Feel the effect of qigong?

呼！
Hoo!

呼！
Hoo!

受益良多，谢谢。
It's done me a lot of good. Thank you.

你发功，我享受免费的暖气。
You emitted heat and I enjoyed heating free of charge.

…

*When a person is practising qigong he emits heat or qi from his body,which is called 发功.The qi from his body is supposed to have an effect on a target person and help cure that person's illness. The word 功 also means "skill",hence the pun in the following conversation.

换我来发功，喝！
Let me do it.Ya!

我什么都不惊！向前行！
I walk on without fear!

你发的这算是什么功？
What kind of skill is that?

唱“功”！
Singing skill!

我再发功一次，让你看清气功的奥秘。
I'll do it once more,so that you can get the knack of it.

看清楚了吧？
Did you see clearly?

喝！
Hey!

…

的确看得一清二楚，摸清师父的底细。
Yes,Master,I saw very clearly.Now I know everything about you.

…

门牙四颗装的是义齿，后面六颗统统有蛀牙。
You have four artificial teeth in front and six decayed teeth at the back.

我虽不会发功，但发气倒还可以。
Though I cannot 发功*, I am able to emit qi.*

喝！
Hey!

哇！受不了的臭……
Waw!The foul air is unbearable...

哈！
Ha!

再发这种气，其实也不容易。
To let off this kind of qi is not easy either.

…

蒜头一斤涨到四百多，而且还缺货。
The price of garlic has risen,and it is still in short supply.

你资质有限，变化术学不来，只好改学驾御动物之术。
You lack the intelligence to master the art of transformation.I think you'd better switch to the study of animal control.

当不了魔术师改当驯兽师也行，咱们应从哪里开始？
Failling to be a magician, I think it's not bad to be an animal trainer, Where do we begin?

第一课："与动物相处"！
Lesson One: Mixing with animals!

哇！
Waw!

吼！
Roar!

吼！
Roar!

世上的动物有千万种，你想驯哪一种动物？
There are thousands of animals in the world.Which kind do you intend to train?

中国以龙为尊，我就来当个驯龙师傅吧。
Chinese people have always worshipped the dragon.I will be a dragon trainer.

不错不错，人小志气不小……
Not bad,this boy is quite ambitious...

只怕对象太大你驯不了……
But I'm afraid your charge is too big for you...

*The Chinese word 虫 means "insect"or "worm".A "learned man "in Chinese is 文人, so a "learned insect"is 文虫, which is pronounced the same as 蚊虫 -mosquito.

**The Chinese for "dental caries"is 蛀牙.The word 蛀 is often associated with insects.

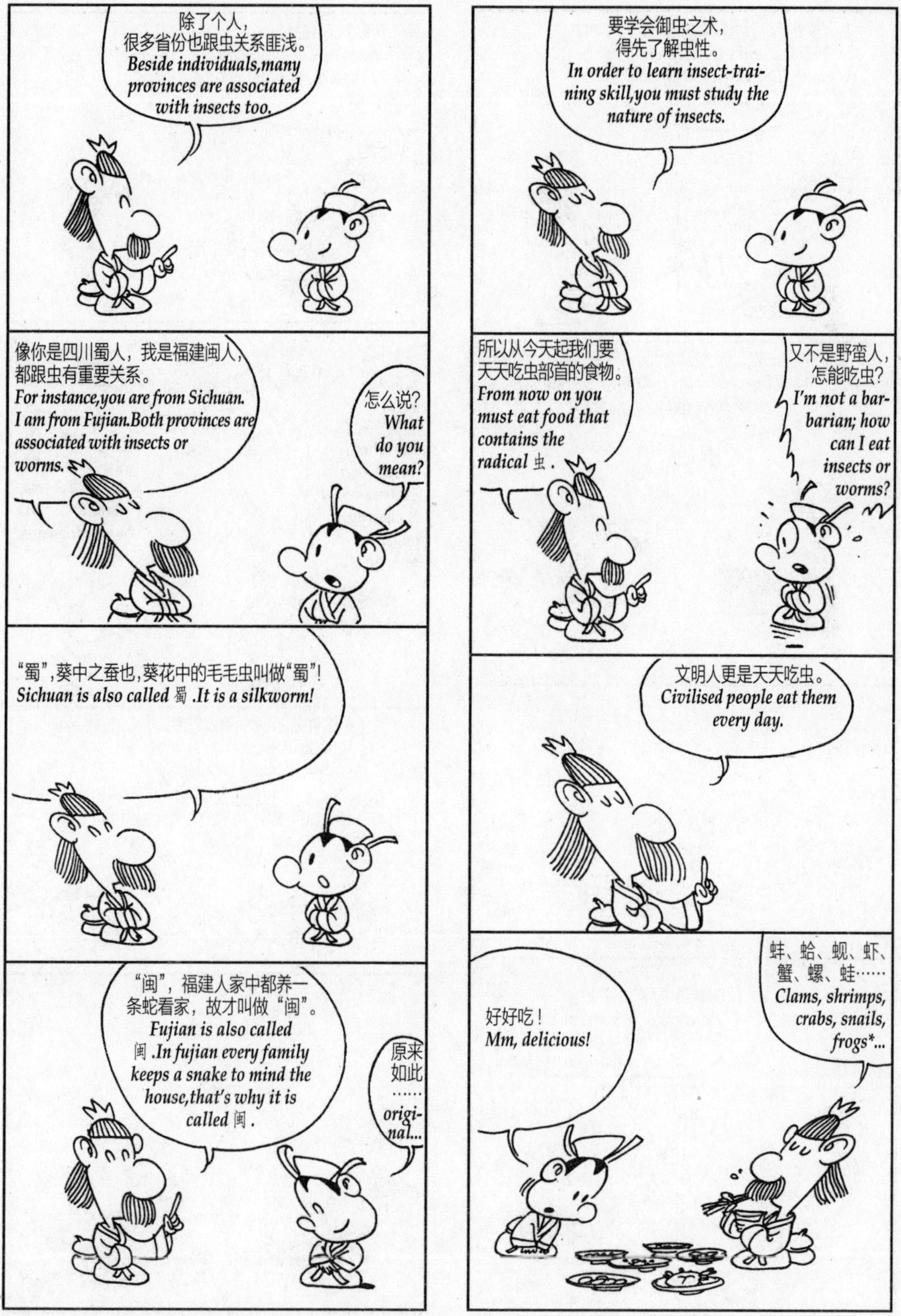

除了个人，
很多省份也跟虫关系匪浅。
Beside individuals,many provinces are associated with insects too.

像你是四川蜀人，我是福建闽人，
都跟虫有重要关系。
For instance,you are from Sichuan. I am from Fujian.Both provinces are associated with insects or worms.

怎么说？
What do you mean?

“蜀”，葵中之蚕也，葵花中的毛毛虫叫做“蜀”！
Sichuan is also called 蜀 .It is a silkworm!

“闽”，福建人家中都养一
条蛇看家，故才叫做“闽”。
Fujian is also called 闽 .In fujian every family keeps a snake to mind the house,that's why it is called 闽 .

原来
如此
……
origi-nal...

The Chinese words for these are 蚌，蛤，蚬，虾，蟹，螺 and 蛙，all with the radical 虫 that means "worm".

这支百年御虫神笛送给你。
This is a century-old insect-controlling magic flute.I give it to you.

神笛一吹，虫就应声而出……
When insect hear the flute they will come out...

虫果然出來了，
神笛内百年来的蛀虫……
Insects have indeed come out—the insects that have lived in the flute for 100 years.

我来示范吹笛引虫！
I'll demonstrate how to attract insects by playing the flute!

风
Wind

古文风从虫，笛一吹虫就来了。
The word for "wind"in old Chinese script is classified under the radical 虫.

风怎能算虫?
What does wind have to do with insect or worm?

风不算虫，少吹一撇总是虫！
Nothing.But take one stroke from it and it becomes an insect!

虱
虱—*the louse.*

*This is the original complex form of the word now simplified as 虫.

**A 瞌睡虫 is a sleep-inducing insect.It is also used to mean a person who is always sleepy.

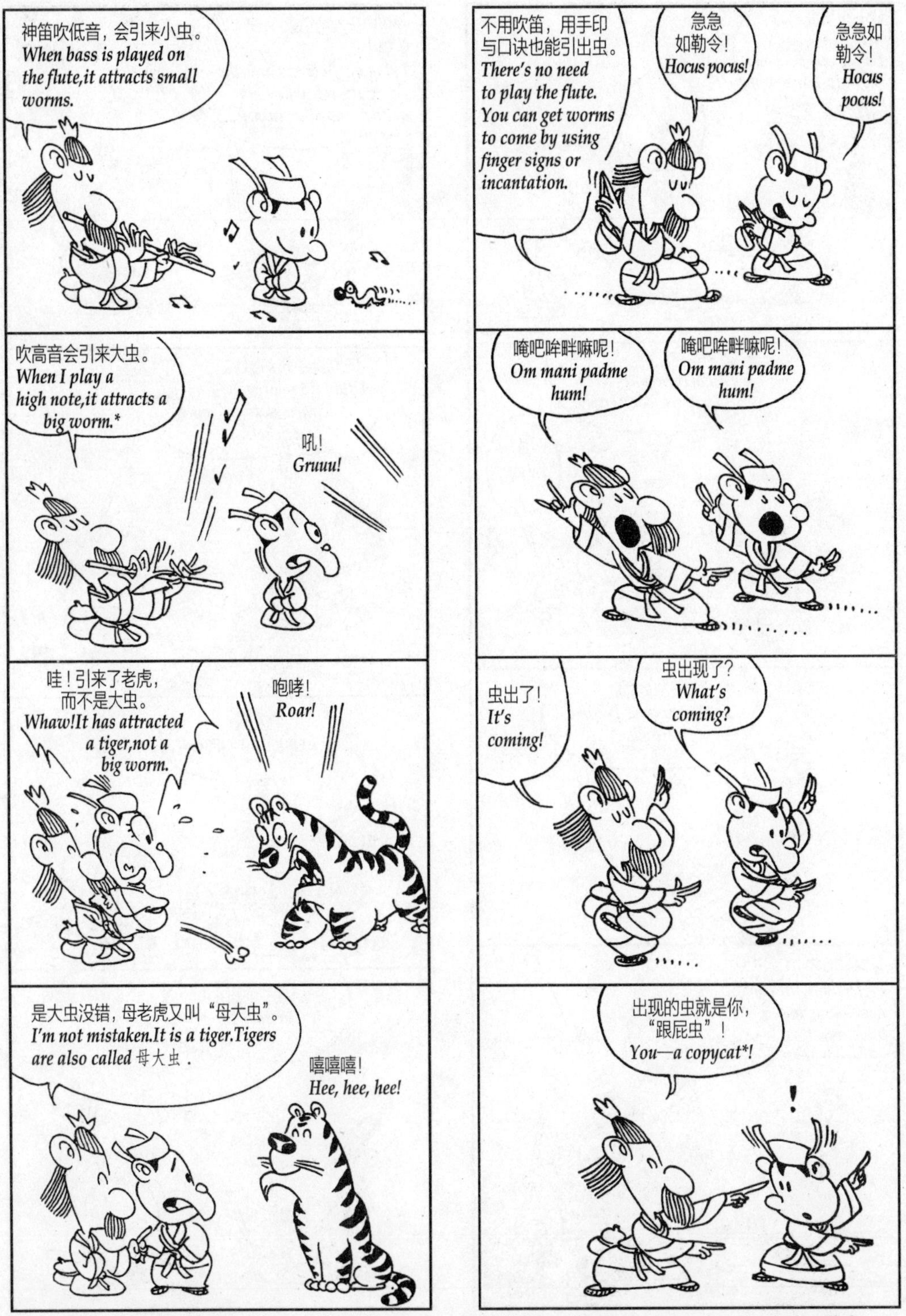

神笛吹低音，会引来小虫。
When bass is played on the flute,it attracts small worms.

吹高音会引来大虫。
*When I play a high note,it attracts a big worm.**

吼！
Gruuu!

哇！引来了老虎，而不是大虫。
Whaw!It has attracted a tiger,not a big worm.

咆哮！
Roar!

是大虫没错，母老虎又叫“母大虫”。
I'm not mistaken.It is a tiger.Tigers are also called 母大虫 *.*

嘻嘻嘻！
Hee, hee, hee!

The literal translation of 大虫 is "big worm",but the Chinese term usually refers to a tiger.

***A person who apes someone else is jocularly called a 跟屁虫 in Chinese.*

急急如勒令，嗡吧咩吽嘛呢，虫出来！
Hocus pocus! Om mani padme hum! Come worms!

咒语无效，虫不肯出洞来！
Your incantation does not work.Worms won't come out of their hole.

洞里是冬眠的虫，要用特别的咒语才有效。
The worms in the hole are hibernating. You need a special incantation to draw them out.

起床啦！
Get up! Get up!

零零零！
Ring-a-ling!

神笛仅能招来这些蚊蛆小虫吗?
Does the magic flute only attract these tiny insects and worms?

吹短音！会引来短短的小虫……
When you play short notes,short worms will come...

吹长音，会引来长虫?
And when I play long notes,long worms will come?

没错。
Quite right.

蛇！
Snake!

上古时代人结草而居，住屋里外多蛇类。
In ancient times people lived in thatched huts.There were lots of snakes in and around their homes.

当时蛇叫做它，人们碰面时不问吃饱了没，而问："有它吗"？
At that time snakes were called 它 (pronounced "tuo" or "she"). People greeted each other by asking "Are there snakes?"

蛇叫做它，好奇怪哦……
How strange...

不奇怪，它是象形文字。
Not strange at all. 它 is an ideogram.

不像蛇呀！
But it doesn't resemble a snake!

把它拉长就像极了。
Stretch it out then it looks exactly like a snake.

哇！
Waw!

蛇其实不可怕，
它还是中国人的祖先呢！
Actually snakes are not fearsome.They are our ancestors!

女娲捏泥造人，中国人的始祖是女娲呀，怎会是蛇？
Our first ancestor is Goddess Nüwa,who created Man.How can a snake be our ancestor?

女娲看起来像似人……
Nüwa looks like a human being...

女娲图
Portrait of Nüwa

……但她是人头蛇身的蛇神！
...but she is a snake goddess with a human head and the body of a snake!

蛇有的有毒，有的没毒，头呈三角形的有毒，色彩鲜艳的有毒……
Some snakes are poisonous and some are not. Those with triangular heads and colourful skin are poisonous...

哪一条蛇最毒？
Which snake is the most poisonous？

会说话的这条蛇最毒。
The one that speaks.

…

这呆瓜呆头呆脑的，也学得会降蛇术？
Can this stupid-looking blockhead learn to subdue snakes?

这条最毒没错，说话好毒！
You are quite right—this snake is the most poisonous.Its words are really venomous!

人类喜欢分善恶，白是纯洁，黑是邪恶。
Man like to distinguish the good from the bad.White is pure and black is evil.

白蛇是好蛇，黑蛇是坏蛇。
White snakes are good snakes and black snakes are bad snakes.

而黑白相间的雨伞节是好蛇又是坏蛇？
And snakes with black-and -white bodies are both good and bad?

没错。
That's right.

咬人时算是坏蛇，被人吃时算是好蛇。
When it bites it is bad,but when it is eaten by people it is good.

音乐能控制蛇，令它闻声起舞！
Music can control a snake and make it dance!

我也来试试。
Let me have a try.

咦？我吹就没效果，它不肯出来跳舞。
Eh? It refuses to come out when I play the flute.

因为你吹的是催眠曲。
Because you played a lullaby.

唵吧叶呢嘛，万蛇朝宗！
Om mani padme hum.All snakes come to pay homage! Huh?Not a single one!

咦？连一条蛇都没来报到……
Huh? Not a single one...

这需要一条正在蜕皮的蛇做引导。
We need a snake that is shedding its skin as a guide.

蛇皮清凉秀免费参观
Free Skin-shedding Show

果然效果不错，蛇潮热滚滚。
good result! Wave upon wave of snakes have come.

要了解蛇性得进入蛇堆中与蛇长时间相处。
In order to know the nature of snakes you should live with them for a long time.

我知道这是要考验我的胆子。
I know you want to test my courage.

不是考验胆子，而是考验你的鼻子……
Not to test your courage, but to test your nose...

蛇类腥臭难闻，看你能忍不能忍。
I want to see if you can stand the awful stench of snakes.

*The words 性 "nature" and 姓 "last name" have the samp pronunciation.

天地六合三界鬼神听令！蜀人邓甲茅山学道有成，特封天师！
Listen gods and ghosts in Heaven and on Earth!Deng Jia,a native of Sichuan, has completed his study of Taoism on Maoshan Mountain.I hereby bestow on him the title of Master!

恭喜邓同学毕业，得天师学位。
Congratulations,Mr Deng! You've completed your study and earned the title of Master.

谢谢。
Thank you.

师父！请问为什么叫做天师呢？
Master, may I ask what is the meaning of Master?

天师为人求雨、消灾、解厄，因为靠天吃饭所以叫天师！
A master prays on behalf of others for rain,to ward off adversity and to dispel bad luck.

…

茅山学道三年苦学出师，成为邓天师，是师字辈人物了！
*After three years' hard work,I have graduated and become Master Deng,one with a title of "shi"!**

今后的地位将与律师、医师一样是高收入者。
From now on my status equals that of doctors and lawyers. I'm in the high-income class.

不是所有的师字辈人物都是高收入！
Not all people with "shi" in their titles are highly paid!

天师的工作是传道济世，与老师、牧师、法师一样低收入。
The duty of a master is to transmit wisdom and do good for society.Like teachers,clergymen and priests, masters are paid very little.

**The Chinese word 师 (pronounced"shi")is used in titles like doctors 医师 ,lawyers 律师, teachers 老师 ,clergymen 牧师 ,priests 法师 ,etc.*

从此你就是茅山第二十七代传人，衣钵就传给你。
From now on you are the 27th-generation inheritor of Maoshan. I pass on my mantle to you.

这是五雷蛇令、打蛇鞭、招魂旗、还魂丹……
Here are the Flag of Five-thunder Snake Command,Snake-thrashing Whip,Spiritcalling Pennant,Life-reviving Pill,...

我已经把茅山所有的宝物全部移交给你点交清楚。
I have transferred to you one by one all the treasures of Maoshan.

谢谢师父如此大方……
Thankyou,Master,for you generosity...

可否把这座茅山的产权也一并过继？
Can you also transfer to me the ownership of this mountain?

师父！弟子要下山去江湖闯荡，有何事项要弟子去办？
Master,your pupil is now leaving the mountain to wander in the world. Is there anything you'd like me to do for you there?

如果有机缘，请替我找几颗长生不老丹。
If you have the opportunity, please get me a few longevity pills.

找长生不老药很简单，有钱就可买到。
That's easy,as long as you have money.

...

这是瑞士制造的防止老化胎盘素，一针八十万元。
This is an anti-aging placental essence made in Switzerland.Each shot costs 8,000yuan.

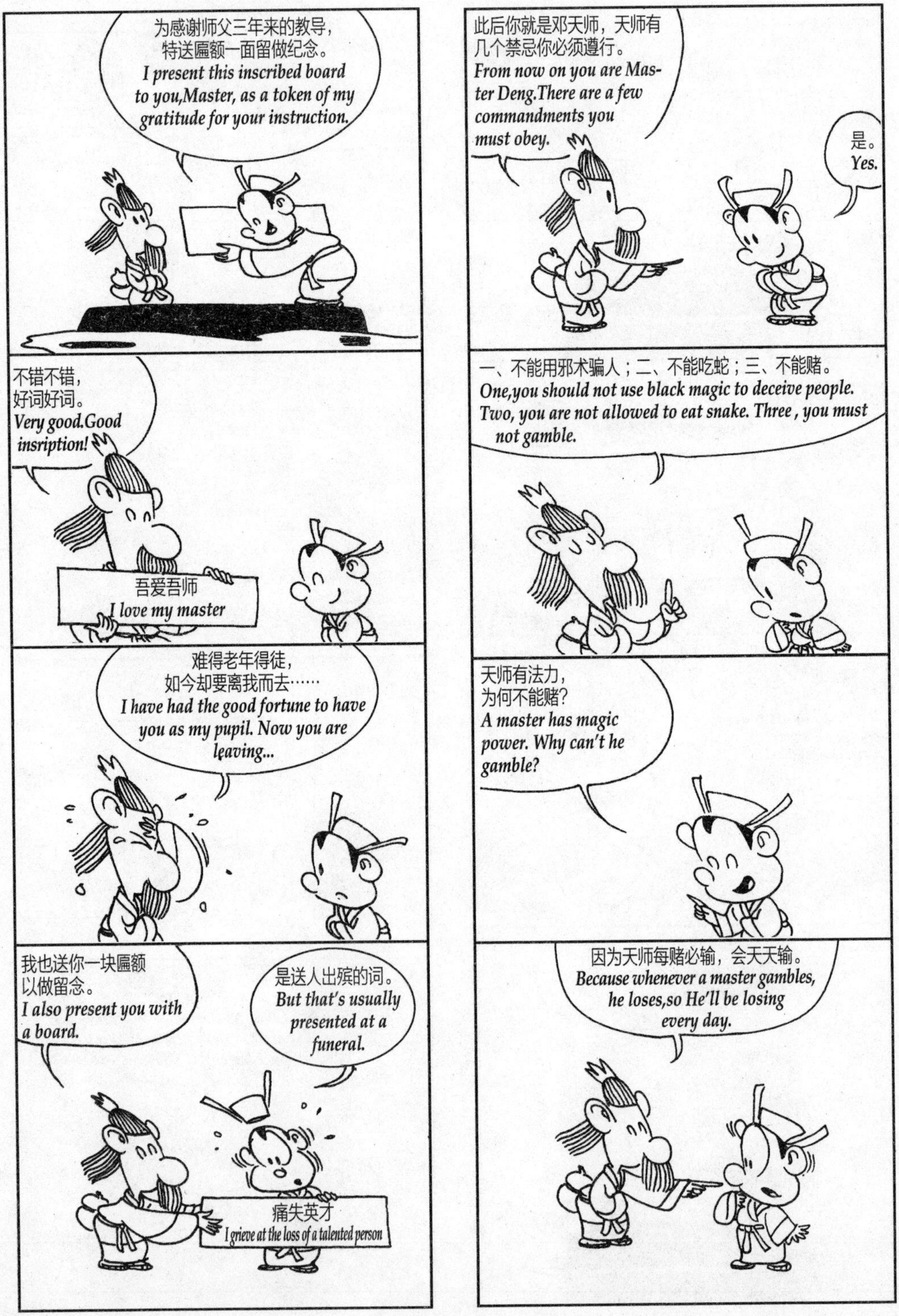

为感谢师父三年来的教导，特送匾额一面留做纪念。
I present this inscribed board to you,Master, as a token of my gratitude for your instruction.

不错不错，好词好词。
Very good.Good insription!
吾爱吾师
I love my master

难得老年得徒，如今却要离我而去……
I have had the good fortune to have you as my pupil. Now you are leaving...

我也送你一块匾额以做留念。
I also present you with a board.
是送人出殡的词。
But that's usually presented at a funeral.
痛失英才
I grieve at the loss of a talented person

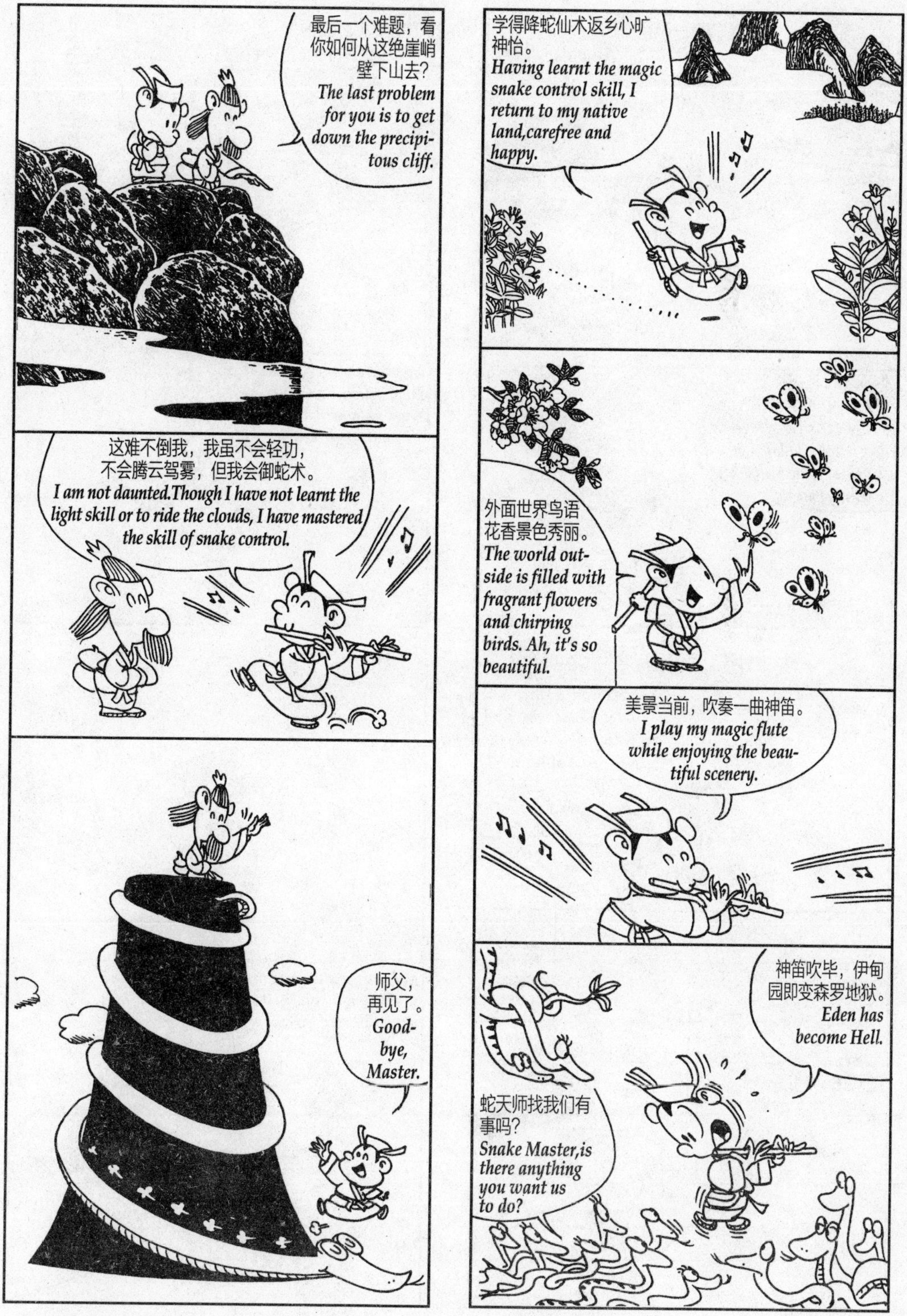

最后一个难题，看你如何从这绝崖峭壁下山去？
The last problem for you is to get down the precipitous cliff.

这难不倒我，我虽不会轻功，不会腾云驾雾，但我会御蛇术。
I am not daunted.Though I have not learnt the light skill or to ride the clouds, I have mastered the skill of snake control.

师父，再见了。
Good-bye, Master.

往江南
To South of Yangtze
往四川
To Sichuan

先到江南玩好呢？还是先返四川省亲的好？
Shall I go and have a good time in the south first,or shall I return to Sichuan to see my parents?

我要往东或往西，抛石头决定前程。
I'll throw a stone and let it decide whether I travel towards the east or the west.

往江南
To South of Yangtze
往四川
To Sichuan
不东不西留在原地？
Neither east nor west. I should stay where I am.

往江南
To South of Yangtze
往四川
To Sichuan
先去江南还是先回四川左右为难。
I'm in an awkward predicament.

你赞成到江南玩，还是回老家四川去？
What do you think,to the south or go home?

我赞成先到江南！
I am for going to the south!

赞成到江南的占百分之百，本次行动是依民意测验决定。
My action is decided by a public opinion poll.To the south got 100% support.
往江南
To South of Yangtze
往四川
To Sichuan

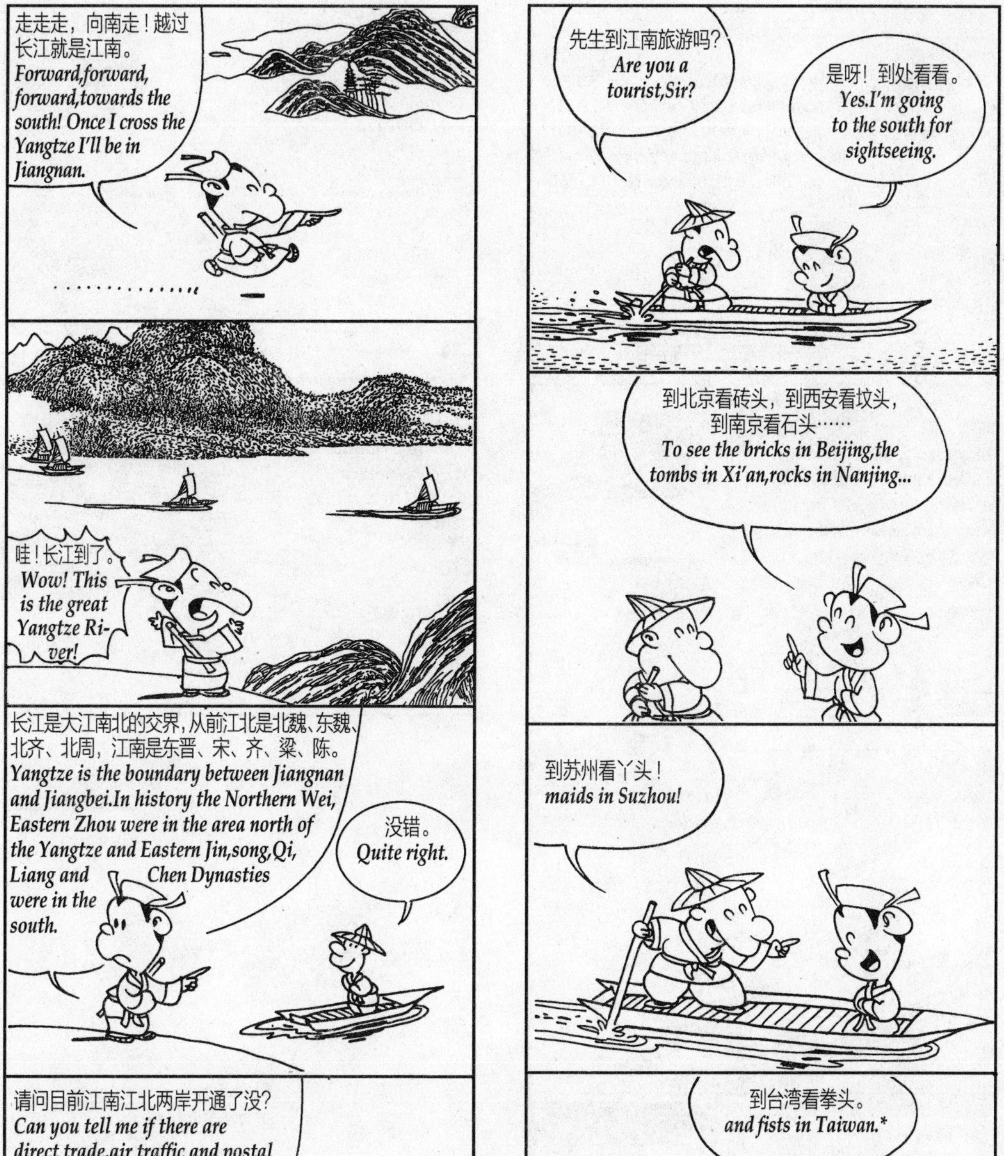

走走走，向南走！越过长江就是江南。
Forward,forward, forward,towards the south! Once I cross the Yangtze I'll be in Jiangnan.

哇！长江到了。
Wow! This is the great Yangtze River!

长江是大江南北的交界，从前江北是北魏、东魏、北齐、北周，江南是东晋、宋、齐、梁、陈。
Yangtze is the boundary between Jiangnan and Jiangbei.In history the Northern Wei, Eastern Zhou were in the area north of the Yangtze and Eastern Jin,song,Qi, Liang and Chen Dynasties were in the south.

没错。
Quite right.

请问目前江南江北两岸开通了没？
Can you tell me if there are direct trade,air traffic and postal communication links between the south and north?

*This is a play on words,as the Chinese words for "brick"(砖头),"tomb"(坟头),"rock"(石头),"maid"(丫头)and "fist"(拳头)all include the character 头.

长江上游是白帝城，再过去是赤壁古战场，景色壮丽……
Along the upper reaches of the Yangtze the scenery is magnificent.See the small town built on the cliffs?It's called Baidicheng.A little downstream is the site of the historic battle of Chibi..

往前下游是金陵石头城，曾是东吴、东晋、宋、齐、梁、陈六朝的国都。
As we reach the lower reaches of the river you'll see the rocky town of Jinling,which was capital of six dynasties: Eastern Wu,Eastern Jin, Song, Qi, Liang and Chen.

船到岸了，船资三文。
Here we are. The fare is three wen.

便宜……
Very reasonable...

另收导游费一百文！
On top of that, you're to pay me 100 wen for being your tour guide!

江南风光，山岚秀丽，烟雨蒙蒙……
The mountains in Jianguan are scenic and covered in mists...

有云烟处湿气重，要注意身体。
It's damp here amidst the clouds and mist. I've got to take care.

咳咳咳！
Ahem,hem, hem!

原是二手烟，怪不得呛鼻。
So I was choked by second-hand smoke.

江南秀色一等一，到处有柳絮。
The beauty of the scenery in Jiangnan is first-rate.I see willow trees everywhere.
你们江北人称它柳，我们江南人可叫它为小杨。
You people from the north call this tree willow, but we in the south call it little poplar.
柳枝向下而垂"流"，杨枝向上"扬"，柳怎么可叫做杨？
Willow branches "flow" down and poplar branches grow upward. How can you call willows poplars?
杨我们叫蒲柳，柳我们叫小杨！
We call poplars catkin willows, and we call willows little poplars!
算了，越说越糊涂了。
Forget it! The more you explain the more confused I become.

黄河水浊，流声"可可可……"的，所以叫"河"。
The water flowing in the turbid Yellow River sounds like "ke,ke,ke" so the river is called 河 (pronounced "he").
江水清，长流声"江江江"的，所以叫"江"。
The Yangtze is clear,so the water sounds like "jiang,jiang,jiang";that's why it is called 江（pronounced "jiang"）.
水湾处成巷，所以叫……
The river bend forms a lane, so it is called...
"港"！
... 港（harbour）！

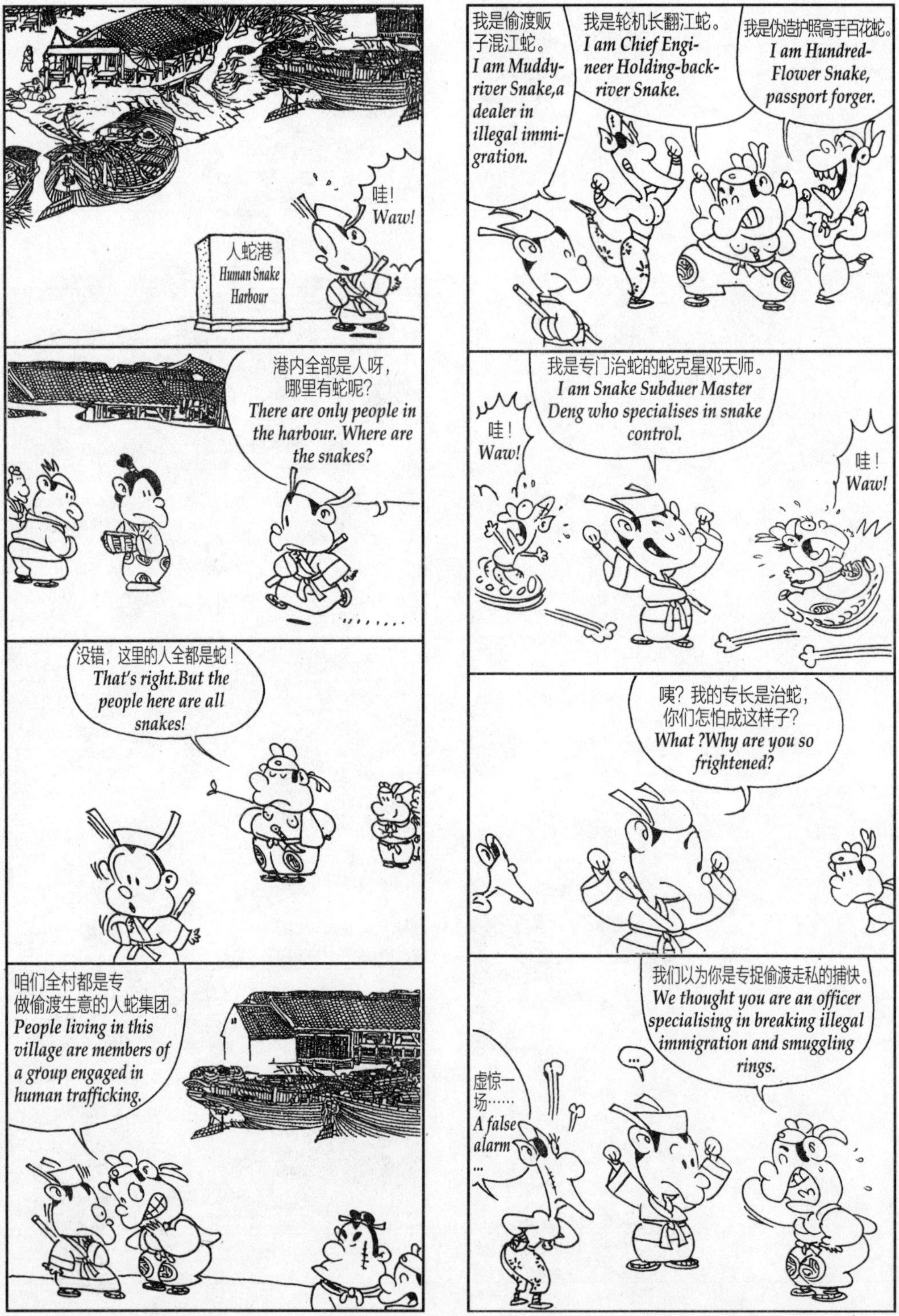

哇！
Waw!

人蛇港
Human Snake Harbour

港内全部是人呀，哪里有蛇呢？
There are only people in the harbour. Where are the snakes?

没错，这里的人全都是蛇！
That's right.But the people here are all snakes!

咱们全村都是专做偷渡生意的人蛇集团。
People living in this village are members of a group engaged in human trafficking.

你是蛇天师，
来我们村子干吗？
Why did you come to our village, Snake Master?

一来到处观光；二来顺
便捉蛇治蛇赚外快。
For sightseeing. And to make some extra money on the side by catching snakes.

可惜我们村子全都是人，
没有蛇可抓。
It's a pity there are only humans in the village. There are no snakes for you to catch.

放心，只要有人聚落的
地方就有蛇！
Don't worry.There are snakes wherever there are human communities!

什么蛇？
What snake?

“地头蛇”!*
*Local bullies!**

…

**The Chinese colloquial term for a local bully is* 地头蛇.

治蛇专家蛇天师
Snake Control Expert—Snake Master

就在这里立招牌招揽生意……
I'll put up a sign here to attract customers....

枯坐半天没半个人影，真不景气……
I've been sitting here for half a day and haven't seen a single customer.Business is really bad...

或许是招牌的文案有问题……
Maybe something's wrong with the wording of my sign...

杀蛇专家蛇天师
Snake Killing Expert—Snake Master

招牌改一个字人潮就来到……
Just by changing one word, I have attracted a sea of people...

你会杀蛇，也会杀虎吗？
You kill tigers,too?

什么时候要杀蛇？
When are you killing snakes?

蛇天师，求求你替我治治我家中可怕的老婆……
Snake Master,please subdue that terrible wife of mine, I beg you...

抱歉！我只会治虫治蛇，不会治你家中的母老虎、河东狮。
Sorry! I can only subdue worms and snakes, not the female tiger in your home.

可是她的确也是蛇……
But she is actually a snake...

哦？
Oh?

生肖属蛇！
She was born in the year of snake!

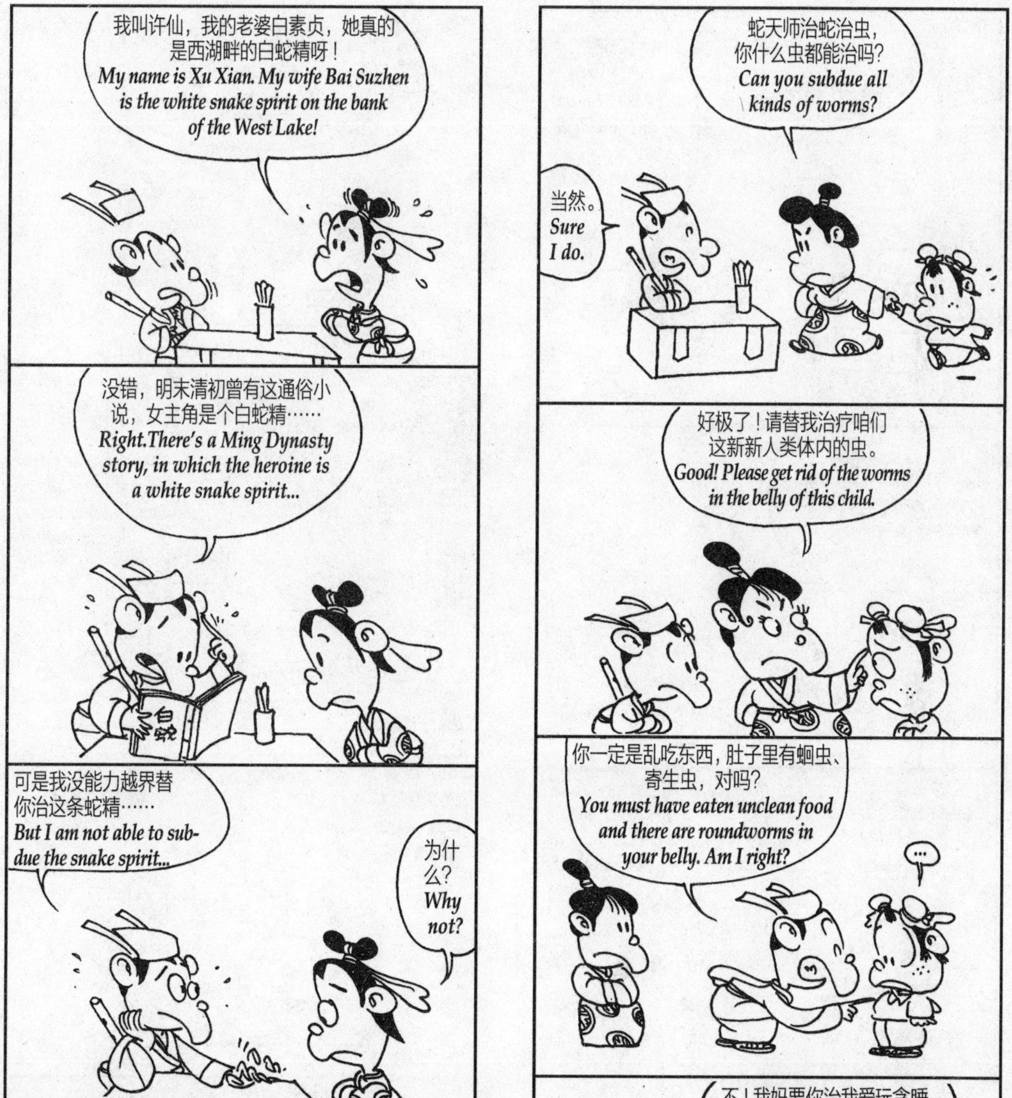

我叫许仙，我的老婆白素贞，她真的是西湖畔的白蛇精呀！
My name is Xu Xian. My wife Bai Suzhen is the white snake spirit on the bank of the West Lake!

没错，明末清初曾有这通俗小说，女主角是个白蛇精……
Right.There's a Ming Dynasty story, in which the heroine is a white snake spirit...

白蛇

可是我没能力越界替你治这条蛇精……
But I am not able to subdue the snake spirit...

为什么？
Why not?

因为现在是唐朝，而你是明朝人物，跑错了年代！
Because it is now the Tang Dynasty and you are a Ming Dynasty character.You've come at the wrong time!

…

杀蛇专家蛇天师
Snake Killing Expert—Snake Master
蛇天师你除蛇怎么收费？
Snake Master, how much do you charge for getting rid of snakes?
降伏一条蛇收费五文钱！
Five wen for subduing each snake.
哇！
Waw!
除一条蛇五文钱也贵吗？
Is that too high?
一条五文是不贵……
Five wen for one snake is not high...
但我要除一千多条蛇就贵了……
But the cost is horrendous as I want to get rid of more than 1,000 snakes...
我父亲华老爹生前爱蛇，收养了各种蛇类一千条……
My father kept snakes as pets. He adopted more than 1,000 snakes of all kinds...
爹过世后我想把房子改建，这一千条蛇变成了大问题。
Now that he's dead, I want to rebuild my home.The snakes are a serious problem for me...
可依一个法案办理。
You can solve the problem according to the law.
什么法案？
What law?
依《老旧眷村改建条例》要它们搬出去。
According to the Regulations Concerning the Rebuilding of Old Villages,you can ask the snakes to move out.
眷村改建
Rebuilding of Old Villages

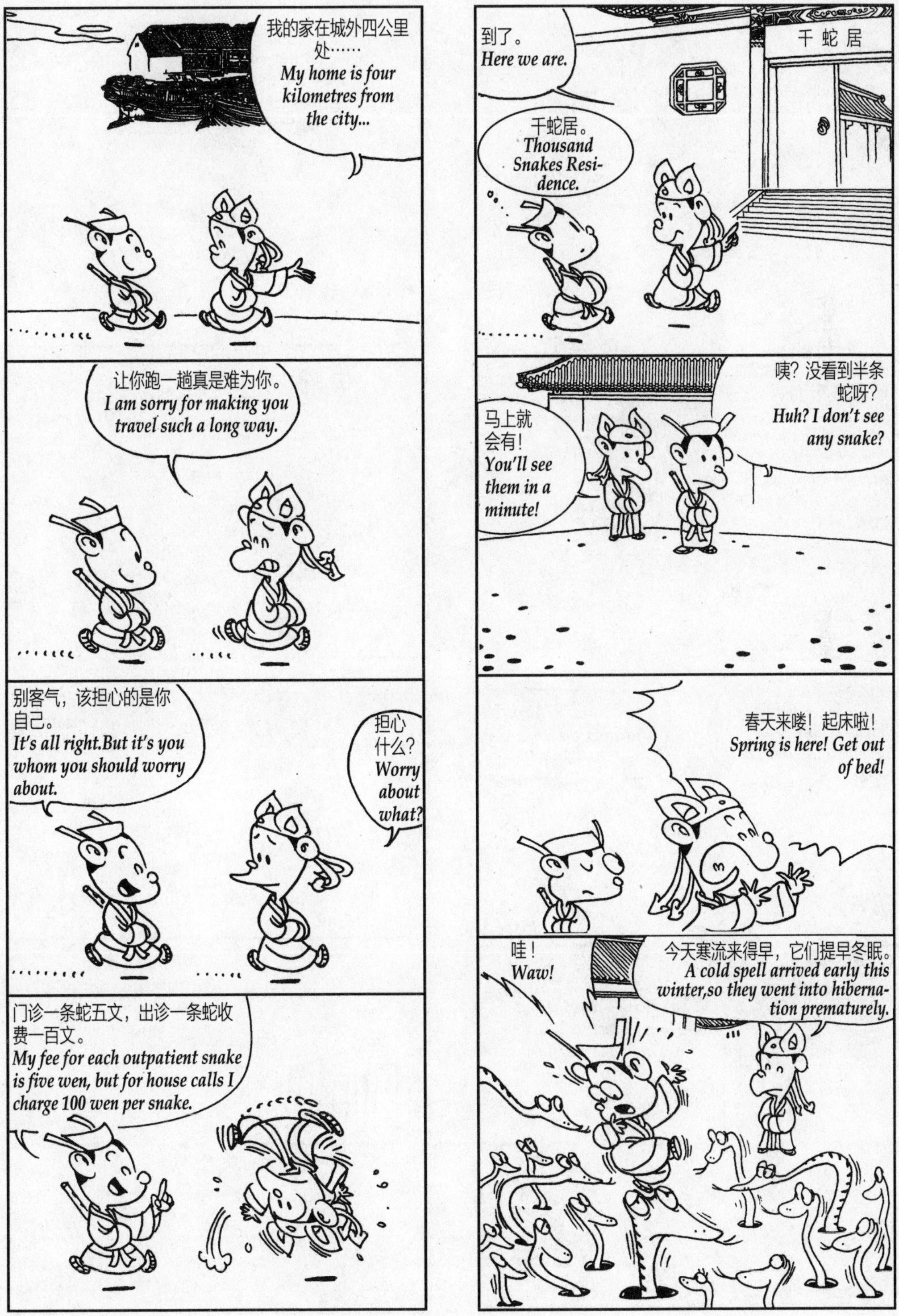

我的家在城外四公里处……
My home is four kilometres from the city...

让你跑一趟真是难为你。
I am sorry for making you travel such a long way.

别客气，该担心的是你自己。
It's all right.But it's you whom you should worry about.

担心什么？
Worry about what?

门诊一条蛇五文，出诊一条蛇收费一百文。
My fee for each outpatient snake is five wen, but for house calls I charge 100 wen per snake.

各位蛇兄蛇姐，养育你们的华老爹不幸过世了！
Dear snake brothers and sisters, I inform you in sorrow that Granddad Hua who raised you has passed away!

依据惯例房子由华公子继承，你们无权再住这里。
According to convention, this house goes into the possession of Granddad Hua's son. You no longer have the right to live here.

可是华老爹答应这栋房子留下来给我们住的。
But Granddad Hua promised to leave the house to us.

可有华老爹的亲笔证明？
Do you have any proof in the old man's handwriting?

千蛇居

门上的招牌就是华老爹的亲笔证据。
The board above the door is evidence left by Granddad Hua.

咱们不是平白要你们搬出去，而是按先建后拆办理。
We are not asking you to move out for nothing. We are doing this according to the regulations concerning the pulling down of old houses.

每蛇可先分配一间独立住房！
Each of you will get your own residence!

条件还真不错，可以接受。
The conditions are fair and acceptable.

可能是独立门户的花园别墅呢！
Maybe we'll each get a villa with a garden!

是现代的钢筋住房。
It's a modern house built with reinforced bars.

好吧！你们既然不自动搬出去，
我就吹降蛇曲对付你们！
OK. Since you refuse to move out voluntarily, I am going to deal with you by playing the snake-subduing melody!

可怕！
Terrible!

恐怖……
Dreadful...

快受不了听
不下去了。
It's unbearable. I can't stand it any longer.

像这样
吹才是。
You should play it like this.

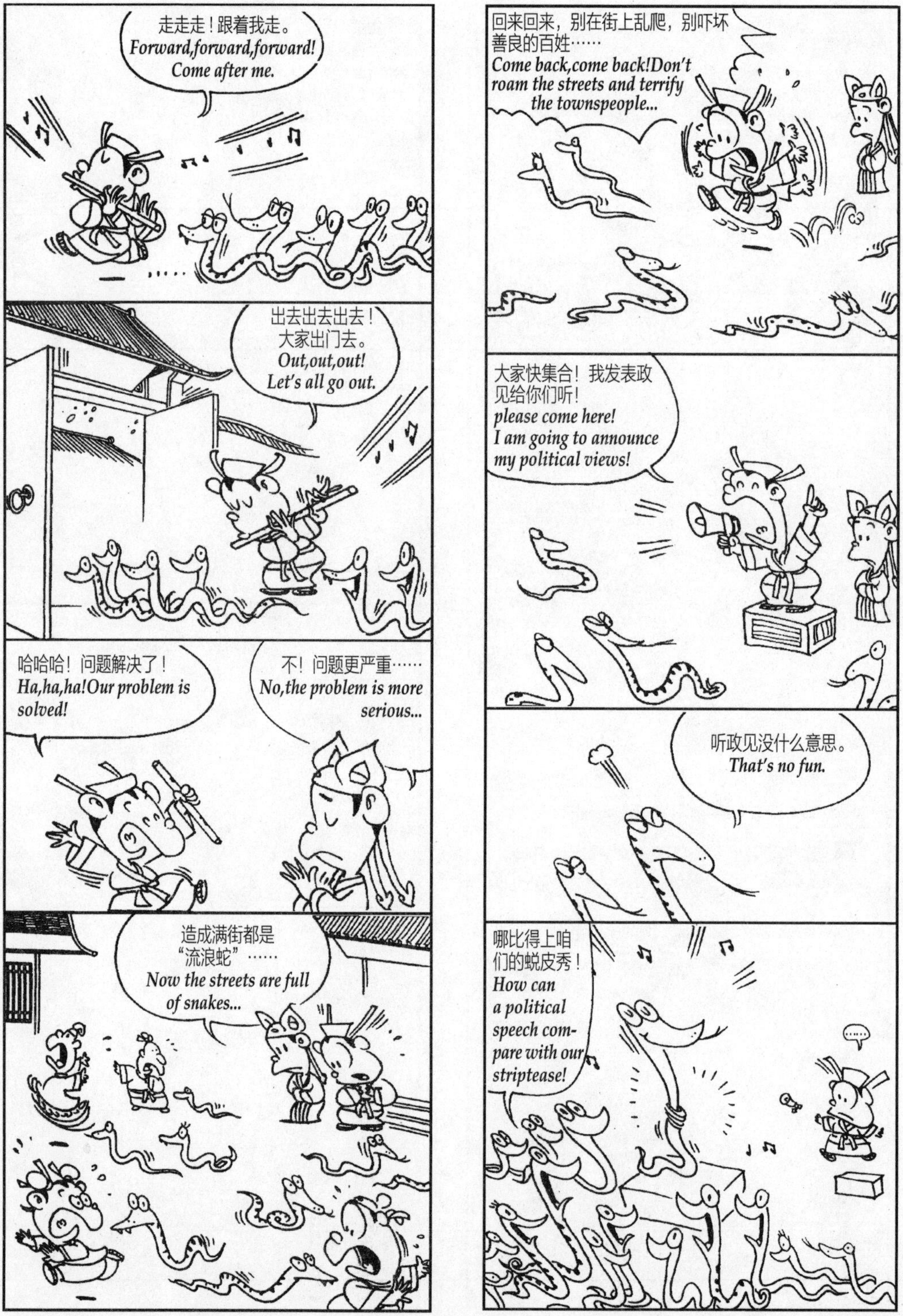

走走走！跟着我走。
Forward,forward,forward!
Come after me.

出去出去出去！
大家出门去。
Out,out,out!
Let's all go out.

哈哈哈！问题解决了！
Ha,ha,ha!Our problem is solved!

不！问题更严重……
No,the problem is more serious...

造成满街都是"流浪蛇"……
Now the streets are full of snakes...

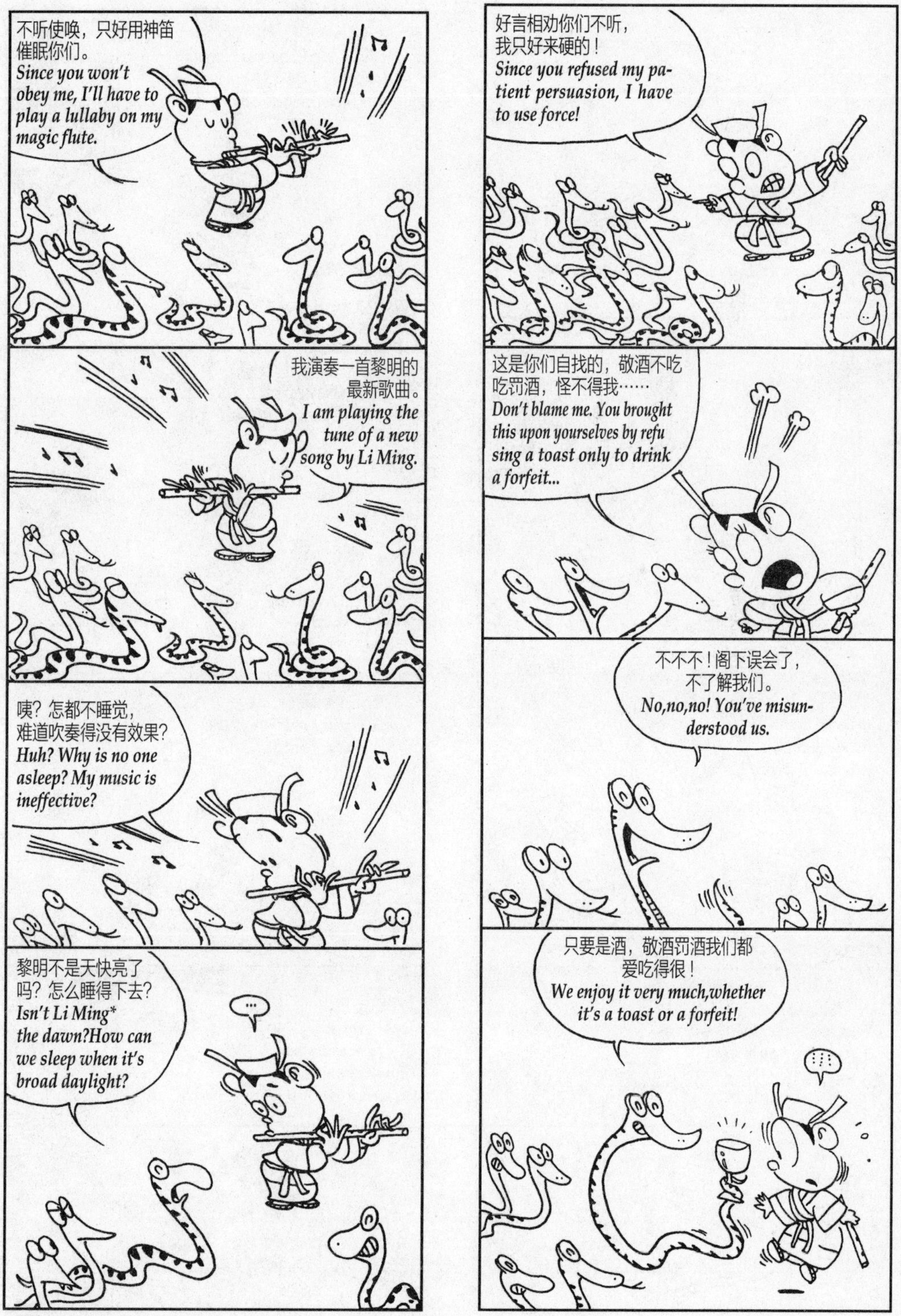

不听使唤，只好用神笛催眠你们。
Since you won't obey me, I'll have to play a lullaby on my magic flute.

我演奏一首黎明的最新歌曲。
I am playing the tune of a new song by Li Ming.

咦？怎都不睡觉，难道吹奏得没有效果？
Huh? Why is no one asleep? My music is ineffective?

黎明不是天快亮了吗？怎么睡得下去？
Isn't Li Ming the dawn?How can we sleep when it's broad daylight?*

* 黎明 *Li Ming is the name of a popular singer and the two characters also mean "day break".*

好吧！软的不吃，我就来硬的。
Since you yield neither to persuasion nor to coercion I'll use force.
亮出绝招斩蛇剑对付你们。
As a last resort I'll deal with you with my Snake-chopping Sword.
硬的来，咱们就软的挡！
You resort to a hard measure,then we counter it with something soft!
法令在眼前，来硬的也不怕！
With the law right here, we're not afraid of your tough measure!
稀有动物保护法
Law on Rare Animal Protection
…

蛇天师！你受聘驱蛇还不快将它们赶出去！
Snake Master! You were hired to drive away snakes.Hurry up and drive them away!
千蛇居
一对一千，这仗难打……
One against 1,000. It's an impossible battle...
一千零一对一，这仗简单。
One thousand and one against one.This is an easy battle.
哇！
Waw!
蛇兄弟们，大家再回千蛇居去。
Snake brothers, let's go back to the Thousand Snakes Residence.
千蛇居

千蛇居
你明知这房子要改建，为何又把蛇带回来？
You know very well that the house is going to be rebuilt. Why did you bring the snakes back?
流浪蛇之家
建筑物不用改，只要改个招牌就成。
The house doesn't have to be rebuilt.All you need to do is change the board above the gate.
改建房子为的是赚钱，我可不是收容流浪蛇的慈善家！
I am rebuilding the house to make money. I am not a philanthropist running an asylum for snake vagrants!
观光蛇园
把流浪蛇之家改成观光蛇园，还是可做生意赚钱。
Just change the name to Snake Garden for Tourists. You can still make money out of it.
你受雇驱蛇没完成任务，休想得到任何酬劳。
Don't expect to get paid till you have fuifilled the task you were hired for.
…
我送你一宝贝，不让你白忙一场。
I'll give you a precious gift so that your efforts were not made in vain.
谢谢你的大礼，请问这是什么宝贝？
Thank you very much.What is this precious gift?
哇！
Waw!
是我的心肝宝贝！
It's my very dear darling!

观光蛇园
Snake Garden for Tourists

观光蛇园的各位蛇兄蛇妹们，我走了，再见！
Good-bye,snake brothers and sisters!

他就是专门治蛇的蛇天师。
He is Snake Master,the snake-sub duing expert.

但他学艺不精治蛇失败，只是半瓶醋功夫！
But he's just a dabbler. He failed to subdue the snakes.

是吗？
Is that so?

所以蛇天师应改名为蛇天输！
So his title should be changed to Snake Loser!

对极了，蛇天输！
Quite right! snake Loser!

蛇天师无能治蛇，怎能靠治蛇游走江湖？
As a Snake Master without the skill to subdue snakes, how can I make a living?

还好我还会吹笛，可以改行吹笛卖艺。
Fortunately I learnt to play the flute. I can earn a living with the flute.

各位客官有钱捧个钱场，没钱捧个人场……
Ladies and gentlemen,pay for my music if you have coins to spare,if not , your presence is also a source of support to me...

笛一吹，蛇就来，破坏了吹奏卖艺的生意。
My music attracted all these snakes and my performance is ruined.

*The Chinese colloquial term for a talkative woman is 长舌妇, As 舌 and 蛇 are homonyms,the author is using a pun here.

附录·延伸阅读

APPENDIX Further reading

此部分为本书图画页的延伸阅读，各段首所示的页码与图画页对应。

P84　唐代传奇：陈鸾凤（雷公传）

话说唐朝元和年间，在海康这个地区有个力士叫做陈鸾凤，由于他生性耿直，对人讲义气，胆子奇大无比，根本就不把鬼神之说放在心上，因此，同乡的邻居亲友给他取了一个“现代周处”的外号。当地有一间雷公庙，乡民因崇信鬼神，向来非常重视祭拜之礼，且据说雷公庙非常灵验，求财得财，求子得子，只要心诚，凡事皆成，因此香火鼎盛。

海康地方有一风俗，在每年听到第一声雷响的那一天，各行各业都不能做生意，必须休息沐浴净身后到雷公庙上香祈福，如果不心存敬意，或没有准备丰盛的祭品，一定会遭到雷公击毙。这种崇信鬼神的观念早已根深蒂固在海康人民的心中，他们对于雷公的法力是深信不疑的，当然也有例外的人、出状况的时候！那当然就是我们的主角陈鸾凤喽！

有一年刚好遇到海康发生大旱灾，当地人民准备了贡品，膜拜祭祀求雨，可是天空依然是一片晴朗，艳阳高照，没下半滴雨。陈鸾凤很生气地说：“我的家乡，应该是受到雷神庇佑的地方，如今做神的不造福百姓，却还受到百姓如此的膜拜祝祷。今天所有的农作物都烤焦了，所有的农田、池塘都干掉了，所有的牲畜也吃光了，遭逢这么大的天灾却求不到甘露，这样的庙还用来干什么！”于是点了一把火，把雷公庙给烧了。

当地还有一个习俗，据说是雷公的规定，就是不能把黄鱼和猪肉混在一起食用，否则会被雷公劈死。有一天陈鸾凤手中拿着一把柴刀，跑到田野中间，故意将黄鱼和猪肉混在一起，弄熟后吃了下去，等着看会有什么事情发生。果然有怪事发生了，一时之间狂风大作、乌云密布，电闪雷鸣、狂风暴雨齐下。陈鸾凤不假思索，立即以刀刃向上挥过去，结果砍断了雷神的左大腿，雷神中刀掉落到地面上来。

雷神的原形长得像熊又像猪，还有长毛状的角，一副青面獠牙的模样。手里拿着短柄的石斧，受伤的大腿处血流如注。就在这个时候——怪云消逝，风雨也停了。鸾凤心里明白，原来“雷”是这样的怪物而不是神祇，于是赶快跑回家，告诉他的家人亲友。说他把“雷”的腿砍断了，要大家一起去看个究竟。没想到大家都吓了一跳，心惊胆战地一同前往，果然看见“雷”被砍断了左腿。

陈鸾凤又拿起刀，想把雷公杀了，把它的肉剁成肉酱，却被乡人阻止。他们说：“这妖怪是天上的灵物，你只是凡间俗人，倘若将它杀害，必定会连累我全乡的人遭到灾殃。”于是大家一起捉住陈鸾凤，让他不能得逞。过了一会儿，又是怪云又是雷声，带着受伤的怪物和被砍断的腿离开了人间。接着下起滂沱大雨，从中午一直下到傍晚。

陈鸾凤被所有在场的亲友乡人痛骂了一顿之后，不许他返家。于是他手里拿着刀，走了三十里路，来到他舅兄家中投宿，可是当夜却遭到雷击，把他睡觉的房间给烧光了。于是他气得拿着刀立在庭院中，一副正气逼人的样子，“雷”终究是拿他没办法，不能加害于他。没一会儿工夫，有人把今天以来所发生过的事情，一五一十地转告给鸾凤的舅兄知道。结果他又被人赶了出来。

接着他又到寺庙投宿，同样也遭到雷击，借宿的房间又被烧毁了。鸾凤知道自己不论走到哪里都一样会遭到报复，于是连夜拿着火把，跑到山洞里面躲了起来。就这样雷再也打不到他，也没有再发生烧房子的事件。结果他在山洞里躲了三天三夜才回家。从此以后，若遇到海康发生旱灾，当地人民就会重金聘请陈鸾凤，让他拿着刀，带着黄鱼和猪肉两种食物到田野间食用，就像前一次一样。

结果每次都会下起大雨来，解除旱情，二十几年来皆如此。于是大家都尊称陈鸾凤为雨师。直到唐朝大和年间，刺史林绪听到这样的事情，便召见陈鸾凤，问他事件的始末缘由。鸾凤回答说："我年轻的时候，年轻气盛，一身是胆，不信鬼神雷电等物，只要是没有好好照顾百姓的，我宁愿牺牲自己的生命，来解救天下苍生，就算是玉皇大帝也不能放纵雷鬼到处惹是生非。"

林绪听了陈鸾凤一番话，对于他的义行十分欣赏，于是赏给他很多金银财宝，希望他能继续维持正义，作为乡里的表率。后人于是封陈鸾凤为雨师、雨伯，请他代雷公职位，专门掌管人间降雨一事，因此特别受到江南地区农民的爱戴。

P132 唐代传奇：邓甲（蛇天师）

唐朝宝应年间，有一个叫邓甲的人，为求得仙术，四处寻访名师，一日终于达成心愿，拜茅山道士峭岩为师。峭岩是一个真正懂得法术的人，可以点石成金、使符咒召用鬼神。邓甲拜师非常诚恳用心，一点儿也不觉得累，甚至连晚上都不敢沉睡，白天更不敢赖床偷懒。

峭岩看在眼里，非常感动。但是邓甲的天资似乎不足，这个法术也学不会，那个法术也不行。点石成金、符召鬼神更是不用说了。因此峭岩道士认为他和这两种法术没有缘分，不可强求。所以另外教他一种神奇的召蛇术，据说世界上只有他一个人会，经过数年的苦学，邓甲终于学成下山了。

邓甲行至乌江畔时，碰巧遇到会稽的县令，因为被蛇咬到，痛苦难当，哀嚎之声震惊四周的邻居，请各地名医，也都束手无策，因此邓甲决定帮他医治。他先用符咒保住县令的心脉，痛楚马上就停止了。邓甲又说："一定要找到咬你的那条蛇，取它的毒液来治疗你，不然的话，你的脚就保不住了。"

但是蛇类不愿接近人类，因此邓甲便走到数里外，在一片桑园林中开起了一个神坛，神坛广场约四丈长宽，用红色的布条将四边围住，准备召来附近的毒蛇。十里内的蛇群，不断地从四面八方涌来，堆积在神坛之上，大约有一丈多高，不知道有几万条。蛇群后方有四条大蛇，每条长约三丈，体围像水桶一般粗大，盘附在蛇堆上。

这个时候虽然是盛夏时节，但百余步附近的花草、树木全都变黄枯萎，可见毒气冲天。邓甲光着脚，攀附神坛边缘，爬到蛇堆上面，用青色的藤条敲打那四条大蛇的脑袋说："派遣你们做地方的霸主，掌管附近的蛇群，不得用毒伤人，愿意听从的就留下，不愿意的就叫它走。"

语毕，邓甲纵身向后跳下，蛇堆顿时崩倒，大蛇先行，小蛇紧随在后，蛇群转眼间便走得精光。只剩下一条小蛇，体呈土色，约尺余长，不敢离开，邓甲于是叫县令过来，把脚放下，叫小蛇把毒收回，起初小蛇畏畏缩缩的面有难色，邓甲再出声吆喝，小蛇被吓得缩成几寸长，而且汗流浃背，不得已之下只好张开口，从县令的伤处吸吮出毒液。

县令突然觉得脑袋里面，好像有东西如针似的往下蹿，小蛇跟着皮开肉绽化为一滩血水，只剩下一条白细的脊椎骨留在地上，县令的病痛也跟着好了，于是赠送许多金银财宝给邓甲作为厚礼。

那时有个叫维扬的人，常常玩蛇取乐，他家的蛇有上千条，因为很有钱，故建有大宅第，他死了以后，他儿子想把宅院卖了，可是却对那些赶也赶不走的蛇群莫可奈何，于是重金礼聘邓甲，于是邓甲给了他一道符，结果那些蛇很快地全都跑出城外去了，大宅第也就顺利卖出。

邓甲后来到了溪梁县，时值春季，茶园里面向来就有毒蛇横行，人们都不敢进去采茶叶，因为被毒蛇咬死的已经有好几十个人了，人们知道邓甲有召蛇的神术，因此赠予金银财宝、绫罗绸缎，请他来为民众除害。邓甲于是开坛设法，调召此地的蛇王，结果有一条约丈余长的大蛇，体粗如人的大腿，体色呈锦色闪闪发亮到来，而且身后还跟着约万余条的蛇群。

这时大蛇单独攀登上神坛，要与邓甲一较高下。大蛇昂首而起，高约数尺，想要高过邓甲的头部。这时邓甲利用一根手杖，顶着他的帽子举起，高度胜过大蛇。结果大蛇因为不能高过邓甲所举起之帽，顿时化成一滩血水，尾随在后的蛇群跟着也都暴毙而亡。幸好如此，不然蛇首若高过邓甲的话，今天化为血水的将是邓甲而非大蛇了。从此以后，茶园之内再也没有毒蛇作怪了。邓甲后来归隐茅山研习道术，相传到今天依然存活。

少林寺
Shaolin Temple

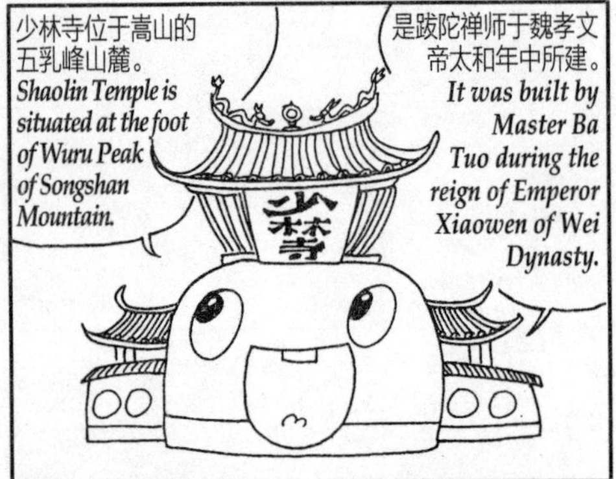
少林寺位于嵩山的五乳峰山麓。
Shaolin Temple is situated at the foot of Wuru Peak of Songshan Mountain.
是跋陀禅师于魏孝文帝太和年中所建。
It was built by Master Ba Tuo during the reign of Emperor Xiaowen of Wei Dynasty.

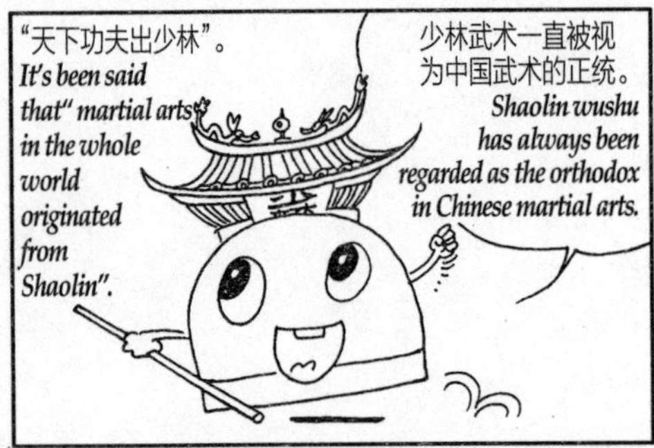
"天下功夫出少林"。
It's been said that" martial arts in the whole world originated from Shaolin".
少林武术一直被视为中国武术的正统。
Shaolin wushu has always been regarded as the orthodox in Chinese martial arts.

少林寺有嵩山少林与泉州少林，俗称南北少林。
There are two branches of Shaolin—Songshan Shaolin and Quanzhou Shaolin, also known as northern and southern Shaolin.
北
南

行！
OK!
当当当当！
Dang, dang, dang, dang!
打赢的出场演这档漫画剧。
The winner will start in this cartoon drama.
北
南

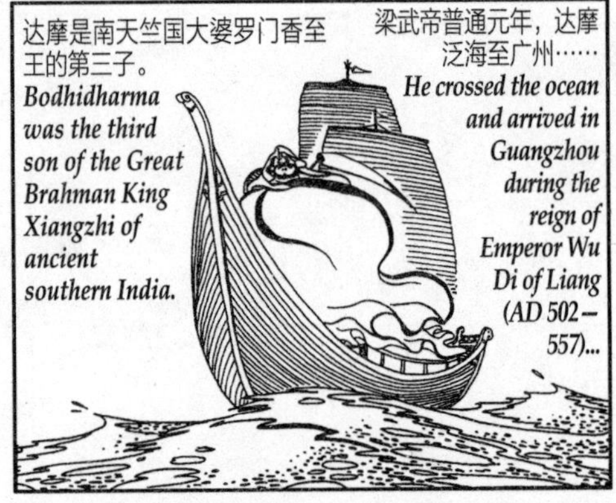
达摩是南天竺国大婆罗门香至王的第三子。
Bodhidharma was the third son of the Great Brahman King Xiangzhi of ancient southern India.
梁武帝普通元年，达摩泛海至广州……
He crossed the ocean and arrived in Guangzhou during the reign of Emperor Wu Di of Liang (AD 502–557)...

梁武帝派遣使者迎接他到南京。
The emperor sent an envoy to bring him to Nanjing.

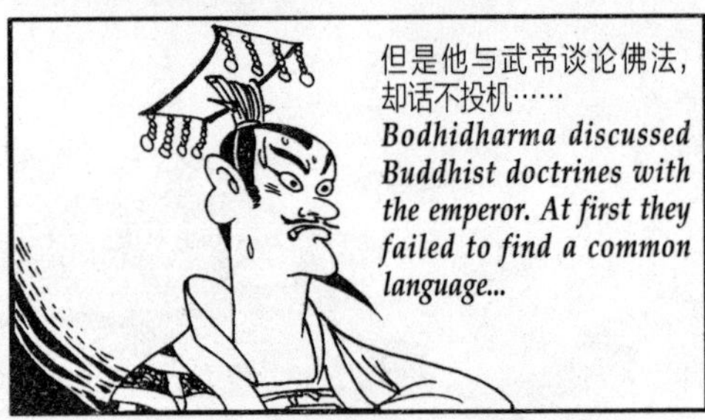
但是他与武帝谈论佛法，却话不投机……
Bodhidharma discussed Buddhist doctrines with the emperor. At first they failed to find a common language...

有没有听懂啊？
Any idea what he's saying?

达摩自知跟梁武帝的法缘不合，就北上到魏。
Bodhidharma knew there was no rapport between him and the emperor, so he went north to Wei.

天竺来的高僧呢？
Where's the monk from India?!
走了。
He's left.

陛下真是视其人而没能看见，会其人而没能会到，太可惜了。
It's a pity Your Majesty looked at him without seeing him, received him without meeting him.
有什么可惜的？
Why?

信奉他所传的教，或许能得到牛油、面粉和衣服的补助啊！
We may get aid in the form of butter, wheat and clothes by converting to his religion!

同年十一月十九日，达摩即从梁渡过长江进入北魏。
On the 19th day of the 10th month in the same year, Bodhidharma crossed the Yangtze River and entered the northern State of Wei.

哇，不用坐船，一苇渡过长江呢！
He crossed the river on a sheaf of reeds!
好神奇！
Terrific!
好棒！
Wow!

是印度的瑜伽钢丝特技，一点也不神奇。
It's no miracle! It's the tightrope walking skill of yoga.

达摩渡过长江，便来到河南的嵩山少林寺。
After crossing the Yangtze River, Bodhidharma came to Shaolin Temple in Henan Province.

你来此有何贵干？
What's your purpose in coming here?
我来自天竺，到中土弘扬佛法。
To propagate Buddhism in China.

佛法乃人之大事，欲登涅槃之岸，莫要太迟！
Buddhism is of great value to humans. Don't miss this chance to enter the world of Nirvana!

可是你却来得太迟，寺僧全都去了天竺。
But you're the one who's late. All the monks here have gone to India.
!

这时有位姓姬的俗家人，特地来到少林寺求见达摩祖师。
At this time, a man called Ji Guang-guang came to Shaolin Temple to see Bodhidharma.

请收我为徒，教我佛法吧。
Please accept me as your disciple and teach me Buddhism.
想拜我为师，得法缘相合才成。
To be my disciple, you've to be in rapport with me.

我天生有佛缘，命该做和尚。
I am a born Buddhist. I'm destined to be a monk.
何以证明？
How can you prove it?

我从小顶上光光不长一毛，不正是天生的和尚命？
I was born bald. Doesn't that prove I'm destined to be a monk.

师父！求求您收我为徒吧！
Please accept me as your disciple, Master!

!

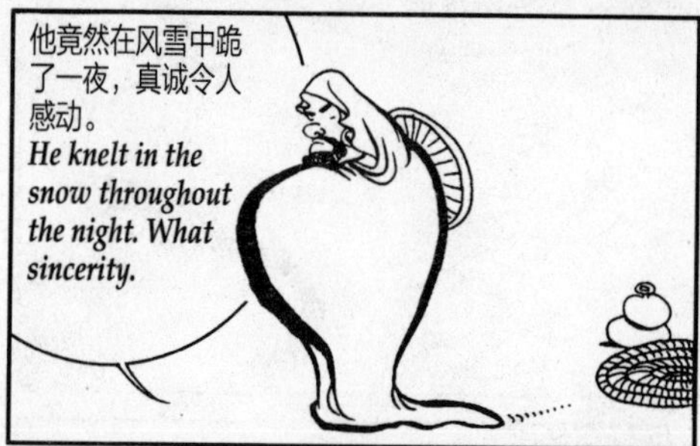
他竟然在风雪中跪了一夜，真诚令人感动。
He knelt in the snow throughout the night. What sincerity.

?

师父您再不答应，我就断臂求法！
If you still refuse to accept me, I'll cut off my arm.

诸佛为求法，不把身体当身体，不把生命当生命，你断臂求法，我也不会答应！
To attain enlightenment Bodhisattvas think nothing of their bodies and lives. I'd still say no even if you cut off your arm!

好吧，穷则变，变则通……
Well, then! Desperation leads to a desire for change, and change brings about success...

你答应，还是不答应？
Will you accept me?
哇！我答应！答应！
Wah! I will! I will!

* Electrocardiogram

我替你落发受戒，
正式收你为徒。
I'll shave your head and initiate you into monkhood, and formally accept you as my disciple.

今后你即是出家之人，应守戒律不杀生，不吃肉。
Now that you're a monk, you should abstain from killing animals and eating meat.

可是我原本光头，
无发可落啊……
But I am bald. There's nothing to shave...

肉吃不得，
皮可穿得？
Eating meat is not allowed. Is wearing leather allowed?
不成！
Of course not!

剃度仪式是非
做不可的。
This ritual is indispensable.

凡是有情众生身躯的
任何部分，皆不可用。
Using and body part of and living creature with feelings is not permitted.

这瓶生发水你拿回去擦，
待长出头发再来剃度吧。
Rub this hair lotion on your pate. Come for the shaving ceremony when your hair grows.

可是师父的拂尘不也是
马尾做的吗？
But Master, isn't your whisk made of horse tail?

《般若心经》是佛学中最重要的经书，我来教你念！
The Prajnaparamita Heart Sutra is the most important Buddhist classic. I'll teach you to recite it.

空中无色。无受想行识。无眼耳鼻舌身意……
There are no senses in the void. No thoughts, actions or knowledge. No eyes, ears, nose, tongue, body, ideas...

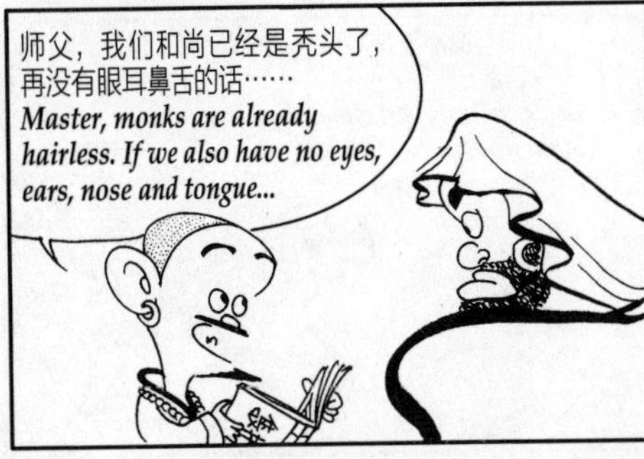
师父，我们和尚已经是秃头了，再没有眼耳鼻舌的话……
Master, monks are already hairless. If we also have no eyes, ears, nose and tongue...

那岂不变成蛋头了？
...wouldn't we become eggheads?

我要重振少林，弘扬佛法！
I want to rebuild Shaolin and spread Buddhism!
好极了！
Great!

可是没有经费啊！
But you lack funds!

人的自身，一切既足，不假外求。经费由我来筹。
Man is self-sufficient; no outside assistance is needed. I'll raise the money.

达摩画像，自产自销，每张只卖二十两。
Portrait of Bodhidharma, self-produced and marketed. Only 20 taels each.
我买一张！
I'll buy one!

一天就卖了二十多张，
筹得经费四百多两。
More than 20 copies were sold in one day. More than 400 taels have been raised.*
20
×22
440

师父的造型独特，有个性，我来想办法将它商品化。
Master, you've a unique image and character. I'll turn it into a commodity.
应该怎么做？
How do you go about it?

这个问题交给我来办！
Leave it all to me!

新开发产品，新奇不倒翁玩具。
Newly developed product—a unique roly-poly.
好棒！
I'll have one.
我买一个！
Wow, how nice!
嘻嘻 Hee, hee.

重振禅门立下招牌招收学生吧。
To restore the prestige of Buddhism, let's put up a sign to enrol students.
免费教授《楞伽经》
Free instruction on Lankavatara Sutra

一个学生也没有……
Not even one student...
免费教授《楞伽经》
Free instruction on Lankavatara Sutra

穷则变，变则通！
变换一下广告词吧。
Desperation leads to change, and change leads to success! Let's change the wording.

哈哈哈，
果然立竿见影。
Ha, ha, ha, ha. It produces instant results.
免费教授西文
Free instruction on Western language
楞伽经

哇，来报名的很多……
Wow! So many are signing up...

师父！来了好多学生！
Master, many students have come!
我去瞧瞧……
Let me go and have a look...

咦？怎么都是些高龄老翁？
Mmm? Why are they all old men?

考了五十多年考不上秀才进士，和尚总考得上吧？
We've been flunking the imperial exams for more than 50 years. We won't fail this exam, will we?

慧可，你深得我髓，今将禅门衣钵传给你。
Hui Ke, you've got the essence of my thoughts. I'll pass my mantle on to you.
!

师父不可！弟子的确不适合，请传给别人吧。
No, you shouldn't do that! I am unfit for it. Please give it to someone else.

为师法眼绝不会看错，由你接此衣钵最适合不过了。
With my exceptional insight, I can't be wrong. You are just the one to take over my mantle.

但确实尺寸太大，不合身呀！
The size is really too large. It doesn't fit me!

此后由你接引学僧，为人师者要有威严，才足以信服别人。
From now on you will guide the novices. Being a teacher you must be dignified so that people will have faith in you.
像这样？
Like this?

不对，应该这样！
No. Like this!

这种眼神学不来啊……
I can't produce that look...

这样子成吗？
Will this do?
蛋壳
Eggshells
!

今天起我要入关面壁，少林寺就交给你了。
I'm going to shut myself up and meditate. Shaolin Temple will be left in your care.

我在洞里准备了声光画壁，师父的日子就好打发了……
I installed an audiovisual system in the cave, so that my master will spend a nice time there...

!

天天要看这种肥皂剧，犹如置身地狱……
Watching these soap operas every day is like being in hell...
哇……
Waa...

师父闭关多日，
一切无恙吧？
I trust you're
well, Master.

师父您一切还好吧？
How have you been,
Master?

大概是睡着
了吧？
He must be
asleep.

睡不着……
I can't sleep
...

** The Chinese character for "Buddha" is made up of a basic structural part that means "Human", and another part that looks like the mirror image of the money sign $.*

出家人须断绝红尘俗事，
心如止水，不再想亲属。
A Buddhist should cut off ties with the mortal world. His heart should be as calm as stagnant water. He must never think about his family.
弟子早已断念，
绝无谎言。
I assure you that I have given up all thought about the mundane world.

我来试一试便知。
I'll test the truth of your statement.

没错，果然是铁石心肠。
Quite right. You are indeed a man of iron.
锵！

学佛须守禅门清规戒律，
还得诵经吃素，非常辛苦。
A Buddhist must observe Buddhist discipline, like studying scriptures and abstaining from meat. It's a hard life.

弟子从小至今一直
都是吃素。
I have been a vegetarian since childhood.

你还真是个有心人，
从小就做好准备工作。
You are really a conscientious person, starting your preparations so early.

不不不，只因家贫买不起肉食。
No, no, that's not the case. My family is poor and can't afford to buy meat.

好吧，我就收你为徒，传你正法眼。
OK, I'll accept you as my disciple and teach you the essence of Buddhist doctrines.

此后我即是佛门弟子了。
From now on, I'm a follower of Buddhism.

错了，错了！小沙弥要拿大拂尘。
Err...A novice should take a large whisk.

妈妈……
Mummy...

啊?!
Ah?!

咚咚咚咚!
Tock, tock, tock!

可以让我敲敲吗?
May I have a go?
当然可以!
Certainly!

谢谢你,真舒服!
Thank you. That feels great!
咚咚咚
Tock, tock, tock!

咯咯……
Tock, tock, tock!

哎呀! 木鱼有蛀虫……
My! There are worms inside!

真难得很认真地在敲木鱼呢!
He's dong it in earnest. How wonderful!
……咯咯!
Tock, tock, tock!

咯,咯,咯,咯!
Tock, tock, tock, tock!
嘻嘻嘻!
Hee, hee, hee!

哎呀！
Oh no!

应该这样……
Do it like this...

嘻嘻……
Hee, hee...
谢谢您。
Thank you.

瑜伽教室
Yoga Room

请上座吧！
Sit down please!

谢谢！
Thank you.

……

回来!
Come back!
!

走开！走开！
Get lost!
Scram!

能吃得苦中之苦，方可成佛……
Only if you can stand the hardest of hardships can you become a Buddha...

来吧!
来吃晚餐吧。
Come have your dinner.

!

立佛站着拜……
Stand straight up when you do obeisance to a statue of a standing Buddha...

坐佛坐着拜……
Sit down when you do obeisance to a sitting Buddha...

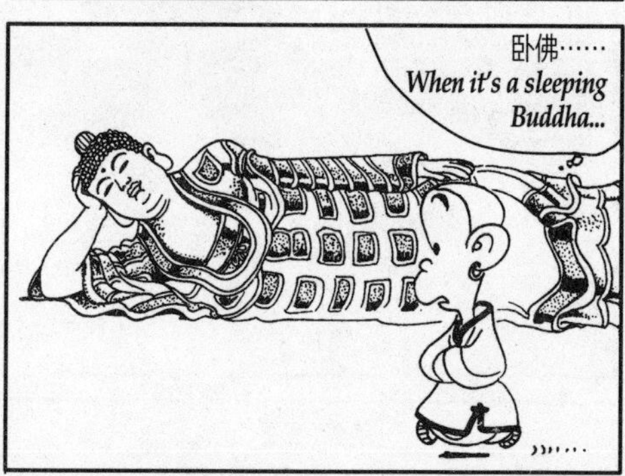
卧佛……
When it's a sleeping Buddha...

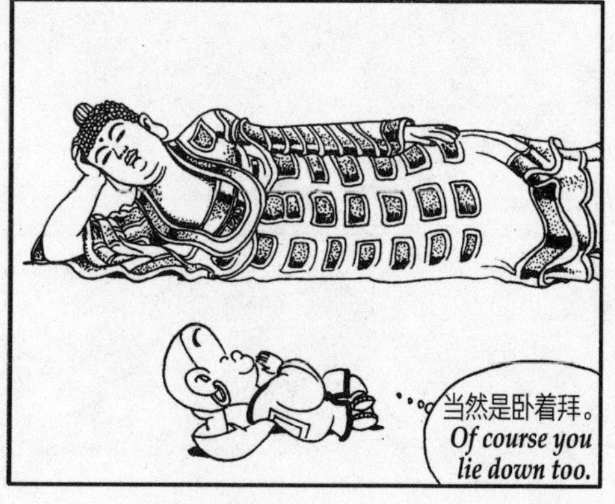
当然是卧着拜。
Of course you lie down too.

呱呱呱呱……
Croak, croak, croak...
呱呱呱呱……
Croak, croak, croak...

夜听蛙声是不错，若是听虫声将更美。
Hearing the croaking of frogs at night is not bad, but it would be even better to listen to the chirping of insects.
没问题！
No problem!

换一卷带子。
Let's change the tape.

零零
Ling, ling...
零零
Ling, ling...

经云："一切声音是佛声。"
It is said in the scriptures:"All sounds are the voice of Buddha."

若得纯真的无心妙用，任何声音皆是佛唱声。
All sounds are the singing of Buddha if your heart is pure.

夜里听昆虫的声音，便会使人心更静。
Listening to the sounds made by insects at night will make you feel even more tranquil.

但不是所有的昆虫声……
But not all insect sounds...
嗡
Buzz...
嗡
Buzz
嗡
Buzz

溪声便是广长舌。
A mountain scene means peace and quiet.

山色岂非清净身。只要悟得这道理。
The sound of a mountain brook is the sound of a long flat tongue.

处处皆是佛唱声！
Once you've realised this, the Buddha's singing can be heard everywhere.

!
呱，呱，呱……
Croak, croak, croak...

自然的
Natural

自然的箫声
演奏会
Natural
Flute Music
A Recital

嗡

喝！
Hey!

万物皆有佛性，不得杀生！
All things are endowed with Buddha's nature. I mustn't take its life!

世事无常，万相皆空，
奉劝施主快入佛门。
This world is everchanging, and the universe is a void. Please convert to Buddhism as soon as possible.
!
素食之妙
Advantages of a Vegetarian Diet

色即是空
The world of senses is a void.

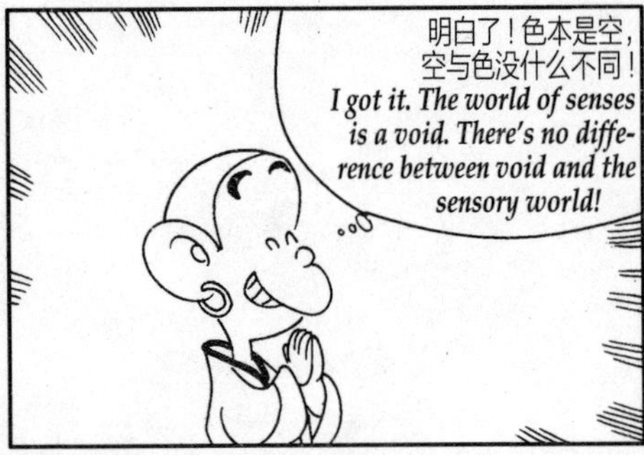
明白了！色本是空，空与色没什么不同！
I got it. The world of senses is a void. There's no difference between void and the sensory world!

空即是色！
Void is the sensory world!
!

不明白……到底空是色，还是色是空？
Now I'm confused. Is the sensory world a void or is void the sensory world?

奇怪……账目不符，怎么少了一两银……
These figures don't tally. I'm short of one tael of silver.

一定是摆在哪儿忘了，找找看……
Must have misplaced it somewhere...

哈！果然找到了三两银。
Ha! I've found three taels.

奇怪……账目不符，怎么多了二两银……
Well, the figures still don't tally. There's a surplus of two taels now...

除夕子时，上山敲除夕钟报春音。
At midnight on New Year's Eve, I ascend the hilltop and sound the bell to usher in spring.

咚咚咚……
Dang, dang!
除夕钟新年快乐……
Happy New Year ...

当，当！
Dang, dang!
当，当！
Dang, dang!
喝！是紧急钟声。
Hey! It's an alarm.

当，当！
Dang, dang!
当，当！
Dang, dang!
当，当！
Dang, dang!
哇！别跑！
Wah! Stop right there!

今天我要讲的佛理是“无”。
My lecture today is no Nothingness.

师父请讲，弟子洗耳恭听。
Please go ahead, Master. I am listening attentively.

你还坐着干吗？我能讲的也是“无”啊！
I've nothing to say on the subject of Nothingness. Why are you still here?
…

禅者无心三昧境，要无心地看，
无心地听，此中包含禅的真谛。
A Zen believer achieves enlightenment without using his senses and reason. He looks and listens without intention. Herein lies the essence of Zen.

师父讲无字公案，
寺里到处贴满了“无”。
Master is lecturing on Nothingness. I see the word" Nothingness"all over the place.
無
無
無

连午饭也“无”！
There is nothing for lunch!
無
無

事实是因为米缸里早已空“无”一物……
The rice vat has nothing...
無
米

真“空”无相、无形、无声，
所以应舍弃佛见法见。
True void is without appearance, shape or sound. Thus, the idea of Buddha seeing with his magic power should be discarded.

是什么声音?
What's that sound?
!

是“空”的声音。
It's the sound of void.

果然“空”也有声啊！
So void does have a sound!
咕噜……

** Here the author makes a pun with the Chinese character 空. When pronounced in the first tone, it means empty or void, but when pronounced in the fourth tone, it means free.*

寒流来了，天气转凉了……
A cold spell has arrived...

你们将自己所证悟的写成偈子，有谁真已悟道便得衣钵。
Write down as a hymn what you've realised through meditation. Whoever has really attained enlightenment will inherit the mantle.

加一件衣服吧，免得着凉。
Put on another jacket, so that you won't catch a cold.

好深奥的禅偈啊！
How profound!
没读过书还能写禅偈，真难得呀。
It is rare that someone who's never been to school can write a Buddhist hymn.

加一件衣服吧，免得着凉。
Put on a coat, so that you won't catch a cold.

hé běn míng pú
chù lá jíng tì
rě wú yí běn
chér yī fei wú
ai wù tāi shù
...
深入浅出。
The profound meaning is expressed in simple terms.

从此你将承传少林衣钵，我会将少林武学全传给你，你想先学什么？
Now you will inherit the mantle of Shaolin. I will teach you everything about Shaolin martial arts. What do you want to learn first?

我想先练少林第一巨著！《少林易筋经》！
I want to work on the greatest work of Shaolin, the Muscle Change Classic.
选得好，只怕你底子太弱，承担不起这巨著。
Good! But I'm afraid you lack the physical condition to begin with.

少林易筋经
第一式练手劲，双手举经半个时辰。
Let's first strengthen your hands. Hold up the sutra with both hands for half an hour.

纵算是武学巨著，也不需要编成这么大本书啊！
Though it's the greatest Shaolin classic, it's unnecessary to print it as such a big book!
少林易筋经

大本巨著不但不容易被偷，还有其他的好处。
A large book like this does not get stolen easily. And it has other advantages too.
少林易筋经

第二式
还可边看边练，眼睛不模糊。
You can read it easily while exercising.

再来是练轻功，首先要种一棵小树……
Now, practise the Light Skill. First, plant a sprig.

随着树的成长，轻功自然跟着进步。
Your skill will improve with the growth of this plant.

五年后……
Five years later...
果然还是能跃过树梢。
Indeed! Now I can leap over the top of the tree.

当初种错了品种啊……
You planted the wrong king of tree...

少林拳讲的是快速勇猛，速度快才有劲道。
The characteristic of Shaolin wushu is its speed and force.

容易！
That's easy!

太极拳刚好相反，动作要慢，慢才能厚实。
Taiji is just the opposite. Movements are slow, but with slowness comes solidity.

难啊……
This is tough...

蛇拳！
The snake punch!

猴拳！
The monkey blow!

熊掌！
The bear paw!

!
?
熊掌？熊掌在哪里？
Bear paw? Where is it?

少林齐眉棍法。喝！
The Shaolin pole skill. Hey!
嗬！
Hey!

我将打通你任督二脉，
把我的真气传到你体内。
I'll open up your veins and pass my vital breath into your body.

我将毕生修行全部转移给你，
这时候务必格外小心谨慎……
I'll pass on to you all that I've acquired through a lifetime of cultivation. Now, be very cautious...

喝！啊！
Hey! Ah!

否则万一走火入魔，
后果可不堪设想。
If you overdo it and go astray, the consequences would be disastrous.

好累啊……
休息一下吧。
Oh, I'm exhausted! Let's take.

喝！啊！
Hey! Ah!

真舒服！
It feels very good!

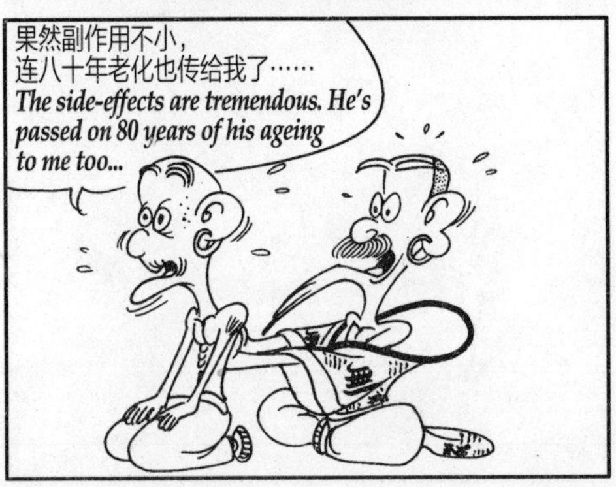
果然副作用不小，
连八十年老化也传给我了……
The side-effects are tremendous. He's passed on 80 years of his ageing to me too...

练武必须练就眼明手快的功夫。
You should train to become sharp-eyed and deft-handed.
嗡
Zirr

眼到心到手到，全部动作一气呵成。
Your eyes, mind and hands should move in coordination.
我也来试试看！
Let me try to do it!

哈哈，没那么简单吧？
Ha, ha, ha! It's not so easy, is it?
哎呀！
Aiya!
嗡

...
抓小的抓不成，抓大的也成。
I couldn't catch the small one but I can catch the big one.

习武者要充分利用自然环境，武器也就信手拈来……
While practising wushu you should make full use of nature, taking whatever is at hand as your weapon...

吃西瓜时，瓜子就是武器！
When you are eating watermelon, melon seeds are your weapons!
~噗噗噗
~Pooh pooh pooh

这叫做“自然武器”，学会了吗？
This is called the “natural weapon”. Have you learnt it!
地瓜
Sweet pota-toes

哇！
Wah!
学会了！
Yes, I've learnt it!
噗噗……
Pooh, pooh...

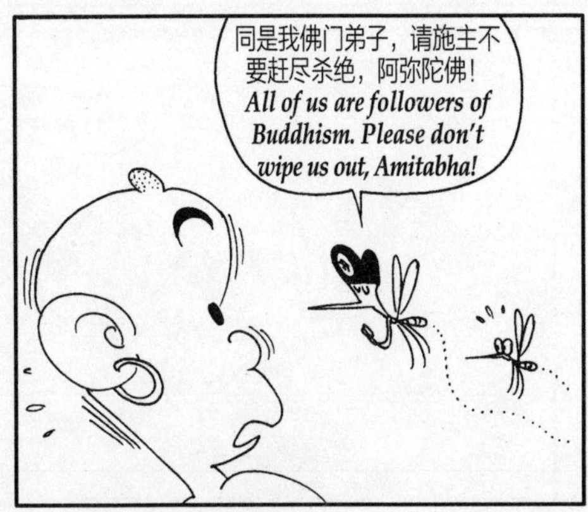

* Shaolin Buddhist Sutra Hall

1 *18 Bronze Men of Shaolin*
2 *The Semi—gods and the Semi—demons*

这些书都是武学经典之著，江湖中人经常到少林盗书。
These are all martial arts classics. Wushu practitioners often come here to steal them.
哦？
Oh?

今天起，你就睡在这里，保护这些书。
From now on, you'll sleep here to safeguard the book.
是。
Yes, Master.

像这两本枪棍秘笈就被偷盗了……
For instance, these two books on the skill of using poles and spears were stolen...

哼！有我在此护着，保证万无一失！
Humph! With me around, they are perfectly safe!

这两本明明还在啊，哪里被盗？
But they are still here. Why do you say they've been stolen?

挖墙鼠辈们，休想到此猖狂偷书！
Thieving rats, don't think you can swipe our books!

被盗版了！
They've been pirated!
三本一百元！
Three books for 100 yuan!
5折书

这里没得混了……
We can't stay on...
赶快搬家吧。
Let's move out...

* This is the literal translation of the Chinese expression which means"commit adultery".

这次受委托到少林寺盗取这批书……
I was entrusted with the job of stealing these books from the Shaolin Temple...
代理
Procuration

少林寺警戒森严，要如何潜入？
The temple is heavily guarded. How do I get in?

这问题难不倒我，就借用这张委托书。
No problem. I'll make use of this trust deed.

这里就是藏经阁……
This is the Buddhist Sutra Hall.

先找武学第一巨著《少林神拳》。
I'll look for the number one classic Magic Boxing of Shaolin.

哈！一眼就看到了！
Ha! It's right here!
少林十八铜人
少林神拳

这部巨著不愧是少林镇山之宝，分量十足……
This book is indeed worth its weight in gold...

谁说少林寺警戒森严？半个少林弟子都看不到。
Who says Shaolin Temple is heavily guarded? I see no one here.

盗贼你别高兴得太早！少林护经弟子如影随形，随身在侧！
Don't rejoice too early, Robber General. The guardian of Shaolin classics is following you like your shadow!

谁？你躲在哪里？有种出来！
Who's that? Where are you? Step forward if you have the guts!

在这里！
I'm here!

大胆狂徒！竟敢潜入少林盗经，还不快认错！
Cocky fellow! How dare you steal from us! Kneel down and ask for forgiveness!

古德说："职业无高低，行行出状元。"
It is said:"All professions are equal; every profession produces its own leading authority."
没错！
True!

先贤说："人要尽其本分，要努力认真工作。"
Sages in the past also said:"Every man must give full play to his telents and work conscientiously."
没错！
True!

那么我是个小偷，每晚辛苦认真工作，何错之有呢？
Then, as a thief why shouldn't I work hard every night?
没错……
True...

挖壁跳墙的小偷也敢强词夺理？看拳！
Resorthing to sophistry? Watch out for my fist!
哈！来得好！
Ha! That's great!

到寺外来比画比画吧！
Let's fight outside!
好！
OK.

杀！
Attack!
喝！
Hey!

看我的"夺命三绝拳"。
Watch out for my Three Fatal Punches.
哇……
Wah...

寝室肃静
Silence to be maintained in the dormitory

师弟的功夫学得不够道地，一急招术就忘光了。
The young monk has not learnt his tricks well. He forgets the movements when he gets excited.
我们做点弊助他一臂之力吧。
Let's resort to a little cheating to help him.

寝室肃静
Silence to be maintained in the dormitory

大本书就有大本的好处。
A big book has its advantages.
哇！
Wah!

古德说："至动无动，至言无言，至射无射，是以不射。"孙子说："不战而屈人之兵，善之善者也。"
A Buddhist ancestor said: "The utmost action is inaction; the ultimate expression is silence; the best shot is not shooting; therefore, do not shoot." Sunzi said: "Defeating enemies without fighting is the best tactic."

这次来到少林除了盗经外，还顺道送比武大会的邀请函来，希望你派人参加！
Besides stealing sutras, I came with a letter of invitation to the martial arts tournament. I hope you'll send a participant.
比武大

比武大会上再见了，在下告辞。
See you at the tournament then. Goodbye!

盛衰无常，石火光中争什么长短？少林寺不会派人去参加比武的。
What's the point of striving for temporary superiority in this fleeting and everchanging world? Our temple won't be sending a representative.

慢着！休想一走了之，接着！
Wait! Don't think you can walk away just like that! Take this!

武当长老说得没错，他早料定少林寺不敢参加！
The Wudang Temple abbot was right. He predicted you won't dare take part!
啊？！
What?!

金钱飞镖……
Coin darts...

可恶的武当牛鼻子！敢嘲笑我少林无能，我偏要参加，与你较雌论雄！
That wicked Wudang ox muzzle dared sneer at us! We shall take part and see who's stronger!

请先替我徒儿到比武大会报名，先交报名费。
please sign up for my disciple and pay his registration fee.

明天你就代表少林，去参加比武大会吧。
You shall represent Shaolin in the tournament.
是。
Yes, Master.

啊！有流星，快趁这个时候许愿吧！
Ah! A shooting star! Make a wish!

请保佑我在比武大会得胜而归……
Please bless me with success at the...

不是流星，是流星飞镖！
It's not a stooting star, but a shooting dart!

你快去准备行李，明早好上路。
Pack your things, so you can set out early tomorrow morning.
是。
OK.

内衣！
Underwear!
棉被。
Quilt.
干粮。
Food.

出门远行一切要靠自己，东西要准备周全。
On a long journey, you've only yourself to rely on, so take everything you need.
是。
Yes.

准备齐全了。
I've got everything I need.
又不是要搬家……
Are you moving house...

这五两银子给你当旅费，拿去吧。
Five taels of silver for your travel expenses.

五两银子怎么够生活一个月，太少了吧？
Five taels of silver is too little. It's not enough to cover my living expenses for a month.

咱们出家人吃素，只吃青菜不吃肉，用钱比较省。
We monks are vegetarians. Your food won't cost much since you are not going to eat meat.

师父真是不知道行情，现在菜价贵过肉价，吃素比吃荤多花钱啊！
Master, you are not aware of present market prices. Now vegetables cost more than meat!
青菜 80
牛肉 20
猪肉 30
Veg. 80
Beef 20
Pork 30

师父请多保重，弟子走了……
Goodbye, Master. Please take care...

想到要离开师父这么久，弟子实在不忍心……
I feel sad when I think of being separated from you for so long...

我也舍不得你走啊！我看还是别去参加了……
I'm reluctant to part with you too. Maybe you'd better stay...
哇！

不不不！我马上就走！
No, no, no! I am setting off at once!

武当山
Wudang Mountain

话说武当山掌门人张三丰外号叫“通微显化真人”。
The head of the school on Wudang Mountain was called Zhang Sanfeng, nicknamed True Man of Tongwei Xianhua.

喝！
Hey!
张三丰本来学的是少林拳……
Zhang Sanfang began his career by learning Shaolin wushu.

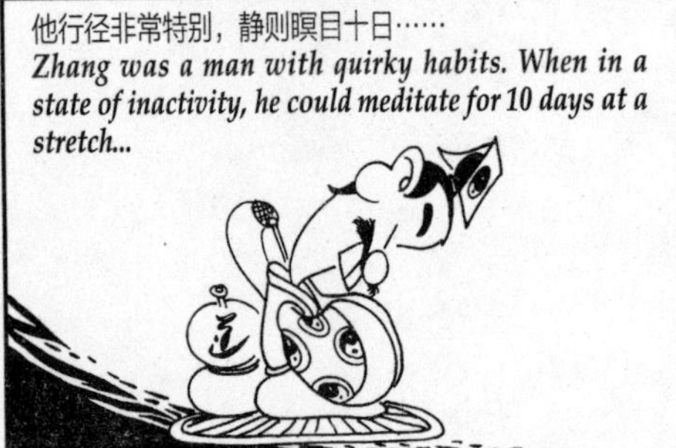
他行径非常特别，静则瞑目十日……
Zhang was a man with quirky habits. When in a state of inactivity, he could meditate for 10 days at a stretch...

这招学得真好！
You've learnt this move well!
谢谢师父！
Thank you, Master!

动则日行千里……
When active, he'd travel 1000 miles a day...

后来因见蛇鹰相斗而自创出武当拳。
Later, he got inspiration from a fight between a hawk and a snake and created wushu of the Wudang style.
呱！

我在全国各地开连锁道观，为了生意来来去去，情非得已。
I've set up a chain of Taoist temples all over the country, so I have to travel back and forth on business.

这招学得真好！
This move is well done!
谢谢师父！
Thank you, Master!

张三丰又见臭鼬与犬相斗而创出了“臭弹神功”……
Zhang also saw a weasel fighting a dog and created the Magic Skill of the Stinking Pellet.

...
有种靠过来试试看！
Try this if you have the guts!

又巧遇虎龟相斗而创出“王八护身大法”。
Once, seeing a tiger attacking a turtle, he created the Turtle's Skill of Self-defence.

出来！
Come out!
大丈夫说不出来就不出来！
Being a true man I stick to my word. I'm not coming out!

张三丰有位嫡传弟子，名叫“大醉侠”。
Zhang had a disciple whom he taught personally-Big Drunk Hero.

能有幸跟我修学功夫，是你前世修来的福。
You have the good fortune to have me as your gongfu master, thanks to your self-cultivation in your previous life.

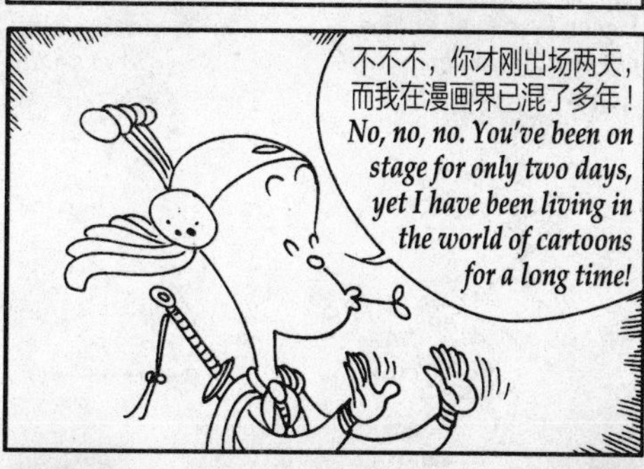
不不不，你才刚出场两天，而我在漫画界已混了多年！
No, no, no. You've been on stage for only two days, yet I have been living in the world of cartoons for a long time!

能有幸演我大醉侠的师父，是你前世修来的福。
You earned the good fortune to play the role of my master through self-cultivation in your previous life.

大醉侠以醉为名，当然是终日以酒为伍。
As the word"drund"in his name showed, he spent all his days guzzling alcoholic drinks.
酒
酒
酒

大醉侠！我来与你拼酒，看谁的酒量大！
Big Drunk Hero, I dare you to drink with me and see who can hold more liquor.

酒？我一听到酒字就醉了！
Liquor! I am drunk as soon as I hear the word!
这么不能喝酒？
Is your capacity so small?

我如果能千杯不醉，怎么会叫做大醉侠？
If I could stay sober after drinking 1000 cups, would I be called a"drunk"hero?
果然不虚“醉”名……
So the word "drunk" in your name is indeed true...

想当年我见了蛇鹰相斗，体会出以柔克刚的功夫……
I recall that when I saw a snake fighting a hawk, I realised that the soft could overcome the hard...

于是自创出以守为攻的武当拳术。
Thus I created the Wudang punck of attack by means of defence.

喔喔喔
而今你见了公鸡振翅，体会了什么心得？
Now what do you realise when you see a cock flapping its wings?

我想到了炸鸡翅加薯条和饮料，可开快餐连锁店。
It reminds me that with fried chicken wings, French fries and a beverage, I can establish a fast-food chain.
M

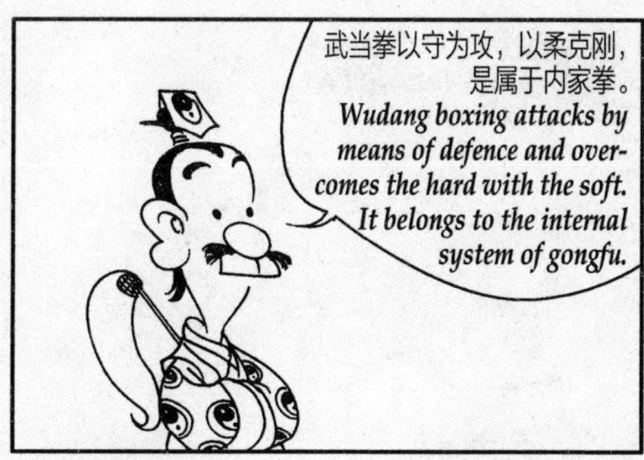
武当拳以守为攻，以柔克刚，是属于内家拳。
Wudang boxing attacks by means of defence and overcomes the hard with the soft. It belongs to the internal system of gongfu.

这种内家拳是当今江湖中的最佳拳术。
The internal system is now the most popular in gongfu circles.

但江湖中人却公认少林拳最好。
But insiders generally acknowledge Shaolin gongfu as the best.
胡说！
What rubbish!

少林拳将失传于世，而武当拳将发展成太极拳独步江湖。
Shaolin gongfu will be lost from the world, while Wudang gongfu will develop into taiji boxing and become unrivalled.

这日张三丰突然心血来潮，于是掐指一算……
One day Zhang Sanfeng had a brainwave. He calculated on his fingers and predicted...

哎呀不好！
My goodness!

师父您算出了什么大事要发生？
What have you foretold, Master?

没什么事情，只是手指抽筋……
Nothing! I have cramps in my fingers...

江湖中正有一场比武大会，
少林也派出弟子参加了。
A wushu tournament is being held and some Shaolin followers are participating.

咦？你的师兄大醉侠呢？
Where's Big Drunk Hero?
他正潜心勤练功夫。
He's engaged in intensive training.

他在后堂已练了一天一夜了……
He's been practising round the clock...
孺子可教也，我武当有望了。
A promising young man! There's hope for our Wudang school.

功夫不分大小，样样都重要，
现在我正在练“应酬功夫”。
All skills are important, be they major or minor skills. I am now practising the "socialising skill".

竟喝成这样，不成体统！
This is downright outrageous! You're soused with liquor.

真是世风日下，一代不如一代，应该要好好地教训教训你。
The world has gone to the dogs. Each generation is inferior to the previous one! I must teach you a good lesson.

喝！
Hey!

想当年我一喝就是几百斤，
哪像你一次只喝几瓶就醉醺醺！
In the old days, I drank several hundred catties of liquor at one go. Look at you, a few bottles have made you tipsy!

** These are phrases people shout when they play the finger–guessing game while drinking.*

最后关头，紧急传你武当拳中最厉害的“小九天拳”。
Now, I'll teach you the Little Nine-Day Boxing, the most powerful Wudang boxing skill.

“小九天拳”是超级慢速拳，一趟拳得打九天！
It is a super-slow boxing movement. Each set of movements takes nine days.

他先被打败了……
He's already defeated...
Z Z z

攻过来！我把压箱绝活传给你。
You attack and I'll teach you my secret skill.
是。
Yes.

喝！
Hey!
哎呀！
Aiya!

师父要传授的是挨打的功夫？
Are you teaching me the skill of taking a beating?

不！是狗皮膏药的疗伤功夫。
No. I'm teaching you the skill of using dogskin plaster to heal a bruise.

行家一出手，便知有没有。
As an expert, I can assess your skill as soon as I see your opening move.

是。
Yes, Master.
你对我打一掌，我便知此行是否能马到成功。
Hit me once. I'll know if you'll enjoy instant success at the tournament.

看掌！
Watch this!

太阳丘饱满，事业线顺畅，大吉大利。
I see a smooth career line on your palm. You are blessed with luck.

不过以你这种功夫，到了大会也打不出名堂。
But with your skills now, you won't achieve anything at the tournament.

功夫好坏不会影响参加这场比武大会的意义！
That won't lessen the significance of participating in the tournament!

你明白参加比赛的意义？
Do you know the significance?
明白。
Sure.

志在参加，不在得奖！
My purpose is to participate and not to win!

大醉侠，你今晚要沐浴斋戒，
明天好上路。
Big Drunk Hero, bathe and fast tonight, so that you can set out tomorrow.
是。
Yes, Master.

大醉侠啊！此去定要认真比武技！
Big Drunk Hero, you must take the tournament seriously!
是。
Yes, Master.

弟子定为武当争气，
夺回奖杯得第一！
I vow to win credit for Wudang and bring back the most trophies!

酒

哇！
Wah!

吹牛皮的功夫
倒真是天下第一！
Your bragging skills are truly the best in the world!

比 武 大 会

The Tournament

往韩山去，应走哪条路啊？
Which is the way to Hanshan?

投石问路，不就明白了吗？
Throw a stone. Then you'll know the way.

多谢指路。
Thank you for showing me the direction.

等一等，你要到韩山比武？
Wait! Are you going to Hanshan for the tournament?
是啊。
Oui.

小弟也要到韩山，正好同路。
I am going there too.
刚好有伴。
I'll have company then.

在下大醉侠，是武当弟子，阁下是哪里来的？
I am Big Drunk Hero from Wudang. Where are you from?
看我的头也知道我从哪里来的。
You'll know where I'm from by looking at my head.

我明白了，是刚从“龟山监狱”出来的？
Oh, I see. Just been released from the Guishan jail?
...

*This is a kind of children's game.

* *A dumpling is made of glutinous rice wrapped in bamboo or reed leaves shaped like a pyramid.*

话说江湖中有家“韩江烤肉”非常有名……
It is said that there was a famous restaurant called Hanjiang Barbecue...
酒

韩江主人平时喜欢研读功夫……
The restaurant owner is an avid student of gongfu...
咳

本店各种肉类都烤，要吃什么就烤什么。
We serve all kinds of roast meat. Whatever meat you wish to eat is available.
牛肉 羊肉
鹿肉 马肉
熊肉
Beef Mutton
Venison
Horse meat
Bear meat

啐！
Pooh!

我想来份烤人肉，行吗？
I wish to have roast human meat. Is that OK?
行！
Certainly!

哇！
Wah!
材料自备！
You'll provide the ingredients!

偶然机会证得绝技，成为一代宗师。
By chance he acquired a unique skill and became a master.
专授
吐痰神功
一代宗师韩江主人
Instruction in the Magic Skill of Spitting Master of great learning Master of Hanjiang

到这家店
吃饭吧。
Let's eat at this restaurant.
酒

出家人不吃荤，来点素菜吧。
Being a monk, I don't eat meat. We'll have a vegetarian dish.
好。
Coming right up.

就来些韩国泡菜，
青菜总是素菜吧？
Have some Korean pickles. It's made of green vegetables.

葱、韭、蒜等有辣味的蔬菜
也是荤菜啊。
But we Buddhists are forbidden to eat strong-smelling vegetables like onion, leek and garlic.
真麻烦……
So annoying...

那么喝碗青菜汤
下饭吧？
What about a pakchoi* soup to go with rice?
谢谢。
Thank you.

这碗汤也是荤的，
吃不得……
No, we can't drink the soup...

青菜豆腐汤怎会是荤菜？
There's nothing besides pakchoi and bean curd in the soup. Why can't you eat it?

还是活的呢！
It's still alive!
苍蝇！
A fly

* Cabbage

这是本店招牌菜
“人参汤”好吃又营养。
This is ginseng soup, our house specialty. It's delicious as well as nourishing.

哇！
Wah!

我佛慈悲，原谅我看到不该看的。
Merciful Buddha, please forgive me for seeing what I shouldn't have seen.
人参汤也见不得？
Ginseng soup?

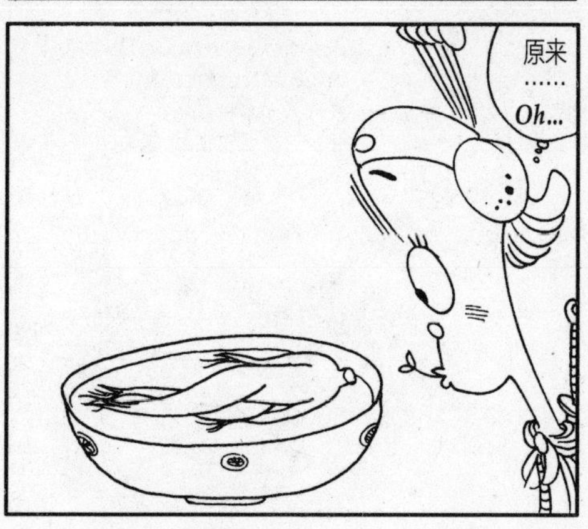
原来……
Oh...

两位想必也是来参加擂台大赛的？先与小弟比划一下如何？
You two must be here to participate in the tournament. How about having a contest with me first?

这人是四川暗器唐门的弟子，任何东西一经他手，皆可成为暗器！
He's from the Tang school of Sichuan that specialises in secret weapons. They can turn anything into secret weapons!

难道嘴中吃鱼也能变成暗器？
Ha, how can he turn the fish he's eating into a secret weapon?

鱼刺……
Fish bones...
当然可以！
We sure can!

我也以暗器对付你。
I can also use a secret weapon against you.
哈!
Ha!

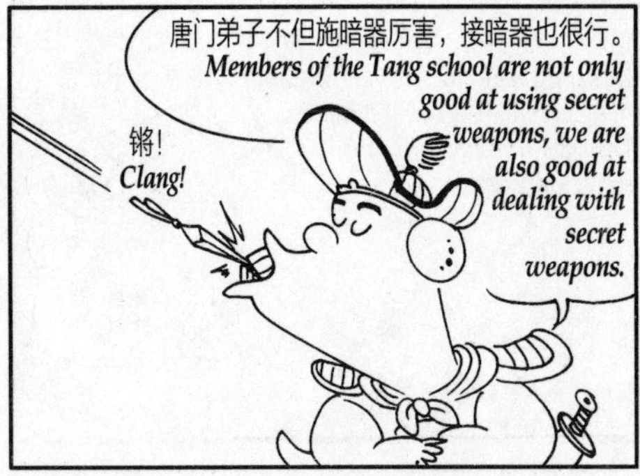
唐门弟子不但施暗器厉害，接暗器也很行。
Members of the Tang school are not only good at using secret weapons, we are also good at dealing with secret weapons.
锵!
Clang!

用嘴接住暗器，这招厉害。
That's powerful, catching a secret weapon with his mouth.

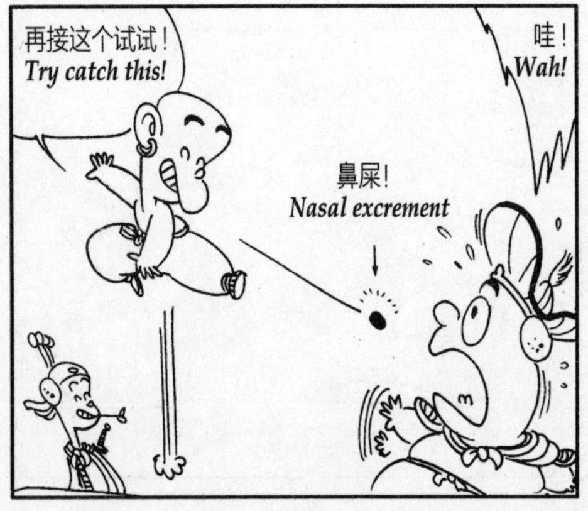
再接这个试试!
Try catch this!
哇!
Wah!
鼻屎!
Nasal excrement

游侠江湖最恨暗箭伤人，施暗器实在令人不齿。
Using secret weapons is what we roving heroes hate most. We despise people who do this.

兄台所言甚是，暗器伤人确实不够光明……
You're quite right. It's ignoble to hurt others by underhand means.
所以我暗器门人已经自律改正这个缺点。
Therefore, I have mended my ways.

看镖!
Watch out!

施放暗器前一定先喊“看镖”，让人先听清楚。
I warn my opponent before I let loose my secret weapon, so that he is prepared for it.
哇!
Wah!

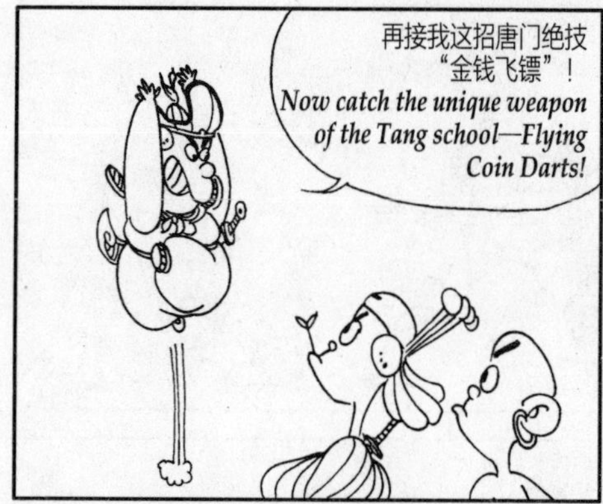

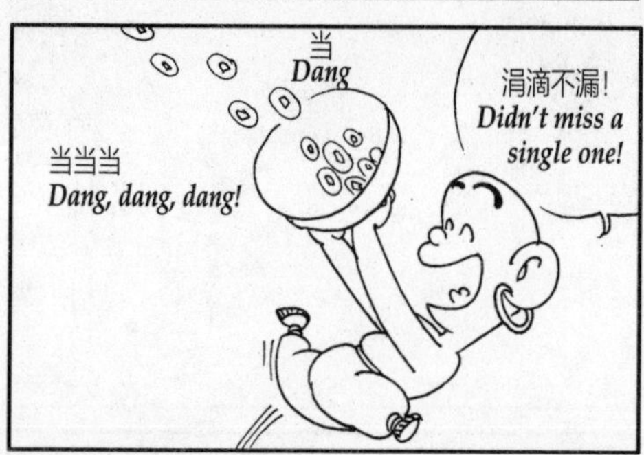

*This is a derogatory Chinese term for a voluptuous woman!

看椅！
Watch out!
这招容易应付。
This is easy to deal with.

看碗！
Watch out for the bowl!
这招也不难应付！
This is not difficult either!

看账！
Watch out for the bill!

这里由你善后，小弟先走一步！
I have to go. You settle the affairs here!
这招可应付不了……
This move is tough...

两桌的账一共二百一十二两银。
Altogether 212 taels of silver.
小意思，由我来付。
A mere trifle. I'll pay.
不不！我来付。
No, no, I'll pay.

浑蛋！应该我来付。
I will pay, you idiot!
当！
Dang!
胡说！应该由我来付。
Nonsense! I must pay.

可恶！
Despicable!
当当当
Dang, dang, dang!
酒

啊！我的账还没付清啊！
Hey! The bill hasn't been paid!
快逃！快逃！
Run! Run!
嘻嘻！
Ha,ha!

本座乃是魔教教主是也，本教创教已经三十年，但……
I am Chief of the Devilish Sect. My sect was founded more than 30 years ago, but...

江湖九大门派竟然一直不肯承认我魔教的存在！
The nine major schools in the martial arts circle have refused to recognise us.

为争取我魔教的法律地位，只好进行恐怖活动！
In order to win legal status for our sect, we've had to resort to terrorism!

嘻嘻！
Hee, hee!
哇！恐怖！
Eeeek! How gross!

江湖各帮派忽视我的存在，所以我要对付他们。
I must hit back at the other schools for ignoring our existence.

存在！
We exist!
存在！
We exist!
存在！
We exist!

有什么比存在更重要呢？
What is more important than existence?

教主！"存在主义"早已不再流行了，现在流行"后现代主义"。
Chief! Existentialism is no longer in fashion. The fad now is postmodernism.

密函到，请收件。
Confidential letter. Please sign here.
怎么是张白纸？
Why is it a blank page?

用火烤字就出现了。
The words will show when you warm the paper over a fire.
果然！
Indeed!
武林比武大会
The Tournament

哇！白脸！
Way! A featureless face!

用火烤脸就出现了。
The features will show when the face is warmed over a fire.

密函指出韩山庄要举行比武大会，江湖各帮派都会参加。
It says a tournament is being held at Hanshan Village. All schools are sending repressentatives to take part.

嘿嘿！这是我们活动的好机会。
Hee, hee. It's a good chance for us.
趁这个绝佳机会做一票！
We must seize this opportunity!

你知道要怎样做吗？
Do you know how to go about it?
当然明白。
Of course I do.

到现场去卖盒饭饮料，赚他一票。
Sell beverages on the premises and make money.
!

笨笨笨笨笨笨大笨瓜！
Stupid, stupid, stupid, stupid fool!

杀手屠夫何在？
Where's Killer Butcher?
弟子在此。
I'm here.

魔教要进行的是恐怖活动，而你只想到小利！
Our purpose is to carry out terrorism, and you only think of making a little profit!

久未派你执行任务，如今要借重你的屠刀功夫。
It's been a long time since I've assigned you a job. I need the help of your butcher's knife.

卖盒饭饮料也是恐怖活动，只是其中加点料。
Selling beverages is also terrorist activity. All we have to do is add something in them.

弟子这段时日，一刻也不曾荒废取命术。
I have not for a moment let my life-taking skill fall into disuse.
好极了！
That's very good!

悄悄地在盒饭饮料中加点毒药……
We can add some poison in the beverages...
聪明！
Clever fellow!

每天都到市场杀鸡七十只。
I kill at least 70 chickens in the market a day.

可悲啊，要进行恐怖活动，
来个杀鸡客有何用？
How pathetic! What's the use of a chicken-killer in the terrorist activities I'm about to conduct?

把这些鸡卖进韩山庄，
就是非常好的主意。
Selling chickens in Hanshan Village is a great idea.

叛逆！怎么可能跟敌人做生意？
Turncoat, how can you do business with the enemy?

如此就能引起当地农民的抗议而进行自力救济，这就是恐怖活动啊。
In doing so, we can arouse the farmers to protest and start selfrelief, which is a terrorist activity.
好计！
Good idea!

三大杀手听令！
Listen, great killers! Here are my instructions.
弟子恭听御旨。
Your disciples are awaiting your decree, Master.

令你等三人至韩山庄比武大会中伺机进行恐怖活动。
Go to the tournament at Hanshan Village and wait for an opportunity to conduct terrorist activities.

这个任务对各位而言只是牛刀小试。
For you people, this task is just a small display of your expertise.

行动闲暇之余，
顺便在场外卖点黄牛票。
You can also scalp some tickets when you have free moments during the action.

比赛的场地都安排好了……
The contest ground is ready...

奖品奖杯也都准备齐全了。
The trophies are all here.

第一个冠军诞生了！
The first champion is born!
比赛都还没开始，哪来的第一？
The contests have not even begun. Where is the champion from?

第一个完成报到手续！
The first one to complete registration.
...
报到
regis-tra-tion

报到第一不能颁奖杯给你。
There's no trophy for the registration champion.

就送你十斤高丽民族的名产当奖品。
But you'll be awarded 10 catties of Korea's most famous product.

能得十斤人参也不赖。
Wow, not bad! Ten catties of Korean ginseng!

不不！是十斤高丽菜。
No, no. It's ten catties of cabbage.

报到处
Registration Area

抱歉！你的资格不符，不得报名参加比赛。
Sorry! You lack the necessary qualifications. You can't enter this contest.

和尚也是人啊，为何不得参加？
A monk is also a man. Why can't I sign up?

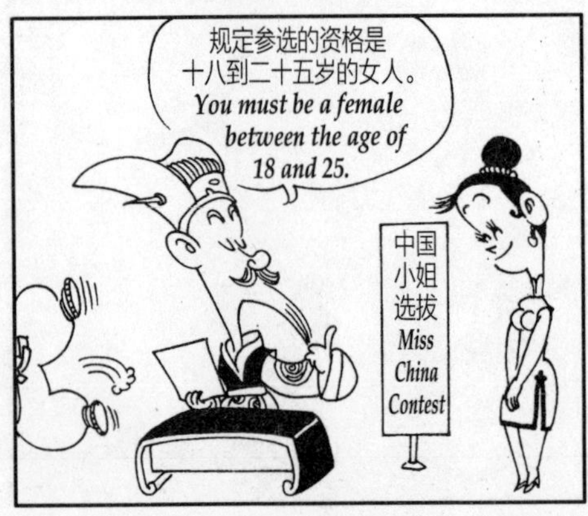
规定参选的资格是十八到二十五岁的女人。
You must be a female between the age of 18 and 25.
中国小姐选拔
Miss China Contest

赛前还得过磅量体重呢！
The contestants have to be weighed!
65 公斤！
Sixty-five kilos!

37 公斤！
Thirty-seven kilos!

恭喜你得到大会的第一个奖杯。
Congrats! You're the first to receive a trophy at the tournament.
?
轻功第一
Took the first

你在所有与赛选手中体重最轻，得第一。
You are the champion as far as body weight is concerned.
轻功第一

为防范恐怖分子，
大会警戒森严……
Strict precautions were taken against terrorists at the tournament grounds...
从门经过。
Please walk through the frame.

通过。
Pass.

铃！
铃！
铃！
你身上有枪弹武器！
You have firearms of ammunition on you!

六个枪疤，子弹还留在体内。
Six bullet—wound scars. The bullets are still inside.

参加搏击的选手，
个个人高马大。
Those taking part in wrestling are heavy-set.

这么瘦小也想参加搏击？
This puny man dares to participate in wrestling?

太重了，
不合规定。
Too heavy! Disqualified.

还得回去
减肥才成。
Have got to lose some more weight.
超轻量级
35 公斤
Weight limit of 35 kilos for super featherweight
不合规定
Disqualified

来自江湖各地的队伍，把大会挤得人山人海。
The grounds were packed with teams of participants and spectators from all over the country.

各帮派精英倾巢而出……
The cream of all schools in the martial arts world turned up at the tournament.
不得奖牌，誓不回去！
We swear not to go home without medals!

有的帮派只来了高级干部……
Some sects sent only high-ranking cadres...
志在观光，不在得奖。
We came for sightseeing, not to win medals.

明早就要比赛了，先参观一下比赛场地……
The competitions will begin tomorrow. I'll go look at the sports ground.

砰！
Bong!
哎呀！
Ouch!

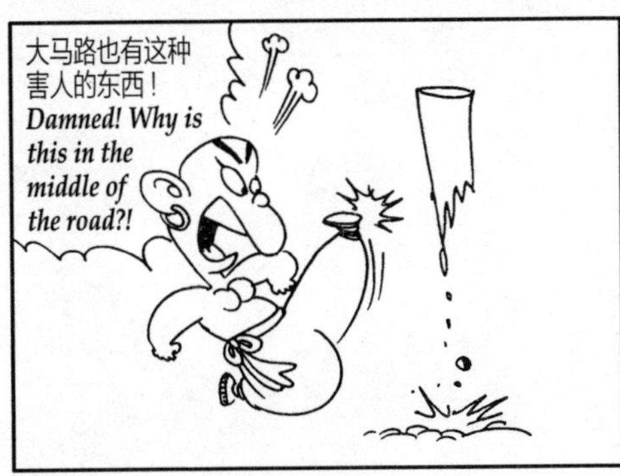
大马路也有这种害人的东西！
Damned! Why is this in the middle of the road?!

为何破坏比赛设施梅花桩？
Why have you destroyed the tree stump installed for the stump-walking race?
…

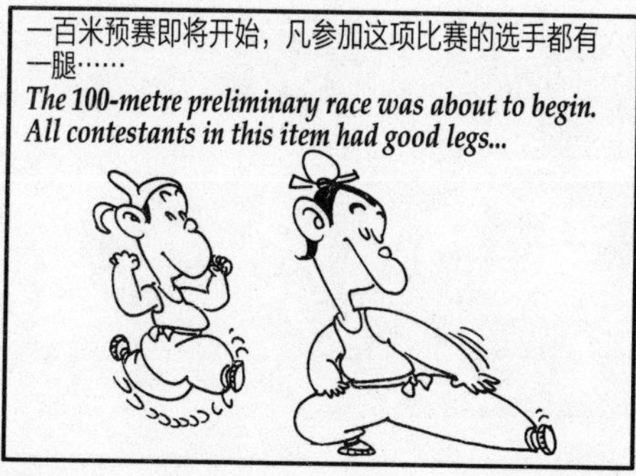
一百米预赛即将开始，凡参加这项比赛的选手都有一腿……
The 100-metre preliminary race was about to begin. All contestants in this item had good legs...

我的是“弹簧腿”！
Mine are spring legs.
哇噻！这招厉害。
Wow! That's fantastic.
蹦！
Bong!
蹦！
Bong!
蹦！
Bong!

我帮你装个“爆炸腿”……
Let me fit you out with an explosive leg...

这下够快了吧？
Aren't you fast?
哇！要爆炸了！
Wah! I'm going to explode!

百米A组预赛
Group A 100-metre preliminary...

砰！
Bang!

好快啊，第一终于产生了！
The number one has emerged. So soon!
真是丢尽了帮门的脸……
What a shame for the whole school!
好没面子！
Disgrace!

第一个弃权的选手……
Number one to give up...

* This is a corruption of a Chinese saying:"The frontiersman loses his horse—a blessing in disguise."It is from a parable about a frontiersman whose strayed horse returned, accompanied by a better horse.

预赛成绩 9 秒 6。
I ran 9.6 secs in the preliminary.
预赛成绩 20 秒 8。
I ran 20.8 secs.

我身轻如燕，决赛你是赢不了的。
I'm as light as a swallow; you have no hope of winning in the finals.

请手下留情，这个请收下。
Please take this and be lenient in the finals.
金子我收下，但不会让给你。
Thanks, but I won't make any allowances for you.

这下可实力相当，势均力敌了。
Now we are equally matched.

百米决赛开始，大醉侠一马当先冲出去……
The 100-metre final began. Big Drunk Hero dashed forward and took the lead...

水准差太远了，足足领先了 10 秒。
He's far behind. I'm at least 10 secs ahead of him.

太藐视人了，竟利用这空当睡午觉……
That hoitytoity fellow is taking a nap...
Z

到！
I've reached the finishing line!

接下来的项目是
"百米木桩竞走"。
The next item is the 100-metre stump-walking race.

走木桩战战兢兢，如临深渊如履薄冰。
I'm walking with great care, as if on the brink of an abyss or treading on thin ice.

对胖子而言，走木柱如履平地。
For a fat man like me, walking on stumps is just like walking on level ground.

哇！木桩都踩平了！
Wow! They have been pushed into the ground!

哈哈，领先！
Ha, ha. I'm ahead of you!

休想赶过我！
Don't think you can catch up with me!

哇！赶过了头了！
Wah! I've overshot!

接下来的项目是
“轻功比试”。
Now comes the Light Skill contest.

我先来一招“蜻蜓点水”。
I'll demonstrate the skill of Dragonfly Skimming the Water Surface.

哇!
Wow!
这种功夫也要献丑……
He's making a display of his poor skill...
轰!
Bang!

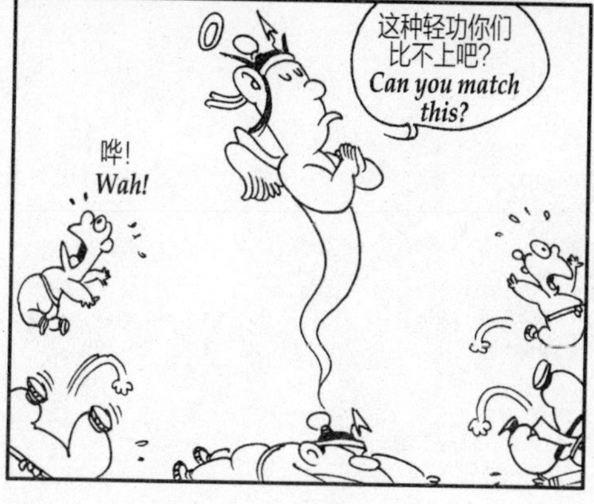
这种轻功你们比不上吧?
Can you match this?
哗!
Wah!

旱地拔葱!
Pulling Up a Scallion from Dry Land!
哗!
好厉害!
Wow!
Terrific!
哗!
Wow!

我俩联手合作，一定能打败他。
We can definitely beat him if we cooperate.
可是我的弹性不好啊……
But, I'm afraid my bounce is no good...

哇!跳得比我还高……
Wah! He jumps higher than I did...
哗!
Wah!
好棒的弹性!
Wonderful!

弹性好的是我的肚皮!
It is my paunch that is bouncy!

* Strike to defend the weak and helpless.
* Kill to wipe out all evildoers.

第一阶段拳脚功夫，
现在宣布比赛开始！
The first stage of the boxing contest begins now!

我是少林弟子，哪位想先上来领教少林功夫？
I am from the Shaolin school. Who would like to have the first taste of Shaolin gongfu!

传闻少林神腿毫无瑕疵，在下想见识见识。
I hear that the leg skill of Shaolin is flawless. I'd like to see it.

恭敬不如从命，在下就为你露一腿吧！
I'll gladly oblige. I shall now exhibit my leg!

在下想领教几招！
I'd like to learn a few moves from you!

你是和尚，我也是和尚，你是少林弟子，我也是少林弟子！
You are a monk, so am I. You are a Shaolin follower. So am I.

这次大赛少林寺只派我一人来，你是哪来的冒牌货？
I'm the only one sent by Shaolin Temple. Where are you from, imposter?
当然不是冒牌货。
I am definitely not an imposter.

你是嵩山少林弟子，
我是泉州少林弟子。
You are a follower of the Shaolin at Songshan, and I, a Shaolin follower from Quanzhou.

少林弟子对少林弟子！
Shaolin versus Shaolin!
和尚对和尚，光头对光头。
Monk versus monk and baldy versus baldy.

南少林决战北少林。
Southern Shaolin in a decisive battle with northern Shaolin.

同样是光头，我的内容比较好。
Both of us are hairless, but I have better stuff inside.

这种少林神腿不够地道。
This is not the genuine Magic Shaolin Kick.

当！
Dang!

让你尝尝正宗少林腿的滋味！
I'll let you have a taste of the real thing.

同样是光头，我的外壳比较硬。
Both of us are hairless, but my crust is harder.
砰砰！
Bong, bong!

抵抗不了吧？
You can't take it, can you?
哇！受不了……
Wah! I can't stand it anymore...

少林弟子果然有两把刷子，
让我来会会你。
The follower of Shaolin is indeed remarkable. Let me take you on.

香帅公子加油啊！
Come on, Fragrant Handsome Master!
加油！
Come on!
谢谢。
Thank you.

何不请你的啦啦队代你上台与我对阵？
Why don't you ask your cheering squad to come up and confront me?
恭敬不如从命，小心接招了！
I'll gladly oblige. Watch out!

加油！加油！
Go, go, go!
这招你可消受不了吧？
This is something you can't stomach.

少林弟子果然纯洁得可爱，
在下万分佩服。
Followers of Shaolin are so pure and adorable. Your humble servant is filled with utmost admiration.

在下风流一世，有朝一日也想到少林出家。
I have lived all my life in pleasure-seeking. Maybe one of these days I'll renounce the mundane world and become a disciple at Shaolin Temple.

这个容易！
That's easy!

少林剃刀神掌，
成全你的心志。
The Magic Shaolin Razor Palm has fulfilled that wish of yours.

嘻嘻嘻！
Hee hee, hee!
哇！
Wah!

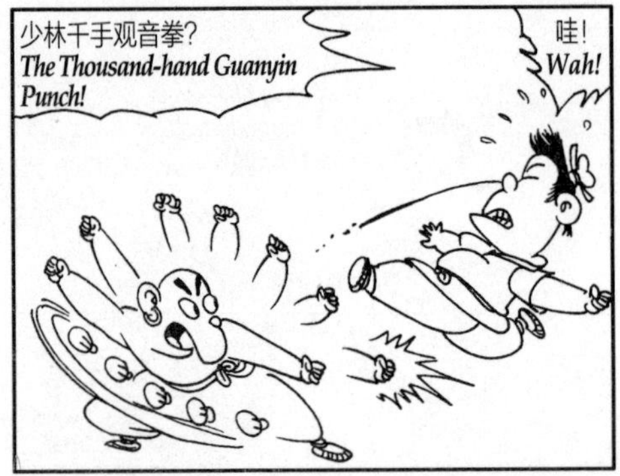
少林千手观音拳？
The Thousand-hand Guanyin Punch!
哇！
Wah!

还有哪位高手想接接我的剃刀？
Are there other heroes who wish to have a try of my razor?
我来。
I do.

还有哪位敢上台领教少林千手拳？
Who else would like to try the Thousand-hand Guanyin Punch!

阁下剃刀神掌果真厉害，在下特来请教。
Your Magic Shaolin Razor Palm is fantastic. I want to try it.
请。
Fine.

指定代打，去将他打下台。
We appoint a surrogate boxer to swipe him off the platform.

拜托你服务了。
Thank you for your service.
…

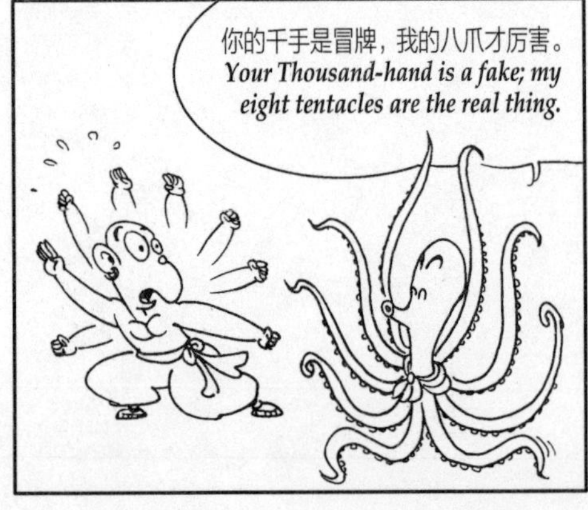
你的千手是冒牌，我的八爪才厉害。
Your Thousand-hand is a fake; my eight tentacles are the real thing.

在下来自东瀛，特来中原领教中国剑。
Your humble servant is from Japan. I came to the Central Plains to learn Chinese sword skills.

来个真剑比试。
Let's use real swords.
行。
Fine.

我上去教训这倭人国来的家伙。
Let me go up to teach this fellow from Japan a lesson.

他的刀长，拔出不易，应用近身肉搏战！
It's difficult for him to pull out his long sword. I'll use hand-to-hand combat tactics.

行家一出场高低已分，胜负立判。
When an expert appears on stage, one can immediately distinguish the winner from the loser.

杀！
Strike!
叱！
Attack!

高
Tall.
低
Short.

不是长刀是短剑，你输。
You lose. Mine is only a short dagger.

* This Chinese saying warns that someone who refuses to cooperate will be dealt with more harshly.

在下“金钱飞镖”敬请指教。
Your humble servant, Gold Coin Darts, begs to learn from you.
行。
OK.

飞镖一出手，百发百中！
My darts never miss the bull's-eye!

明明是百发不中！
Apparently they never hit the bull's-eye!
当！
Dang!
当！
Dang!
当！
Dang!

射中了！
I've hit the target!

当！
Dang!
“小猪”接零钱，恰恰适宜。
My piggy bank is just the thing for coins.
当！
Dang!

当当当
Dang, dang, dang!
嘻嘻，谢谢奉献！
Hee, hee! Thanks for your contribution!

哎呀！钱没了。
My! I've run out of coins.
现在你还有什么招？
What other tricks do you have?

以人头担保向你借点钱救救急……
I pledge my head to borrow some money from you to meet an urgent need...

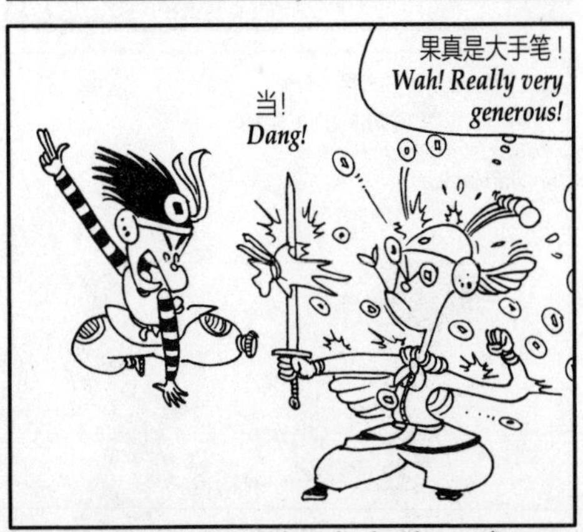

* Zhuge Liang once sent out 20 boats lined with straw figures to meet Cao Cao's troops in a fog. As predicted, the enemies fired arrows relentlessly. Zhuge Liang managed to collect about 150000 arrows.

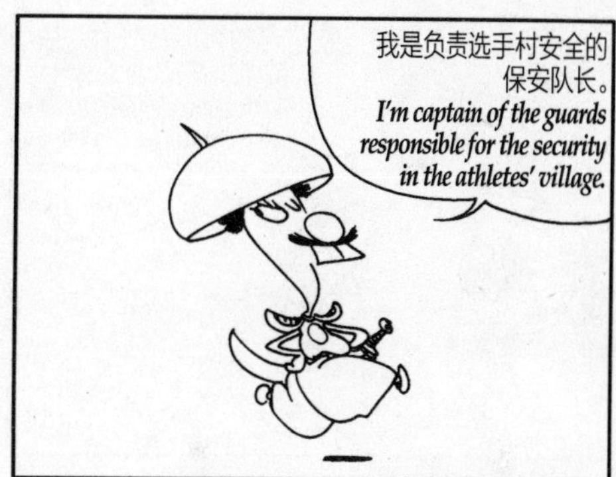

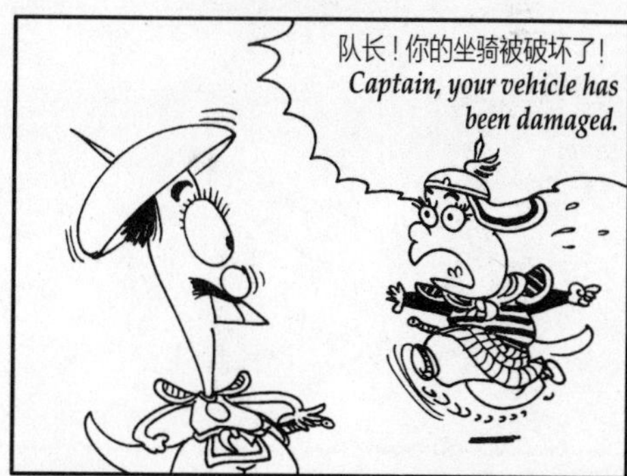

* *As in the previous line, the author is using stock market jargon.*

选手村有我在此把关，任何破坏分子休想越雷池一步！
With me guarding the athletes' village, it's impossible for amy saboteur to elude me!

!

飞天遁地都逃不过我的耳目，出来！
Nothing escapes me! Come out!

!

各位住在选手村，由我负责各位的安全。
Friends, I am responsible for the safety of all athletes staying in the village.

如发现任何坏蛋潜入，请向我报告，谢谢合作。
Please report to me if you find anyone sneaking into our village. Thank you for your cooperation.

报告！选手村刚刚混进了两个坏蛋。
Report! Two villains are slipping into the village.
在哪儿呢？
Where are they?

它们没经过批准，正要飞进去。
They are flying in without a permit.

小师父慈悲为怀，
是否愿意助人？
Young master,you're a kind person.Would you help us?
出家人行善不后人。
Being a monk, I never hesitate to do kind deeds.

想借用小师父的项上人头一用。
I'd like to borrow the head on your shoulders.
!

放心，保证不伤你半根毫毛。
Don't worry. I'm not going to harm you at all.

这生发剂确实有效，准许它进口吧。
This hair lotion is so effective! Issue an import licence for it.
!
是。
Yes, sir.

这种天气热得受不了。
根本睡不着。
It's sweltering! I can't sleep.

鬼！
Ghost!

你来得正好，刚好替我解决了问题。
You've come in time to solve a problem for me.

阴风冷气机，省电又便宜。
A"sinister airconditioner"that saves electricity and money.
...

大醉侠，为师来为你加油鼓劲。
Big Drunk Hero, I am here to cheer you on.
师父！
Master!

选手村警戒森严，师父怎么进来的？
The athletes' village is closely guarded. How did you get in?

这部戏我一人演二角，戴起帽我演保安队长。
I am playing two roles in this drama. With my hat on, I play captain of the guards.

脱下帽我演师父。
And with the hat off, I play your master.

这次比赛有什么问题？
Any problems in the competition?
比赛场次太密，身体酸痛得不得了。
The schedule is too tight. I fell sore all over.

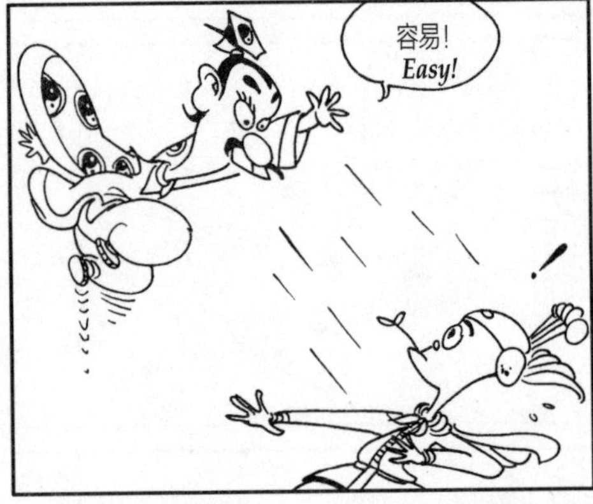
容易！
Easy!

师父！你干什么？
What are you doing, Master?!

针灸治疗。
Treating you with acupuncture.
不错，果真有效。
Not bad. It's really effective.

这次比赛太重要了，以你的功力不足以全胜……
This is a very important tournament. You may not gain complete victory with your skills.

为确保你得冠军，我将毕生的修为全传入你体内。
To ensure that you become the champion, I am transmitting into your body my accomplishment of a lifetime.

大醉侠何德何能，让师父做这么大的牺牲？
What have I done to deserve such a great sacrifice on your part, Master?

因为我把武当的全部庙产押注在你身上，赌你赢！
Because I have betted the entire property of Wudang on you.

还有什么问题需要我解决的？
Is there anything else you want me to do?
住选手村太吵，每天都睡不好。
It's too noisy in the athletes' village. I can't sleep at all.

比赛期间不能用药物……
Drugs are prohibited during the tournament.
所以安眠药不能吃。
I can't take sleeping pills then.

放心，我替你带来了自然的安眠药。
Don't worry. I've brought you a natural sleep-inducer.

这种自然饮料我最喜欢！
Mmm...Wine is still the best!

好酒!
Good wine!

酒弱的人……
He has no capacity for wine...

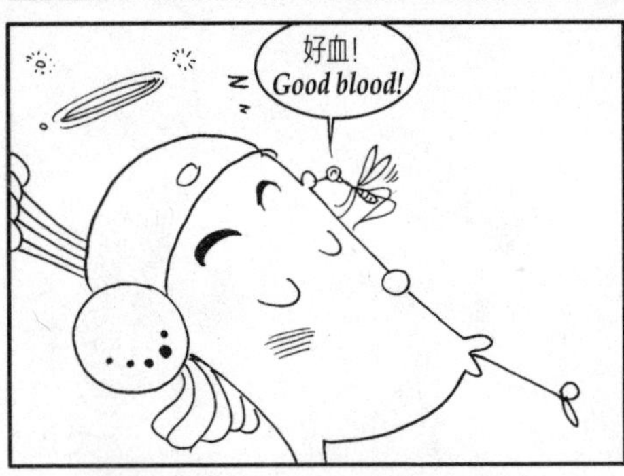
好血!
Good blood!

酒弱的蚊……
It has no capacity for wine...

夜深人静，正好进行破坏活动。
The dead of night is the best time for sabotage.

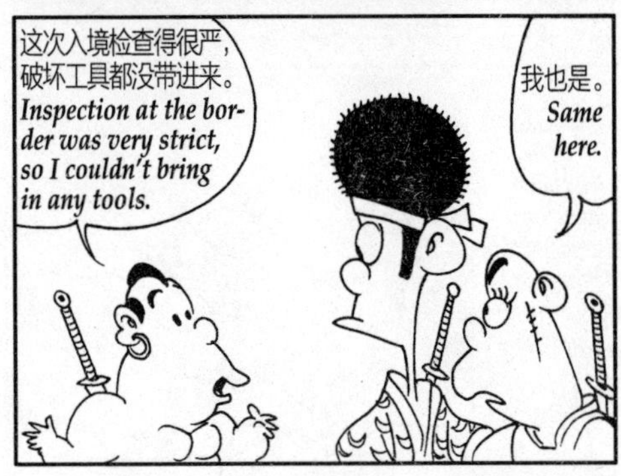
这次入境检查得很严，破坏工具都没带进来。
Inspection at the border was very strict, so I couldn't bring in any tools.
我也是。
Same here.

这要靠自己动脑想办法……
We have to use our heads...

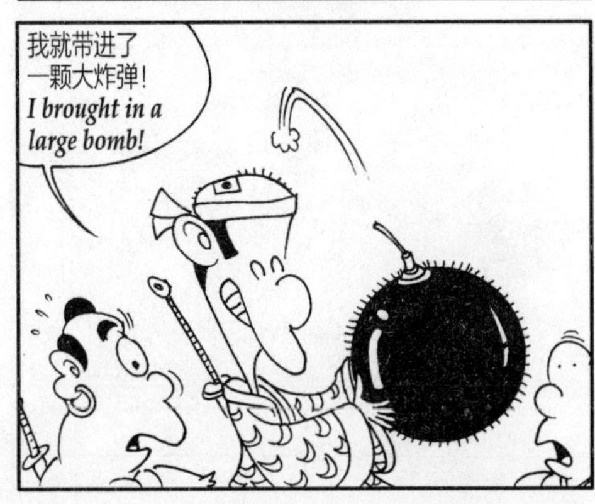
我就带进了一颗大炸弹!
I brought in a large bomb!

你们在此把风，我进去下毒。
You two keep watch here. I'm going in to dispense the poison.

传闻韩山庄机关密布，要小心。
Hanshan Village has many traps. Better be careful.

啊！机关陷阱！
Ah! A trap!

布这种陷阱未免太藐视人……
Laying a trap like this is so insulting...
$100

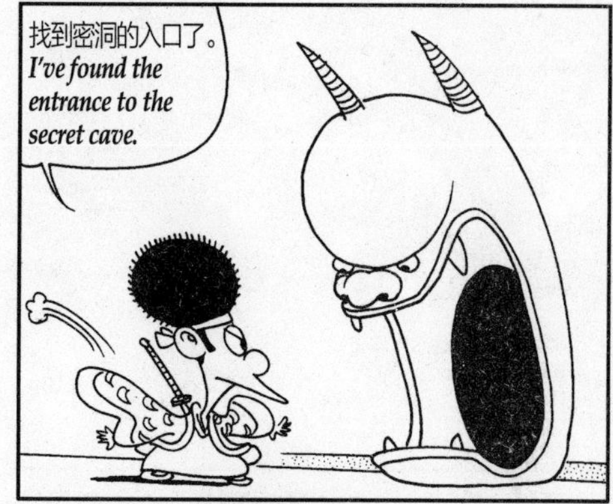
找到密洞的入口了。
I've found the entrance to the secret cave.

咦……
Mmm...

警戒松散，半个警卫都没有。
Such laxity! Not a single guard here.

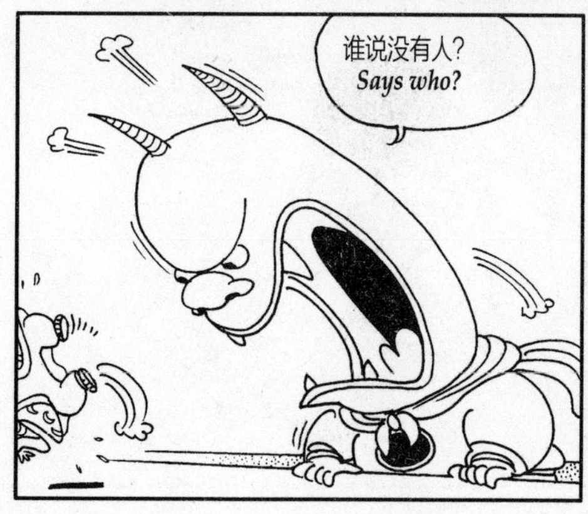
谁说没有人？
Says who?

过这道机关要胆大心细，
步步为营。
It takes both courage and caution to get through this trap. I've got to watch my step.

嘿! Hey!

安全着陆。
Safe landing.

还是被暗算了……
Oops, I didn't quite make it...

嘿嘿，终于到厨房了。
Hee, hee! I've finally reached the kitchen.

偷偷下毒在水里，
神不知鬼不觉。
I'll add poison in the water.
No one will notice it.
水

!

...
...

下毒计划失败了，
快点离开此地。
My plot has failed. I've got to leave this place at once.

睡得真死，可以放心跑过去。
That fellow is fast asleep. I can sneak out without any danger.

谁说我睡着了？
Who says I'm asleep?

运用一点脑力，略施小计，
你果然自投罗网！
I play a little trick and you walk right into my trap.

!
站住！
Hold it!

双手难敌四拳，你还是快快投降。
Two hands are no match for four fists. Surrender now.

你找来帮手，
我也带了位朋友帮腿。
You have an assistant. So do I!

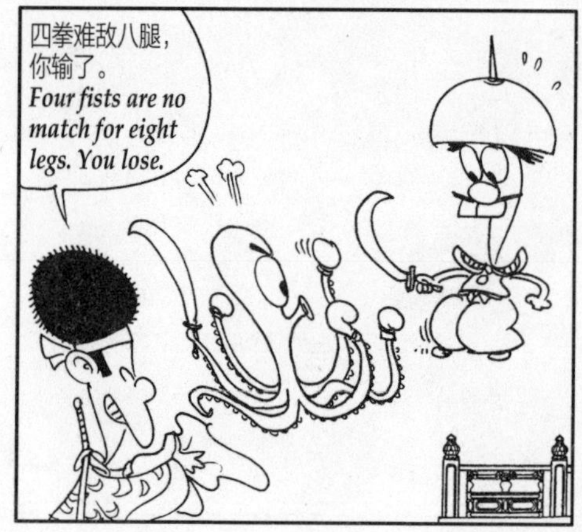
四拳难敌八腿，
你输了。
Four fists are no match for eight legs. You lose.

退后！否则我要放催泪瓦斯弹了！
Stand back! Otherwise, I'll use tear gas!

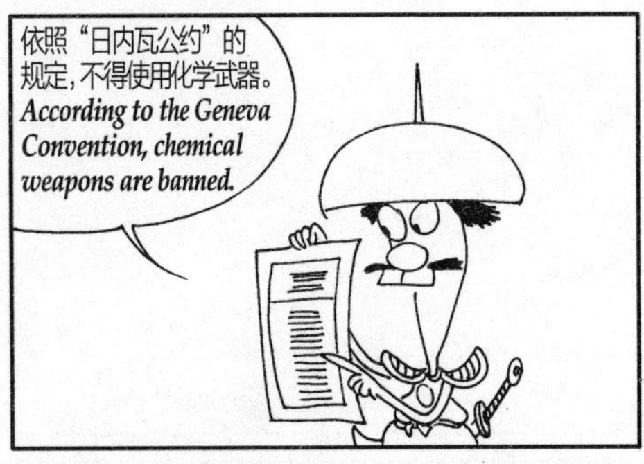
依照"日内瓦公约"的规定，不得使用化学武器。
According to the Geneva Convention, chemical weapons are banned.

恭敬不如从命。
I'll gladly oblige.

改用自然的烟幕弹。
I shall use a natural bomb then.

哇！
Wah!
看机关翻板！
Look out for the trapdoor!

救命啊！
Help!
只有这些骷髅真能救你了。
There are only skulls to help you.

谢谢你的提醒！
Thanks for reminding me!
!

这些好兄弟每人助我一头之力。
They helped me make headway out of here.

要走不难，先得过
我这关，拔刀吧！
If you want to go, defeat
me first. Draw
your sword.

兵乃不祥之器，
先拔刀者不利。
Weapons are baneful
things. One who draws
his sword first will meet
with ill fortune.

气候不对，拔刀者
都不利。
One who draws his
sword in unfavou-
rable weather is at
a disadvantage.

雷雨天，更是拔刀
不利。
It is even more
disadvantageous to
draw one's sword in
stormy weather.
轰！
Rumble!

对付这些小喽罗，
撒一把十字钉便成。
These small fry can be effectively
dealt with by throwing out a
handful of nails.

再不然用金子，效果更佳。
Or else use gold, the result
will be even better.

哇！
Wah!

铁暗器，金暗器，
不如一个香蕉皮。
Your iron and gold secret weapons are not as effective
as a banana skin.

* A swordsmith from the Warring States Period.

看我的快速神拳！
Watch my high-speed magic gongfu!

你打我三拳，我还你一拳。
You struck at me three times and I'll give you one back.

这种内家拳打人，毫毛不伤。
Your internal gongfu has not harmed a hair of mine.

不伤毫毛，只伤内脏！
Right. It hurts only your internal organs!
!

用妖术使你血溅五步。
I'll use sorcery to spill your blood.

这种幻术唬不了人。
Your illusions can't scare anyone.

看我货真价实的真功夫。
Watch my genuine skill.

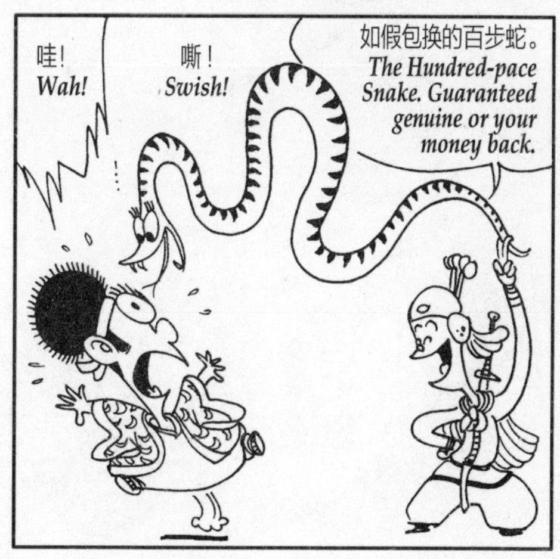
哇！
Wah!
嘶！
Swish!
如假包换的百步蛇。
The Hundred-pace Snake. Guaranteed genuine or your money back.

使出真正的法术。
This is genuine magic.

这种妖术好对付。
This is easy to deal with.

剪刀、石头、布！
Scissors, rock and cloth!
输了！
I've lost!

报告班长，坏人捉到了。
Captain, I've caught an evildoer.
功劳又被抢去了。
He's stolen the credit.

是不是该颁个奖鼓励鼓励？
Aren't you giving me an award?
应该。
Sure.

恭喜你又得个第一。
Congrats! You've won yet again.
谢谢。
Thank you.

!
抢戏第一
First Place in Stealing the Show

擂台又开，不速之客抢先上台。
The contest is restarting.

本人不请自来，是因为这里人山人海。
I came here without an invitation as saw a huge crowd here.

此行目的有二，一是比武；二是招收弟子。
I have two aims in coming here. First, to compete in the tournament. Second, to recruit disciples.

学琴的小孩不会学坏，请赶快报名。
Children who take music lessons will not get into trouble. Sign up now.
暑假儿童音乐班
八月开课
Music lessons for kids
Starting in August

老夫魔音琴功厉害非凡，有哪位想先领教？
My name is True Man of Magic Music. My skill is terrific. Who'd like to hear it first?

哇！引起公愤了？
Wah! Have I aroused public indignation?
咻！
Whoosh!
咻！
Whoosh!
咻！
Whoosh!
咻！
Whoosh!

嘿！ *Hey!*

歌曲点唱单……
Song requests...
快乐出帆
舞女
补破网

魔音琴一弹，石破天惊，鬼哭神号，无人抵抗得了。
When I play my Magic Zither, rocks break up and Heaven shakes.

我行走江湖，闯荡武林，就仗着这把名琴。
Ghosts wail and gods howl. Nobody can resist it.

这把琴绝对可称天下第一……
I rely on my zither to roam the world and make a living in martial arts circles...

天下第一破琴！
This instrument is number one in the world!

既然比的是这种音乐，我也敢上台。
World's number one lousy instrument! If this is the standard of this contest, I think I qualify.

你学过多久音乐，敢上台与我比试？
You? How long have you been studying music?

就是没学过，才可怕呀！
Screech! I am formidable precisely because I've never studied music.

嘎
Screech!
嘎
Screech!

魔音琴弹出独门绝技“摇篮曲”……
A unique lullaby was played on the Magic Zither.
嘎

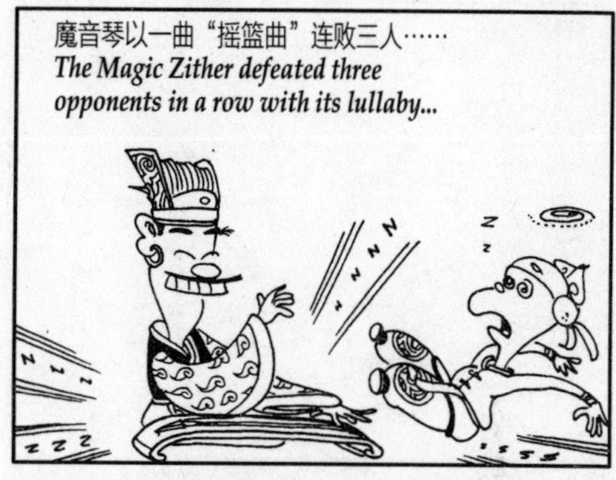
魔音琴以一曲“摇篮曲”连败三人……
The Magic Zither defeated three opponents in a row with its lullaby...

大醉侠抵抗不了，马上躺地……
Unable to withstand the music, Big Drunk Hero immediately lay down on the floor...

每个人一听他的音乐便睡着了。
Every one of them fell asleep as soon as they heard the music.
晚上睡觉时，我用佛门魔音对付他。
I'll use the Magic Buddhist Music to deal with him tonight.

胜负已分，大醉侠输了！
It's obvious that Big Drunk Hero has lost.
不！魔音琴没赢，大醉侠没输。
No! The Magic Zither hasn't won and Big Drunk Hero hasn't lost.

南无南无 南无南无 南无南无 南无南无 南无南无
Namo, namo, namo, namo, namo...
咚，咚，咚……
Tock, tock, tock...

魔音真人也抵抗不了自己的催眠曲。
True Man of Magic Music also could not withstand his own lullaby.

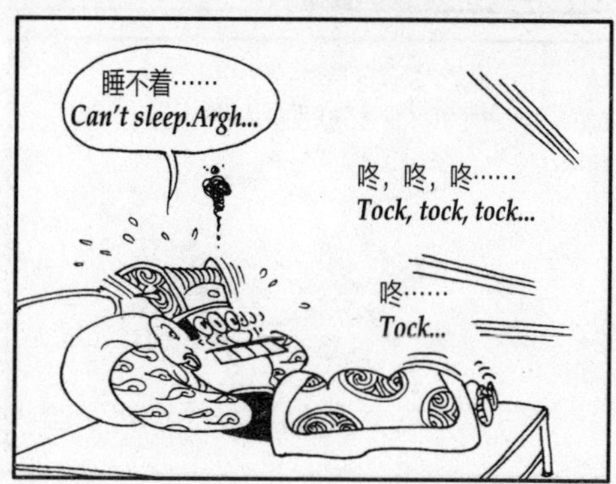
睡不着……
Can't sleep.Argh...
咚，咚，咚……
Tock, tock, tock...
咚……
Tock...

还有哪位愿上台指教?
Who else wants to come up?
我来领教几招?
I do.

好，接招!
Fine Ready?
当!
Dang!
当!
Dang!
当!
Dang!

承让了。
Thank you for yielding to me.
哗!
哗!
哗!
没看到对手啊……
Where's the oppo-nent?
奇怪?
How odd...

师父!我被打下擂台了……
Master, I was thrown off the platform...

吴钩双刀上台领教几招。
Can I have a bout with you using my double swords?

这是真剑比武，上台怎么不带刀?
This is a contest with real weapons. Why are you here without your sword?

带了。
They are here.

黑色的胡须刀?
Black moustache swords?
当!Dang!

当！
Dang!
当！
Dang!
当！
Dang!
当！
Dang!

吴钩黑刀锋利无比，现在可领教到了吧？
Now you know how sharp my curved black swords are!
当！
Dang!
当！
Dang!
当！
Dang!
当！
Dang!

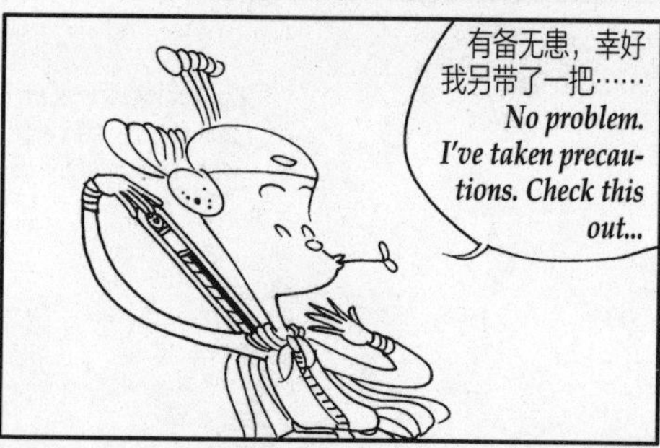
有备无患，幸好我另带了一把……
No problem. I've taken precautions. Check this out...

不怕断的美工刀！
An art knife that doesn't snap!

再接一招！
Let's have a nother go!

啊！下大雨了……
Ah! It's raining...

为照顾多数人的利益，请到下面比。
For the sake of the majority, please fight off stage.

连日梅雨，
不能比赛……
Thanks to the rainy weather, the contests have to be cancelled...

宝剑锈了不少。
My sword is corroded by rust.

连日梅雨不停……
It's been drizzling for days.

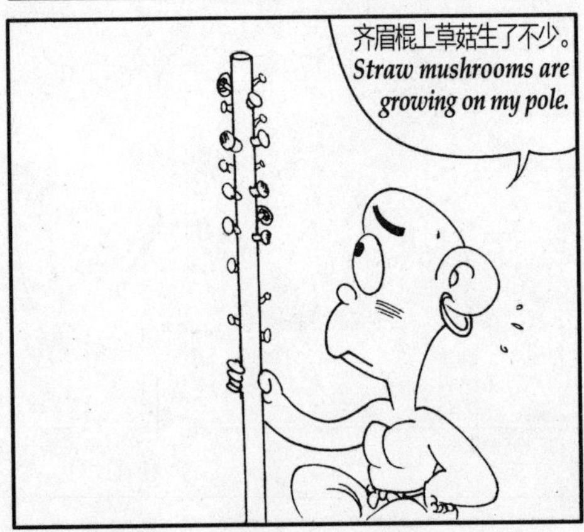
齐眉棍上草菇生了不少。
Straw mushrooms are growing on my pole.

接下来木桩比武，被打落水的便算输。
The next item is combat on tree stumps. When a contestant falls off the stump, he loses.

我先上台走一圈，
便知妙不妙。
Let me take a walk on the stumps.

如何？
What do you think?
木桩排列得富创意，
有朝气。
The arrangement of the stumps is creative and has a youthful spirit.

是根据迪斯科舞步设计的。
It's designed in accordance with disco steps.

在下想与你单挑，上台比一比。
I'd like to compete with you one to one.
行。
All right.

高手一上场，轻重高低便分明。
When experts face each other, who's the stronger is immediately seen.

轻功不行！
His Light Skill is no good!
扑通！

足下功夫不如人，手上功夫可不输人。这样就下台万万不服。
My foot skill is not as good as yours, but my hand skill is not inferior. I won't give up.

在下愿领教一下阁下的手上功夫。
I'd like to see your hand skill.

行！
OK!

高竿？
Huh?

唐家三少，上台领教。
I, Third Young Master of the Tang Family, am here to challenge you.

对付幼齿，一只手便可以。
To deal with a child, one hand is quite enough.
可恶！欺人太甚！
Damn! You're too much!

用兵以奇，先送你一个见面礼。
One should resort to unusual moves in combat. I'm giving you a present on our first meeting.

当！
Dang!
哇！
Wah!

哇！
Wah!

双方实力相差太多了。
The two sides are ill-matched in terms of strength.
可是大醉侠已经让了不少。
But Big Drunk Hero has dealt with him leniently.

果然是个幼齿！
A young master, indeed!

嘻嘻！
Hee,Hee!

在下“铁链金钩”，请指教。
Your humble servant the Iron-chained Shrimp begs to compete with you.

呼呼呼呼……
Whirr...

铁链只有一个，其他是幻影，找空隙杀进去。
There is only one chain. The others are all illusions. Find a chink and thrust in your sword.

全身布满链影，攻不进去……
He's hidden inside the whirling chain. I can't find a point to attack...

好机会！
Here's my chance!

全身被缠住，动弹不得……
Oops, I can hardly move...

是五倍分量，所以没空隙。
My weapon is five times heavy duty, and has no chinks.

打败强敌令人雀跃不已！
I've beaten a strong opponent. Hurray!

利用这空当来点余兴节目……
I'd like to use the interval for some entertainment.

卡拉 OK，高歌一曲！
I'll sing a karaoke song!

金燕子来会会你。
I, Golden Swallow, am here to compete with you.

别因为我是女孩而手下留情，尽管杀过来！
Don't make allowance for my being a girl. Strike as hard as you can!

对付女孩当然要用软性武器。
When dealing with a girl, a soft weapon should be used.

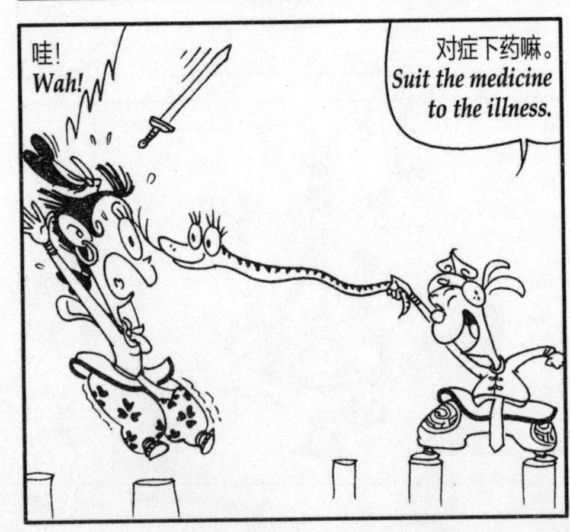
哇！
Wah!
对症下药嘛。
Suit the medicine to the illness.

接招！
Catch this!

这些破铜烂铁，我看不在眼里！
This junk is not worth my attention!
当！
Dang!

再试试这个！
Then, try this!

投降！
I surrender!
对于贵重的武器，没有抵抗力。
She cannot resist a valuable weapon.

我输得不服气，重新再比。
I can't accept my defeat. Let's do it again.
再给你一次机会。
I'll give you another chance.

用两根长针要怎么比？
How do you compete with two long needles?

比赛织毛衣。
We'll have a knitting contest.

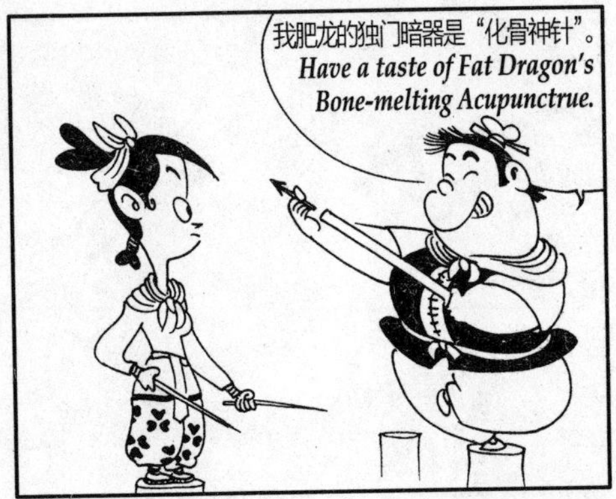
我肥龙的独门暗器是“化骨神针”。
Have a taste of Fat Dragon's Bone-melting Acupunctrue.

这次一定成功，接招！
This time I'm sure of success. Watch out!
啊！
Ah!

哇！
Wah!
接招！
Watch out!

咻咻咻……
Shuu, shuu, shuu...
哇！
Wah!

化骨神针见血封喉，不服解药一定会死。
A prick by my needle causes bleeding and blocks the windpipe. If the antidote is not taken, death is imminent.

嘻嘻嘻，对不起！管子塞住了……
Hee, hee, hee. Sorry, the tube is blocked...

幸好我脸部化妆厚，伤不到我的皮肤。
Fortunately I have thick make-up on my face, so my skin is not hurt.

你的神针对我来说只是小针美容。
Your magic needle is a beauty treatment for me.

对付女孩怎能用这种狠毒的暗器？
How can you use such a pernicious weapon against a girl?
马上就改。
I'll correct my mistake.

再试试这个！
Then try this.

改用洞箫对付你。
I'll use a flute to deal with you.
这还差不多。
That's more like it.

哇！怎么可以使用火箭炮？
Wah! How can you use a bazooka?

啐啐啐！
Toot, toot!

是大型吹箭化骨针。
It's a big blowpipe for Jumbo Bone-melting Needles.

口水当暗器可够软性了吧？
Is spit soft enough for you?
...

赢女孩不足喜，
有种跟我比！
Defeating a woman is not a feat worth rejoicing. Take me on if you dare!
行。
Fine.

念你因为左脚受伤，
我只用一根小指对付你。
Since you hurt your left foot, I'll use only my pinkie to deal with you.

当！
Dang!
当！
Dang!
哇！
Wah!
当！
Dang!

可恶！看我修理你！
Outrageous! See how I'll handle you!

这种暗器怎能伤得了
我分毫？
This kind of secret weapon cannot harm me in the least!

当！
Dang!
当！
Dang!
当！
Dang!

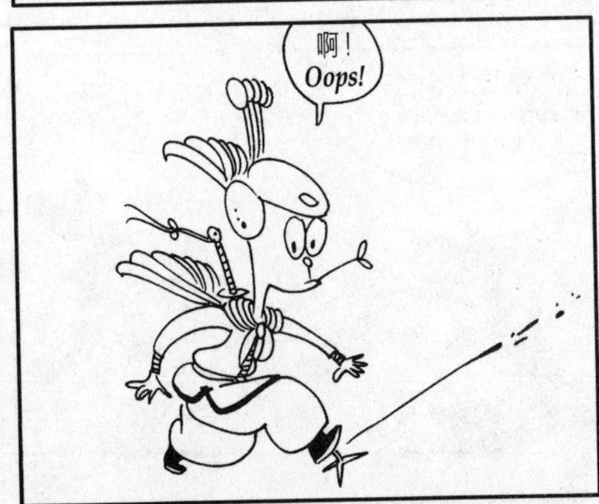
啊！
Oops!

不错！不错！
指甲修得真整齐。
Not bad! Not bad! My nails have been neatly manicured.

使出真功夫，巨剑回龙对付你。
Here's the real thing, the Huge Spiral Dragon Sword.

剑气凌人有魄力，无法抵抗……
The sword looks formidable. I can't handle it.

哇噻！这招正中我的要害……
Wah! He has hit right at my weak point...

香气逼人，无法抵抗。
What an aromal! I can't resist.

现在由大醉侠与少林小子对打，谁赢了就是总冠军。
Now Big Drunk Hero will compete with Shaolin Kid. The winner will be the champion.

不公平！我六胜，而他只三胜，应该算我赢。
That's not fair. I have six victories and he has only three. I am the winner.

抱歉，本漫画演的是少林寺，而不是大醉侠。
Sorry. This comics is about Shaolin Temple and not Big Drunk Hero.

本漫画的主角就算零胜，也有权最后出场，争取总冠军。
The protagonist of this comics is entitled to compete for championship even if he has zero victory.

*This saying jeers at the mentality that foreign people or things are superior.

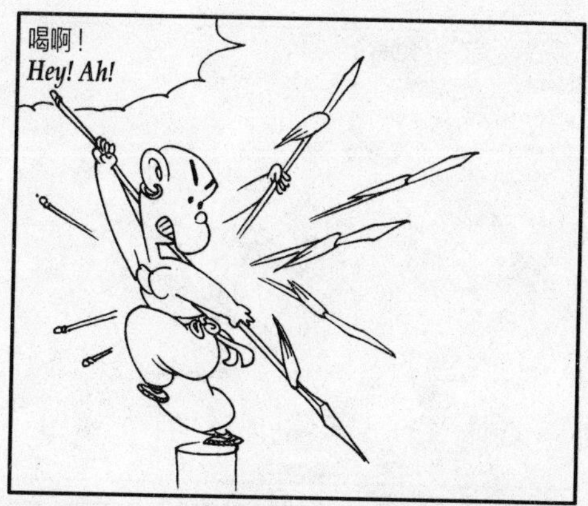
喝啊！
Hey! Ah!

少林十八般武艺样样犀利，你对付不了。
We Shaolin followers are trained in all combat skills. You can't cope with them.

俗语说："矛盾相克"，以矛攻来，以盾挡之。
As the saying goes:"The spear and the shied work against each other."You attack with a spear and I'll ward it off with a shield.

这种造型的盾你不敢碰吧？
Dare you attack shields shaped like these?

当！
Dang!
当！
Dang!
当！
Dang!

再接这支"子母离魂镖"！
Now be ready for the Mother-and-Son Dart.

照接不误，一点都不稀奇。
Big deal. I can catch it for sure.

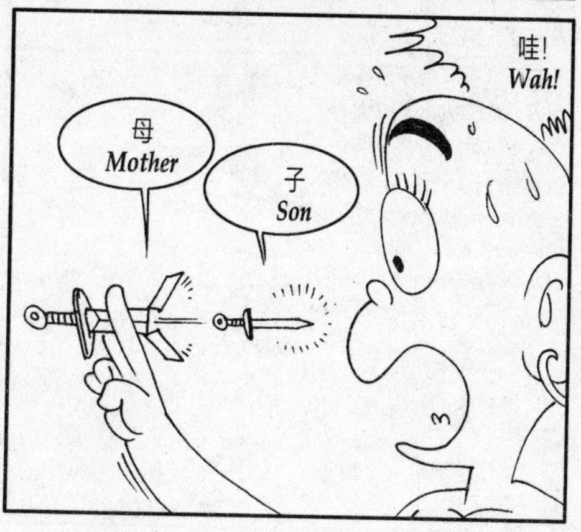
哇！
Wah!
母
Mother
子
Son

当！
Dang!
当！
Dang!
当！
Dang!

再接
这个！
Take this!

哇！
Wah!

对症下药，和尚不敢碰女体！
Suit the remedy to the cause. Monks won't dare touch a female body!

现在颁发前三名奖牌。
Now I'm going to award medals to the winners.
1
2

冠军颁发纯金奖牌一面。
The champion is awarded a medal of pure gold.

就算金价上涨，也不该小气到这样啊！
Even though gold prices are rising, they should not be so stingy!

全世界的黄金百分之六十被台湾和日本买去了，韩国金子缺货。
Sixty percent of the gold in the world is bought by Taiwan and Japan. So there's a shortage in Korea.

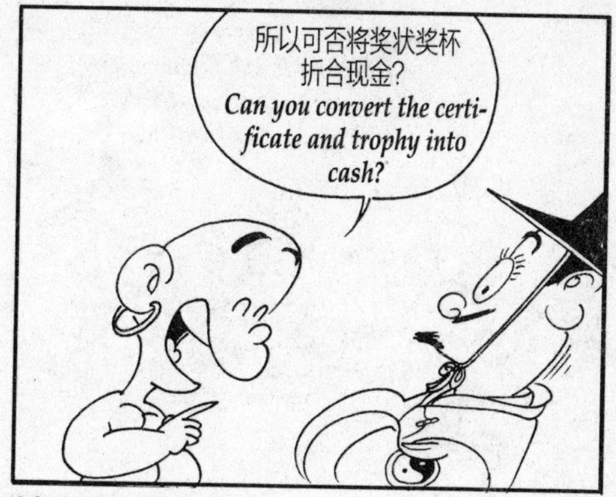

*See note on page 13.

武当山得六个冠军，
所以是第一！
Wudang wins first place with six championships.
少林寺得三个冠军是第二。
Shaolin Temple is second with three championships.
冠军
Champion
冠军
Champion

韩山庄得了十个冠军最多，
才是第一！
Hanshan Village should be in first place. It won 10 championships.

韩山庄根本就没派人出场比赛，何来这么多冠军？
Hanshan Village did not send any contestant. How did it win 10 championships?

当然有！服务冠军、保安冠军、伙食冠军、卖票冠军……
Of course it did! Champion in service, security,catering, ticketing...

恭请总冠军替我签名。
May I have your autograph, chief champion?
好啊！
Sure.

也帮我签名留念。
I'd like to have your autograph too.
好好好……
一个一个来。
All right. Let me do it one by one.

请你在这里签个名。
Please sign here.
行。
OK.

答应就不能反悔，多少钱都行！
You agreed to sign. Now you must keep your promise. It doesn't matter how much money you give.
…
捐款同意书
捐款人：
Contribution Pledge
Name of donor

今晚来个庆功宴！
Let's celebrate tonight!
不醉不归。
We shan't go home till we're dead drunk.
酒
酒

干杯！
Cheers!
干干干！
Bottoms up!

恭喜你又多得了一个冠军。
Congrats! You've won another champion-ship.
冠军

酒量冠军！
Drinking champion!
酒量冠军
!

真希望能留下冠军奖杯啊！
I wish we could keep the trophies!
就是啊！
So do I!
哈哈哈！
哈哈哈！
冠军
冠军

马上可以办到。
That wish can be fulfilled at once.

请缴所得税百分之八十。
Please pay 80 percent income tax.
所得税80%

这不是留下奖杯了吗？
We've managed to keep the trophies, haven't we?
...
冠军

这次失败了，四年后再来吧……
We failed this time. Let's come back four years later...
带点土回去留念……
Let's take home some earth as souvenir.

比赛结束了，什么奖也没捞到……
The tournament is over and we did not win any prize...
回去很难交代！
We'll have difficulty justifying our returning emptyhanded!

呜……下次一定要赢才行。
We've got to win next time.

各位别担心，我们也为没得奖的选手考虑到了。
Fret not, friends. We've made provisions for those who did not win.

谁允许你们挖土回去的？
Who gave you permission to take home our earth?
土又不值钱，带点回去作纪念又何妨？
Earth is worthless. What's wrong with our taking some home as souvenir?

本会准备了很多奖杯，能让没得奖的选手也能有个交代。
The committee has prepared extra trophies, so those who didn't win any can take some home.

土地一坪两百多万，这些土当然值钱！
This land is worth over two million a ping. The earth is of course valuable!
…

奖杯热卖，大的十两，小的五两。
Large ones 10 taels each, small ones five taels each.
好棒！
Ha, ha!
我买一个。
I want one.
Yippee!
冠军
冠军
冠军
Champion
买两个杯。
I'll take two.

要把这么大的奖杯搬回去，也是够辛苦的。
It's so strenuous to lug such a huge trophy home.

双手扛得累死了。
My arms are sore from holding the trophy.

奖杯带回去只能充门面,其实也没多大用途。
It has no practical use; it only keeps up appearances.
是啊！
That's right!

两位乖乖地把奖杯交出来，否则在下可要不客气了。
Hand over the trophies or I'll get tough with you.

啊！下雨了……
Ah! It's raining...

你想要就拿去吧。
Take them if you like.
还真大方呢！
You're so generous!

还是有点用途的。
They do have a bit of use.

让他替我扛一阵子，等一下再抢回来。
I'll let him carry it for me for a while. I'll snatch it back later.

我已经休息够了，现在把奖杯还给我吧！
I've had enough rest. Now give the trophy back to me!

除非把我杀了，否则休想夺回奖杯！
Over my dead body!
冠军

我乃是本届功夫擂台冠军，要杀死你还不容易?
Being the gongfu champion at the recent tournament, I can easily kill you.

台北人寿
国泰人寿
北山人寿
旧光人寿
我投保了终身寿险，想杀死我得看他们同不同意。
I have taken out life insurance policies. You need their agreement to kill me.
冠军

台北人寿
国泰人寿
北山人寿
旧光人寿
我每家投保五百万，故他们不会让我被杀死的。
I have an insurance policy of five million at each of these companies, so they won't let me be killed.

在商言商，商人好应付。
Businessmen will be businessmen. They are easy to deal with.

每家寿险公司我也各投保终身寿险三千万。
I'll take out a life insurance for 30 million at each of your companies.
太好了！
Wonderful!

三千万的客户得好好保护，五百万的休管他死活。
A client worth 30 million ought to be well protected. We don't care if the one worth only five million should die.
人寿
人寿
国泰人寿
台北人寿
!

大主顾，决斗前请服现代仙丹维他命。
Dear customer, please take these Modern Elixir Vitamins before the duel.
国泰人寿
人寿
人寿

吃这种东西有效吗？
Do these work?
实验证明效果很好。
Good results were seen in experiments.

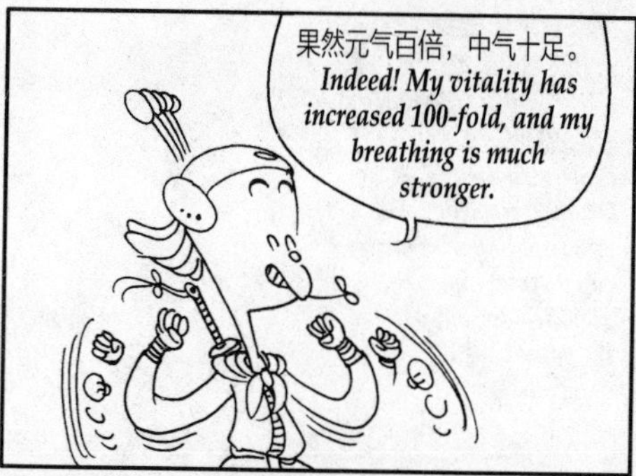
果然元气百倍，中气十足。
Indeed! My vitality has increased 100-fold, and my breathing is much stronger.

小草都开花了，养分真足！
Look, the grass has bloomed. It's so nourishing!

求求你将这冠军杯卖给我，让我回去好交代……
I beg you to sell me this trophy, so that I can face my folks back home...

冠军应凭真本事得来，怎可以用钱购买？
A championship should be earned. How can you buy it with money?

其实你也有个本事堪称武林冠军，无人能比。
Actually, you have a matchless ability good enough to earn first place in the martial arts circles.
是什么，我怎么没发现？
What is it? Why haven't dicovered it?

厚脸皮冠军！
Champion of thick skin!

终于回到了武当山。
Finally I'm back at Wudang Mountain.

咦？师父怎么不在……
Mmm? My master is not here...

糟了！师父一定还在韩山庄没回来。
Good gracious! He must be at Hanshan Village.

搭你的便车，一路跟着你回来啦！
I took a ride and came back with you!
哇！好诈……
Wha! A sly old...
冠军
Champion

你果真不负师命，夺得锦标归来。
You brought back a prize and didn't let me down.
这个杯够大，正合我需要。
This trophy is big enough to suit my purpose.

用它来当酒杯，气派十足。
I'll look dignified when I use it for drinking wine.
是啊！
Quite right!

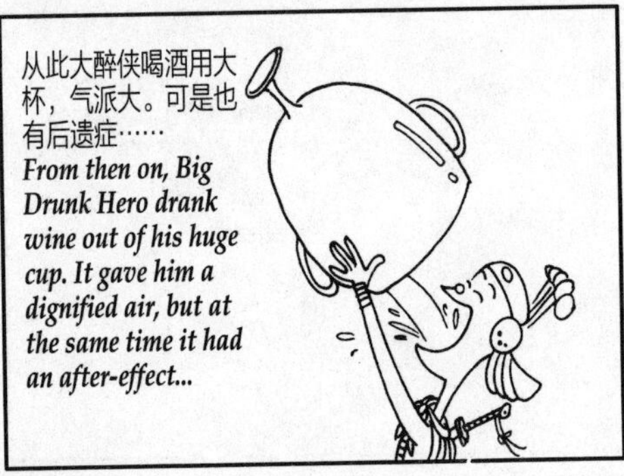
从此大醉侠喝酒用大杯，气派大。可是也有后遗症……
From then on, Big Drunk Hero drank wine out of his huge cup. It gave him a dignified air, but at the same time it had an after-effect...

大醉侠从此改名叫"大肚侠"。
Big Drunk Hero's name was changed to Big Paunch Hero.
…

没得冠军，夺得亚军，也不赖。
I did not win first place, but was good enough to be runner-up.
亚军 runner-up

师父他们一定大开庆功宴，迎接我回来！
I'm sure they will hold a celebration party to welcome me home.
亚军 runner-up

咦？空荡荡，不见半个人影……
Why, the temple is empty...

被放鸽子啦！
I've been left out!
本寺全体员工到汉城参观奥运会少林寺休馆两周
Closed for two weeks. The staff of this temple has gone to Sydney for the Olympics.

附录·延伸阅读
APPENDIX Further reading

此部分为本书图画页的延伸阅读，
各段首所示的页码与图画页对应。

P218　少林寺位于嵩山五乳峰下。嵩山，位于河南省登封县，自古以来有许多不同的名称；《尚书》称为“外方”，《诗经》称为“嵩高”，《尔雅》称为“中岳”，《汉书》称为“灵高”，《史记》称为“太室”，《山海经》则称为“半石山”。

少林寺之所以闻名于世，有两大原因：其一，是因为印度僧人菩提达摩，在此首创禅宗，为我国佛教的发源地。其二，少林寺的武功可说是武林重镇，要学武功、要研究武学，绝不可遗漏少林寺。

P219　第一个在少林寺建筑寺庙的其实不是菩提达摩，而是另一位印度僧人跋陀禅师，于北魏孝文帝太和二十年所建。

佛教自汉代传入中国，经过历代君主的提倡，到了南北朝时达到全盛。北魏孝文帝承明元年（西元四七六年），孝文帝命人选拔青年男女百余人，亲自为他们讲经说法，并亲自为他们落发，及各赠僧衣或尼衣一套。

P220　至西元四七七年，孝文帝将年号改为太和，三月时，京城内已有佛寺百余所，僧尼七万七千二百五十八人，而从天竺（今之印度）来的僧人，更受尊崇。

跋陀禅师就是这个时候到了洛阳，建了少林寺之后，并在寺之西台建有舍利塔，塔后造翻经台。他除了在少林译经外，并传授小乘佛教，是地宗论的鼻祖，后来被派至嵩岳寺做住持。

P221　菩提达摩，简称达摩，西域南天竺国人，是大婆罗门国王第三子。

南朝梁武帝时，达摩渡海东来中国，会见了这位中国历史上最护持佛教的皇帝，有了如下的对话——

帝问：“朕即位以来，造寺、写经、度僧，不可胜记，有何功德？”达摩兜头就是一盆冷水：“并无功德。”那么，“如何是圣谛第一义？”“廓然无圣。”不死心的梁武帝，问了最后一个问题：“对语者谁？”达摩依然冷冷答道：“不识。”于是，武帝与达摩，终究只落得“见之不见，逢之不逢，遇之不遇”。

P222　● 小憩

《心经》，全称为“摩诃般若波罗蜜多心经”，全部经文仅二百六十字，是佛教最短的经文。

般若波罗蜜多，意译作“慧到彼岸”，即照了诸法实相，而穷尽一切智慧之边际，度生死此岸到涅槃彼岸的菩萨大慧。

心，指心脏，含有精要、心髓等意。《心经》系将六百卷之《大般若经》，浓缩成为表现“般若皆可”精神的简洁经典；全经举出四谛、五蕴、六尘、十二因缘等法，以总述诸法皆空之理。

P223　● 小憩

一般人常说的“色即是空，空即是色”一语，即是出自本经。

P224　达摩与梁武帝不契合，乃以一苇渡过长江，于北魏孝明帝太和十年到了少林，进石洞修壁观，一坐就是九年。

后来达摩传法给慧可，创建禅宗，史称达摩为中土之初祖，少林为祖庭；从此以后，禅法盛行于中国。

P225 《指月录》云：世尊在灵山会上，拈花示众。是时，众皆默然，唯迦叶尊者，破颜而笑。世尊曰："吾有正法眼藏，涅槃妙心，实相无相，微妙法门，不立文字，教外别传，咐嘱摩诃迦叶。"

这是传说中禅宗的开始；所以，禅是言语道断，以心印心，不立文字的。

P226 "禅"是从印度的"禅那"这个词翻译过来的，是"禅那"的简称，意译是思惟修或静虑，指的是佛教中一种修行的方法，如参禅打坐、凝神静坐。

其实，禅宗是反对参禅打坐的，也反对从文字上学习佛教和佛学，可以说是注重思惟修的，禅宗的名字也是因此而来的。

P227　● 小憩

在印度佛教的戒律上，如果是具足"不见不闻不疑"这三个条件的三净肉，是允许比丘肉食，而不一定要全面禁肉的。

所谓不见者，不自眼见为我故杀是畜生；不闻者，不从可信人闻为汝故杀是畜生；不疑者，是中有屠儿，是人慈心，不能夺畜生命。

P228　● 小憩

而中国僧尼全面禁绝肉食，是源自南朝梁武帝，请光宅寺法云讲解禁酒肉的《大般涅槃四相品》后，他认为"佛教究竟说，是断一切酒肉的"。

于是颁布《断酒肉文》，与诸僧尼共同约誓，断一切肉，若不遵守之僧尼，并要加以问罪，因此形成中国出家人有别于世界各国的独特现象—— 素食。

P229 神光慧可，河南人，少年稍通世学，壮年在龙门香山出家。后入嵩山少林寺拜谒达摩开示，并请为入室弟子，遂在门外伫候。

时值风雪漫天，神光为示求法决心，断臂立雪中直至雪没及腰，达摩终于开门问他："汝究竟来此所求何事？"

神光答道："弟子心未安，乞师安心。"

达摩喝道："将心拿来，吾为汝安！"

P230 神光慧可愕然地说："觅心了不可得！"

达摩居然答："吾与汝安心竟。"

神光慧可当下大悟。

P231 达摩在魏地居止九年，一天忽向众门人说："我欲西返天竺，时将至矣，汝等盍各言所得？"道副对曰："如我所见，不执文字，不离文字，而为道用。"师曰："汝得吾皮。"尼总持曰："我今所解，如庆喜见阿闳佛国，一见更不再见。"师曰："汝得吾肉。"道育曰："四大本空，五阴（蕴）非有，而我见处，无一法可得。"师曰："汝得吾骨。"最后，慧可礼拜，依位而立。师曰："汝得吾髓。"

达摩于是对慧可说："昔如来以正法眼付迦叶，而辗转至我。我今以付于汝，汝当护持。并授袈裟，以为法信。各有所表，宜可知矣。"

P232 并说偈曰：吾本来兹土，传法救迷情；一花开五叶，结果自然成。

达摩为中国禅宗始祖，慧可是为二祖。

P233 六祖慧能大师，俗姓卢氏，三岁丧父，家贫，生活艰难，遂打柴以养母。一日负柴至市中，听到有人读诵《金刚经》，至"应无所住而生其心"时有所感悟，于是到黄梅参见五祖弘忍。

五祖问他："你从哪里来？"答："岭南。"

再问："你想做什么？" 慧能石破天惊地一语："唯求作佛！"

为了考验他的根性，五祖故意说："岭南人是獦獠，没有佛性，怎么能作佛呢？"

"人虽有南北，佛性哪里有南北之分呢？" 慧能这个答案，令五祖十分满意。

P234 五祖为了传付衣钵，命众门人作偈。

神秀曰："身是菩提树，心如明镜台，时时勤拂拭，莫使惹尘埃。"

慧能和曰："菩提本无树，明镜亦非台，本来无一物，何处惹尘埃？"

五祖认为慧能已彻悟空性，于是传付衣钵给慧能，是为禅宗六祖，并为讲授《金刚经》，至"应无所住而生其心"而大悟。慧能因说："何期自性本自清净，何期自性本不生灭，何期自性本自具足，何期自性本无动摇，何期自性能生万法。"

P235 五祖传法偈曰："有情来下种，因地果还生，无情既无种，无性亦无生。"并说"衣为争端，止汝不传"，嘱咐慧能尽速离去。

后来六祖慧能辗转到了广州，在一家寺院听人讲经，其时有风，吹动了旗杆上的幡；有人说是风动，有人说是幡动，六祖说："不是风动，也不是幡动，仁者心动。"

此语一出，震惊与会大众，开始了六祖在南方弘传大法的生涯。

P236 禅宗的教育是要打破一切执着的，有一次——

一位在家居士去请教智藏禅师，问道："有天堂和地狱吗？" 禅师点点头，说："有啊！"

居士再问："有因果报应吗？" 禅师说："有啊！"

又问："有佛菩萨和三宝（佛法僧）吗？" 禅师仍然回答他："有啊！"

这位居士听了觉得非常疑惑："禅师，您是不是回答错了？以前我问金山禅师一样的问题，他总是说'无！无！'，为什么您却什么都'有'？"

P237 智藏禅师听了微笑问他："你有老婆吗？" 居士回答："有。"

禅师又问："你有儿女吗？" 居士答："有。"

禅师再问："你有田产房屋吗？" 居士答："有。"

P238 禅师换了一个方式，又问："金山禅师有老婆吗？""没有！"

"有儿女吗？""没有！"

"有田产房屋吗？""没有！"

P239 禅师总结："金山禅师讲"无"，是讲他的境界；我回答你"有"，是讲你的世界啊！"

P240 悠悠千载以来，少林寺留下了许多传说及文化宝藏：

一、立雪亭，是二祖慧可断臂求法处。

二、塔林，共有二百三十余座古塔，有历代各种建筑风格及造型，还有精美的石雕艺术；塔铭中并记载了古代中外文化交流与武术资料。

三、碑林，有唐宋元明清各代杰出书法家的手迹，如苏轼的画梅碑与赞碑，宋代书法家米芾的第一山，及明代董其昌的道公（人名）碑等。另有程绍题少林观武诗碑，为研究少林寺武学的珍贵资料。

P241 四、千佛殿，殿内东西北三面墙上，绘有五百罗汉朝毘卢的彩色壁画，画中虽与打斗无关，然殿内地面上有四十八个凹陷的脚坑，却是过去寺中武僧，长期在殿中练武留下的遗迹。

五、白衣殿，因殿内绘有少林拳谱之壁画，又称拳谱殿。北壁绘寺僧徒手搏击图，计十六组之多；南山墙面主要绘持械格斗场面，计十五组，兵器有棍枪、双刀、剑戟、袖圈等。后壁画面则分四部分：北边为唐初少林和尚救援唐王李世民的故事，南边则为元末时少林寺烧火和尚（紧那罗王）显圣，吓走盗贼。壁画内容对研究少林武术，具有重要参考价值。

P242 少林寺的建筑中，还有一项最值得一提的，就是由元代著名天文学家郭守敬主持建造的"观星象台”。

郭守敬利用这座观星台，观察了二十八个星宿，及一些恒星的位置，并和王恂、许衡等人计算并编出伟大的历法——授时历。

授时历施行达三百六十年，依此计算出一年的长度，比地球围绕太阳转一圈的实际时间，只差二十六秒。而目前通用的阳历，与授时历是一致的，它的制定却比授时历晚了三百年。

P243　少林拳，据说传自达摩祖师。

达摩至少林后徒众日多，大都精神萎靡、筋肉衰惫，每次说法入座时，总是昏沉不振。达摩于是训示徒众说：

佛法虽不重躯壳，然不了解此性，终不能令灵魂躯壳相离；是欲见性，必先强身。盖躯壳强而灵魂易悟，果皆如诸生之志靡神昏，一入蒲团，睡魔即侵，则明心见性之功，俟诸何日？吾今为诸生先立一强身术，每日晨光熹微，即起而习之，始能日进而有功。

P244　于是，达摩为徒众示范一种练习法，前后左右都是十八式，叫做十八法，又叫十八罗汉手，此即达摩祖师之开宗法。

P245　少林武术初显，是于隋朝末年民不聊生，人民皆被迫为盗，形成群雄并起的局面，为了自卫，少林僧众不得不用武力自救。

李渊即位，平定群雄，改国号为唐。李世民被封为秦王，负责讨伐王世充，他怕王世充占据嵩山山区，乃书告少林寺上座寺主及徒众，暨军民首领士庶等。

因此，少林寺僧志操、惠玚、昙宗等出与王世充作战，擒获王世充侄儿，献给唐朝。

P246　当时少林寺僧达两千多人，练武之风尤盛，时人曾作诗记之：

名香古殿自氤氲，舞剑挥戈送落曛；

怪得僧徒偏好武，昙宗曾拜大将军。

P247　北宋初年，福居和尚曾邀集全国十八家武术名家到少林寺，并将各家武艺加以汇总。

经过三年的整理，福居和尚取各家之长，将十八家手法变为五形拳，以龙蛇虎豹鹤为五形，总称为少林五拳。

P248《少林宗法》和《少林拳术秘诀》二书说：“龙拳练神，虎拳练骨，豹拳练力，蛇拳练气，鹤拳练精。五拳学之能精，则身坚气壮，手灵足稳，眼锐胆壮。”五拳的练习要点是：练龙拳时要两肩沉静，五心相印，气注丹田，用意不用力；练虎拳时须鼓全身之气，臂肩腰实，腋力充沛，努目强项，一气相贯；练豹拳时须全身鼓力，两拳紧握，五指如钩铜屈铁；练蛇拳时要注意气之吞吐抑扬，以沉静柔实为主；练鹤拳时须凝精铸神，以缓急适中为得宜。

P249　少林拳术有许多套路，五形八法拳即是其中之一，它是由五形拳和大金刚拳融合而成。

五形包括龙形、虎形、豹形、蛇形、鹤形等。八法则包括：以静坐、站桩为基础的内功法和意念法，以操练打、踢、摔、拿等动作姿势为内容的外功法、拳法、腿法、擒摔法、身步法，还有锻炼气息并配合动作的发声用气法。

这套拳的特点是“猛起硬落、近逼快攻”，动作刚劲有力，节奏鲜明。

P250　少林拳属外家拳，以刚为主，以柔为辅。实际上，少林拳讲求实效，因此朴实无华，既有刚猛有力的外功拳，也有柔和无比的内功拳。

刚法的基本动作是踢、打、摔、拿、扑、撞，力量运用灵活而富弹性，套路紧密细致，虚实并用。快速进攻时“拳有形，打之无形”，“动如风，站如针，犯之如猛虎，守之如处女”。它的特点是“少林拳打一条线”，即拳术套路的起落进退，全在一条线上；另一个特点是“拳打卧牛之地”，即与敌相接，不过前进与进退两三步之间。简而言之，重点如下：

P251 “拳”打一条线，“眼”以目注目，“手”曲而不曲、直而不直，滚如滚出，“步”要轻、灵、稳、固，“身”强调起横落顺；“力量”的运用强调灵活而有弹性，刚健有力、朴实无华的风格，体现一个“硬”字。以刚健为主，刚中有柔，刚柔相济，求其自然。

P252 少林拳有六字要诀：工、顺、勇、疾、狠、真。

工，就是功夫要练到家，拳法要精纯巧妙，变化莫测，要身随心动，机动灵活。

顺，就是顺势，顺敌之势，供敌之力，四两拨千斤。勇，是果断，见机便入，不可犹豫。

疾，是迅速，即“拳有形，打无形”之意，就是拳在蓄势时看得见，出手则疾若闪电、难见其形。

狠，出手无情，攻敌要害。

真，不尚花招，意在攻防。

P253 少林拳除了强调“刚”之外，还强调功与法。有功有法才能刚，功到法到才自然。所谓功，即软、硬、内、外四功；所谓法，即点、擒、卸、治四法。

软功，练习比较困难，初练不见成效，成功相隔数尺，拳不触及身而敌被击倒，世称柔劲阴光，如阳光手，掌心雷。

硬功，练习较易，一蓄力，一运气，便收成效，世称刚劲阳功，如金钟罩、铁布衫。

内功，主练气，也称气功，如蛤蟆气吸阴功。

P254 外功，主练力，也称硬气功，如铁牛功，千斤闸。

如“少林一指金刚法”属硬功，硬功外壮，属阳刚之劲，一指到身能洞胸彻肺。围绕“少林一指金刚法”又有许多基本辅助的功夫，如抱树功、拔针功、四段功、足肘功、双销功、一指禅功、排打功、铁头功、铁布衫功、蜈蚣跳、仙人拳、刚柔法、硃砂掌、洞水术、罗汉功、钻指功、金钟罩等。

P255 如“壁虎游墙术”属软功，软功内壮，又称爬壁功及挂画，又有许多基本功，如琵琶功、流星桩、梅花桩、铁臂功、蛤蟆功、鹰爪功、铁牛功、阳光手、门挡功、龟背功、跳跃功、轻身术、石柱功、铁砂掌、飞行功、分水功、飞檐走壁功、翻胜术、柏木桩、拈花功、推山掌、沙包功、点石功、螳螂爪、布袋功。

这些基本功，往往都是和软、硬、内、外四功相结合的。

P256 少林拳四法：

点穴法，人身各穴属于十二经、四脉、二跷、二堆，共三百七十九穴；经脉外之奇穴，有大小生死之分。大穴一百零八穴，其中麻穴七十二，死穴三十六；小穴二百七十一，其中主晕穴七十二。所以点穴即在麻、晕、死三种穴上作文章，重者丧命，轻者瘫痪、麻木、休克，因之非到万不得已，绝不轻易使用。练点穴的步骤有认穴、寻经、考向指功、点打、眼力、虚劲、透劲、解穴（能伤人必能救人）。

P257 擒拿法，是较古的武功，奇妙实用，可使对方有力而无所用，有拳而不能击，俯首贴耳受制于己。擒拿法可分为拿耳根法、拿太阳法、拿前颈法、拿后颈法、拿前肩法、拿后肩法、拿外肩法、擒拿大臂法、擒拿肘节法、擒拿小臂法、拿手腕法、拿腰筋法、拿小腿法等。

卸骨法，往往与擒拿法并用，可使对方卸骨之后，完全处于被动，陷入瘫痪状态。卸骨分为卸头、卸手指、卸腕、卸腿、卸腰，唯此法今已不传。

P258 治伤法，一般习武者绝不能避免受伤，因之少林拳术中亦设有治伤法，如气血阻滞、神态昏迷、额心伤、太阳穴伤、大肠伤、心脏伤、肾脏伤、膀胱伤、两肋伤、血凝伤、气眼伤、肩背伤、筋断骨折、扭伤、血流不止、五官破损、刀斧伤、断喉伤、破腹伤、烫伤、刑杖伤等，都要能治能解。

P260 武当山，又称太和，位于湖北省均县南方。南雍州记：“武当山，山高峨峻，若博山香炉，千霄出雾。”与地纪：“武当山上，有七十二峰，三十六岩，九泉，二十四涧，其峰最高者，曰天柱，曰紫霄。”此山之所以称为武当山，是因元偈傒斯所作之《大五龙万寿宫碑》云：“元武神得道于此中，故名武当，即谓非玄武不能当也。”

武当山，不止景色奇伟，更是道教名山。它的历史最早可溯至唐代贞观年间，相传均州太守姚简祈雨于此山，见五龙从天而降，求雨得雨，乃在此山兴建五龙祠。至宋代，建筑规模不断扩大。

P261 元代成宗大德年间，在展旗峰的半山中，兴建了太子岩，殿侧有太子崖。但现存建筑多为明代所建。

明代永乐十年，成祖命工部侍郎郭进，督军工三十余万人在武当山兴建宫观，历时十二年，从北端的争乐宫到天柱峰顶的金殿，共七十余公里，建有八宫、二观、三十六庵、七十二岩庙、十二亭、十祠。

P262 在武当山这座道教名山中，有几个特别的宫殿：

玉虚宫，在武当主峰的西北，相传明末李自成曾在此处扎营，故又名老营宫。此宫有大殿、启圣殿，另有许多堂、祠、坛、庙，建成二百余间，是八宫二观中，规模最大的一处。

遇真宫，在武当山北麓，建于永乐十五年，有真仙殿、山门、斋堂等殿宇近三百间，是为纪念元末明初的著名道士张三丰。真仙殿内供奉的张三丰坐像，形象生动。

P263 磨针井，在登山道旁，相传当年真武进山修炼，日久思归，偶遇一老妇持铁杵研磨。真武问其磨铁杵何为？答以磨针，又问铁杵岂能磨针？老妇云：“功到自然成。”真武顿悟，复还山苦炼，终于修炼成仙，后人因建磨针井以为纪念。磨针井殿内供真武年轻时塑像，四壁绘画以真武修炼为题材；殿前阶下，立铁杵二根，高约四尺，象征老妪欲磨成针之铁杵。

五龙宫，在武当山主峰以北，始建于唐，现仅存水火将塑像，及真武铜像，殿右有元代碑刻，附近有飞云瀑布及陈希夷诵经台等名胜。

P264 金殿，又称金顶，座落在武当山主峰峰顶，是武当山最突出、最足以代表道教的建筑。整个大殿，除殿基是用花岗石铺垫外，其余全部用铜铸成。由于外镀赤金，因此金碧辉煌、光彩夺目，建于永乐十四年，是全中国现有最大用铜建成的金殿。殿内供真武大帝，披发跣足，风姿魁伟，左右侍立金童玉女，乃水火二将，均系铜铸而成。五百年来，虽经风雨雷电的侵蚀，仍宏丽如新。欲上金顶，必须攀千年旧铁索始能抵达。

P265 武当山不特为道教名山，也是武当山太极拳的发源地。

太极拳，昔称绵拳，相传为宋末张三丰所创。据南雷集王征南墓志铭所载：“宋之张三丰为武当丹士，徽宗召之，路梗不能进，夜梦元帝授之拳法，厥明以单丁杀贼百余。”

据明史方伎传载：“张三丰，辽东懿州人，名全一，一名君宝，三丰其号也；以不修边幅，又号张邋遢，颀而伟，龟形鹤背，大耳圆目，须髯如戟，寒着惟一衲蓑，所啖升斗辄尽，或数日数月不食，一日千里，善嬉戏，旁若无人，尝与其徒游武当，筑草庐而居之。洪武二十四年，太祖闻其名，遣使觅之不得。”

P266 又据明郎瑛七修类稿内载：“张仙名君宝，字全一，别号玄玄，时人又称张邋遢，天顺三年，曾来谒帝，予见其像，须发竖立，一髻背垂，紫面大腹，而携笠者，上为赐诰之文，封为通微显化真人。”

P267 有人说，张三丰之技出于道家冯一元；也有人说张三丰乃古时坐道隐士，因观鹊蛇之斗，忽有会心，于是发明了太极拳。

但根据清代大儒黄宗义的说法：“少林以拳勇名闻于天下，然而终有机可乘之时，以搏人为主。内家（拳）以静制动，可以立即击倒来犯者。因此可与少林外家拳区别。”黄宗义之子黄百家撰《百家拳法》则说：“张三丰既精于少林，复从而翻之，是名内家。”

P268 传之今世，太极拳已广为流行，最著名的有十三家：宋氏太极、南宗太极、江西太极、陈氏太极、杨氏太极、吴氏太极、武氏太极、郝氏太极、孙氏太极、快速太极、简易太极、双边太极、张氏太极等。

太极拳之发明，以自然为旨，拳非遇危不发，发则乘其旧力已过，新力未生之时。故所当必靡，犯者应手即仆。其内修，呼吸调元，其动作，以柔克刚，以静制动。简言之，有三法：

（一）柔、缓、松。（二）巧、软、绵。（三）引进落空，粘连不脱，四两拨千斤。

以此九种方法对敌，就能轻灵自然，随屈就伸。随人之来势，以借人之力，制服刚强，此即太极拳。

P270 武术一词，最早见于南朝梁昭明太子所著《文选》，中有诗云："偃闭武术，阐扬文令。"此处武术，泛指军事技术，在此之前则称为武艺和技击，被归入兵家的兵技巧类。

武，是属于会意字，从止从戈，即合止、戈二字为武，因此有所谓"止戈为武"，《汉书·武五子传赞》云："以武禁暴整乱，止息干戈，非以为残而兴纵之也。"

P271 技击的说法，在春秋战国时就非常流行了，《荀子·议兵篇》中有："齐人隆技击。"注："齐人以勇力击斩敌者，号为技击。"《汉书·刑法志》则说："齐愍以技击强。"注引孟康语说，技击即"兵家之技巧。技巧者，习手足，使器械，积机关，以立攻守之胜。"

武艺一名，在汉代已有用例，西晋陈寿《三国志·蜀志·刘封传》记载："（刘封）有武艺，气力过人。"

技击和武艺一直被泛指骑射、击刺和徒手搏斗等攻防实战技术。到了明代，出现了"花法武艺"和"套子武艺"两种说法，意指花拳绣腿、绣花枕头之喻的，无实用价值的武艺。

P272 戚继光《纪效新书》中，将"周旋左右，满片花草"、"徒支虚架以图人前美观"者，称为花法武艺；何良臣著《阵纪》，则把"花刀、花枪、套棍、滚杈之类，诚无济于实用，虽为美看，抑何益于技"者，称为套子武艺。

P273 武术的起源，可远溯至原始人类为了求生存，而抵御野兽的侵袭及与他部落的战争，于是有了兵器，所谓"以石片砍物为器，以石片格斗为兵"。

到了黄帝时代，九黎族首领蚩尤"与轩辕斗，以角牴人，人不能向"，则出现了模仿动物的特征，蚩尤即模仿牛以角牴人；这种较力斗硬的"角牴"，虽无攻防、奇巧可言，却孕育了未来的徒手格斗。

P274 到了西元前一〇七五年，已出现了训练兵械击刺技能的具体方向。

《十三经注疏·尚书·牧誓》载："夫子勗哉。不愆于四伐、五伐、六伐、七伐，乃止齐焉。"伐，为击、刺；戈谓击兵，矛谓刺兵，就是记述西周军队以戈、矛击刺之法相配合，所进行的训练方法。

当时，还将攻防动作制成武舞，用于教育。《礼记·内则》中有要求"成童（年满十五岁的少年）舞象"。所谓象，指象武或象舞。

P275《十三经注疏·毛诗正义·卷十九》注云："象舞，象用兵时刺伐之舞，武王制焉。"又说："此乐，象于用兵之时刺伐之事而为之舞，故谓之象武也。"

P276 ● 小憩

象形拳是武术中的一种，凡模仿动物，或模仿特定环境中的人物形态所创出的拳术，皆属此类。

例如，猴拳和螳螂拳等是模仿动物的拳术，醉拳是模仿人在喝醉时的形态所构成的拳术。象形拳的种类和内容很多，基本的规律有四：

（一）象形制拳。象形拳的核心是攻防技术，是借被模仿者之形态，融入攻防，转化为拳技、编成拳术。若离攻防，则可能沦为"禽戏"或"拟兽舞"，而不是象形拳。

P277 ● 小憩

（二）仿形为艺。象形拳必须升华为艺术化，蕴攻防术于其中，外形则栩栩如生，不同于穷凶极恶的兽斗形象。

（三）借形显意。象形拳是抓住被模仿对象的特点，将其形态动作人格化，显出人的意志个性。例如模仿猴，在于抓住其轻灵善变的动作特点，通过模仿其忽起忽落、忽击忽嬉、变化莫测的动作，展示出人是世间最灵巧之物；也可以说是，模仿猴而高于猴，胜于猴，而不能使人猿猴化，局限住人的体能和智能。

P278 ● **小憩**

（四）神形兼备。象形拳的神，即神似；象形拳的形，即形似。象形拳要求以形似为基础，以神似为精髓，进而达到神形兼备。因为，离开了被模仿对象形态的“形似”，则拳无所藏，艺无所依，意无所寄；离开了被模仿对象个性特征的“神似”，则形无神主而散，拳无意味而淡。离开了“形神”，就不是技击化、艺术化、人格化的象形拳了。

P279 明代以前，武术以军阵格杀技术为主，训练内容主要是兵械实用技法，而拳术（手搏）占的比例较小。军事杀伐中，兵种的变化（或车兵、或骑兵、或步兵）和兵器的形制、长短、轻重的变化，都影响武术的发展。

直到明代以后，武术才出现了较大的发展演进；可用五种现象得知：

（一）出现了练功、单舞、对搏并重的训练。

（二）出现了以拳术为主体，十八（或十七）种兵器为锻炼器械的技术体系。

P280（三）总结出了较为系统的武术基本理论。

（四）出现了广泛吸取传统文化的某些精神，来促进武术发展，增浓了武术文化色彩的趋势。

（五）武术的健身价值受到重视，审美价值得到有意识的运用，不再仅着眼于杀伐的纯军事技术。

P281 明代抗倭名将戚继光，在《练兵实纪》中说：“舞（单舞）、对（对搏）二事全然不通，与未习者为不知。”又说：“能舞而不知对，能对而不知舞，虽精只作中。”还说，先自跳舞，舞毕即以花枪对之，次以木刀对砍。

所谓舞，就是程式化动作的单练；所谓对，就是相互搏斗。戚继光认为，单舞和对搏应皆能，缺一不可；他并编成了“三十二势”拳术套路，作为活动肢体，惯勤手足的学武入门之术。

在《练兵实纪》中，戚继光还列了练心力、练手力、练足力、练身力等锻炼方法。

P282 在明代，少林拳已享盛名，并出现了与少林拳风格特点不同的“内家拳”。

此外，还流传有宋太祖三十二势长拳、六步拳、猴拳、化拳、温家七十二行拳、三十六合锁、二十四弃探马、八闪翻、十二短、巴子拳等。

同时，还出现了一批擅长某一拳技的名手。例如，擅长短打的有“绵张”、“吕红”、“山西刘”；擅长踢法的有“山东李半天”、“曹聋子”；擅长打法的有“张伯敬”；擅长拿法的有“王鹰爪”、“唐养吾”；擅长跌法的有“千跌张”。

P283 十八般武艺，初见于宋代戏文《张协状元》，泛指各种武艺，并非是指武艺的十八种内容。

明代戚晋叔辑《元曲选·逞风流王焕百花亭》中有：“若论著十八般武艺，弓弩枪牌，戈矛剑戟，鞭链挝锤。”

元朝施耐庵著《水浒全传·第二回》上说：“那十八般武艺：矛锤弓弩铳，鞭简剑链挝，斧钺并戈戟，牌棒与枪扒。”

P284 明万历年间谢肇浙《五杂俎》则说：“十八般：一弓、二弩、三枪、四刀、五剑、六矛、七盾、八斧、九钺、十戟、十一鞭、十二锏、十三挝、十四殳、十五叉、十六把头、十七绵绳套索、十八白打。”清代褚人获《坚瓠集》和陆凤藻《小知录》，二书中所记十八般武艺，内容与《五杂俎》相同。

后世还出现了“九长九短”、“六短十二长”，以及“大十八般”、“小十八般”等武艺的内容说法。经整理后，十八般武艺内容如下：

（一）抛射兵器——弓、弩、箭矢、铳。

P285（二）长兵器——戈、矛、枪、棍、殳、杵、杆、杖、棒、斧、钺、戟、（长杆）大刀、耙头

（把头）、扒、挝、铲。

（三）短兵器——剑、（短柄）刀、鞭、锏（简）、钩、镰、锤、枴、环（圈）。

（四）软兵器——链、流星、绵绳套索。

（五）属徒手的武艺，统称“白打”。

P286 何良臣《阵记》一书，在教学训练方面，理出了学习武艺要“先学拳”、“次学棍”的原则。

吴殳《手臂录》则说明了练习枪法，要先学“一戳一革”，然后学“连环”，最后学“破法”等循序渐进的教学训练法则。

P287 武术的分类，帮助人们对武术的技法特征，多了一些了解。

例如，将兵器分为长兵和短兵，在战国时有“长兵以卫，短兵以守”的战法；到明代就发展出了“长兵短用”和“短兵长用”的技法。

又如明清之际的“内家拳”，仅是王征南承传的一个拳种，“外家拳”仅指少林拳。到近代，发展成为凡“主于搏人”、“亦足以通利关节”者，概称外家拳；凡注重“以静制动”、“得于导引者为多”者，概称为内家拳。

P288 再如，以江河流域分派，南派、北派的分法，都指出了武术的分布情况，以及地理气候对拳术之形成的影响。

P289 武术的分类，还有一较特别的分类法，就是“竞赛分类法”，例如中国大陆所颁布的《武术竞赛规则》分列如下：

一、长拳。二、太极拳。三、南拳。四、剑术。五、刀术。六、枪术。七、棍术。八、其他拳术：除规则规定的自选拳术内容以外的拳术。如——第一类，形意、八卦、八极；第二类，通臂、劈挂、翻子；第三类，查、花、炮、红、华拳，少林、各式太极拳和南拳等。

P290 九、其他器械：除规则规定的自选器械项目内容以外的器械项目。如——第一类，单器械；第二类，双器械；第三类，软器械。十、对练项目：徒手对练、器械对练、徒手与器械对练。十一、集体项目。

P291 武术功法，包括有提高肢体关节活动幅度及肌肉舒张性能的“柔功”；锻练意、气、劲、形，完整一体的“内功”；增强肢体攻击力和抗击能力的“硬功”；发展人体平衡能力和翻腾奔跑能力的“轻功”等。

P292 “硬功”很早就受到重视。

《史记·殷本纪》记有帝武乙，做偶人，“与之搏”。偶人是土木做成的人像，与偶人搏斗，很像后世“木人功”锻炼法。这类提高击打能力的硬功功法，发展到明代，则有打动靶和打静靶两类。

唐顺之《武编·卷五》记有悬米袋或蒲团，或在平地上立三尺长凳或石墩为靶，以钻腿、桩腿、蹴腿、弹腿等腿法，进行踢击练习。这与现代的“吊袋功”、“踢桩功”基本相似。

P293 硬功中提高抗击、抗压能力的功法，在唐代已较为流行。

唐睿宗时的杂技表演，已有“卧剑上舞”。唐武宗时，有个名叫管万敌的供奉，颇有膂力，他奋力用拳击一麻衣人，却“如扣木石”。

当时，医家用于自我按摩的“拍击法”，是以指环、手、拳拍击身体，与后世“排打功”的初步练法相似。近代的“排打功”及“钢刀排身”、“卧叉”等表演，很可能就是承袭唐代。

P294 硬功中，提高力量的锻炼法，在汉代有“扛鼎”（举鼎），晋唐间有“翘关”（推举铁棒），清代流行有“舞刀”。

舞刀是以铁制大刀为械，进行推举和舞花等力量练习，很像是举铁棒进一步结合武术技术形成的。清代将一般练力法结合武技形成的功法很多，如“石锁功”、“鹰爪功”等。

P295 轻功，也是较早受到重视的功法。

例如，战国时《列子·汤问》中，载有将木桩“计步而置，履之而行，趣走往返，无跌失也”的练习方法；很像后世“梅花桩”、“跑桩”等功法。

又如《梁书·羊侃传》记，南北朝时的羊侃，“尝于兖州，尧庙蹋壁，直上至五寻，横行得七迹。”《朝野佥载》记唐代柴绍之弟，“尝著吉莫靴走上砖城，直至女墙，手无攀引。又以足趾蹈佛殿柱至檐头，捻椽覆，上越百尺楼阁，了无障碍。”这些记述，很像后世所谓“飞檐走壁”。

P296 再如《陈书》中载，南北朝时黄法氍步行，日三百里，距跃三丈；陈灵洗“步日二百余里”。

明代戚继光《纪效新书》述此类练法云：“如古人足囊以沙，渐渐加之，临敌去沙，自然轻便。”这些话和练法，同于后世的“陆地飞行术”。

P297 内功，是武术技法与气功结合的产物。

宋代已流行的八段锦，采用左右开弓、攒拳怒目、四面卫击等武技动作，进行以气助势、以气助力的练习，是早期内功的练法。

明代天启四年，《易筋经》问世，使内功的修炼达登峰造极的阶段。它强调内壮与外壮统一，追求通过内外俱炼，“使气串于腹间，护其骨，壮其筋”，达到“并其指可贯牛腹，侧其掌可断牛头”的效能。

P298 ● 小憩

清代少林寺将《易筋经》作为习武的必修内容，认为少林武技之精，皆赖《易筋经》之功。

晚清刻本《易筋经·潘霨伟序》云：“至今少林僧众谨以角艺擅场，是得此经之一斑也。”

近代，少林寺方丈妙兴，传出的数十种少林功法，大都是《易筋经》行功理法的繁衍。

《易筋经》是明天启四年天台紫凝道人所著，内容包括儒家的养气，医家的“引导按跷”、按摩拍击，道教服丹药以助功效的修炼法等。

P299 ● 小憩

在养气方面，《易筋经》旨在积气，以追求能增力助力的“浩然之精气”，例如书中云：“气积而力自积，气充而力自周，此气即孟子所谓至大至刚、塞乎天地之间者，是吾浩然之气也。”

而《易筋经》中对人体进行揉、拍、大杵捣、木槌捶、石袋打的锻炼，旨在凝气于中、积气充固、运气畅达，追求“气至则膜起，气行则膜张，能起能张，则膜与筋齐坚齐固矣”。以获得全身“无一处惧打，无一处不打人”的能力。

P300 ● 小憩

古代道教修炼时服食丹药，旨在借助药效加速修炼，追求驻形延年、长生不老、肉体成仙。《易筋经》在行功前后配合内外用药，是借助药力加强功效，促进内壮外强，消除热毒，软肤活络。

P301 柔功，是锻炼提高柔韧素质的基本方法，历来受到习武者的重视。

明代唐顺之在《峨眉道人拳歌》中，说道人练拳时“百折连腰尽无骨”。戚继光的《纪效新书》则说：“学拳要身法活便，手法便利，……腿可飞腾……活着朝天，而其柔也。”

P302 格斗，泛指两人在一定条件下，遵照一定的规则，进行徒手或器械的对抗练习和实战竞赛。内容包括徒搏（散打、推手）、短兵、长兵三项。

徒搏可以追溯到较力斗硬的“角牴”，而后发展成“始乎阳，常卒乎阴”、“举手击要，终在扑也”的相搏，继而又发展出了“相错畜，相散手”的手搏。

P303 手搏，是一种以打为主的搏斗，也有摔法、踢法、拿法的徒手格斗。

据说，在战国时代，已有专门传授手搏的人；至汉代，手搏流传更广。例如西汉人甘延寿，曾经经过手搏比试，取得军职“期门”；汉哀帝不好声色之娱，却常观手搏。

发展到宋代，手搏的竞争性、娱乐性更高。宋太祖时，王嗣宗与赵昌言争状元，“太祖命二人手搏，约胜者与之”。河南渑池县令世卫，曾“下令较手搏”，乘“倾城人随伍观之”的机会，约众举庙梁上山。

当时，民间将手搏称为“打擂台”。

P304 擂台比试有一定的规矩，先由一高手立擂，打擂者须先立生死“文书”，再上台较量。

比试时，先由“布署”（裁判）检查双方是否夹带暗器，宣布“不许暗算”等条例，然后双方才进行比赛。

P305 短兵运动可溯至战国时代，纯为观赏娱乐的斗剑。战国时赵文王喜剑，剑士日夜相击于前，死伤者岁百余人。

因为太过残忍，便以无刃杆杖代替利剑。三国时魏文帝曹丕与奋威将军邓展的一场较量，就是以蔗代剑进行的。

晋代则出现了以木剑代刃剑的情况。这种木剑主要用于装饰佩戴，有时也用于格斗；《南史·陈始兴王叔陵传》中，有“取朝服木剑以进”应付仓促变故。

P306 发展到后来，木制刀剑成了代替利剑铁刀的器械，例如明代戚继光《练兵实录》中记有“以木刀对砍”的文字。

P307 武学，广义而言是泛指武术教学活动，狭义则是指古代培养军事人才的专科学校；现代一些武术学者则将中国武术学问简称为武学。

校，本为养马之地，在夏代逐渐演变为进行角斗、比武和考校的场所，发展成了高官显贵及其子弟学习军旅武技的教育机构。

武学始于宋代庆历三年，是专门培养军事人才的学校；至清代武生附入儒学，武学的教学内容包括兵法、武艺、前世忠义等。《武经七书》、《百将传》、《教法格并图像》及《四书》都曾被列为武学教材。

P308 春秋战国时，甘绳、卫飞、养繇基等，是出自民间的高超射手。越女、袁公、鲁公、鲁石公等，是出自民间的高超剑术家。

历代著名武将中，多有从师民间拳师学得武技者，例如宋时岳飞学于周侗，明代俞大猷从赵本学习技，戚继光吸取民间十六家拳法之长，才编成势势相承的三十二势长拳。

清代民间拳门林立，少林拳、太极拳、形意拳、八卦拳、通臂拳、八极拳等，都出自民间武人之手。民间拜师学艺和家传形式的武学，虽未入史册，却是中国武术绵延发展的主要形式。

P309 ● 小憩

古代武术专书亡佚颇多，例如，收入《汉书·艺文志》的《手搏》六篇，《剑道》三十八篇；收入《隋书·经籍志》的《马槊谱》等都只残存片简只言或序言。

近代运用较多的古籍，除了《吴越春秋》的“越女论剑”，及《庄子》的“说剑”等少量远古武技文论外，主要是明清两代的著述。

P310《武经七书》又名《武学七书》。

北宋元丰三年，宋神宗下诏校定《孙子》、《吴子》、《六韬》、《司马法》、《三略》、《尉缭子》和《李卫公问对》，号称七书，定为武学教科书。

宋朝南渡后，宋高宗明文规定：“凡武学生习七书兵法”，武举考试以七书命题。

明清两代，仍沿袭宋代旧制，武科用《武经七书》试士。为了科举考试的需要，武生以七书为晋身阶梯，刻苦研习，促进了兵法与武术技法的融合。

P311《武编》为明代唐顺之编著，编录于《明史·艺文志》中。

《武编》共十卷，分前后两集，前集六卷，后集四卷。其前集卷五有牌、射、弓、弩、拳、枪、剑、刀、简、锤、扒、镋十二篇。在拳的部分，记述了当时流行的拳术流派，还辑录了一些练功方法和技法。

P312《正气堂集》为明代名将俞大猷所著，亦由《明史·艺文志》所编录。

本书中有余集和续集，在余集的卷四中所载《剑经》，主要是讲述棍法诀要。其中提出了“顺人之势，借人之力”、“(乘他）旧力略过，新力未生”等技击法则。

俞大猷并提出了“刚在他力前，柔乘他力后；彼忙我静待，知拍任君斗”等具有普遍意义的战术原则，对后世各派拳术都有极重要之影响。

P313 《纪效新书》乃明代抗倭名将戚继光编著，编录入《明史·艺文志》中，有十四卷本和十八卷本两种刊本。

其中包含有射、棍、枪、钯、牌、筅、拳等武艺技法，还介绍了当时武术的流派，论及了民间武术和军旅武术的差异，以及拳法在军事技术训练中的作用等若干问题。

此书卷十《长兵短用说篇》、卷十二《短兵长用说篇》、卷十四《拳经捷要篇》等，甚为后世拳家所推崇。

P314 《耕余剩技》是明天启元年程宗猷著，包括《少林棍法阐宗》三卷、《蹶张心法》一卷、《长枪法选》一卷、《单刀法选》一卷。

一九二九年，吴兴周由廑取家藏天启本影印问世，易名为《国术四书》。书中论述了套路运动形式对掌握攻防技术，提高攻防技能的作用，首次采用图解记叙武术套路的连贯练法。

P315 《易筋经》始见于天启四年，出自天台紫凝道人。清道光以后，先后有傅金铨、来章氏、宋光祚等辑本《易筋经》问世。

《易筋经》的主要内容，包括：易筋经总论、内壮论、内壮神勇、外壮神勇八段锦、十二势图等。

在理论上，《易筋经》并提出了“内壮”与“外壮”统一的观点，制定了“内壮既熟”，再练外壮的锻炼顺序，并创编了“内外兼修”的“内壮揉腹功”、“易筋经十二势”、“外壮神勇八段锦”等功法，本书在少林寺僧和武术传习者中流传甚广，被视为武术气功文献的代表作。

P316 《易筋经》一书，旧题为《达摩撰》，般剌密谛译文；据清人凌廷堪《校礼堂文集》、周中孚《郑堂读书集》、近人唐豪《旧中国体育史上附会的达摩》等文考证，晚明始见的《易筋经》，不是南北朝时天竺僧达摩的遗作。

P317 《手臂录》为明遗民吴殳著，亦编录于《明史·艺文志》中，本书共分四卷及附卷上下。其中除卷三《单刀图说》、卷四的《诸器总说》、《叉说》、《狼筅说》、《藤牌说》、《大棒说》、《剑诀》、《双刀歌》和《后剑诀》等篇外，其他内容皆为枪法。

本书对明代至清初流传的石家枪法、马家枪法、沙家枪法、杨家枪法、峨眉枪法、梦绿堂枪法、程宗猷枪法等多家枪法，加以注释与辨析，总结了枪法要诀，被后世视为集枪法之大成者。

P318　● 小憩

峨眉派，可说是武术中极重要的一支，以峨眉山为发祥地。明人唐顺之《荆川先生文集·峨眉道人拳歌》云：“浮屠善幻多技能，少林拳法世稀有，道人更自出新奇，乃是深山白猿授。”依此说法，峨眉道人的拳术是在少林拳的基础上，模仿猿猴或受猿猴特点之启示，而创编的新奇拳术。

明末安徽人程真如得峨眉山僧普恩禅师传枪法，并命此为“峨眉枪法”。据说近代传习的白眉拳，始自峨眉山的白眉道人；鸭形拳创自峨眉绿雅（一说绿鸭）道人。

P319　● 小憩

此外，峨眉僧道中亦不乏原来精通民间武术者。例如，在河南天幢寺击败窃金者张某的峨眉僧人，是内家拳师单思南的再传弟子（见《清朝野史大观·清代述异》）；峨眉人曹洞宗第三代妙钢和尚是武举人出身；峨眉九老洞遇仙寺道人李长叶是八卦掌鼻祖董海川的再传弟子。

今人习云泰著《中国武术史》，将四川流传的黄林派、余门拳、白眉拳等“土生土长的拳术”，当作峨眉派武功的基本内容。

P320 ● 小憩

另有人将近代四川风行的僧、岳、杜、赵、洪、化、字、会八门，及黄林、点易、铁佛、青城、青牛五派拳术，统归为峨眉派拳术，即《峨眉拳谱》所谓“五花八叶扶”。

其中，僧、岳、杜、赵称四大家，洪、化、字、会称四小家。五派是指流传于四川境内五个地区的五术，这五个地区指荣昌和隆昌两县交界地区（黄林派），涪陵县点易洞地区（点易派），青城山地区（青城派），云顶山、铁佛寺地区（铁佛派），丰都县青牛山地区（青牛派）。

P321 ● 小憩

一般拳术都是在中国大陆发源，唯有“僧门”例外。僧门，是四川地方拳种，蜀称四大家之一，也称申门。申系猴，取猿猴肩臂敏捷之意，传说源自台湾少林，明末时由湖北传入四川。

僧门的早期代表人物有曾五、孙草药、苏三等，相传清嘉庆年间由马朝柱（外号赵麻布）传至四川。

僧门的拳法多虚步高桩，刚劲有力；技击上靠挤靠擒拿，贴身近打，腿法不多，仅以虚腿诱人，或低发腿，要求“十腿九虚，腿不过膝”；主要套路有大练、单鞭、虎豹、缠丝、六通等。

P322 《拳经·拳法备要》为明代少林寺玄机和尚所传授，明末陈松泉再传，张鸣鹗编撰。清代康熙初年张孔昭补充，乾隆年间曹焕门又增补。

本书含拳经、拳法各一卷，包括问答歌诀、周身秘诀、下盘细密秘诀、少林寺短打身法统宗拳谱、少林短打推盘步法。

P323 《内家拳法》是清代黄百家著，编录《清史·艺文志》。

书中记述了内家拳源流、练手法、练步法，内家拳的套路“六路”和“十段锦”，还介绍了内家拳的禁犯病、打法、心法、穴法等内容；此书是研究明代内家拳史和技术体系的重要资料。

P324 《太极拳经》是清人武禹襄自称于一八五二年在河南舞阳盐店偶得。此谱作者署名为山右王宗岳，原名《太极拳谱》，民国初关百益尊之为经，故沿袭称“经”。

《太极拳经》的内容包括：十三势论、太极拳论、太极拳解、十三势歌、打手歌、十三势行功心解、十三势名目。

P325 ● 小憩

《太极拳经》云：太极者，无极而生，阴阳之母也。动之则分，静之则合，无过不及，随曲就伸，人刚我柔谓之走，我顺人背谓之黏，动急则急应，动缓则缓随，虽变化万端，而理为一贯，由着熟而渐悟懂劲，由懂劲而阶及神明，然非功力之久，不能豁然贯通焉。

虚领顶劲，气沿丹田，不偏不倚，忽隐忽现，左重则左虚，右重则右杳，仰之则弥高，俯之则弥深，进之则愈长，退之则愈促，人不知我，我独知人，英雄所向无敌，盖皆由此而及也。

P326 ● 小憩

斯技旁门甚多，虽势有区别，概不外乎壮欺弱，慢让快耳；有力打无力，手慢让手快，是皆天然之能，非关学力而有无也。

察四两拨千斤之句，显非力胜，观耄耋能御众之形，快何能为，立如平准，活似车轮，偏沉则随，双重则滞，每见数年纯功，不能运化者，率自为人制，双重之病未悟耳；欲避此病，须知阴阳相济，方为懂劲，懂劲后愈练愈精，默识揣摩渐至从心所欲，本是舍己从人，多误舍近求远，学者不可不详辨焉。

P327 讲到练武，就不能不提到丹田，丹田究竟在哪里呢？

丹田分为上丹田、中丹田、下丹田；葛洪《抱朴子·地真》中说丹田的位置：“子欲长生，守一长明，……或在脐下二寸四分下丹田中，或在心下降宫全阙中丹田也，或在人两眉间，却行一寸为明堂，二寸为洞房，三寸为上丹田也。”

也有人认为丹田是培育“丹”的田地，丹是练功获得的一种特殊能量物质，因此只要能由锻炼产生丹的地方，就是丹田。故有“人身无处不丹田”的说法。

P328 而我们通常说的“气沉丹田”、“丹田发力”、“气归丹田”、“丹田气”等用语中的“丹田”，皆指下丹田，即小腹。

P329 武术中的传说，非常多，迷宗拳就有一段故事。

迷宗拳是长拳的一种，又称燕青拳、迷踪拳、猊猔拳、迷踪艺，传说创自宋代燕青，燕青是梁山泊一百零八条好汉的一个，话说他雪夜逃往梁山时，一边前行，一边以树枝扫去足迹，后世于是将此拳取名燕青拳及迷踪拳。

又有人说燕青的拳法学自要猴人“半夜仙”，是取猊猔猴灵敏善跃的特点编成的，故名猊猔拳；还有一种说法，是说这种拳法是取各家招法编成，难明其宗，故名“迷宗拳”。

P330 无论如何，这些说法都没有史料佐证，比较确定的是，近代迷踪拳传自清嘉庆前后的孙通。

孙通是山东岱州人，初从兖州张某习武，旋入嵩山少林寺习技达十多年，学得多种拳械，擅长点穴术、卸骨术、擒拿术；离寺后，设教于山东青州一带，嘉庆年间定居河北沧州，设教传徒。青州一带传人称其技为燕青神捶，沧州一带传人称其拳为迷宗、迷踪、猊猔拳。

P331 迷宗拳经过陈善、张耀庭、霍元甲等历代门人增添招法、结合内功，形成了丰富的内容。

此拳眼法要求，既要注视一点，又要顾盼八方；手型有拳、掌、勾；手法有冲、砸、劈、崩、撩、穿、勾、搂等；步型有弓、马、仆、虚、歇；步法强调闪展腾挪、窜纵跳跃、注重插裆套步；腿法有踢、蹬、弹、缠；身型要求头顶颈直、直腰、敛臀；身法有靠、闪、挺、缩。

在劲力上，要松紧交替，讲究出手如棉，触身似铁；在节奏上，要动静分明，讲究静如泰山、动如狂风；运动特点表现为姿势舒展，架式端正，动作圆活，轻灵敏捷。

P332 迷宗拳流传的拳套，有练手拳、罗汉拳、三步架、小进拳、五虎拳、豹拳、绵掌拳、八折拳、八打拳、燕青拳、秘宗长拳等。

P333 ● 小憩

侠，是指中国古代社会中品德端正、见义勇为、主持公道的人，俗称侠客。

“侠”一般都有高超的武功，这些人轻死重义，其言必信、其行必果、己诺必诚，为了“义”，不忌“以武犯禁”，不惧杀身成仁、为知己死。

P334 ● 小憩

抱拳礼

古代习武者相见，以抱拳为礼。不以握手为礼，意在避免对方猜疑，也避免对方的暗藏杀机，如擒拿中即有趁伸手相握时擒住对方的招式。

抱拳礼的含义，右手握拳喻“尚武”、“以武会友”。以左掌掩右拳，喻拳由理来，屈左拇指，喻不自大。左掌四指并拢，喻四海武林同道团结齐心，发扬武术。

P335 ● 小憩

武侠小说中，常有“刀如猛虎，剑似飞凤”的说法，是喻指单刀和单剑的特点。

单刀舞练起来，如程宗猷于《单刀法选》中所言，“刀不离身左右前后，手足肩臂与刀俱转，舒之可刃人于数步之外，敛之可转舞于座间。”因刀快步疾，故以虎猛之性喻刀。在《越女论剑》中，提到单剑练舞起来“内实精神，外示安仪”，“杳杳若日、偏如腾兔，追形逐影，光若仿佛，呼吸往来，不及法禁，纵横顺逆，直复不闻”。因剑势轻灵，变化多端，气势贯串，故以凤之飞态喻剑。

P336 戳脚，是一种以腿法为主的拳术，相传起源于宋代，典型动作是玉环步、鸳鸯腿。

《水浒传》中，描写武松醉打蒋门神时，就用了玉环步、鸳鸯腿。

《太平天国野史》中，记述太平军石达开部将对敌时，“俟敌踵至，疾踢其腹脐下。如敌劲，则数转环踢之”，亦似玉环步、鸳鸯腿的打法。

太平军林凤祥部北伐失利后，战将赵燦益隐居河北饶阳一带，将“戳脚”传给段老绪，此后逐渐传至京津、东北、西北。

P337　● 小憩

武举，是中国古代科举制度中，为选拔武官而设的考试科目，始自唐长安二年；考科目有长垛、马射、步射、平射、管射、马枪、翘关（试举重）。

宋代武举增加了兵书义理，或《论语》、《孟子》大义等理论考试，称为“内场”。至清时，考试分为童试、乡试、会试、殿试四级。

光绪二十七年，武举制度废除。

P338　传说通臂拳起源于战国，传者姓白，名士口，字衣三，而“士口衣三”四字恰巧合成“猿”字，即通臂拳传自白猿。近代流传的通臂拳，主要有祈家通臂、白猿通臂、劈挂通臂三种。

祈家通臂是清道光时，浙江人祈信在河北固安、冀县、涿县一带传出；弟子中以其子太昌和涿州人陈庆为著。

白猿通臂，清末山东黄县人任十，将此拳传北京石鸿胜，经石氏及其弟子努力，此拳盛传于北京牛街回民聚居区。

P339　劈挂通臂则为劈挂拳，因特点与通臂拳相近，故被归为其中一支。

P340　● 小憩

穴位，又名腧穴、穴道、气穴、孔穴、骨穴等，是人体脏腑经络之气输注于体表的处所，更是内气与外气沟通之处。

人身有三百六十个穴位。点穴法是透过这些穴位的制人之术和解救之法。

P341　● 小憩

经络，是穴位与脏腑间的联络线。

经络包括经脉和络脉两种，经脉上下直行，络脉左右横行。经络计有十二经脉、奇经八脉、十二经别、十二经筋、十二皮部、十五络等。